PRAISE FOR ROBERT DUGONI'S TRACY CROSSWHITE SERIES

Praise for *Close to Home*

"An immensely—almost compulsively—readable tale . . . A crackerjack mystery."

—*Booklist* (starred review)

"In bestseller Dugoni's nail-biting fifth Tracy Crosswhite mystery . . . [he] embellishes this clever procedural with well-developed characters and an interesting exploration of Navy criminal justice."

—*Publishers Weekly*

"*Close to Home* [is] another thrilling addition to Dugoni's Crosswhite series."

—Associated Press

"Dugoni's twisted tale is one of conspiracy and culpability . . . richly nuanced and entirely compelling."

—Criminal Element

Praise for *The Trapped Girl*

"In Dugoni's outstanding fourth Tracy Crosswhite mystery, the Seattle homicide detective investigates the death of Andrea Strickland, a young woman whose body a fisherman finds in a crab pot raised from the sea . . . In less deft hands this tale wouldn't hold water, but Dugoni presents his victim's life in discrete pieces, each revealing a bit more about Andrea and her struggle to find happiness. Tracy's quest to uncover the truth leads her into life-altering peril in this exceptional installment."

—*Publishers Weekly* (starred review)

"Dugoni drills so deep into the troubled relationships among his characters that each new revelation shows them in a disturbing new light . . . [A]n unholy tangle of crimes makes this his best book to date."

—*Kirkus Reviews*

"Dugoni has a gift for creating compelling characters and mysteries that seem straightforward, but his stories, like an onion, have many hidden layers. He also is able to capture the spirit and atmosphere of the Pacific Northwest, making the environment come alive . . . [A] nother winner from Dugoni."

—Associated Press

"All of Robert Dugoni's talents are once again firmly on display in *The Trapped Girl*, a blisteringly effective crime thriller . . . structured along classical lines drawn years ago by the likes of Raymond Chandler and Dashiell Hammett. A fiendishly clever tale that colors its pages with crisp shades of postmodern noir."

—*Providence Journal*

"Robert Dugoni, yet again, delivers an excellent read . . . With many twists, turns, and jumps in the road traveled by the detective and her cohorts, this absolutely superb plot becomes more than just a little entertaining. The problem remains the same: Readers must now once again wait impatiently for the next book by Robert Dugoni to arrive."

—*Suspense Magazine*

Praise for *In the Clearing*

"Tracy displays ingenuity and bravery as she strives to figure out who killed Kimi."

—*Publishers Weekly*

"Dugoni's third 'Tracy Crosswhite' novel (after *Her Final Breath*) continues his series' standard of excellence with superb plotting and skillful balancing of the two story lines."

—*Library Journal* (starred review)

"Dugoni has become one of the best crime novelists in the business, and his latest featuring Seattle homicide detective Tracy Crosswhite will only draw more accolades."

—*Romantic Times*, Top Pick

"Robert Dugoni tops himself in the darkly brilliant and mesmerizing *In the Clearing*, an ironically apt title for a tale in which nothing at all is clear."

—*Providence Journal*

Praise for *Her Final Breath*

"A stunningly suspenseful exercise in terror that hits every note at the perfect pitch."

—*Providence Journal*

"Absorbing . . . Dugoni expertly ratchets up the suspense as Crosswhite becomes a target herself."

—*Seattle Times*

"Dugoni does a masterful job with this entertaining novel, as he has done in all his prior works. If you are not already reading his books, you should be!"

—Bookreporter

"Takes the stock items and reinvents them with crafty plotting and high energy . . . The revelations come in a wild finale."

—*Booklist*

"Another stellar story featuring homicide detective Tracy Crosswhite . . . Crosswhite is a sympathetic, well-drawn protagonist, and her next adventure can't come fast enough."

—*Library Journal* (starred review)

Praise for *My Sister's Grave*

"One of the best books I'll read this year."

—Lisa Gardner, bestselling author of *Touch & Go*

"Dugoni does a superior job of positioning [the plot elements] for maximum impact, especially in a climactic scene set in an abandoned mine during a blizzard."

—*Publishers Weekly*

"Yes, a conspiracy is revealed, but it's an unexpected one, as moving as it is startling . . . The ending is violent, suspenseful, even touching. A nice surprise for thriller fans."

—*Booklist*

"Combines the best of a police procedural with a legal thriller, and the end result is outstanding . . . Dugoni continues to deliver emotional and gut-wrenching, character-driven suspense stories that will resonate with any fan of the thriller genre."

—*Library Journal* (starred review)

"Well written, and its classic premise is sure to absorb legal-thriller fans . . . The characters are richly detailed and true to life, and the ending is sure to please fans."

—*Kirkus Reviews*

"*My Sister's Grave* is a chilling portrait shaded in neo-noir, as if someone had taken a knife to a Norman Rockwell painting by casting small-town America as the place where bad guys blend into the landscape, establishing Dugoni as a force to be reckoned with outside the courtroom as well as in."

—*Providence Journal*

"What starts out as a sturdy police procedural morphs into a gripping legal thriller . . . Dugoni is a superb storyteller, and his courtroom drama shines . . . This 'Grave' is one to get lost in."

—*Boston Globe*

A STEEP PRICE

ALSO BY ROBERT DUGONI

The Extraordinary Life of Sam Hell

The 7th Canon

Damage Control

The Tracy Crosswhite Series

My Sister's Grave

Her Final Breath

In the Clearing

The Trapped Girl

Close to Home

The Academy (a short story)

Third Watch (a short story)

The David Sloane Series

The Jury Master

Wrongful Death

Bodily Harm

Murder One

The Conviction

Nonfiction with Joseph Hilldorfer

The Cyanide Canary

A STEEP PRICE

ROBERT DUGONI

THOMAS & MERCER

This is a work of fiction. Names, characters, organizations, places, events, and incidents are either products of the author's imagination or are used fictitiously. Any resemblance to actual persons, living or dead, or actual events is purely coincidental.

Published by Thomas & Mercer, Seattle

www.apub.com

ISBN-13: 9781503954182
ISBN-10: 1503954188

Cover design by David Drummond

Printed in the United States of America

To all the women who have suffered from breast cancer and have fought the good fight. Hopefully, someday, research will break through and we finally will have a cure.

CHAPTER 1

Tuesday, July 10, 2018

It had been more than a year since Seattle homicide detectives Del Castigliano and Vic Fazzio had worked a case in South Park, but the reason for their visits hadn't changed. Someone had been murdered.

On their last case, two attorneys trying to flip homes and spur redevelopment had been shot in one of their properties—a subtle message.

South Park wasn't interested in change.

"A world unto itself," Del said, repeating a Seattle Police Department mantra as he drove their pool car across the South Park Bridge over the green-gray waters of the Duwamish River. Just after 4:00 p.m., a July sun reflected diamonds of sparkling light across the river's surface, and the temperature in Seattle had risen above eighty-five degrees, without a cloud in the sky.

The bridge deposited them onto Cloverdale Street. "I thought South Park might get redeveloped when the bridge reopened," Faz said.

South Park had what those in real estate considered the most important criteria for redevelopment: location, location, location. Situated twenty minutes south of downtown Seattle, it was also a stone's throw west of Boeing Field and close to the Seattle-Tacoma Airport. The South Park Bridge had been condemned in 2010 and did not reopen for more than four years; nobody seemed to be in a great rush. If South Park's toxic topsoil and polluted waters did not dissuade redevelopment, crime usually did. South Park's population included a large contingent of Sureño gang members out of Southern California—foot soldiers for the Mexican drug cartels.

"I thought some developer would start buying up property and raise rents, especially with this housing market," Faz continued. "Now I'm thinking that's as likely as me losing weight." At six foot four, Faz tipped the scale at 270 pounds. He glanced at Del. "You actually look like you put on a couple pounds."

Del, an inch taller, had lost fifty pounds since starting a relationship with Celia McDaniel, a King County prosecutor. "I'm eating some carbs again," Del said. "Celia says she likes me better at this weight."

"I like you better at this weight. We were starting to look like Laurel and Hardy," Faz said. "Did Billy call and get us some help?" Billy Williams was the A Team's sergeant, and Del and Faz the homicide team on call for the week. Ordinarily, Tracy Crosswhite and Kinsington Rowe, the other two detectives on the four-person team, would provide support. Crosswhite, however, had been sitting in a homicide trial in King County Superior Court for more than a month.

"He said he'd get somebody." Del made a right turn and slowed as they approached a stream of parked police vehicles. A crowd stood on the south side of the street—men and women of all ages dressed in tank tops, shorts, and flip-flops. They fanned themselves and shielded their eyes from the glare of the afternoon sun. "The circus has come to town," Del said, continuing past the CSI van and a fire truck, while looking for a place to park.

"Four o'clock on a weekday—this is better than a movie," Faz agreed. "Park in front of the ambulance."

Del pulled into an angled spot in front of a two-story redbrick apartment building. Faz slid from the passenger seat of the air-conditioned car and slipped a lightweight blazer over his long-sleeve shirt and tie. “I can already feel myself starting to sweat.”

“I’ve been sweating since the day I was born,” Del said. He, too, wore a suit, though he’d removed his tie as a concession to the heat.

Faz looked up when he heard the thrum of a hovering news helicopter. First thing they’d need to do, if Billy hadn’t done it already, was to get the helicopter the hell out of the area. They badged the officer holding the police log, scribbled their names, badge numbers, and time of their arrival in the log, and ducked beneath yellow-and-black crime scene tape. Most of the officers had congregated around a small playground in the center courtyard of the U-shaped apartment building. The body lay beneath a blue sheet near a green jungle gym. Billy stood talking to one of several uniformed officers but he broke off the conversation when he saw Faz and Del.

“You call in about the helicopter?” Faz asked.

“Yeah,” Billy said, not sounding optimistic his call would do any good. News helicopters could only be fined for being in a police no-fly zone. If the story were big enough, the station would stay and pay the fine.

“Any chance we can argue the apartment is in King County?” Del said.

“I wish,” Billy said.

Some of the streets in South Park were within the King County Sheriff’s jurisdiction, and the running joke between the two agencies was that officers rolled bodies across streets to put them in the other’s jurisdiction. Though he meant it as a joke, Del refrained from smiling. With the union trying out body cameras on their uniformed officers, humor no longer had any place at a crime scene. They’d all be on Zoloft by the end of the year.

Billy adjusted his driving cap, which shielded his shaved head from the sun. "This one could get ugly, fast. The decedent is Monique Rodgers." He paused, as if the name should mean something to them. "You might have read about her or seen her on the news, advocating against gangs and drugs in South Park."

"The activist?" Faz said. He recalled something on the news about an African American woman speaking to the city council about drugs and gangs in the South Park community.

"Would-be activist," Billy said. "She didn't get all that far."

"Could be the reason she was shot in broad daylight," Faz said. "Someone sending a message."

"Likely," Billy said.

"I'm assuming someone saw it?" Del asked.

"One would think, wouldn't he?" Billy said. "I'm told there were half a dozen moms out here with their kids, but so far everyone is doing the 'see no, hear no, speak no English' act."

"They're scared," Faz said.

"Anyone else hurt?" Del asked.

Billy shook his head. "Nothing reported."

"So then we're assuming she was the intended victim?" Faz asked the question as he considered two brick pony walls along the sidewalk, which would have made for good cover if two rival gangs had started shooting at one another—South Park was also home to the Crips and to a couple Asian gangs, though in far fewer numbers than the Sureños. If two gangs had opened fire, Rodgers could have been an innocent victim caught in the cross fire.

"We are," Billy said, "given that no one else was shot, and witnesses said they only heard the one shooter." He glanced up at the news helicopter, still hovering. "TV is going to play up big the fact that it was broad daylight with kids around."

"Where's her family now?" Faz asked.

"Grandmother got the kids out of here and took them into the apartment." He pointed to a corner of the U-shaped building. "Husband has apparently come home from work and is also with them."

"Is anyone saying anything?" Faz asked.

Billy shook his head. "We can't even get confirmation on the number of shots or from what direction they were fired. One woman told the responding officer she thought she heard three shots coming from over there." Williams pointed to a corner of the building.

"They find shell casings?" Del asked.

"None," Billy said.

"So the witness either got it wrong," Faz said, "or the shooter used a revolver."

"I got patrol searching for casings," Billy said. He pointed again to the apartments. "And Anderson-Cooper is going door-to-door."

Desmond Anderson and Lee Cooper worked out of the B Team. Since *the* Anderson Cooper had become CNN's regular nightly news anchor, the detectives in Violent Crimes referred to the two-man detective team in the singular.

"We're going to need the video unit," Faz said. "One of the businesses around here might have picked up the shooter fleeing or getting into a car." The street was mixed-use, with apartment buildings, small homes, and corner stores.

"Already on their way," Billy said.

"How much did the kids see?" Faz asked.

"All of it," Billy said.

Faz turned to the sound of trumpets and guitars—Mexican music—coming from the street. A cherry-red, two-door Chevelle with black stripes and gold hubcaps bounced up and down as it drove past the apartment complex.

"Send in the clowns," Del said.

The man in the passenger seat had a shaved head and a thin mustache that extended to a goatee. Dark sunglasses hugged his face, giving him fly's eyes. His right arm, heavily tattooed, hung out the window. The car slowed and the man removed his sunglasses, staring at Faz.

"Little Jimmy," Faz said. "All grown-up."

Ten years earlier, Faz had put Little Jimmy's father in prison. Big Jimmy lasted six months. A rival gang member killed him with a shiv.

Little Jimmy smiled, then he made a gun with his thumb and index finger and took aim at Faz, imitating the kick of the barrel as the gun discharged.

CHAPTER 2

Tracy Crosswhite grimaced as the defense attorney, Leonard Litwin, tilted the plastic pitcher from the counsel table. A miniature waterfall cascaded into his paper cup, the splatter the only sound in the courtroom. Ostensibly, Litwin needed to quench his thirst, but from her seat on the elevated witness stand, Tracy suspected Litwin had a different motivation for leaving the lectern. Litwin was stalling, like a battered and beaten prizefighter desperate to reach the final bell.

Ordinarily, Tracy wouldn't have cared what Litwin did, or how long it took him to do it, but for thirty-seven of the fifty-three minutes since the court had last recessed and she had retaken the witness stand, she'd had to pee. Really pee. It seemed unlikely that Litwin, or anyone else in the courtroom, could detect Tracy's urgent problem, or the sixteen-week baby bump causing it, but that didn't change Tracy's circumstances. Judge Miriam Gowin certainly wasn't going to rush a defense attorney representing a client facing the death penalty, and Tracy wasn't about to bail out Litwin by asking for an early recess. With each passing minute, however, she thought of Beth Duchance, the poor girl who'd wet her pants in the second grade. Duchance had forgotten her homework and when pressed by their teacher, responded like a frightened miniature poodle before the alpha dog. For the remainder of what had to have been an eternal eight years, Beth Duchance suffered the humiliation only immature boys and nasty grammar school girls could wreak—they called her Beth "Wet My Pants." Tracy had no desire to become similarly etched in the memories of courthouse personnel.

Litwin tilted the cup to his lips and drank in painfully slow gulps. Rather than set the glass on the counsel table, he carried it to the lectern and methodically considered pages of notes and testimony in his binder.

"Detective Crosswhite, you said . . ." Litwin looked as if he were about to read, but turned another page, and another. In her peripheral vision, Tracy noted several jurors glancing at the large wall clock across the room. The second hand buzzed and lurched past the twelve. Finally, Litwin continued, "You said that . . . that you found no fingerprints on the knife. Is that correct?"

Tracy paused to allow the prosecutor, Adam Hoetig, time to object. She'd answered the question twice before. But Hoetig sat with his head down, as if he had taken a sudden interest in his loafers.

"That's correct," she said.

"So you have no evidence the knife belonged to the defendant—isn't that also true?"

Tracy's bladder begged her to let the question go, but she couldn't bypass the opportunity to take another shot at Litwin and his client. "Other than the fact that the defendant told me the knife matched the set of knives in the kitchen drawer? No."

Her response drew sidelong glances from several of the jurors.

Litwin's back stiffened. "I'll rephrase. You have no evidence, Detective Crosswhite, that the knife was used to . . . no forensic evidence the knife was used to stab his wife."

This is like shooting fish in a barrel. "Other than the fact that the knife handle was sticking out of Mrs. Stephenson's chest and she had seven stab wounds? No."

The number of glances multiplied. Several jurors smiled.

Litwin bristled. His cheeks splashed a splotchy red. "Detective, you have no forensic evidence linking the murder—"

Tracy cut him off to speed up the process. "The defendant's fingerprints were not found on the knife sticking out of his wife's chest. That is correct."

Predictably, Litwin turned to the bench. "Your Honor, the defense requests that you admonish Detective Crosswhite to allow me to complete my questions before she answers."

Gowin glanced at the clock before directing her gaze to Tracy. "Detective, let counsel finish his question." For one interminable moment, Tracy thought Gowin might allow Litwin to continue. Then she said, "Counsel, it's four fifty-four. Do you believe you will complete your cross-examination of Detective Crosswhite within the next six minutes?"

Not a chance.

"I estimate that I have another hour," Litwin said.

He didn't, but Litwin and Tracy were both about to get a much-needed reprieve.

"Then we'll end for the day," Gowin said, "and pick up tomorrow morning with Detective Crosswhite on the witness stand."

When the last of the jurors had collected their belongings and departed to the jury room, Tracy hurried from the witness stand to the courtroom doors. In her peripheral vision, she saw Hoetig fast approaching, likely to set a time to meet and discuss Litwin's expected areas of cross-examination in the morning.

"I'll call you," she said, deflecting Hoetig's advance before he could speak, and hurried out the courtroom door.

CHAPTER 3

Faz watched the red Chevelle until it drove out of sight, the music lingering for several more seconds.

"Little Jimmy's not so little anymore," Del said. He wiped the sweat from his brow with a handkerchief.

"Yeah, he's now a grown-up shithead," Faz said. "Amazing how the garbage never falls far from the trash can."

"He seems to remember you," Del said.

Little Jimmy had been fourteen when Faz put Big Jimmy in prison. "And he was already a punk then."

Big Jimmy had run drugs in South Park. A rival gang out of Los Angeles tried to step in. A war erupted. Thirteen gang members died in two weeks. Faz's investigation led to the arrest of eight Sureño gang members, including Big Jimmy, though Big Jimmy never pulled a trigger. The jury determined that Big Jimmy had ordered the hits on the rival gang members, and King County prosecutor Rick Cerrabone convicted him under the Racketeer Influenced and Corrupt Organizations Act. A jury sentenced Big Jimmy to twenty-five years in prison.

"I don't like guys pointing a gun at me, fake or not," Faz said. "Maybe we pay Little Jimmy a visit, determine whether that drive-by was a message to those watching from across the street."

"Little Jimmy can count on it," Del said.

Faz turned from the road and walked to the body. He crouched, lifted a corner of the sheet, and considered Monique Rodgers. He guessed early thirties. A deep-red stain had blossomed on the front of her shirt, and blood ran along the cracks in the concrete. Faz lowered the sheet and stood, his knee cracking when he did. He turned to Billy while eyeing the apartment complex. "Which apartment?"

Williams pointed to a corner of the horseshoe-shaped building. A police officer stood on the exterior landing. "Last door."

Faz followed Del up a concrete-and-wrought-iron staircase to a second-floor breezeway cluttered with chairs and charcoal barbecues. Residents stood in the open doors of their sweltering apartments. Several gave Del and Faz the stink eye.

"Feeling the love?" Del said.

"I'm all warm and fuzzy inside," Faz said.

Chatter spilled from the speaker clipped to the officer's shoulder, and he reached to turn down the volume as he handed the clipboard to Faz.

"How are they doing?" Faz scribbled his name and badge number and handed the board to Del. "Are they talking?"

The officer frowned. "Not a lot."

"Anyone in with them now?" Faz asked.

"No," the officer said. "They're in the kitchen. I told them that detectives wished to speak to them."

Faz and Del stepped inside to a living room of worn furniture. To their left, an African American man sat at a kitchen table looking stunned. In his lap, a young girl pressed against his chest, her thumb in her mouth. Across the table, a woman, perhaps early fifties, held a young boy. A third seat, bathed in a stream of light from a window, remained empty. The room smelled of burned coffee.

"Mr. Rodgers?" Faz introduced himself and Del. "I'm very sorry about your wife, sir."

The woman got up from her seat carrying the boy. She held out her free hand to the father. "I'll take her?"

"Where?" Rodgers shook his head. "Where are you going to go that's safe?"

"The other room," the woman said. "I'll take them to the bedroom." She paused, but when the little girl ignored her hand, she departed with the boy. Faz and Del would talk to the woman in private and determine what she had seen and heard on the playground.

Rodgers shifted his attention to Faz. "So, what are you going to do about it?" He arched his eyebrows in question.

"We're going to work very hard to find the persons responsible." Faz chose his words carefully with a child still in the room.

"And then what?"

"We'll work very hard to arrest them."

Rodgers shook his head, as if bemused. "The guy who did this . . . A nobody. Likely a wannabe gang member and this was his initiation. Kill the squeaky wheel." Faz didn't disagree. "Getting *him* won't do anything." Rodgers grimaced as if it hurt to say the words. "It's not going to get rid of the drugs, and it's not going to get rid of the gangs, and it isn't going to bring Monique back."

Faz proceeded delicately. "If the shooter was following orders, we can bring charges against the person who gave that order. We used that law to get rid of Big Jimmy when he was running drugs down here ten years ago."

"Yeah? And who are you going to get to testify?" This time it wasn't a question.

"We'll take it one step at a time," Faz said.

"You said *Big* Jimmy," the man said. "Little Jimmy's father?"

"You know Little Jimmy?"

"Everybody down here knows Little Jimmy. He runs the drugs and he runs the gang. He's the problem."

"I understand your wife was a community activist?"

Rodgers fought back tears. His daughter pressed her head to his chest. "Didn't start out that way," he said. "Monique just wanted to get the community together to get rid of the drugs and the guns, to build a better place for our kids. She pushed the community leaders and the supervisors to establish after-school programs so the kids weren't on the street where the gangs can get at them."

"Had she been threatened by anyone?"

Rodgers chuckled, but it had a sad quality to it. "All the time, man. All the time." He shook his head. Then he repeated himself. "All the time . . . But Monique . . . She didn't care. She just went about her business. The gangs used to follow her home. They'd drive by with their music blaring."

Faz glanced at Del. Little Jimmy's drive-by had been more than a flippant display of disrespect. It had been a warning.

"Monique set up a community watch program so people could report things they saw to the police."

"What was the community's reaction to her efforts?" Faz asked.

"They were scared," Rodgers said without hesitation. "She set it up so that everything was anonymous, but people were still scared."

"Was she getting *any* traction?" Del asked.

"They shot her, didn't they?" Rodgers looked away, his gaze not focused on anyone or anything. "Mothers and kids were out there playing," he said, voice soft, "but they don't care. They don't care who they kill."

He lowered his chin, resting it on his daughter's head, clutching her, holding her tight. Faz knew it was a poor substitute for a mother's embrace.

CHAPTER 4

Tracy's walk from the courthouse to Police Headquarters on Fifth Avenue wasn't far, but it was uphill, and the heat gods had decided this would be the week Seattle burned. By the time she reached Police Headquarters, she was sweating, and her bladder beckoned yet again. When she stepped off the elevator to the seventh-floor lobby, she nearly collided with Kins. Her partner wore his jacket, preparing to go home. Since his hip replacement four months earlier, Kins had been easing his way back into work.

"Tracy. Hey, I'm glad I caught—"

"Give me a minute." She hurried past him in the direction of the bathroom. When she pushed in the door, she almost hit a woman standing on the other side. "Sorry," Tracy said.

"Detective Crosswhite." The woman spoke Tracy's name as if they knew one another. After several high-profile cases, many officers in the department knew Tracy. She'd also become a mentor to some of the younger female officers, especially those who needed shooting training to pass their qualifying exam. She didn't recognize the woman with shoulder-length auburn hair.

The woman extended a hand. "Andrea Gonzalez." The name also did not ring any memory bells.

Gonzalez looked down at Tracy's stomach. "How far along are you? Six months?"

Tracy pulled closed her suit coat. She'd only told Kins the news. SPD rules mandated that a pregnant officer be put on limited duty, which basically meant desk duty. *No thanks.* "Who told you?"

The woman shrugged. "No one. I can just tell. Though you look great."

Tracy didn't look great. Her face was puffy from water retention, and her hair had wilted from the heat. She'd also put on ten pounds and felt fat. Gonzalez, on the other hand, looked as fresh as if she'd just come in to work. Maybe she had. She wore creased black slacks and a matching jacket over a blue shirt that accentuated what Faz would have referred to as well-developed assets.

"I guess I'll be taking your place when you're out on maternity leave." Gonzalez's voice inched higher, as if she meant it as a question, though it came out a statement.

"What do you mean taking my place?"

Gonzalez smiled. "I'm just assuming that's why they hired me." She paused. "I'm sorry, I thought your department would have told you I was starting this week. I'm the A Team's new fifth wheel."

No one had told Tracy anything. "What about Ron Mayweather?"

Gonzalez shrugged. "Who's he?" She moved to the counter, checking her appearance in the mirror, then turning on the water and washing her hands.

"He's our fifth wheel, has been for several years."

"I don't know. I was just told to report to the A Team, today." Gonzalez glanced at Tracy's reflection in the mirror. "So I guess we'll be working with each other—for a few months, at least." Gonzalez dried her hands and deposited the towels in the trash. "Nice meeting you," she said and departed.

Tracy watched the door swing shut. She looked at her reflection in the mirror, focusing on the baby bump. She'd bought several shirts and jackets cut to hide her pregnancy. No one in the office had mentioned anything to her. Then again, she worked with three men who wouldn't ask a woman if she was pregnant unless she was giving birth. Still, the ease and the rapidity with which Gonzalez noted Tracy's condition made her wonder if someone had told her. And if someone had, it made her wonder if that was why Gonzalez had been hired—not to fill in, but to take Tracy's place.

CHAPTER 5

Tracy tossed a paper towel into the garbage bin and stepped from the bathroom to the lobby. Kins leaned against the wall, trying to look engaged on his phone.

"Did you know about this?" she asked.

Kins nodded like a busted teenager. "I didn't know she was in the bathroom, but . . . That's what I wanted to talk to you about. She just showed up this morning. Nolasco introduced her, said she was starting as our fifth wheel."

"She knows I'm pregnant." Tracy lowered her volume as more people entered the lobby. "How the hell does she know I'm pregnant?"

Kins shook his head. "I don't know. I didn't tell her." He looked around the lobby and nodded for Tracy to follow him down the hall. They slipped into a conference room and he shut the door.

"Look, I'm heading to South Park. Del and Faz got a murder and need help with interviews, so I don't have a lot of time. Did Gonzalez say how she knew?"

"No. She said she could tell, which I find unlikely since we've never met."

"And she said she was taking your place?"

"She said she assumed that's why she'd been hired."

"I'm sure she meant it was just for your maternity leave," he said.

"So then why did Nolasco move Ron? Why not just let him step in, like when you went out for your hip?"

"Ron's been reassigned to the C Team."

"When did that happen?"

"I just found that out late this morning when Gonzalez showed up. Apparently, Arroyo is retiring in January."

That news caught Tracy by surprise. "Arroyo is retiring?"

Kins shrugged. "Apparently."

They were getting off topic. "Ron's been working with us for three years," she said. "Why would Nolasco reassign him?"

"Maybe because none of us is going anywhere. You're not, are you?"

"What does that mean?"

"It means I assume you're coming back, after you have the baby. You are, aren't you?"

"This is no different from your hip surgery. You were out, Ron filled in, now you're back."

"Yes, but I didn't have to leave my hip at home, Tracy."

For a moment she didn't speak, uncertain of Kins's point. Then she said, "What?"

"You know how it is. That's your baby you're leaving at home. And you don't have to work. We all know Dan does well . . . better than well."

Tracy and Dan had married a year earlier. "Dan just hired someone so he could spend more time at home. I'm not planning on quitting, Kins." Kins had a strange expression, like a man standing on the edge of a cliff, terrified to jump. "What?" she asked.

He shook his head. "Nothing."

"What?"

"Nothing. I got to go."

"If you think I'm acting irrationally, tell me."

He looked at his watch. "Okay, look, just promise not to bite my head off, all right? This is just a friend talking to a friend—someone who's been down this path before."

Kins had three sons. "Fine," Tracy said.

Kins laughed uneasily. "Tracy, I know you. You're listening but you're ready to take me down and remove my gallbladder with your hands."

She pulled out a chair and sat, crossing her legs. "I'm calm, okay? And I'm listening."

Kins took a moment to either gather his thoughts or his courage. He stepped off the ledge. "This is your first child, so I think it's safe to say that you can't fully predict how you're going to feel when the baby is born."

"I know—"

Kins raised a hand. "Just hear me out."

She raised both hands as if to say, *Fine, continue.*

"I know that when you have a kid you think nothing is going to change, that work isn't going to change, but it does. Everything changes, and not for the worse. It just changes. That's the hard part—leaving the best part of you at home, with someone else. The best part of you is being raised by someone else. I didn't want that. Neither did Shannah. So she quit her job and stayed home even though we couldn't really afford it. And, even with Shannah at home, it was still hard as hell for me, Tracy. I'd get to work and I couldn't wait to leave, to get back home and see my boys."

Tracy knew from years working together what Kins's boys meant to him. She'd watched them grow and heard the stories.

"I couldn't wait to coach them in Little League and to go to their high school games. I loved it. I've loved every minute of it. Now, in a couple months, we'll be taking Connor off to college and I'm already dreading that day because I know it's going to hurt. It's going to hurt to know he's not sleeping in his bed, that he has another bed and another life, with people I don't even know." Kins's voice choked and Tracy knew he was fighting to suppress his emotions. After a pause, he blew out a held breath. "I know every parent goes through it. Every parent has to say good-bye, but trust me, that doesn't make it any easier. So I'm just telling you, it goes by so fast. Before you know it, and much sooner than you ever expected, you'll be driving them off to college and saying good-bye. And you'll ask yourself, *Where did the years go?* You'll look at pictures and you can't even remember when they were that small, and you'll wish they still were; that you could go back to those days and just have them home again. So what I'm telling you is, don't look at staying home as some punishment, Tracy, because if you do, you'll regret it and . . . look, I got to go."

Kins pulled open the door and departed without finishing the sentence, but he didn't have to. Tracy knew what he was thinking but didn't say.

And this might be your only child.

—

After leaving the conference room, Tracy grabbed a decaffeinated coffee from the kitchen, which she thought best given her current agitated state, and headed to her desk. She felt flushed, as warm as she'd felt walking up the hill to Police Headquarters. Her conversation with Andrea Gonzalez kept filtering through her mind.

How far along are you? Six months?

God, did she look that big already?

Kins, too, had surprised her. She knew he loved his three boys, without question, but he'd also told her the unflattering stories: the stupid things the boys did, the pandemonium in the house, the trips to school because one of the boys was in trouble or failing a class. It had been hard to watch him in the conference room, on the verge of tears because one of his sons was leaving for college. It was raw emotion, something police officers didn't let out often with other officers, if at all.

Tracy stepped into the A Team's bull pen. Andrea Gonzalez sat at Tracy's desk, which simply was never done at SPD. Desks and cubicles were sacrosanct. Fifth wheels sat at computer terminals in the back of the room. Gonzalez looked like she'd moved in. She'd hung her jacket in Tracy's cubicle closet and a Starbucks coffee cup with red lipstick on the rim rested on Tracy's desk pad.

"Excuse me," she said. Gonzalez turned. "What are you doing at my desk?"

"What?"

Tracy pointed to her desk. "What are you doing at my desk?"

Gonzalez looked as if she didn't understand the question. "I understood you were testifying in court all day. Captain Nolasco told me to get caught up on your case files."

Tracy looked at the computer and saw a document on the screen. "How'd you get into my case files?"

"Captain Nolasco had IT provide me with a generic password."

Tracy clenched her teeth, afraid of what she might say. She should have known Nolasco would have something to do with this. Nobody would be happier to have Tracy leave.

"Let me clear out," Gonzalez said. She stood and grabbed her coffee. "Listen, I'm sorry. I didn't know this was a breach of some protocol. In LA, we often just picked a desk not being used and logged in."

Tracy wasn't interested in the debate. "I need to make a phone call."

Gonzalez checked her watch. "I feel like we're getting off on the wrong foot here. Can I buy you a beer?" She cringed and glanced at Tracy's stomach. "I'm sorry. Maybe something nonalcoholic?"

Tracy suppressed her anger, thinking it better directed at Nolasco than Gonzalez. Maybe her hormones were just out of whack. "Thanks, but I can't. I'm in trial and I need to contact the prosecutor to prepare for tomorrow."

"Right. I heard that. Anyway, sorry about using your desk."

Gonzalez departed the cubicle.

Tracy sat and hit the space bar. The computer went to her password-protected screen, as it always did when the keyboard remained idle for a prolonged period. She typed in her password and the computer screen came back to life. She was looking at a file Del had apparently opened on the South Park shooting, though it was still blank. Her e-mails, too, had been opened. She checked the Sent folder, but nothing had been sent from her computer since she'd last used it the prior afternoon.

Her desk phone rang. Now fully paranoid, she deliberately did not use her normal greeting, which included her name, in case the call was for Gonzalez. "Hello," she said.

"Oh, uh, I'm trying to reach Detective Crosswhite?"

A female voice, but not one Tracy recognized. "This is Detective Crosswhite."

"Tracy?" The caller sounded confused. "It's Katie. Katie Pryor."

"Katie. Hi. Sorry. I was . . . I was just busy with something and . . . never mind. Hey, how do you like the new job?"

Six months earlier, Talia Greenwood had retired from the missing persons unit after more than thirty years. Tracy had recommended Pryor for the job. Pryor, a mother of two young girls with a husband who liked her at home, had told Tracy one afternoon at the shooting range that she was looking for something with more stable hours.

"I like it . . . well, as much as anyone can like searching for missing persons. The structured hours allow me to better plan my time at home with the kids."

There had been a time when just the mention of the words "missing person" caused a visceral reaction in Tracy. Her sister, Sarah, had been abducted and her whereabouts unknown for more than twenty years. With time, she'd become more accepting.

"Listen, I don't want to keep you," Pryor said. "I know you're in the Stephenson trial, but I got in a report from a woman who thinks her roommate is missing and I don't have a good feeling about it. I ordinarily wouldn't bother you without more information, but my captain is in Europe for the next two weeks, and the woman who made the report is leaving the country to live in London. I thought it best to have someone in Violent Crimes talk with her before she goes. The person missing doesn't sound like someone who'd just take up and leave."

"How old is she?" Tracy asked.

"Twenty-four. The two women shared an apartment in the University District near the UW campus."

"Students?"

"Graduates. The missing woman was apparently applying to medical schools."

Most missing persons tended to be either in a high-risk profession, like prostitution, or have high-risk circumstances—the addicted, mentally challenged, or the elderly suffering from Alzheimer's or dementia.

"This woman making the report was her roommate?" Tracy asked.

"Up until recently."

"What happened recently?"

"The woman who made the report got married in India, unexpectedly from the sound of it. She didn't even get the chance to tell her roommate about it until she got back. She's the one moving to London."

"Okay, so why does she think her roommate's missing?"

"She can't reach her on her cell, and she isn't responding to text messages or e-mails. She said she's just disappeared. It's complicated."

"How long has she been gone?"

"Getting close to twenty-four hours."

Tracy knew twenty-four hours could be an eternity to a family but not to SPD, though that, too, was changing. SPD used to wait forty-eight hours before considering a person missing, but they'd become more vigilant after a recent case in which a nurse met a man online and went missing. They found her body parts scattered in garbage bins throughout the city.

Pryor continued, "She said they've been friends since childhood and that she wouldn't just run away." Tracy heard Pryor rustling papers. "Sorry, this is confusing. The one making the report is named Aditi Dasgupta."

"Indian."

"Yes. Dasgupta said she and her roommate, Kavita Mukherjee, have gone to school together since they were kids, and they've lived together in an apartment in the U District the last two years. Both had been planning on attending medical school."

"I'm not following."

"Neither was I. The officer who took the report said the one filing the report . . . Dasgupta . . . recently got married in India—an arranged marriage, apparently. The missing roommate, Kavita Mukherjee, didn't know about the wedding."

"She didn't know her roommate got married?"

"Apparently not. Anyway, Dasgupta said the roommate, Kavita Mukherjee, was pretty upset when she found out."

"Could she just be upset and need some time alone to process everything that has happened?"

"Maybe, but Dasgupta doesn't think that's the case. She said it's not like her."

"Have you filled out an EMPA yet?" Tracy asked, referring to an Endangered/Missing Person Alert.

"I haven't had the chance. I've been making telephone calls to the family and several friends, and to her employer. No one has heard from her."

Tracy looked at the clock in the lower right corner of her computer screen. She'd hoped to get home at a decent hour. She also knew Nolasco would never let her take a missing persons case, not without more substantial evidence of a violent crime, and not with Del and Faz pulling a murder in South Park and likely needing support.

"Are you still in your office?" Tracy asked.

"I am."

"I'll stop by on my way home," she said. "I have to make a phone call. Can you stay for a bit?"

"I'll stay," Pryor said. "You want me to send you what I have?"

Tracy didn't, given that it was unlikely Nolasco would agree to let her run with it. "Print out the report for me. I'll pick it up when I stop by."

"I appreciate it. I know you're busy but . . . You know how you get a sense about these cases, when something just doesn't seem right?"

Tracy did, all too well.

CHAPTER 6

Anderson-Cooper went door-to-door at the apartment complex in search of witnesses to the shooting, while Del and Faz canvassed the local businesses for videotape that might have captured the killer fleeing the scene, or getting into a car, anything. It was already early evening, and some of the businesses had closed. Faz kept a log of those that had, so detectives could return first thing in the morning. If the business had video, they'd want to get there before that video was recorded over. He'd also called the traffic division and asked that traffic cameras in that area be checked and film preserved. Monique Rodgers's mother said she'd heard shots fired on the east side of the apartment complex. If correct, South Cloverdale, which ran parallel with the building, would have been a natural escape route for the shooter.

The owner of a gas station at the end of the block said his camera focused on the gas pumps but it might have recorded a portion of the street. To keep things moving, Del and Faz left a detective from the video unit to go through the footage while they drove to a convenience store across the street, which was also a good bet to have videotape.

Faz pushed open the glass door, causing a string of bells tied to the inside handle to rattle. A man tall enough to look him in the eye, and as wide as Faz and Del combined, greeted them with a scowl.

"Can I help you?"

The man had a bun of curly black hair. He folded meaty arms across his chest and rested them on an ample stomach. Elaborate tattoos encircled biceps as big as most men's legs. He wore shorts, a T-shirt, and flip-flops.

Faz and Del introduced themselves and explained the reason for their presence. The owner had a soft handshake and a voice higher-pitched than Faz would have imagined for a man his size. He introduced himself as Tanielu Eliapo but said, "Guys, call me Tanny. It's easier. I heard about what happened to that lady."

"How'd you hear?"

"It was on the news, man." He turned and pointed to a small television hanging above the checkout counter where a woman, who also looked to be of Polynesian descent and was also very big, sat on a wooden stool eyeballing them with a sullen expression. An oscillating fan on the counter rotated left to right and back, causing the woman's floral dress and strands of hair to flutter.

"Hey!" Tanny turned and shouted at two Hispanic kids near a magazine rack at the storefront. They flinched and looked up at him. Tanny pointed to a sign on the wall. "If you're reading it, you're buying it. Make a choice." Then he pointed to a mounted camera hanging from the ceiling. "Surprise, man. You're on candid camera! If I don't catch you, the camera does, and then I finish you."

Tanny continued to eye them until they put the magazine back on the rack and walked to the register carrying soda and candy. He turned back to Faz. "I heard people are afraid to talk to the police."

"Where'd you hear that?" Faz asked, doubtful it was from the news.

"Word on the street spreads fast, man."

"What else have you heard?" Del asked.

"I heard Little Jimmy is getting the word out that he doesn't want anyone talking to you."

So Faz's assumption that Little Jimmy had some involvement appeared accurate. "You know him?" Faz asked.

"Know of him. Ricardo Luis Bernadino Jiminez." Tanny said the name quickly and made a face like he'd detected a bad odor. "He's a punk. I've heard that his father, Big Jimmy, was a big deal here in South Park—that he did a lot for the people. Little Jimmy isn't a big deal, though he thinks he is. Heard he's working for one of the Mexican cartels. Back then Big Jimmy was dealing pot. Little Jimmy's dealing heroin. Bad shit, man. That stuff will kill you."

Faz glanced at Del, who'd lost his niece to a heroin overdose less than six months earlier. Del didn't say anything.

"You're not afraid of him?" Faz asked.

Tanny scoffed liked the question was ridiculous. "What's he going to do? He knows if he touches me or my business, the Bruddahs will not be happy. Trust me, he don't want nothing to do with the Bruddahs, man."

Faz could see why, given Tanny's size—not to mention the woman behind the counter. She looked like she could eat glass shards and shit a stained-glass window. He pointed to the ceiling. "You have video?" he asked.

Tanny nodded to the woman. "Pika likes to look at the video every night. She can watch on her phone. She sees anybody steal anything, the next time they come in . . . it's not so good for them. Me, I don't like people who steal. Pika, she's biblical about it." He shrugged and gave them a broad smile.

"Can we look at the tape for today, about three o'clock, maybe a little before?" Faz asked.

"You want to see?" Tanny asked.

"Absolutely," Del said.

"Pika, I'll be in the back." He nodded to two young men who'd walked in the front door. "Watch those two. If they steal anything, break their arms." He smacked a meaty fist into his palm and grunted before leading Del and Faz through a door at the back of the store to a computer set on a folding table. The room was cluttered with boxes and cleaning supplies and had the sharp smell of ammonia. In the corner, the wooden handle of a mop protruded from a metal bucket and leaned against the edge of a large sink. The lone window above the computer was fogged glass, barred on the inside.

"You like my office?" Tanny laughed and spread his arms wide, as if showing off the place. "It's a dump, man." He typed at the keyboard with stubby fingers, then circled with the mouse. "You said around three o'clock today?"

"Approximately," Faz said, slipping on cheaters to see the screen clearly.

Tanny typed again. A black-and-white image appeared on the screen with a date and time bar in the bottom right corner. He used the mouse to advance the video, stopping at 2:33 p.m. Then he let it run at regular speed. The image on the computer screen focused primarily on the interior of the store—and the counter where Pika sat—but it also showed the glass door entrance and a portion of the parking lot and the street. Still, Faz's barometer that the video had captured anything useful remained "doubtful." They watched the video as people entered the store, bought items, and departed. Faz paid close attention to the street, cars passing the store and pulling into and out of the parking lot, people walking.

Nearly fifteen minutes had passed when Del said, "Can we speed it up? If we see anything we can stop and go back."

"No problem, man," Tanny said.

He hit the "Fast Forward" button and the tape speed increased, though not dramatically. "You want to go faster, man?"

"No, this is good for now," Del said.

After several minutes, Faz said, "Wait. Go back."

"You see something?" Del asked.

"I don't know."

Tanny rewound the tape.

"Right there. Stop it. Now go forward," Faz said. "Stop. You see?" he said to Del. He pointed a finger at the right corner of the screen where someone had appeared, though the image was fuzzy.

"Yeah, I see," Del said, not sounding impressed.

"Play it," Faz said, leaning closer to the screen. The person jogged into the picture and across a patch of lawn, toward the street, too far from the camera for them to see any features. "Stop it," Faz said. He leaned in closer. "What's he wearing over his face?"

"I see him," Tanny said, pointing with his index finger. "That's a hoodie, man. You know, a sweatshirt. He has the hood up. You see?"

"Yeah, I see," Faz said. "I think you're right."

"He's got it pulled tight around his face," Tanny said.

"It had to be ninety degrees today," Del said.

"Eighty-five," Tanny said. "It's crazy, I know, but they wear them all the time around here. Hoodies and tank-top T-shirts."

"Tied shut like that?" Del asked.

"That I don't see so much," Tanny said.

Faz looked for identifying characteristics—a team logo, something to distinguish the hooded sweatshirt. If there were any, the distance was too great for them to see clearly. He glanced down at the time in the lower right corner of the computer screen, then up at Del. "Right time."

"Right location," Del said. The path to the street would have been from the back of the apartment complex.

Tanny looked between the two of them. "You think this could be your shooter?"

"Hard to tell," Del said. "Might be nothing."

"How you going to identify him wearing a hoodie like that?" Tanny said.

"Don't know," Faz said. "Continue playing it."

Tanny hit the button and the man stepped from the curb. He stumbled, as if he'd twisted an ankle and, to maintain his balance, placed his left hand on the hood of a parked car. Then he righted himself and limped across the street, dodging southbound traffic. He nearly ran out of the picture frame before he climbed into the passenger seat of what looked to be a white SUV or truck—Faz couldn't tell—a split second before the vehicle drove out of the camera frame.

"Did you see that?" Faz asked.

"I saw," Del said.

Tanny hit "Stop" and looked to Del and Faz. "So what you think, Bruddah?"

Del spoke to Faz. "I doubt we can get a license plate on the white SUV even if we get the tape enhanced. It's too far and not enough frames for them to work with. But we might be able to get the plate of the parked car he put his hand on."

"Maybe," Faz said. "Traffic cameras could have picked up the white vehicle he got into. And just in case we should check local hospitals—see if anyone came in with an ankle injury."

"Doubt it, but worth a shot," Del said.

Faz pulled out his cell phone to contact the video unit detective. He turned to Tanny. "I'm going to have somebody come down here and retrieve the video."

"No problem, man." Tanny shrugged.

Faz held out a business card. It looked as small as a postage stamp in Tanny's hands. "I know you're not afraid of Little Jimmy, and I don't want to tell you what to do, but I'd keep this quiet," Faz said. "Little Jimmy might be a punk, but if he's running the Sureños, that could quickly become a problem for you."

Tanny smiled. "I ain't stupid, man. What you seen out there?" He pointed with his thumb to the door leading to the interior of the store. "That was just for show, man. You can't show fear around here. You show fear and people will steal you blind. But in here, yeah, Bruddah, I understand. I ain't looking to take no bullet. Like I say, Little Jimmy, he's crazy loco."

CHAPTER 7

Tracy hung up after speaking to the prosecutor, Adam Hoetig. They'd discussed her testimony, as well as possible areas that Leonard Litwin would attempt to attack her in his restructured cross-examination. She also told Hoetig she had a bladder infection and would appreciate a break midmorning—if Litwin planned to go longer than an hour. Since Tracy was the last witness scheduled to testify, and Hoetig didn't anticipate rebuttal witnesses, he begged off meeting in person so he could work on his closing argument.

After the call, Tracy made her way to the outer offices. She wanted to catch Nolasco before he went home. She wanted to ask him about Ron Mayweather, and about Arroyo's apparent impending retirement, as well as get a feel for whether Nolasco knew about her pregnancy and had told Gonzalez. The blinds to his office windows were lowered and pinched shut, preventing her from seeing inside. Tracy knocked on a closed door, heard Nolasco say, "Enter," and pushed the door in.

Nolasco sat behind his desk holding a mug of tea. Across from him, Andrea Gonzalez sat in one of two chairs. She turned to look at Tracy.

"You two have met?" Nolasco said.

"Yeah," Tracy and Gonzalez said at the same time.

Tracy looked to Nolasco. "I'll come back."

"No." Gonzalez stood. "I'm just on my way out. Thanks, Captain. I'm on it." She smiled at Tracy as she stepped past her.

"You need to hear this too." Nolasco spoke before Tracy had taken a step inside his office. "You heard about the shooting in South Park?"

Tracy nodded. "Yeah, from Kins when I got in from court."

"Someone shot into a playground at an apartment complex and killed a mother of two. She'd been outspoken against the drugs and gangs down there. The news is all over it, which means they're all over us. I'm sending anyone I can to help Del and Faz canvass the area. Where are you at in your trial?"

"Back on the stand tomorrow morning."

"Who's after you?"

"No one, unless Hoetig calls someone on rebuttal, or Litwin changes his mind overnight. Hoetig thinks he'll give closing late morning or early afternoon."

"Del and Faz are going to need your help as soon you're finished," he said. The lead detective in a homicide trial typically sat with the prosecutor at counsel table from pretrial motions until the jury delivered its verdict. It was intended to give a human face to the state's case.

"Are we operating under the premise that the killing was retaliatory?" Tracy asked.

"We are."

"That's Sureño territory down there," Tracy said. She'd had two gang killings in South Park.

"I want you to call Del and Faz as soon as you're done and find out what they need." Nolasco lowered his head, apparently thinking their conversation had concluded. He looked up when Tracy didn't leave. "Something else?"

"Did you provide Gonzalez a password to get on to my computer?"

"No. I told her to check with IT for a temporary password."

"You know she has a computer back in administration, right? She didn't have to use mine."

"With Del and Faz gone, and you and Kins in trial, I wanted someone in the bull pen. And I wanted her to get familiar with your files so she could hit the ground running."

"Yeah, but using my computer with a temporary password she could access my privatized files, my report files." Detectives could all access the unit files, but only the lead detective on any particular case could open the report files, or "privatized" files. Any unauthorized access of those files was reported to the lead detective in a V-mail, which stood for Versaterm.

"All of you are too attached to your terminals. Files are supposed to be open so the work is collaborative. I don't understand the problem," Nolasco said.

Tracy couldn't be sure if Nolasco was pushing her or not. She decided to push him. "Ron *knew* what was going on?"

"What's that supposed to mean?"

"Ron was our fifth wheel and he was up to speed on our files."

"Yeah, and we had an opening on C Team. Arroyo is retiring end of the year."

"I heard."

"Did you hear that Ron wanted the position, which left an opening for a fifth wheel on A Team?"

"Ron wanted to move teams?"

Nolasco stared at her. "Anything else?"

"You hired Gonzalez awfully quickly."

"No, I didn't. That took place above me and has been in the works since Arroyo told the brass he was leaving." He paused. "You know, most detectives would have thanked me."

Tracy said, "For what?"

"For putting the quality of your team first and getting someone quickly up to speed."

Tracy nodded. "Well, then, thank you."

"Anything else?"

Tracy shook her head. She wasn't going to get anything more out of Nolasco, and Katie Pryor was waiting for her at the Park 95 complex.

"As soon as you're free, give Faz and Del a hand," Nolasco said.

Tracy drove to the Park 95 complex, the department name for the concrete buildings on Airport Way that housed much of the Seattle Police Department's forensic units, CSI, and specialty units such as SWAT. She made her way to the missing persons unit. Well after six o'clock, most of the building's cubicles were empty, without voices, telephones ringing, or the tapping of keystrokes.

Tracy knew the missing persons unit from her time working with CSI in the same building. She'd also worked with Talia Greenwood, Katie Pryor's predecessor, on several missing persons cases. Greenwood had told Tracy that the unit never considered a case hopeless or closed. Greenwood either found the missing person, or the case lingered in an open file on her computer. Tracy thought that a depressing and thankless task—a job you brought home at night; a job that could consume you each time you read or heard that another person went missing or a body was found; a job you could never escape.

Greenwood once told Tracy she was only partially correct.

As emotionally taxing as the job could be, Greenwood said she'd also experienced many good moments. Most people reported to be missing weren't actually missing; they'd often been arrested and sent to the county jail, or they'd been hurt and taken to a hospital. Others just wanted to get lost for a short while, when everyday life became too much for them to bear, which was perhaps insensitive to those who loved them but not illegal. And therein lay the first problem. How long did a young woman need to be missing before she was considered missing? What circumstances had to exist for a person to be missing and not just taking a break from life? SPD constantly seemed to be refining the answers to those questions.

"Knock, knock," Tracy said.

Pryor swiveled her chair, stood, and gave Tracy a smile and a hug. "Tracy. Hey. Thanks for coming down." Her voice was soft, high-pitched, and reminded Tracy of a schoolgirl's. It had only been a few years since Tracy met Pryor at the shooting range to help her to pass her qualification exam, but already Pryor's laugh lines were a bit more pronounced and her hips fuller.

"Sorry it took longer than expected. How're the kids?" Tracy asked.

"Everyone is doing well. Can you believe my oldest will be starting middle school in the fall?" Pryor shook her head the same way Kins had when he'd told Tracy that his oldest was leaving for college.

"You ever think about that, where the years went?" Tracy asked.

Pryor laughed. "Only on special occasions—like birthdays and Christmas. On a day-to-day basis, my husband and I are just trying to keep the ship afloat. This job has really helped. I can plan around my kids' schedules, be home to help them with homework, and pick them up after their practices. It's been a godsend; it really has."

"I'm glad to hear it," Tracy said, and then, maybe because they'd broached the topic of kids, she added, "Because I'm going to be faced with that problem soon."

"You're pregnant?" Pryor asked, her voice rising with disbelief. Tracy knew that part of Pryor's surprise related to Tracy's age, and likely a perception that Tracy had either chosen not to have children or couldn't conceive.

"I just completed my sixteenth week."

Pryor smiled. "Oh my God," she said. "That's fantastic." She looked down at Tracy's belly. "I never would have guessed. You look terrific."

Coming from a mother of two, Pryor's comment made Tracy wonder again how Gonzalez had so quickly deduced her pregnancy. "I don't always feel terrific," she said. "And I'm keeping it quiet for now."

"I won't say anything. Do you know the sex?"

"No," Tracy said. "Dan doesn't want to find out. He said it's the last real surprise in life and I guess I agree with him."

Pryor smiled. "I'm happy for you."

"It will complicate things," Tracy said. It already had.

"Don't worry about work, Tracy. You're not the first woman with a job who has had a child. Did I tell you the story about the time when I was seven months pregnant with my second and still working patrol?"

"I don't think so."

"My sergeant, who had a gut out to here," Pryor said, extending her arms and hands to simulate a bulging stomach, "actually had the nerve to ask how I was going to put on my gun belt. You know what I told him?"

"No," Tracy said, though she was already laughing.

"I said, 'The same way you do, Sergeant.'" They both laughed. "We never had that conversation again," Pryor said. She looked up at the clock on the wall. "Okay, I know you're pressed for time. We can talk more about babies later. I got you a seat."

Tracy wheeled the chair closer to the computer and sat beside Pryor, who handed her a multipage document, then turned to her keyboard and typed. Tracy studied the missing person's report, which also appeared on Pryor's screen. Soft music played from Pryor's computer.

"The missing woman's name is Kavita Mukherjee," Pryor said. "Twenty-four years old, a graduate of the University of Washington with a degree in chemistry."

"I like her already," Tracy said. She'd been a high school chemistry teacher before joining the police force. "So, no dummy."

"Definitely not. Her former roommate, Aditi Dasgupta, sent me the photograph you're looking at."

Pryor enlarged the photograph on her computer screen, which was clearer and less grainy than the printed copy. Mukherjee reclined on a couch. She wore a black T-shirt and jeans with holes in the knees. Her toenails were painted a bright red.

"Beautiful girl," Tracy said.

"She's five feet, ten inches tall and a hundred and thirty pounds with dark-brown hair and blue eyes."

"Blue eyes? That's got to be rare for her nationality."

"I thought the same thing. It's uncommon for someone of Indian descent, but it does happen."

"You said she and the roommate were friends?"

"Since childhood. The past four years they've been roommates."

Tracy sat back, content to let Pryor tell her what she'd learned.

—

The front door to the apartment opened slowly. Kavita Mukherjee, reclining on the sofa in the living room, slapped closed the novel she'd been reading, tossed it into the air, and shouted, "Aditi!"

She jumped from the couch and rushed the door, ignoring Aditi's suitcases and embracing her best friend in a bear hug. Aditi had left earlier that summer to attend a cousin's wedding in India, then had stayed several months, traveling. She and Kavita had rarely been apart since childhood.

"It's so good to have you back," Kavita said. "Was it really twelve weeks? It feels as if you have been gone forever. And look at you!" She touched the silk of Aditi's green-and-yellow sari. "You look so different. Did you buy this over there? Let me guess. Your mother bought it for you." Kavita laughed and rolled her eyes. "She never gives up, does she?"

"No," Aditi said, smiling. "She never does."

They were both twenty-four years old, Kavita the older by a couple of months, and already their mothers were harping on them to "settle," which meant "get married." Forget that neither had a serious boyfriend. In fact, that was preferred. It made Kavita and Aditi that much more attractive to the list of suitors their mothers had started to compile even before they'd completed their undergraduate education. Not that Aditi or Kavita were having any of it.

"Here, let me help you." Kavita picked up the last of three large suitcases still in the hall.

"No. It's—" Aditi said, reaching for the case.

"It's so light," Kavita said. "Someday you'll have to teach me to pack."

She set the suitcase down beside the two in the entryway and pulled Aditi into the living room. They'd rented the apartment in the University District after their sophomore year at the UW. They lived in the dorms their first two years but wanted something of their own. The furnishings were a hodgepodge of borrowed and gifted furniture and what they could get for next to nothing—a gray leather couch, a brown cloth chair, and an assortment of lamps, which they rarely used in the summer months when it stayed light past nine at night. From their fifth-floor, eastern-facing apartment, they had views of the UW campus, Lake Washington, and, on clear days such as this, the snowcapped Cascade mountains. Tonight, the sound of buses and cars filtered up from the Ave through the open windows.

"So, come on." Kavita sat, folding her bare feet beneath her. She wore jeans with holes in the knees and a purple University of Washington T-shirt. "Tell me all about your trip. How was your cousin's wedding? Did you get sick from the food? I'll bet it was hot. You must have been out of Internet range because I didn't get any of your messages the last two weeks. I'm just so glad to have you back." She leaned forward, and the two women embraced.

"It was nice," Aditi said. She looked understandably tired after traveling halfway around the world.

"Nice? It was nice?" Kavita laughed. "Always the woman of few words." She slapped at Aditi playfully. "Tell me about the wedding. Was the rest of your family surprised to see you? I'll bet they were surprised at how much you've matured."

"They were surprised," Aditi said. She dropped her gaze to her hands, which she'd folded in her lap. Kavita got an uneasy feeling that something

was wrong. Aditi was more than a friend and a roommate; the two women were like sisters. They knew each other's moods.

"What's wrong? What's the matter?" Kavita asked, but even as she spoke, her eyes, no longer filled with excitement, considered Aditi more carefully, and she fixated on the gold necklace with the black beads, then noticed the red dot just beneath Aditi's hairline. Kavita looked down at Aditi's open-toed sandals. Rings adorned several of her toes, much more than a young woman's fashion statement.

The realization hit her like a punch to the gut. She could barely get the words out, suddenly nauseated. "You're married?" She said the words as if not believing them, not wanting to believe them, wanting to be wrong.

Aditi raised her gaze to meet Kavita's. Tears trickled down her cheeks, but she tried to smile through them.

Kavita let go of her friend's hands. "I don't understand." She quickly added, "Is that why you went home?"

Aditi shook her head. "No. No, Vita. It was just a visit, to attend my cousin's wedding."

"But . . . what happened . . . my e-mails . . ."

"I met Rashesh at the wedding and, afterward, just a day or two, he came and spoke with my father. My relatives arranged it all."

"Who is he?" Kavita said.

"He's an engineer," Aditi said, "from Bangladesh, but he works in London. His father and my father have been friends since they were boys. They grew up in the same village. That's why his family was at my cousin's wedding."

The information seemed as if it was assaulting Kavita from a dozen different angles. She felt dizzy and disoriented. "An arranged marriage?" She shook her head, disbelieving. "But we said we would never agree to it. We both said we'd never agree to it." They'd sworn an oath—a silly little oath in a fort they'd built in the state park when they'd been schoolgirls, but an oath they had renewed over the years. It had become a lifeline that had provided them strength when their parents persisted in trying to arrange their weddings and, when Kavita and Aditi refused to acquiesce, when their parents would no longer pay the apartment rent or for postgraduate study.

Aditi gripped Kavita's hands, speaking softly, as if talking to a hurt little girl. "We were just kids, Vita. We were just little girls."

Kavita pulled her hands away and wiped tears from her cheeks. She looked at the suitcases. Another shock wave rolled over her. "They're empty, aren't they? You're not here to move home. You're here to move out."

Aditi nodded, now openly weeping. "My parents and . . . my husband are waiting downstairs. I asked them to let me break the news to you. I'm sorry, Vita . . . I can pay the rent until you find someone to take my place. I can—"

Kavita stood and turned from her. The word "husband" had not rolled off Aditi's tongue naturally. It sounded awkward, like she was pronouncing a foreign language and was uncertain she'd got it right. "It's not about the rent, Aditi. We agreed. We—"

"I'm not like you, Vita. I'm not as strong as you. I . . . I can't do what you're doing."

Kavita turned to her. "What about medical school?"

"I have my place now."

"What place? Following a man around you hardly know? Moving in with his family and cleaning up after them, waiting on them like some servant? Like the good Indian wife?"

Aditi looked as if the last words pierced her. "I'm sorry, Vita. I know you don't understand—"

"Of course I don't understand. My best friend goes home for a visit and comes back married . . . and . . . and you didn't even invite me?" It was like another punch, a round of blows threatening to knock her down.

"I didn't go to India intending to get married, Vita. You have to believe me. It was only after we met at the wedding . . . and I liked him. A week later, the invitations were printed. Two weeks after that we were married."

Kavita paced before the open windows. "My invitation must have gotten lost in the mail." Another thought gained clarity and she turned to her friend. "You ignored my e-mails. The Internet was fine. You just didn't want to answer them because you didn't want to lie to me."

Aditi remained seated. "I didn't invite you, Vita, because you wouldn't have understood. You would have tried to talk me out of it."

"You're damn right I would have tried to talk you out of it. This is insanity. You were going to be a doctor. We'd talked about it for years. Pediatricians. Opening a practice together. I would have asked you if you'd lost your mind, if your mother had slipped something into your drink when you weren't looking. I would have called the embassy and told them you were being held captive against your will. What were you thinking?"

"I wasn't thinking, Vita. Not about getting married . . . Not until I met him."

Kavita stopped pacing. She didn't want to hear it. "Please don't tell me this was what, love at first sight?"

"Love comes in time."

"Stop. Just stop! Do you hear yourself? My God, you sound like your mother. Like my mother." She switched to a Bengali accent. "No man marries willingly, Kavita. He does it out of attraction, or for money, or to keep a family obligation. Money is spent, attraction fades, but stability is built through family." She dropped the accent. "So what was it, Aditi? Money? Did your parents sell you off to him, a big dowry he couldn't resist, or was it to keep a family obligation?"

Aditi lowered her gaze, weeping. Kavita gritted her teeth, regretting what she'd said. She'd always been quick to anger, a bad trait when accompanied by a sharp tongue that cut before she could curtail it. She sat and pressed her forehead to her best friend's, the way they had always done, the way they did when they'd made their pact. "I'm sorry, Diti. I didn't mean it. I'm just so . . . stunned . . . I didn't mean it."

After a moment, Aditi raised her gaze. "I like him, Vita. I liked him from the moment I saw him."

Kavita shook her head. "But do you love him, Diti? Are you hopelessly in love and you can't fathom living a day without him? Do you feel that way about him, Diti? Do you?"

Aditi sat back. Her words came with a bite. "And how has that worked out for you, Vita? How has it worked out for me?"

"We're only twenty-four! We were going to graduate school."

"How many boyfriends have I had, Vita?" Aditi persisted.

"What?"

Aditi shook her head but maintained her gaze and her resolve. "I'm not like you. I don't look like you and I don't have your personality. I didn't do as well as you in school. You are going to medical school, Vita, but what if I don't get in? What if my MCATs are not as good as yours? What then?"

"You're beautiful, Diti, and you're smart. Of course you'll get in."

Aditi's voice rose in volume and increased in intensity. "No, Vita. I'm not." She took a deep breath that fluttered in her chest. "I'm not smart, not like you. I just work harder. And I'm not beautiful, especially not here."

"Aditi—"

Aditi raised her hand. "Stop, Vita. We go out and men flock to you and your light skin. Me? They talk to me because I'm there, like a houseplant. They think that if they talk to me long enough they might get the chance to talk to you."

"That's not true."

"Yes, Vita, it is true," she said, her voice becoming ever more adamant. "Look at you. You're tall and thin and you have fine features, and those blue eyes. Men love your blue eyes. You can talk to anyone about anything and they'll listen." She shook her head. "I'm the awkward obligation, the person they have to talk with if they want to talk to you. It's been that way all our lives. All my life I've taken a backseat to you, and I was happy to do it, happy to just be your friend." She tapped her chest with a closed fist. "But this man, Rashesh, he saw me and he liked what he saw. Do you know how that made me feel?"

Kavita didn't want to hurt her friend. She didn't want to tell her that Rashesh might not have liked what he saw at all. In India it was not about love at first sight. It wasn't even about love. It was about societal pressure placed mostly on girls, and their parents, but also on men. The older a young woman got, the greater the apprehension that she would not marry, and the greater the suspicion that she had been ditched by some other suitor because she was too ambitious, because she wasn't wife material, or because there was some dosh *in her* kundali. *(The stars weren't appropriately aligned at the time of her birth.)*

Something.

Kavita spoke, her voice barely above a whisper. "But he doesn't even know you, Diti."

"Exactly, Vita," her friend said, eyes widening. "That is exactly my point. He didn't even know me and yet he liked me. He liked my dark skin and my flat nose, and my overweight body. He didn't talk to me just so he could talk to you. So why can't you be my friend now, Vita? Why can't you just be happy for me?"

"Because I hate to see you throw your life away like this."

"But it's my life, Vita!" Aditi said, striking her chest. "It's my life and I can do with it as I please. Now who sounds like my mother, telling me what is best for me?"

"But you're not Indian, Diti. I'm not Indian. We're American. We were born here in America."

"I am Indian, Vita. To my very core, my very essence, I am Indian. Yes, I call this home but why? My relatives do not live here and I don't fit in."

"Yes, you do, Diti."

"No, Vita. No." She shook her head. "I'm a minority here. You're a minority. Here, everyone notices the color of my skin. If I do well in school it's dismissed as neurotic studying forced upon me by my compulsive, over-achieving parents. Yes, I was born in this country, but I am still a stranger here. At least in India no one questions the color of my skin. At least in India the color of my skin is admired and respected and yes, even liked. Men

talked to me not because I was standing next to you. Not because I am the ugly sidekick they must get past. They talked to me because they liked me. Rashesh liked me."

They sat in silence and the full ramifications of Aditi's decision began to wash over Kavita. "So you're moving to London? You're going to live there?"

"Yes."

"With his family?"

"Yes."

Kavita wiped the tears from her eyes and inhaled and exhaled several deep breaths. "I'm sorry, Diti. I'm sorry if I made you feel bad about yourself. I didn't know how hard it's been for you. I never meant—"

Aditi grabbed Kavita's hands and squeezed. "I know you didn't." She smiled and again lowered her forehead until it touched Kavita's. "You can't help it if you're gorgeous."

Kavita laughed through her tears. "Are you happy, Diti? Really happy?"

Aditi smiled—a genuine smile. "I am, Vita. I am happy. Would you like to meet him, my husband?"

Kavita thought she would, in time, but she didn't want to see Aditi's mother, not now, not today, maybe not ever. Aditi's mother would be beaming, gloating. She'd throw Aditi's marriage in Kavita's face, and in her mother's face. My God, she'd take great pleasure in extolling that Aditi was married, and to someone in their samaaj *(same religion and caste), while Kavita was still traipsing from one unfulfilling relationship to another. She'd gloat to Kavita's mother that Aditi would provide her with grandchildren—the fact that those children would grow up halfway around the world, and that she would see them maybe once or twice a year, was irrelevant when one was gloating, driving home a point like driving a stake through a vampire's chest.*

"I can't right now," Kavita said. "I'm sorry, but I just can't. I'm going to leave so that you can move your things. So that I'm not in the way."

"You're never in the—"

Kavita leaned forward and gripped her friend in a fierce embrace, knowing it would likely be years before they saw one another again. "I'm going to miss you, Diti," she whispered.

"And I'm going to miss you. I'm going to miss you more than my parents and my brothers," Aditi said.

"I am your sister, Diti, and you're mine. You were the sister I never had. The only sister I will ever have."

Weeping, Aditi said, "Promise me you will meet him. Promise me you will come to London and see me."

Kavita pulled away, overcome with emotion. "I can't . . ."

Aditi clutched Kavita's shoulders. "Yes, Vita, you can. Please say it. I can't bear the thought of never seeing you again. Say it, please. Say you will come and visit me."

Kavita stifled her sobs long enough to answer. "Of course, Diti. Of course I'll come."

They released their embrace. Kavita stood. She knew leaving would be painful, but not as painful as a prolonged good-bye. "I have to go," she said, and she hurried from the apartment, her body racked with sorrow, fighting not to sob. She'd lost her sister.

—

Tracy blew out a short breath. "That had to be a lot for somebody to take in, especially from someone she'd been friends with for so many years."

Pryor nodded. "Dasgupta said there were a lot of tears, but that Mukherjee eventually expressed happiness for her."

Tracy glanced at the clock on the computer. She knew she'd kept Pryor from her family long enough and she, too, was anxious to get home. "So Dasgupta thinks she's missing because she can't reach her on her cell?"

"It goes straight to voice mail. And she hasn't responded to text messages or e-mails."

"And we know that she's not at her parents' or staying with a friend?"

"I called the family and I've reached most on the list of friends Dasgupta provided. Dasgupta also told me it was not likely Mukherjee would be with family. She said Mukherjee was estranged from her parents and rarely went home."

"Because she wouldn't submit to an arranged marriage."

Pryor nodded. "Dasgupta said Mukherjee was headstrong about it. So, apparently, is the mother. It's at a standoff."

Tracy continued through the missing persons report. "Has anyone been to the apartment to see if her luggage or clothes are gone?"

Another nod. "Dasgupta went by the apartment when she couldn't reach Mukherjee by phone. She said nothing looked to have been taken, and there was no sign of a forced entry or of a confrontation in the apartment."

"Mukherjee hadn't been back to the apartment?"

"No, she apparently had been. That's what made Dasgupta so concerned. Dasgupta said she left Mukherjee a note and a gift—a sari she'd brought back from India. She said the note had been opened and the sari was spread across Mukherjee's bed."

"So she'd come home at some point, but she didn't sleep in her bed if the sari and note were still on it?"

Pryor nodded. "That appears to have been the case."

"Does she have a boyfriend?" Tracy asked.

"No."

Tracy pointed to the picture on the screen. "A girl who looks like that?"

Pryor shrugged. "That's what Dasgupta told me."

"What about an ex-boyfriend? Someone who could have harmed her."

Pryor shook her head. "Nothing recent. Dasgupta said Mukherjee didn't have the time to get serious with anyone. After their families cut them off financially, Mukherjee was working whenever she could, trying to save for medical school." Pryor looked at her computer, scrolling down the screen. "That's another thing. I spoke to the employer. It's a clothing store on the Ave. Mukherjee was scheduled to work this afternoon but didn't show up, which the employer said had never happened before."

"Does she own a car? Could she have driven somewhere to get away and be alone?"

"She bought a 1999 Honda Accord after graduation. It's apparently a beater and she never drove it far. According to Dasgupta, it's still parked on the street near the apartment."

Tracy flipped another page of the report, considering the friends Pryor had already contacted. Then she said, "So the roommate didn't have any idea where Mukherjee might have gone? Someplace she might have crashed."

"She called their closest friends. No one has seen or heard from her."

"And I assume you checked the county jail and hospitals?"

"First calls. No luck."

Tracy sat back. "She might have just needed a break to process everything the roommate dumped on her. It's a lot to take in—she's married. She's moving out. She's moving to London."

"I hope that's the case," Pryor said.

"I do too. I'm not sure Nolasco is going to let me work this," Tracy said. "Faz and Del just pulled a murder in South Park, and Nolasco wants me to jump in when I'm out of the Stephenson trial."

"I know you're busy over there," Pryor said. "But like I said on the phone, sometimes you just get a feel for these things, and this one is bothering me."

Tracy gave it another moment of thought. "I should be out of court tomorrow," she said. "Set up a meeting with Dasgupta at the apartment for the afternoon. Tell her not to go in, just in case this is something more than it appears."

CHAPTER 8

Tracy rolled her 1973 Ford F-150 truck up the gravel drive to their stone farmhouse in Redmond. The cloudless sky burned a deep-orange along the horizon, and shadows crept up the surrounding hills and trees. Rex and Sherlock, their two Rhodesian ridgebacks, barked when they heard the truck and bounded off the deck to greet her. Tracy had become accustomed to using the plural to describe ownership of the house and the dogs, after so many years of using the singular pronoun.

She shut off the engine and took a moment to decompress, thinking again of what Kins had said about having a child, about how things would change, that it was inevitable. Just this morning, Dan had fretted about the size of their farmhouse, with its single bathroom, lone bedroom, and tiny kitchen.

"It's a baby," Tracy had said to calm him. "We're not adopting an elephant. We can worry about remodeling, or moving, later."

But she, too, had moments of concern. She'd soon need a new wardrobe—she could no longer button her jeans with the baby bump, and her shoes and bras were tight. She looked around the interior of the truck cab. Though she kept the truck in mint condition, it didn't have air bags or shoulder belts, or any of the other safety bells and whistles. She'd have to get a new car for the baby—something sturdy and maternal, like a Volvo or Subaru.

Dan stepped out the sliding glass doors onto the deck. He held barbecue tongs. Tracy had called to tell him she'd be late, and he'd promised to have dinner waiting. He smiled at her from behind round wire-rimmed sunglasses and clacked the tongs together playfully, as if to pinch her. Barefoot, Dan wore his cargo shorts and a Bruce Springsteen T-shirt he'd bought at *The River* revival concert at Key Arena. Additional concerts would be on hold for a while.

Tracy turned off the stereo and stepped down from the cab. She patted and rubbed the big dogs' heads and sides as they circled her, panting, tongues hanging from their mouths, their fur warm from the sun. Around them, the air buzzed and the brown grass crackled as if with static.

Tracy climbed the steps, and she and Dan kissed. His sunglasses weren't the only similarity to John Lennon, the Beatles founder. Dan wore his hair long. The curls brushed the collars of his dress shirts.

"You're certainly putting this deck to good use," Tracy said. Dan built the deck to give them more room. In the summer, he was usually grilling something. "Put a desk and a computer out here and it could be your office."

"How's our little tadpole doing?" Dan asked, placing a hand on Tracy's stomach.

"Hungry," she said.

"I just put the halibut on. Why don't you change?"

She went to one of the Adirondack chairs where Roger, their cat, lay stretched out. When she rubbed his coat, he startled and scratched at her. "Fine, be that way," she said, shooing him from the chair and taking his place. "But don't come running to me tonight when I'm in bed."

Tracy reached for a glass of iced tea and sipped it, grimacing at the bitter, unsweetened taste. "God, how do you drink this stuff without any sugar?"

"Bad day in court?" Dan asked, clearly sensing her mood.

"Court was fine, except I had to pee every five minutes."

"Still?"

She had questioned her doctor about her urgent need during the most recent exam, but he had assured her that the increased sensation was perfectly normal and caused by pressure on her bladder. It was all very clinical, but of little comfort. "It got worse when I went back to the office."

"Having to pee?"

"My day. I ran into my replacement in the bathroom."

Dan flinched as if he'd been the one pinched with the tongs. His eyebrows inched together above his glasses. "I thought you didn't tell anyone except Kins."

"I didn't, but when I stepped into the bathroom, I bumped into a woman who said Nolasco had hired her to work with the A Team. I know I should be happy to have another woman in the section, but my initial impression is I'm not going to like her much."

A buzzer sounded on Dan's phone. He shut it off, lifted the lid on the barbecue, which emitted smoke and the smell of herbs, and flipped the halibut, along with two ears of corn wrapped in foil. The top side of the halibut now displayed blackened stripes. Dan spoke as he coated the fish with what looked and smelled like butter-and-garlic sauce. "What about Ron Mayweather? I thought he was your fifth wheel."

"He is . . . was. Nolasco said Ron opted to take a permanent position on C Team. One of their detectives is retiring end of December."

Dan gave a small shrug, reset the timer, and closed the lid. "Maybe this woman won't be so bad."

"Maybe. She's a good-looking Hispanic woman, which is reason enough for Nolasco to hire her."

"Don't hold that against her."

"I'm not. But I am wondering if he hired her to replace me when I go out on maternity leave, with the hope that I won't be back."

"You might be giving him a little too much credit, don't you think? How would he know if you hadn't told anyone?"

"She clearly knew."

"She did?"

"Called me on it about five seconds after I met her. Asked, 'How far along are you?'" Tracy looked out at the dead grass. "I don't know. Maybe you're right. Maybe I am making too much out of it. I know I can't hide being pregnant forever."

"No, you can't, but Nolasco also can't fire you or give your position away. He isn't that dumb, is he?"

"I'd like to say no, but . . ."

Dan gave her a knowing look. "Something else bothering you?"

"Maybe it's just my hormones, but I'm tired of fighting this crap, Dan." She rubbed Sherlock's head and kissed his nose.

"What are you saying? You don't want to go back after the baby's born?"

"I'm not saying anything. I'm just thinking things over."

"Are you thinking about quitting?"

She looked up at him. "Why? Do you think I should quit?"

"I think you should do whatever you want."

"Why'd you ask me?"

Dan looked confused. "Because you said you were tired of fighting the bullshit day in and out?"

"I am. And I'd like to tell you that I'd never give Nolasco the satisfaction of quitting, but yeah, I guess I am thinking about what to do when the baby is born."

Dan leaned his back against the railing. "What brought this on?"

"Kins."

"Kins? I would have thought he'd be the one trying to convince you to stay."

"He said things change when you have a baby, that I might want to stay at home." She took another sip of the tea and again grimaced. "Never understand why you don't add sugar," she said.

"Not everyone is built the same, Tracy."

"Are you talking about the iced tea or staying home when the baby is born?"

"Both, I guess."

She stood to change out of her clothes. Maybe she was just hot and tired and hungry. Or maybe it was what Kins had said to her. "Realistically, this may be the only child we're ever going to have. I don't want to miss out on things because I'm working. Kins said that in a few months they'll be taking Connor off to college—"

"Is that what this is about? He's just emotional, Tracy, because his son is leaving."

"No," she said. "He's emotional because his son will no longer be living at home, and he wishes he could have spent more time with him. He told me not to feel bad if I want to stay home with our baby."

"Well, maybe he's right." The alarm sounded. Dan shut it off but didn't immediately raise the barbecue lid. "I certainly don't mind, Tracy. We don't need your salary. But we also don't need to make the decision tonight. If you want to stay home when the baby's born, make that decision then."

"You'd be all right with it?"

"If that's what you decide you want to do."

She nodded to the barbecue. "Don't burn that halibut."

CHAPTER 9

Faz and Del took the convenience store video to Park 95. The video unit would get to work in the morning and try to come up with a license plate number for the parked car, the white SUV, or both.

Faz drove from Park 95 to his home in Green Lake. When he pulled down his driveway, he triggered the light on the cornice of the freestanding garage, and it illuminated the mounted basketball hoop and backboard. There had been years when Faz could not park in the driveway, back when Antonio was still playing basketball at St. John's Grammar School, and later at Bishop Blanchet High School.

Faz had loved those years, especially the summer nights when the neighborhood kids came over, and he and Vera fed them. They would have had half a dozen kids, but it wasn't meant to be. He and Vera had married later in life. Their first date had been set up by their parents, though they were quick to note that it hadn't been a blind date—their families had been longtime acquaintances and had arranged for the two of them to meet for coffee. Faz fell in love at first sight. Vera said it took her longer, three dates. They were married three months from that first date, then decided it best they get to know one another before having their first child. When they'd started trying, Vera couldn't get pregnant. It took another year. After Antonio's birth they tried for a second child, but when Vera again couldn't get pregnant, she went to the doctor. They found a tumor in her uterus that tested malignant and required that she have her uterus removed, which ended talk of any more kids. The doctor said they'd been lucky; that if they hadn't been trying to get pregnant, they never would have found the tumor and it could have spread. Faz said it was love that had saved Vera's life, and they'd poured all of that love into Antonio, who now lived not far from them in Fremont.

Faz stepped from the car, his sport coat draped over his arm. He'd loosened his tie and unbuttoned the collar of his shirt. At the back door, another light triggered. He'd installed that light for Vera, so she wasn't coming home in the dark during the winter months. He was searching for his house key on his key ring when Vera pulled open the door.

"I thought I heard you drive up," she said. "Were you on a phone call?"

"Hey," he said. "No, I was just thinking about all those years we couldn't park in the driveway because Antonio was playing basketball." Faz dropped his watch, keys, wallet, and cell phone in a basket by the back door, a habit so he wouldn't forget them in the morning.

Vera smiled at the memory. "Any leads on the shooter in South Park?" she asked.

Faz had called to let her know of the shooting and that he'd be home late. "Maybe," he said. "Don't I get a kiss hello?"

Vera turned back and kissed him.

He removed his tie and spoke as he walked into the adjacent dining room. He draped both the tie and his jacket over the back of a chair. He told her of the convenience store and the videotape showing the possible shooter. "We might have caught a lucky break. The video unit is breaking the tape down for us tomorrow."

Vera turned toward the stove. "Are you hungry? I made chicken Milano and polenta. Antonio gave me the recipe." Antonio worked as a chef at an Italian restaurant and was saving money to open his own place. He intended to call it Fazzio's. Faz almost cried when Antonio delivered the news.

"How about that?" he'd said to Vera. "I always knew I'd see my name in lights."

"Did you talk to him today?" Faz pulled out a chair and sat at the kitchen table. "How's he doing?" He rolled up the cuffs of his sleeves. "How about that girl he's been dating? Is he ever going to propose?"

"I think he might."

Faz stopped rolling his sleeve. "Yeah?"

"He talked about it," Vera said. "He wants to wait until he has money to buy her a ring."

"That's no reason to wait. He loves her, he should marry her. Like we did. We didn't wait. Turned out okay."

Vera laughed lightly. "You just wanted to have sex."

"Yeah, but that's because I love you."

"Uh-huh," she said. "Don't pressure him. I know you want grandkids, but he has a lot on his plate."

"What pressure? I'm not pressuring him. Just thinking it would be nice if the grandkids put that hoop to good use."

"You want the chicken and polenta?" she asked.

"Do I want the chicken and polenta? Is the Pope single?"

Vera opened the oven door and the room filled with the enticing aroma of lemon, butter, and garlic. Vera never used a microwave to warm Faz's meals. She said it made the chicken rubbery.

"Smells good," Faz said.

Vera set a plate and utensils in front of him. "You tired?"

"More frustrated than tired. I don't understand people anymore. Here a mother of two gets shot in front of her two small kids and everyone in the apartment complex is keeping quiet."

"You said they're afraid?" Vera set the chicken on a pot holder on the table and scooped Faz a breast, then covered it with sauce.

"Looks good," he said, picking up a knife and fork. "There's a punk down there running the drugs. Hey, you remember Big Jimmy? I put him away for twenty-five years. He got stabbed in prison. You remember?"

"Not really."

"Well, the guy running things down there now is Little Jimmy, his son. Word on the street is he's crazy."

"I hate you working the gang cases."

"A convenience store owner told me and Del that Little Jimmy put out the word that anybody says anything they're going to end up like the woman." Faz decided not to elaborate on seeing Little Jimmy, or the hand gesture Little Jimmy had made as the car drove past, which would only worry Vera. He cut into the chicken. Steam rose from his fork and his plate. He took a bite and a burst of flavor filled his mouth. "Tell Antonio he's got another winner. For real. This might be his best."

"You want wine?"

"Yeah," he said. "Not too much though. Del and I are going back out tomorrow morning."

He heard her opening the cabinet behind him and retrieving the bottle of Chianti and a glass, and noticed that Vera had not set herself a plate. Except when he was working night shift, she ordinarily waited so they could eat dinner together. "You're not eating?" Faz asked. When Vera didn't answer, he turned in his chair. She stood at the counter, her back to him. "Vera?"

"I ate earlier," she said, her voice soft. "You go ahead."

He sensed something was not quite right, stood, and moved to her. "You all right? Vera? What's wrong?" She was crying, using a towel to wipe at tears.

"I had my mammogram this afternoon before I saw Antonio."

Faz felt a cold sweat that chilled him to the bone. "That's right," he said, cautious. "Shit, I'm sorry, Vera. I should have asked you right away. How'd it go?" He wasn't sure he wanted the answer, and when

Vera didn't immediately respond, he got a pain in his gut. He put a hand on her shoulder and turned her.

"I have another mass, Vic. I felt it the other day. I didn't want to alarm you until I made the appointment."

Faz felt sick. "What did the doctor say?"

She gave a small shrug. "He said it's definitely a mass and that the mammogram raised some questions."

"What kind of questions?"

"They don't know yet. They called this afternoon. They want me to come back for some additional screening."

"When?"

"Tomorrow morning at eight o'clock."

"I'm coming with you."

"No, Vic. You have that shooting. You go to work; I know how busy you are."

"We got to wait and see if they can enhance the video and get us a license plate," he said. "So I'm going with you." They both paused, and in the silence Faz heard the humming of the refrigerator and the ticks and creaks of a home that had quickly grown old. He looked at Vera, uncertain what more to say. "It's probably nothing, right?"

CHAPTER 10

Wednesday, July 11, 2018

It was noon when Leonard Litwin finally released Tracy and rested his case. Judge Gowin dismissed the jury with instruction to return at 2:00 p.m. for closing arguments. Tracy walked back to Police Headquarters rather than to Hoetig's office. The closing argument was the prosecutor's alone to prepare and deliver, though she would be present to hear it. She'd given him what thoughts she had, for what they were worth.

July had produced another glorious day—clear blue skies with temperatures cooled by a gentle breeze blowing off Elliott Bay and funneling between the high-rises. "God vacations in Seattle in the summer," Kins liked to say. "But he gets the hell out come October."

At Police Headquarters, Tracy reached for the glass door and nearly collided with Ron Mayweather and other detectives from the Violent Crimes Section's C Team, which Mayweather was now calling home. The group looked to be heading off to lunch.

"Ron," she said, stepping back to let everyone pass. "Hey. You got a second?"

"Yeah, sure." Mayweather looked to the other detectives. "Save me a seat. I'll catch up with you in a few minutes." After the others had departed, he turned to Tracy. "You're in Stephenson, aren't you?"

Faz had nicknamed Mayweather "Kotter" because he resembled Gabe Kaplan, the lead actor with the dark curly hair and thick drooping mustache on the television show *Welcome Back, Kotter*. Few, however, remembered the show, and those who did remember it didn't remember Kaplan, but a young actor named John Travolta making his television debut.

"Just finished all the testimony. Hoetig gives his closing at two."

"How did it go?"

"Evidence got in. No real surprises." Tracy stepped closer to the side of the building to get out of foot traffic on the sidewalk. "Listen, I'm sorry to keep you."

"Not a problem. What's up?"

"I wanted to ask you about your decision to move to the C Team," Tracy said.

"Yeah, sorry I didn't get the chance to talk to you," he said. "It came up quickly. I talked to the other guys, but you were in court."

Tracy folded an errant strand of windblown blonde hair behind her ear. "I just wanted to ask why you decided to make the move?"

"Why?" Mayweather chuckled. "Because Nolasco told me to."

Tracy had not expected the answer. "He told you to move to C Team?"

"Yeah," Mayweather said, giving her a slight what-are-you-going-to-do shrug.

"What exactly did he say?"

"He called me in and said Arroyo was retiring end of the year. He said he wanted me to start working with him, so I had a feel for his cases and could hit the ground running when he left."

Tracy gave the comment some thought. "You didn't ask to be moved?"

"No." Mayweather answered like her question surprised him. "I liked A Team, even with Fazzio giving me shit all the time. I had no idea Arroyo was thinking of retiring. No one did, apparently, not even the guys on his team."

"No?"

"He said he came to the decision sitting home one night with his wife. He has enough years in to retire on a full pension and wanted to move on with his life."

The sentiment was not unusual. Once a detective had put in the requisite number of years to pull a full pension, the lure of leaving behind the sick and depraved for a more normal life became much more appealing. "Did Nolasco say anything about me being pregnant?"

Mayweather smiled. "I was wondering when you were going to make that announcement."

"You knew?" Tracy asked.

"Suspected . . . I think most people suspect."

She wondered if Nolasco was among those people.

"But to answer your question, Nolasco didn't say anything. I was wondering whether you'd be coming back after the baby was born though, whether your spot might open up."

"Did you bring that up with Nolasco?"

"I didn't have to. He said he didn't see a spot opening on A Team anytime soon and C Team needed a detective. You are coming back, aren't you?"

That was not what Nolasco had told Kins to justify hiring Gonzalez. "Yeah," she said. "Yeah, I intend to come back."

Mayweather smiled. "Good. We'd miss you around here. Anything else?"

"No. Thanks. Sorry to keep you."

"No worries," Mayweather said, and he started up the street.

Tracy watched Mayweather go. Her team *would* miss him. He was dependable and had a good sense of humor. Anyone who could take

Del and Faz's constant ribbing had to have thick skin and a lot of confidence, but that was not what was foremost on Tracy's mind.

Nolasco had told her that Mayweather asked to take Arroyo's place because there wouldn't be any openings on the A Team anytime soon. That had clearly not been what had happened. Nolasco had moved Mayweather to C Team to open a space for Gonzalez on the A Team, and Tracy suspected she knew why. Once Tracy took her pregnancy leave, it would be much more difficult for her to argue discrimination if Nolasco replaced her with another woman—especially a minority woman, and he could do so seamlessly if Gonzalez was the A Team's fifth wheel. Nolasco was covering his ass. She thought of the prior day, when she'd found Gonzalez in Nolasco's office with the door closed, and how Gonzalez had logged on to Tracy's computer and accessed Tracy's reports. That simply wasn't done in Violent Crimes, and certainly could be interpreted as an indication that Nolasco wanted Gonzalez to take over for Tracy.

Then again, maybe Tracy was just being paranoid, seeing conspiracies where none existed.

Maybe.

CHAPTER 11

The Volkswagen was registered to Doug and Sandy Blaismith of Newcastle, Washington, a town neither Del nor Faz would have predicted for the parked car. First, Newcastle was located twenty-five to forty-five minutes east of South Park, depending on the time of day and the traffic. Second, Newcastle was considered middle to upper-middle class, with an average income exceeding $125,000, and home prices of more than a million dollars. Newcastle's demographics also had little in common with South Park, with roughly 65 percent Caucasian and less than 4 percent Hispanic.

The video unit had not been able to pull a plate from the white SUV, the vehicle into which the suspect had climbed, nor had it been able to find any video of the vehicle on traffic cameras.

Faz received the news over the phone shortly after he'd returned to Police Headquarters, after spending the morning with Vera in the doctor's office. He hadn't wanted to leave her, but Vera had insisted, telling him that nothing good could come from both of them sitting at home worrying.

Del and Faz decided to wait until after 5:00 p.m. before driving to Newcastle, when it would be more likely the car would be at the house. They also decided not to call the Blaismith home ahead of time. They used the time to drive back out to South Park to conduct interviews, including questioning the residents of the apartment complex, and talking to the businesses that had been closed the previous night, but they didn't find anyone with information about the shooting, or any other useful videotapes. While they had been in South Park, Faz had Andrea Gonzalez put a search warrant together and get it signed by the court, in case the Blaismiths got squirrelly.

Faz had hoped to get home at a decent hour and spend time with Vera, but he also knew this could be the one break they needed to find Monique Rodgers's killer, and maybe determine if it had been a hit ordered by Little Jimmy. Before leaving Police Headquarters, he called home to let Vera know he would be late. True to form, Vera told him to do what he needed to do, and that she'd keep his dinner warm. It was clear to him that she didn't want to talk about the doctor's meeting that morning.

"Drugs," Del said as they drove to Newcastle. Drugs had been the first theory that came to both their minds for the car being in South Park. "Opioids, meth, maybe heroin."

"Maybe," Faz said. He didn't much care about the reason the car had been parked near the shooting; only that it had been. They had a bigger fish to fry.

"If we nail the shooter he might start talking. If he does, we could nail Little Jimmy," Del said from behind the wheel. "Wouldn't that be something—like father, like son."

"Let's not get ahead of ourselves," Faz said. "But yeah. That would be something."

The Blaismiths lived in a suburban development of high-end tract homes not far from the Newcastle golf club. Many such developments had been built in the 1980s to accommodate Seattle's expanding population. "Functional" was the word that came to mind when Faz and Del drove past the brick wall bearing the development's name and saw homes squeezed together tighter than molars to maximize the number of lots. Creativity and imagination were clearly not exalted here; the homes varied only slightly in the orientation of the buildings on the lots, and their floor plans. The exteriors were brick and gray-wood siding, and the square footage nearly maxed out the yards, leaving just enough room for a few sculpted hedges and patches of green lawn that could be mowed with two swipes of a mower's blade.

Del parked on a sloped curb in front of the Blaismiths' two-story home. The base of a basketball hoop was embedded in the sliver of yard separating the property from the neighbor's, and the hoop hung out over a pristine driveway, devoid of any cars. Faz hoped the Jetta was parked in one of the three garage bays. Otherwise, it had been a long trip for nothing.

They donned their sport coats and walked a brick path to a beveled glass door beneath a twelve-foot entry. The weather felt warmer than it had in Seattle, despite the shade of trees looming behind the roofline. Del rang the doorbell, setting off a series of chimes followed instantly by the barking of what sounded like a large dog.

"Ten bucks says it's a Labrador." Del removed his sunglasses and slipped them inside his coat pocket.

"Too easy," Faz said. "Specify. Yellow, black, or brown?" He kept his gaze directed at the door.

"Yellow. Definitely yellow."

"I might as well just give you the ten bucks now," Faz said.

A woman pulled open the door, holding the collar of a very excited yellow Lab. The dog looked like he was trying to fly, his front legs elevated and swiping at the air, tongue hanging from the side of his mouth. Del gave Faz a subtle smirk.

"Can I help you?" the woman asked.

Sandy Blaismith appeared to be midforties and impeccably put together in tight jeans, black ankle boots, and a blouse with a plunging neckline that revealed a freckled chest and a gold necklace. Rings adorned several fingers, some with impressive stones. Before Faz could respond, she yelled at the dog, tugging on the animal's collar. "Sit. Seager, sit. Sit."

The dog ignored her, continuing to whine and paw at the air.

"I'm sorry, but if you're selling anything we're not interested, and you really don't want me to let my dog go. He bites."

It was a bluff, and not a very good one. The only damage Seager looked capable of causing was to knock them down and lick them to death.

Faz held up his badge. "We're with the Seattle Police Department. Are you Sandy Blaismith?"

The woman went from looking exasperated to looking concerned. "What is this about?"

"Maybe you could lock the dog out back?" Del suggested.

"Hang on," she said. She yanked the dog inside and flung the door shut. Faz heard her yell to her husband over the dog's barking.

"Doug? Come take your dog and put him in the backyard. I need you to get your dog and put him in the backyard."

"Not an animal lover," Faz said.

"Definitely not," Del said.

"Because there are two Seattle police officers at the front door," Sandy hollered. "Two police officers. I don't know. Just take Seager and put him out back."

Del looked at Faz. "Double or nothing they also have a cat, a son, and a daughter. Instant family. Just add water."

"Won't take that bet," Faz said.

The door reopened. This time Sandy was minus the dog but now accompanied by her husband, who introduced himself as Doug Blaismith. Doug wore the remnants of a suit, as well as success. Several strands of yellow dog hair clung to his navy-blue slacks. He'd unbuttoned the collar of his shirt and rolled the cuffs of his sleeves up his forearms, revealing an expensive-looking gold watch and thick wrist chain. His thinning hair was gelled and combed back from his forehead. A protruding belly indicated he liked to eat but not work out.

"What can we do for you?" he said.

"Do you own a blue Jetta, Mr. Blaismith?" Faz provided the license plate number.

"It's silver," Doug said. "Not blue."

"Is it here?"

"Is something wrong?" Doug said. "Did my son get in an accident?"

"Does your son drive that car?" Faz asked.

"To school mostly," Sandy said, "but it's summer so . . ."

"Is the car here?" Faz asked.

"It's in the garage," Doug said. "Why do you ask?"

Faz thought that was obvious at this point but he decided to indulge Doug's apparent need to feel as though he was in charge. "We'd like to see it."

"What is this about?" Doug persisted, squinting at them. "Do I need a lawyer?"

"We believe," Faz said, "that the car may have been touched by someone involved in committing a crime."

"I'm sorry?" Sandy said. She'd visibly blanched.

"I don't understand," Doug said.

"Let me back up." Faz explained the shooting of Monique Rodgers and what the convenience store video had revealed.

"I read about that in the paper, or saw something about it on the news," Doug said. "But there has to be a mistake, Detectives. My son is the only one who drives that car and there'd be no reason for him to be in . . . Did you say South Park?"

There would be, actually, Faz thought but didn't say. "We have a video," Faz said, removing two snapshots, one of the car parked at the curb and another of the license plate, blown up. He handed both to Doug. Doug considered the photographs, his wife viewing them over his shoulder. Both looked perplexed.

"No one is in trouble here," Faz said, hoping to alleviate their growing concern, although the son might very well be in trouble with his parents. "We're hoping we can lift a handprint from the hood and determine the identity of the person who touched your car."

Doug continued shaking his head. Sandy looked pale.

"That is the car's license plate number, isn't it?" Faz said, hoping to prompt some comment.

Doug scratched at his temple. "I honestly don't know the plate number off the top of my head." He looked at his wife, but Sandy shook her head. "What day did you say it was?" Doug asked.

"You said the car is here?" Faz asked.

"In the garage," Doug said.

"Maybe we can check the plate number with the photograph first, so there's no mistake? If it's not your car we'll be out of your hair." When neither Sandy nor Doug responded, Faz said, "Does your son play basketball?"

Del gave him a quick glance, like he thought Faz had lost his mind.

Doug looked even more confused. "What?"

Faz just wanted to get the couple saying something. "I noticed the basketball hoop in your driveway. My son was a basketball player. I don't think I parked in my driveway for twenty years because he was always out there shooting. I was just wondering if the car is in the garage?"

"Oh, uh, yeah," Doug said. "He plays for an AAU team here on the Eastside, but he had his knee scoped yesterday. That's what's causing the confusion. He had a tear in the meniscus fixed Monday morning. So you see, he couldn't have had the car in South Park yesterday. He couldn't drive."

"It was here all day yesterday?" Faz said. Now he was confused.

"It's been parked in the garage." Doug looked at his wife for confirmation.

"Do you have any other children?" Del asked.

Doug nodded. "A daughter, but she's only thirteen. She doesn't drive."

"We know this is an inconvenience, but if we can just compare the license plate of the car in your garage with this one, maybe we can clear this up," Faz said.

"Hang on a second." Doug turned and shouted up a spiral staircase. "Luke?"

"I'll get him," Sandy said, but she didn't go up the stairs. She went down a hallway. Del gave Faz a glance. He'd noticed it too. Weird.

"Come on in." Doug stepped back to allow Del and Faz to enter the marbled entry. He closed the door. Out back, Faz heard the dog barking. He stepped to the side to see down the hall. The wife had headed toward a kitchen.

"We'll try to make this quick," Del said.

A tall, gangly boy with a mop of blond hair appeared on crutches at the top of the stairs, his right knee in a brace. "Yeah?"

Del started to ease down the hall where the mother had retreated.

Doug made the introductions, and Faz quickly explained the purpose of their visit. The boy started shaking his head when Faz mentioned South Park. "I can't drive. I've been home since I left the doctor's office. Besides, I don't even know where South Park is."

Faz gave Del a subtle nod, and Del went down the hall in search of Sandy Blaismith while Faz continued to question the boy. "No one is in trouble here, son. We just need to determine if the person who placed his hand on the hood left a print we can use."

“That’s fine with me, but I’m telling you I didn’t drive the car. It’s been in the garage.”

“Who took you to get your knee scoped?” Faz asked.

“I did,” Doug said. “The doctor is a friend of mine.”

Faz watched Del disappear at the end of the hall. The barking intensified, as did the clicking of toenails against glass. “Does your wife work?”

“Part-time,” Doug said over the dog’s barking.

“Did she work yesterday?”

Faz heard Del yell from somewhere at the back of the house. He moved quickly down the hall into an expansive kitchen and open family room. The flat-screen television, mounted above a brick fireplace, displayed the local news but the volume had been muted. Outside sliding glass doors, the yellow Lab raced left and right across the yard, crushing flowers and shrubs, barking and jumping up on the glass. Faz crossed the family room and pulled open a door to the garage.

Del was moving toward Sandy Blaismith, who stood at an open cabinet holding a spray bottle of blue liquid and a kitchen towel. When she saw Faz and her husband, her face slumped and her shoulders sagged as if she were melting.

“Sandy, what the hell are you doing?” Doug asked.

Sandy did not answer. She lowered the bottle and her gaze. Del moved between her and the car and took the spray bottle and rag from her hands. She offered no resistance. Faz moved to the car and bent to see the reflection from the overhead light on the hood. From the dust and dirt present, it did not look as though Sandy, or anyone else, had recently touched it.

“Sandy,” Doug said, a little more forcefully. “What the hell is going on?”

CHAPTER 12

Tracy thought the exterior of the Village Place apartment building in Seattle's University District looked too nice to be housing eighteen- to twenty-two-year-old college students whose parents were likely fronting them just enough money to pay their rent and not starve. But the proximity of the building to the University of Washington campus and the inexpensive restaurants and chic clothing stores on University Way made student housing a near certainty.

A red concrete walkway led to a white stone courtyard of potted plants and peaked archways framing ornamental hanging lamps and leaded glass protected by metal bars, a concession to the vagaries of "the Ave." The area attracted a healthy contingent of young homeless people, who sat on the sidewalks with cardboard signs and clung to a counterculture movement that had largely ended on most campuses a generation before they were born.

Tracy entered the front door at just after five o'clock. Closing arguments in Stephenson had gone about as expected, and the case was presented to the jury at just after 4:00 p.m. Hoetig said he thought the jury would be out until Friday, at the latest.

She stepped along a red runner extending the length of a marbled, columned interior. The cool temperature inside provided a respite from the July heat. A man and woman stood talking to Katie Pryor in a room to the left of the entry that resembled the living area of an English manor, with paintings of men in riding gear hanging on the walls over a deep-set fireplace that had likely not been used for decades.

Pryor made the introductions. Thin and small-boned, Rashesh Banerjee had a dark complexion and a heavy five-o'clock shadow. He wore black slacks and a striped, collared dress shirt. Aditi Dasgupta, now Banerjee, wore open-toed sandals, black leggings, and a white loose-fitting shirt that extended below her knees. Both thanked Tracy for agreeing to meet.

"My wife is very worried about her friend Kavita." Rashesh spoke with a hint of a British accent.

"I understand you were roommates?" Tracy said to the young woman.

"For several years," the man said.

Tracy smiled. "Mr. Banerjee, I appreciate you wanting to help, but this will go a lot faster and much more smoothly if I can speak directly to Aditi. Okay?"

"Of course." Rashesh nodded and took a step back while making a hand gesture for Tracy to proceed.

"You and Kavita were roommates?" Tracy asked. Aditi repeated much of the information Katie Pryor had told her the previous afternoon.

Tracy listened, then asked her next question, hoping for the best. "Aditi, is it possible Kavita might have just needed some time to process all of this information? It sounds like it was a fairly significant, and unexpected, change for both of you."

"It's possible," Aditi said, nodding as if she, too, wished it to be so. "I thought the same thing, but . . . Kavita wouldn't worry me like this. She would have called or sent a text to let me know she was going away, to let me know she is okay, no matter how upset she is with me."

Tracy nodded, not wanting to discount what the young woman had to say but still not convinced Kavita Mukherjee wasn't somewhere, trying to process everything. "How was she when you left her on Monday?"

"She was upset. We were both very emotional. We were both crying. It was very difficult for me to tell her, and I'm sure it was very difficult for her to hear. She left the apartment because she did not want to see me pack. She said it would be too hard."

"And you were gone when she presumably returned later that evening?"

"Yes. I came back to the apartment because I was worried about her. Before leaving I placed a note and a gift on her bed." She looked at Katie Pryor. "That's when I noticed that the gift, a sari, was unfolded on the bed and the note had been opened."

"And the check," Rashesh prompted.

"Yes. I left her a check for the rent, but she tore it into pieces. So I know she returned that night."

"She tore up a check?" Tracy asked.

"I told Kavita I would pay the rent until she found another roommate," Aditi said. "I knew paying the rent would be difficult for her."

Tracy considered the fact that Kavita had torn up the check to be a strong signal she was angry with Aditi. "Did she have plans to go out that night, plans that you're aware of?"

Aditi shook her head. "Not that I know of, but I have been gone for almost twelve weeks."

"She didn't mention any plans?"

"No."

"Okay. Do you still have a key to the apartment?"

"We called the superintendent," Rashesh said, stepping forward again. "Aditi is still on the lease. He will let us in."

Minutes later, a superintendent led them to the apartment and unlocked the door. "I'll go in first," Tracy said, slipping on a pair of blue latex gloves and stepping into an entryway of dull light.

—

Kavita Mukherjee unlocked the deadbolt and cautiously pushed open the apartment door. She was not afraid of what she might find inside the apartment, but rather of what she would not find. She paused in the hallway, recalling how excited she and Aditi had been upon their first visit, how Aditi had commented on all the natural lighting.

Kavita tossed her keys into the empty bowl on the table by the door, a habit, and walked into the living room. Aditi had placed her keys to the apartment on the kitchen counter. Otherwise, everything in the living room looked as it had when she left. Kavita figured Aditi and her husband had no need for used furniture in his London apartment.

Kavita stepped from the living room to the kitchen. The dishes and glasses remained in their designated places. They didn't eat at home often. Usually, they'd go out and buy something and split the cost. It had always been that way, Kavita and Aditi, for as long as she could recall. If there was a fraternity party, they attended together. If one needed to study, they walked to and from the library together. For tests, they quizzed each other. Yes, Kavita had always received the higher grades, but it was true that Aditi had been the harder worker. Who would Kavita study with now, in medical school?

Kavita looked out a window at the afternoon sun shining on the roofs of the campus buildings where she'd spent four years and had hoped to someday attend medical school. Now that she would be going alone, she decided she no longer wanted to go to the UW. She wanted to go away, to someplace where she would not have memories, someplace far from her family. The thought made her wonder how much of Aditi's decision to marry was dictated by fear instead of love, the same fear Kavita now felt. The fear of being alone. The fear of failing in medical school and having to return home with her tail between her legs.

Her mother certainly would be of no comfort. She'd already resorted to guilt-inducing phone calls. Love is overrated, *she'd say.* You can choose to love after marriage.

And you could choose not to, *Kavita would frequently retort.*

Had Aditi married out of fear that she would never have another opportunity? Had she been afraid that Kavita would one day marry and leave her alone? Had she decided it was better to cling to someone, to anyone, than to cling to no one at all?

Kavita left the front room and walked down the darkened hallway, where the light from the windows did not reach. Tonight the gray seemed more pronounced. She pushed open the door to what had been Aditi's room. The furniture remained, unneeded, but the bed had been stripped bare and the dresser drawers had been emptied of Aditi's clothes. Hangers hung naked on the closet crossbar, and slatted shadows marked the bare walls.

The emptiness of the room hit Kavita hard, as reality often could. Aditi was gone. Kavita was alone.

Weeping, Kavita shut the door and continued past the bathroom. She had to get ready for her date, and she'd never been so happy to have a distraction, even if she didn't feel like putting on a happy face and going out.

She noticed a pair of dark-blue Bata sandals at the foot of her bed and, neatly folded on top of her down comforter, gold-and-blue fabric. Aditi. It was so like her to bring Kavita back a present. Kavita picked up the fabric—a sari—and marveled at the intricacy of the design. In the United States, such craftsmanship would have cost Aditi two weeks' pay. Not in India.

Kavita allowed the sheer fabric to unfurl as she walked to the mirror mounted inside her closet door. She held the material close to her body and recalled one of the first occasions that she'd worn a sari—to her cousin's annaprashan. *Kavita's mother had lectured her that day, telling her the sari was more than just clothing. It was an Indian woman's means to communicate. She showed her how holding the veil across a corner of her face indicated she was being playful, while a tug of the folds of her shoulder indicated she was feeling demure.*

Kavita had never felt any of those things. To her, the sari was a nuisance that made her feel clumsy and without grace. More often than not, the fabric would slip from her shoulder and the pallu, *the long train intended to be draped over her shoulder and arm, would drag on the floor. When the sari was wrapped tight—to give just a hint of the woman's figure—she felt entrapped in the fabric, claustrophobic.*

Kavita held the material close to her face and admired how the blue brought out the color of her eyes, while the gold reflected her skin tone. Aditi. She was always so deliberate when it came to gifts; Kavita could only imagine how much time her best friend had fretted over the dress before buying it. She felt bad she had not been here to accept it, to thank her in person.

She let the six yards of fabric unfurl to the hardwood floor. A card slipped from one of the folds. Kavita gathered the fabric and picked up the card, taking both to her bed. She sat on the foam mattress and placed a pillow at her back. The envelope was addressed to Kavita in Aditi's beautiful script.

She opened it and pulled out the handwritten note.

> My Dear Vita:
> I saw this sari when I was shopping for my wedding and I marveled at how the blue matched the color of your eyes and the gold your skin.

Kavita laughed. They knew each other so well.

> I went back the following day nervous that it would be gone, that someone would have snatched it up. It is so beautiful I simply had to buy it for you. I know it will never be the same as your jeans with the

holes in the knees and your T-shirts ☺, but you would be so beautiful in it, Kavita. I hope someday you will find an opportunity to wear it, and when you do, that you will think of me, your dear friend Aditi.

I will be leaving for London at the end of the week. Until then, Rashesh and I will be staying with my parents. Family—you know. It is the Indian way ☺. I do hope that you will come and see me and meet my husband before we depart. Though it has only been minutes since you left, I miss you already.

Come to London, Vita. You will love it! And we will have so much fun together! No pressure!

Always your sister,

Aditi

Behind the note, Kavita found a check for Aditi's share of the rent for the next two months. She smiled. So like Aditi to worry about her. She sighed, realizing there was no longer a need to worry, not about finances anyway.

Kavita would be a doctor. Of that, she was now quite certain.

—

Aditi led them on a tour of the apartment. The final room belonged to Kavita. Aditi pointed to the bed, which looked to have been clumsily made, the covers pulled up to the pillows. Scraps of paper littered the down comforter. "That's the sari and that's the note I left her."

"Is that the check?" Tracy asked, noting the scraps of paper.

"Yes. I put the check in the envelope with the note."

Tracy again thought that the torn-up check indicated Kavita had not been fine with Aditi's marriage, far from it. She noticed a backpack leaning beside a bedside nightstand and retrieved it. Inside she found a laptop computer.

"That's Kavita's," Aditi said.

Now this was unusual. Most young people rarely went anywhere without their laptop and phone.

"Do you know her password?" she asked. Aditi did not. Tracy handed the backpack to Pryor. "We'll take this with us and get a warrant to search the computer for her e-mails and her social media." She turned back to Aditi. "Do you see anything out of the ordinary, other than the check?"

Aditi shook her head.

"Okay," Tracy said. "I'm going to take a few pictures. I'll meet you in the living room. Again, don't touch anything."

After taking approximately two dozen photographs using her phone, Tracy went back to the living room.

Pryor was speaking to Aditi but turned to Tracy when she entered. "Aditi told Kavita's parents that we might wish to speak with them."

Tracy checked her watch. "Where do they live?"

"In Bellevue," Aditi said. "Her father works at Microsoft. Do you think something could have happened to Kavita?"

"I don't know," Tracy said. If something had happened to the young woman, it hadn't happened in the apartment, not on first appearance anyway. "Aditi, I have to ask you a difficult question; I'm sorry. Is it possible that Kavita could have harmed herself?"

Aditi shook her head. "Not the Vita I know. No. I don't believe she would."

"Was Kavita the type of woman who'd go to a bar, maybe have a couple drinks, and go home with someone she didn't know?"

Again, Aditi shook her head. "No. That would have been out of the ordinary for Kavita."

"Had you ever known her to do that?"

Aditi paused, and Tracy wondered again if her hesitancy was because of Rashesh's presence—a young woman who perhaps did not want to admit her and her roommate's sexual experiences in front of the man she'd just married. "No."

"Did she drink?"

"On occasion. She liked red wine."

"What about drugs?"

"No."

"No drugs? Not even pot?"

"Maybe a few times in high school and college, but no, not regularly."

"What's the rent here?"

"It's $1,850 a month."

"And you said Kavita's parents had cut her off financially?"

"Yes."

"Could Kavita afford the apartment on her own?"

Aditi shook her head. "That's why I offered to pay until she found a new roommate. I felt bad for leaving her."

"I suggested to Aditi that we pay two months' rent," Rashesh said.

"But she tore up the check," Tracy said, more to herself. "So how did she plan on paying the rent?"

"I don't know," Aditi said. "I assumed Kavita would get another roommate. Are you going to speak with her parents tonight?"

Tracy no longer had a choice. "Yes."

"Then I'll let them know you're coming."

Tracy removed a business card from her pocket and handed it to Aditi. Pryor did the same. "That's my contact information. If you hear from Kavita be sure to immediately call me or Detective Pryor."

"What will you do now?" Rashesh asked.

"We'll get out a missing persons alert to the agencies in the state and provide Kavita's picture and her vital information," Pryor said.

"I'm going to need Kavita's phone number and the name of her cell phone carrier," Tracy said. "We'll ask the carrier to track the phone's last known location. If we find the phone, hopefully we'll find Kavita, or at least we'll know where she's been."

CHAPTER 13

The Blaismiths' neighbors had come out of their houses, curious about the Jetta strapped to the bed of a flatbed tow truck. Faz suspected rumors went around the neighborhood faster than trick-or-treaters on Halloween.

He and Del would follow the tow truck to the vehicle processing room at Park 95. He had already e-mailed Gonzalez and told her to forward the signed search warrant to the Latent Print Unit, also located at Park 95. In the morning, technicians would seek to lift fingerprints from the hood. They might even pick up DNA, though that depended on how long the car had been left in the sun, which could destroy DNA evidence.

Obtaining a usable print and having that print match one in their system remained daunting, but they were at least one step closer.

Faz considered Doug Blaismith, who stood in the driveway of his perfect home in his perfect development. Blaismith looked like a person whose house was going up in flames, with no way to save anything inside. Doug had not offered any protest when Faz told him they were impounding the car. Faz suspected Doug was just as eager to determine whether his wife had been in South Park, though given the wife's reaction, they already knew that was probably the case. Why she would have been there was a whole other question, and Del and Faz might never get that answer or need it. After giving up the Windex and the rag, Sandy Blaismith clammed up tight. When she did speak it was to ask for an attorney.

"Woman's been watching too much *CSI*," Del had said. "I wanted to ask her if she meant a criminal defense lawyer or a divorce lawyer."

Faz and Del had agreed not to arrest Sandy Blaismith for obstruction of justice, given that Del had intercepted her before she could wipe down the car. They didn't really care if she'd been buying drugs or if she'd driven to South Park for some other reason, like an affair. That was between her and her family.

When the flatbed departed, Del and Faz followed in the pool car. Del turned down the radio broadcast of the Mariners game.

"You think it's drugs?" he asked. "You think she was buying?"

"Based on her reaction, the way she went pale, I think it might be more personal than drugs."

"She's cheating on him?" Del said.

"Maybe. Not really our business," Faz said. "There's a family to think about, two kids who are innocent in this."

"Yeah, I know," Del said. "It just pisses me off that she would try to wipe away evidence in a murder investigation to keep her own secret . . . What kind of a person does that?"

"I don't know," Faz said. He thought of Doug Blaismith, standing at the end of his driveway, alone, and with the excitement of the evening having now subsided, Faz's thoughts returned to Vera. He wondered if she was okay, home alone, without him, again. Vera had spent many nights alone during Faz's career, but he'd never worried whether she was okay. He'd just assumed it. He wished now that he had called her more often to check on her, to let her know he'd been thinking of her, that he cared.

"Life is way too short to put up with that crap," Del said.

"Not if he loves her . . . ," Faz started to say, but that's when the emotions of the day, the emotions Faz had been fighting so hard to suppress, tore through the façade, and he broke down, crying.

CHAPTER 14

After leaving the newly married Rashesh and Aditi Banerjee at the Village Place apartments, Tracy and Katie Pryor intended to drive immediately to Bellevue to speak to Kavita Mukherjee's parents, but as Tracy drove down University Way, Pryor pointed out the store, Urban Trekking, where Mukherjee worked.

"Call the parents. Tell them we'll be a few minutes late," Tracy said, figuring she'd kill two birds with one stone, since she might not get another stone, not with South Park heating up. She and Pryor parked and walked up a sidewalk filled with people dressed in shorts and tank tops and soaking up vitamin D.

A bell rang as Tracy and Pryor entered Urban Trekking, though the bell was hard to hear over the technobeat electronic music blasting from ceiling speakers. From a quick survey of the clothing folded on metal shelving and hanging on racks, the store looked to be a college student's paradise—priced-to-sell jeans with holes in the knees and shredded thighs, studded and dyed T-shirts, and tank tops. Tracy wouldn't be shopping here anytime soon.

Two women stood behind the counter folding the clothing and chatting. They glanced in the detectives' direction, even smiled politely, but made no effort to approach, a clear indication they didn't expect a sale. The African American clerk greeted Tracy and Pryor when they reached the counter. The white clerk disappeared behind a partition, and moments later the volume of music lowered.

"Can we help you find anything?"

At least she got an A for effort. "I think I might be a little too old for the clothes in here," Tracy said.

The woman smiled, but it looked forced. "We have women your age shop in here all the time."

Tracy looked at Pryor. *"Ouch,"* she said, making Pryor laugh. She fished out her police ID. "Actually, we're here to follow up on one of your employees."

"Kavita?" the clerk asked, moving closer to the counter.

"You know her," Tracy said.

"Sure," she said. "But she didn't come in today and our boss couldn't reach her. I think he let her go. That's why I'm working." She looked to her colleague, who had returned, for confirmation, but the young woman just shrugged an *I don't know.*

Pryor asked for and wrote down both women's names. The black woman was Charlotte, the white girl with the nose and eyebrow piercings, Lindsay. Both women were tall, five foot seven or five foot eight, and they dressed as if modeling the store catalogue.

"When did you last see her?" Tracy asked.

"We closed the store together Saturday," Lindsay said. "That was the last time."

"How well do you know her?" Pryor asked.

They both shrugged. "She was older," Charlotte said, "so we didn't, like . . . hang out after work or anything."

If they considered Mukherjee older, Tracy was ancient. "So she never mentioned to either of you that she wanted to take time off?"

Dual shakes of the head and a stereo response. "No."

"Did she have a boyfriend?" Tracy asked.

The two looked at each other but it was Lindsay who said, "I don't think so. She never talked about a boyfriend."

"She's a beautiful girl," Tracy said.

"Oh my God," Lindsay said, becoming animated. "She is *so* beautiful. I think our boss hired her because she wore the clothes so well. They're sort of designed for tall girls, you know? Kavita is really tall, like your height."

"Any boys ever come in to talk with her?" Tracy asked.

"All the time," Charlotte said. "They come over from the U and hit on all of us, ask us to their fraternity parties, that sort of thing."

"Did Kavita ever take them up on it?"

"God no," Lindsay said, looking bemused at the question. "But she wasn't rude about it. She'd sort of just lead them on a little bit, though not in a bad way, you know? They'd buy shirts and stuff, thinking that maybe she'd go out with them. But she never did. She'd tell them she had a date or that she had to work."

"Any of them ever seem to take that the wrong way?"

"Wrong way?" Lindsay asked.

"Anybody ever get upset or angry? Say anything?" Tracy said.

"You mean like a stalker?" Charlotte asked.

"Or someone just kind of creepy?" Pryor said.

The two gave each other another painful look before shaking their heads. "Not really. I mean, they knew Kavita was out of their league, you know? Guys know, but some figure what the hell; it can't hurt to try. Why, did something happen to her?" Lindsay asked.

"That's what we're trying to determine," Pryor said.

"You're not here because she's, like, dead or something, are you?" Lindsay asked.

"No," Tracy said. "But there are some people worried about her."

"Her roommate called looking for her," Charlotte said.

"When was that?" Tracy asked.

"Today. Earlier. She wanted to know if Kavita had come in to work."

"How was Kavita the last time you saw her? Did she seem upset?" Pryor asked.

They both shrugged. Charlotte said, "She seemed all right when she was working."

"Were there any clubs or bars she ever talked about, places where she hung out?"

More head shakes. "I don't think she's really into clubbing too much. At least she never talked about it to me," Lindsay said. "Like I said, she's kind of older. She works a lot."

"She's trying to get into medical school," Charlotte said. "She wants to be a doctor."

"How much was she getting paid to work here?"

"Minimum wage. Same as us," Lindsay said.

Tracy quickly did the math in her head. If Kavita was working thirty hours a week at $15 an hour, she was earning $450 before taxes, or roughly $1,800 a month gross. Her rent would have been about $900 when sharing the apartment with Aditi. Tracy had to hand it to the woman for not giving in to her parents' pressure, but tearing up Aditi's check to cover the apartment rent for the next two months did not seem like the best idea. Again, it made Tracy wonder if Kavita had done it out of anger.

Tracy and Pryor handed the women business cards. "We'd appreciate a call if you hear from her or think of anything that she might have said, someplace she might have gone."

"I really hope she's okay," Lindsay said, considering the card. She looked at Tracy. "Will you tell us if anything happened to her? It's kind of creepy, the way she just left."

"Sure," Tracy said. She and Pryor started from the store. Then, realizing how long it might take to drive out to Bellevue, Tracy turned back. "Is there a bathroom I can use?"

CHAPTER 15

Del pulled the car to the side of the road and turned off the Mariners broadcast. He'd seen Faz cry, but on those occasions the tears had been tears of joy, like when Vera had hosted a dinner to celebrate Dan and Tracy's engagement and Tracy had told them all what they meant to her, how they had become her family. That was just Faz being Faz. He said crying was part of his Italian genes, but Del was Italian and he wasn't much of a crier. He sensed that Faz's tears this night were neither tears of joy nor sentimental tears, and seeing his partner this vulnerable made him uncomfortable.

Faz removed a handkerchief from his back pocket, blotted his eyes, and blew his nose. His face had become blotchy, as if from rising embarrassment. The color in Faz's cheeks made Del notice that the bags beneath his partner's eyes were darker and more pronounced. Something was wrong.

Faz sighed as if to let out a batch of bad air, then cleared his throat. "Vera's got cancer."

Faz said the words so quickly, without any buildup or warning, that for a brief instant Del thought he must have misheard his partner, but you didn't mishear certain words, no matter how softly spoken. Certain words refuse to be drowned out, refuse to be ignored or pushed into the recesses of the mind to be dealt with at a more convenient time. "Cancer" is one of those words—it is never convenient; never misheard; never ignored.

"No," Del said. He didn't want to believe it. He and Celia had just been to Faz's home for a barbecue the prior weekend. They'd drunk Chianti and ate a pork loin in the backyard.

Faz nodded, as if also coming to grips with the truth. "She has a lump in her breast." He paused long enough to suck in another deep breath. It shuddered in his chest, like poison. He quickly exhaled. "We went back for additional mammograms and an ultrasound this morning. We were sitting in the doctor's office, waiting, trying not to think about it too much—trying not to jump to any conclusions, you know? Then the radiologist walks in, he pulls up the X-rays on a computer and points with the tip of his pen to this small black area in the breast tissue. This thing, it was like a pebble, Del. It was nothing. But this doc, he don't sugarcoat things. He gives it to you straight so there's no misunderstanding. And this guy, he looks right at Vera and he says, *You have cancer.*"

"Faz, I'm sorry," Del said, at a loss for words and trying to curb his own emotions.

"Just like that," Faz said. "Just like that, he says, *You have cancer.*" Faz turned his head and looked at Del. The area beneath his nose was red and his eyes watery. "You want to get angry, you know? You want to get mad at something, at someone, but you can't, because it's just one of those things, you know? One of those *fucking* things." He slammed a fist against the dash, then the door. The car rattled. Del gave him a moment to vent. Faz spoke quietly. "The luck of the draw." He exhaled, looking out the front windshield, his eyes unfocused. "It just feels surreal to me, like I wasn't really even in that room this morning, and it wasn't my Vera he was talking about. I felt numb. I still do."

Del had sat in a car with Faz for more than twenty years, and during that time they'd never been without something to talk about, but now he was struggling with what to say. What do you say? *I'm sorry* seemed too simplistic, too obvious, what a dullard would say. He remained silent.

"They took a biopsy after that."

"Did they give you the results?"

"We won't get those for a couple of days, but the radiologist didn't pull any punches. He said we should find an oncologist now and decide on a course of treatment."

"Listen, Faz, why are you here, man? Take some time off to be with Vera."

Faz shook his head. "I tried, Del. I suggested to Vera that I take some time off, but she said, the two of us sitting around worrying about it wasn't going to change the outcome or make either of us feel any better. It would just make us more miserable. She told me to go to work, to try to get my mind off it."

"Sounds like Vera," Del said.

"Like I could, you know?"

"Well, maybe she's right," Del said. "We're both better when we're working. Like when I got divorced, you remember? Or when Allie died." Allie had been Del's seventeen-year-old niece who had died of a heroin overdose. "It was better when I was working. I know it's not the same thing, Vera being your wife, but . . . Hell, you spend too much time with Vera and she's liable to not like you anymore, right?"

Faz grinned, but it looked small and painful. "I don't know what I would do without her, Del." His body shuddered and he sat up, as if struggling to hold something horrible inside.

"Don't go there," Del said, but it looked to Del like Faz was already there.

"I hate myself for thinking of me at a time like this, but I'd be lost without her, alone in that house, growing old by myself. I don't have any hobbies, nothing to keep me busy. I work too Goddamned much. What would I do, Del? What the hell would I do without her?"

"Hey, first off, Vera's not going anywhere. Second, you got me, Faz. I'll always be around."

"You'll have Celia," Faz said, glancing at him again, giving him another rueful smile. "And I'm happy that you do. Everybody should have somebody."

Del couldn't help but think that Faz was right, that he'd be lost without Vera. Faz and Vera were like red wine and lasagna. They just went together. "Let's not get ahead of ourselves," Del said. "It's like you said about this investigation. We take it one step at a time. One day at a time. Okay?"

"Yeah," Faz said. "Yeah, okay."

"And Vera . . . I'll tell you this. If I was cancer, I'd be scared shitless of Vera."

Faz wiped at his nose with his handkerchief. "She's tough," he agreed.

"Damn right, she's tough. Toughest woman I've ever known. She won't just beat this thing; she'll kick the crap out of it."

Faz nodded, exhaled. He smiled again and sat up, as if awakening from a nap.

"Come on," Del said. "Let's deliver this car so we can get you home."

CHAPTER 16

As Tracy and Katie Pryor drove east across the 520 bridge, the windows of the opulent homes along the shores of Lake Washington sparkled from the light of a fading sun. In the distance, the Cascade mountain range loomed.

The young women inside the store had confirmed Aditi Banerjee's statement that Kavita had not gone to work, and she had not called her boss to let him know— neither action being in character for the woman Aditi, and the two store clerks, had described—mature, smart, a little stubborn, driven.

As Tracy reached the east end of the bridge, she fought to keep negative thoughts from spinning out of control and instead tried to decide how best to approach speaking with the Mukherjee family. It was rare that Tracy was ever in someone's home to deliver good news. Faz once said that a police detective calling about a family member was like a *60 Minutes* producer calling to invite you on to the show. It was rarely for a good reason, no matter how they phrased it.

The Mukherjees lived in a neighborhood called Cherry Crest. Heavily wooded, the area appeared to be designed for equestrians, and was close to a state park. The homes were situated on large lots enclosed with horse fencing. Tracy turned the car down a road without sidewalks. Slatted shafts of light cut between the branches of evergreen, dogwood, and maple trees, casting shadows on the asphalt. Green and blue garbage cans, neatly aligned for pickup, roughly identified the location of each driveway. Tracy turned at the designated address and parked outside a one-story home of dark wood siding nestled in a grove of trees. The yard was impeccably landscaped with stones and native plants. Water trickled beneath a footbridge that spanned a pond covered with netting to protect spotted black-and-orange koi fish. Tracy and Pryor crossed the bridge to the front door.

Pryor rang the doorbell and Tracy watched through a sidelight as a man approached and answered. He wore shorts, a loose-fitting white shirt over a protruding stomach, and no shoes. A woman came and stood beside him. Also barefoot, she wore baggy brown pants and a long-sleeve matching top. Her hair was pulled back from her face and tied in a long braid. From the picture Aditi had provided, Kavita more closely resembled her mother, who also had light skin, fine features, and expressive eyes, though they were brown, not blue.

"Mr. and Mrs. Mukherjee?" Pryor said, introducing herself and Tracy. "We spoke on the phone."

Both parents, Pranav and Himani, looked understandably tentative.

Pranav Mukherjee adjusted black-framed glasses on the bridge of a broad nose and invited them inside. Tracy detected an aroma of cooked spices. "I hope we're not interrupting your dinner," she said.

"No. Please." Pranav gestured for Tracy and Pryor to proceed to his left. They paused in the entry where shoes lined the wall.

"Would you like us to remove our shoes?" Pryor asked.

"It is not necessary," Pranav said, his accent thick.

Tracy and Pryor stepped into a living room where other presumed relatives waited—an elderly couple seated on the couch; a young man, perhaps in his early twenties, leaning against a wall behind the couple;

and a younger boy, early teens, seated on a red beanbag. The elderly woman on the couch had light-blue eyes.

Grandparents.

Behind the grandparents, a mural of brightly colored birds perched on tree limbs climbed the wall. A picture window provided a view of a wooded backyard.

Mr. Mukherjee made the introductions, starting with a hand gesture toward the couch. "This is my mother and my father, Kavita's grandparents." The elderly couple nodded but did not rise. Nor did they speak. "And these are Kavita's two brothers, Nikhil and Sam." Nikhil, the older brother, had his hands thrust in the pockets of blue jeans and made no effort to remove them or to approach. Trim, he resembled his father, with dark skin, broad features, and wiry hair. Sam, the younger brother, had long hair he swept across his forehead. It partially covered his eyes. Light skinned, he resembled his mother and sister. He wore basketball shorts and a tank top.

Pranav gestured to two open chairs designated for Tracy and Pryor. When Tracy sat, it felt a bit like she was back in court on the witness stand. Pranav and Himani moved to an empty sofa positioned perpendicular to the grandparents and across from Tracy and Pryor. "I'm not sure what Aditi has told you," Pryor said, looking for a place to start.

"She hasn't told us anything," Nikhil said. "Except that she can't find Kavita." His tone emanated more annoyance than concern, and it made Tracy wonder, again, if Kavita had gone missing before.

Pranav raised a hand intended to silence his son. Addressing Pryor, he said, "What can you tell us?"

Pryor shared what she and Tracy had learned. After Pryor had finished, the room remained silent.

Pranav broke that silence. "Kavita and Aditi were very close," he said, looking to his wife for confirmation. "I'm sure the news of Aditi's wedding was very difficult for Kavita to accept."

"I take it that you haven't heard from your daughter," Tracy said.

"No," Pranav said. "We have not."

"When was the last time you spoke to Kavita?" Tracy asked.

Again, the room fell silent, and Tracy sensed this was perhaps a source of embarrassment. She pushed ahead to try to get past it. "Aditi mentioned there was some tension in the family?"

Pranav looked to his wife before he reengaged Tracy. "Yes."

When he didn't elaborate, Tracy said, "About her living on her own?"

"We expected Kavita to move home after graduation," Pranav said. "We told Kavita that we would no longer pay for her apartment or her studies. We considered it an unnecessary expense."

"Aditi mentioned that Kavita intended to attend medical school?" Pryor said.

Pranav nodded but it was Himani who spoke. Her voice was surprisingly strong and, like the son's, it, too, had an edge. Pranav may have been the head of the family, but Tracy suspected Himani had her say. "Kavita is very headstrong." Tracy also suspected this was a trait Kavita had inherited from her mother. "It has always been our intention to pay for each of our three children to attend college. Kavita knew this before she started. She knew that we did not intend to pay for graduate school."

"So Kavita would have to pay for medical school herself?" Tracy said.

"If she desired to attend," Himani said.

"Did she desire to attend?" Tracy thought that if Kavita truly desired to live on her own and to enroll in medical school, it was even less likely she would have walked away from a rent check, as well as from her place of employment.

"That is what she told us," Himani said.

"But not what you expected?" Tracy asked.

Himani said, "We expected Vita to marry."

"And I understood that was the source of some conflict—that Kavita would not consent to an arranged marriage," Tracy said.

"Kavita didn't want to be Indian," Nikhil said.

"Nikhil," the father said over his shoulder, sounding more tired than upset.

"It's true." Nikhil pushed away from the wall and took a step down into the living room. He looked at Tracy. "Vita didn't want to move home and she didn't want Ma to find her a husband. She wanted to be American. And she expected us to support her lifestyle."

"So there was conflict," Tracy said, looking to Pranav.

"Yes, there was conflict," Pranav said, without further elaboration.

"Was the conflict to a point that Kavita would not have called you if she was upset about Aditi getting married?"

Himani said, "Perhaps not."

"I'm not judging anyone here," Tracy said, sensing some reticence. "I'm just trying to determine if Kavita could be upset and taking some time to herself, if that's the reason no one has heard from her. I'm wondering what level of communication each of you had with her and when. You know Kavita. I don't. I need to know if Kavita has ever done this before, run off when upset?"

"No," Pranav said. "Not to my knowledge."

"Was Kavita in a relationship that you were aware of?" Tracy asked.

"Probably," Nikhil said.

Tracy looked at him. "Any that you know of?"

Nikhil shook his head.

"Were any of you aware of any relationships Kavita had in the past?"

Pranav and Himani also shook their heads. "Kavita never told us of anyone," Pranav said.

Tracy deduced that to have been deliberate, and not from a lack of suitors, given Kavita's natural beauty. It also would have been unlikely she'd bring boys home to meet parents to whom she was not speaking.

"So when was the last time you spoke to your daughter?" Tracy asked again.

"It has been several months," Himani said. Again, her voice bore no evidence of alarm or concern.

"We had hoped this was just a phase Kavita was going through . . . like all young people," Pranav tried to explain. "We had hoped she was just flexing her independence and would soon move back home."

"And allow you to find her a husband?" Tracy asked Himani.

The woman seemed to take the question as some sort of a challenge. Her eyes burned. "A proper Indian marriage, arranged by your parents, is blessed by Lord Ganesh and Lord Krishna. You may not understand our ways, Detective."

"I'm trying to," Tracy said.

Himani continued, "Americans believe that a young woman must fall in love for the marriage to succeed, but look at your divorce rate." She paused as if to accentuate the fact. "We only wanted what was best for Kavita."

If Pranav was upset at the insinuation that his wife had not loved him when they married, he showed no outward sign that was the case. In fact, despite the unnerving circumstances—a detective in their home asking questions about their missing daughter—the couple did not show any outward sign of affection. They did not hold hands or otherwise console each other.

"I'm not judging," Tracy said again. "I want to know if there were any men in Kavita's life, or who wished to be in her life, who might have had reason to harm her."

The room again fell silent. Tracy was about to move on when Sam spoke from the beanbag chair. "Vita had a boyfriend."

It was as if someone had dropped an F-bomb in the room. Everyone turned to look at him but seemed too stunned to respond.

"How do you know this?" Pranav finally said. Sam looked tentative.

"You've spoken to Kavita?" Tracy prompted.

"Yes," he said. "Sort of. No. We sent text messages."

"Why did you keep this from us?" Himani sounded upset rather than happy her daughter was not completely estranged from the family.

"Kavita asked me not to tell you," Sam said.

"Did Kavita mention a boyfriend?" Tracy asked.

Sam shrugged. "Not exactly. She said she couldn't come to my soccer game because she had a date."

"You spoke to her?" Himani asked.

Sam looked to Tracy, clearly trying to avoid his mother's piercing stare. "What else did she say?" Tracy asked. "Did you speak to her or was this a text?"

"It was a text," he said.

"What did you say in the text?"

"I just said I had a game and I wanted her to come. I said Baba was traveling and Mom wasn't coming so I wanted Vita to come."

"And did she return your text?"

"Yes."

"What did she say?"

"She said she was upset that Aditi had gotten married. She asked me if Ma was gloating about it."

Himani sat up a little straighter, lips pursed.

"Do you have the text on your phone?" Tracy asked.

Sam shook his head. "No. I erased it."

Tracy suspected she knew the answer to the next question but asked it anyway. "Why?"

"Kavita didn't want Ma reading it." Sam looked again to the couch. "Ma reviews my text messages at night."

This was enough to burst the bubble of anger expanding around Himani and to free her tongue. "I take the phone at night so that Sam studies and is not texting his friends or playing some game. I know many mothers who do the same."

"It's summer," Sam said softly. "I don't study in the summer."

"You should be doing something to improve your mind."

"Again," Tracy said. "I'm just trying to find out what information is available. We can recover those text messages from the telephone company. Did Kavita say she was going away, that she was going anywhere?" Tracy asked Sam.

Sam shook his head. "No."

"But she said she couldn't go to your game because she had a date."

"That's what she said."

"Did she mention any names?"

Sam shook his head.

"Did she say anything else you recall in her text messages?" Tracy asked.

Again, Sam shook his head.

"Did you text her back?" Tracy asked, suspecting Sam had.

Sam nodded. Again, his eyes shifted to the couch. This apparently had been forbidden by his parents, or at least his mother, who sat simmering.

"What did you say to her?"

"I just said that we won and I missed her."

"I also texted Kavita," Nikhil said.

Himani looked as though the entire world was suddenly against her. Pranav looked like he'd been sucker punched.

"How long ago?" Tracy asked.

"I don't know. A few weeks, maybe. I told her that her behavior was very hard on our parents. I told her that for the good of the family she needed to move home, and that she needed to get married."

"Did Kavita respond to you?" Tracy asked.

Nikhil shook his head. "No."

Tracy gave this a moment of thought. It was all very foreign to her. Her parents would have been thrilled if she had opted to follow in her father's footsteps and become a doctor. And she suspected that a very large majority of the American population would be proud of a daughter supporting herself, not seeking anything from her parents except perhaps their emotional support and love, but she wasn't there to judge the Mukherjees or to question their culture. She was there to find leads, and, at the very least, the mention of Kavita being on a date gave them at least one. Aditi had not mentioned a date, but then she might not have known because she'd been gone for three months.

"Can you tell me anything more about your daughter?" Tracy spoke to Pranav and Himani. "You said she's stubborn. Can you see her leaving without telling anyone where she was going?"

Pranav and Himani gave the question some quiet thought. Himani spoke first. "As I said, we haven't been in contact with Vita for several months." She glared at Sam. "I'm not sure she would have tried to call us. But in answer to your earlier question, yes, I can see Kavita leaving and not telling us."

"She's trying to hurt us by being difficult," Nikhil added.

"All due respect, Nikhil," Tracy said, "but this seems to have gone beyond being difficult. Kavita did not show up for work today, which her boss said was unlike her, and it doesn't seem logical she'd pass up a chance to work if she was going to have to pay the apartment rent on her own."

"What is being done to locate her?" Pranav said, now sounding worried.

Pryor sat forward. "Aditi filled out a missing persons report and provided us with a recent photograph of Kavita. That information is being disseminated to law enforcement throughout the state. I think we have enough to issue what is referred to as an Endangered/Missing Person Alert, and to provide that to the data center as well."

"What will it do?" Pranav asked.

"It serves as authority for our missing persons unit to try to find Kavita, and places the information into the Washington and National Crime Information Centers. Can you think of anyone who Kavita might have called or gone to stay with?"

"Only Aditi," Himani said. "And perhaps this date she had."

"I'm assuming if Kavita was not receiving financial support from you that she has her own bank account and debit and credit cards?" Tracy asked.

"Yes," Pranav responded.

"And she pays her own bills?"

"Yes," Pranav said.

"Do you know what bank she uses?"

"She used Bank of America while in school," Pranav said. "It was a joint account. After graduation, she switched to a private account."

"Do you have the number on that account?"

"I might have an old statement around, if I can find it."

"What about Kavita's computer? Does anyone here know her password?" Tracy asked.

Tracy received multiple head shakes.

"Okay. We're also going to get a warrant signed to search her laptop and try to determine if there is anything on there that might be of use, and we'll obtain her cell phone records to determine if she's been using her phone since Monday."

"What can we do?" Pranav asked.

Tracy and Pryor gave the family tasks—telephone calls to relatives and Kavita's close friends in case Kavita showed up. Pryor would keep contacting hospitals, airlines, and rental car agencies. Then Tracy said, "I'm also going to ask where each of you were Monday night; it's procedure." She didn't add that a high percentage of murders were committed by family members.

"I was traveling in Los Angeles," Pranav said. "I returned home very late."

"And I was at home with Nikhil, and Pranav's parents," Himani said.

"Here?" Tracy asked.

"Yes."

"Did you go out?" Tracy asked Himani.

"No. I was reading."

Tracy looked to Nikhil. He said, "I was watching television."

Tracy looked to Sam. "And you had a soccer game?"

Sam said, "At Roosevelt. I spent the night at my friend Peter's house."

When they'd finished, Tracy and Pryor stood. They handed Pranav and Himani business cards, but Tracy looked at Sam when she said, "If anyone hears from Kavita, we'd like an immediate call."

CHAPTER 17

Faz and Del escorted the tow truck to the vehicle processing room, which looked like a large indoor garage, at the Park 95 complex. They arrived after 8:00 p.m. Most everyone had already gone home. While optimistic—or at least hopeful—that Latents could pull a usable print, they knew it was never a certainty. On the drive, Faz had spoken with Desmond Anderson and Lee Cooper, but they had not garnered much in the way of usable information at the apartment complex where Monique Rodgers had lived, or from the neighboring homes and businesses. Faz hated having all of their eggs in one basket, but as Del liked to say, "It is what it is."

"Why don't you get home to Vera?" Del said. "I'll finish checking on the car and fill out the paperwork."

Faz had called Vera when they first arrived. She said she'd spent the afternoon working in her garden and was going to an elderly neighbor's to make banana bread. She visited the woman a couple times a month to keep her company. "I appreciate it," Faz said to Del, "but Vera is out keeping busy and I think we should pay Little Jimmy a visit tonight, shake the tree and see what falls in case Latents can't pull a print."

"We can go first thing tomorrow."

Faz shook his head. "We could, but if Little Jimmy is putting the word out and intimidating people, I want him to think we're already on his ass and not about to let up."

They drove to South Park to conduct a noncustodial interview, which was exactly what it sounded like. They'd question Little Jimmy without taking him into custody. Police detectives favored the interview because it did not require a warrant, nor were they required to read the person his Miranda rights. Defense attorneys argued the interview was intended to intimidate, and Faz and Del hoped it did, though they'd never say so.

Back in South Park, Del parked on a street lined with red muscle cars like the one that had driven Little Jimmy past the apartment building after Monique Rodgers had been shot. It looked like a convention, each car washed and waxed and glistening beneath the street lamps. When they stepped from the car, Faz heard Mexican music echoing throughout the neighborhood. It wasn't hard to find the source. Bright lights emanated from a one-story clapboard home that didn't look to be more than a couple hundred square feet and in need of a good painting. They'd found the party. Men in jeans and tank tops stood outside the home talking to women in cutoff shorts smaller than bikini bottoms. Their bodies had been inked with enough tattoos, some of the prison variety, to start a catalogue. Faz saw various iterations of the number 13: XIII, X3, and *M*—the thirteenth letter in the alphabet. Sureño gang symbols. The attendees drank from red plastic cups and, from the sweet aroma lingering on the stagnant night air, smoked pot. Illicit drugs were also likely.

"Looks like a party," Faz said. "We picked a good night."

"Yeah, they're going to love us," Del said. They crossed a dandelion-infested brown lawn and made their way down a sloped driveway, garnering stink looks and under-the-breath comments from the crowd. A brown wooden gate separated the front from the backyard. Behind it, two men in black bandannas stood like bouncers outside a bar. The more assertive of the two had roped muscles so large he looked like an overinflated sex doll.

"It's a private party," he said.

Faz held up his badge. "Good thing we have our invitations. Looking for Little Jimmy. He knows me. He waved to me today from his car. Tell him Detectives Fazzio and Castigliano would like a moment of his time."

Steroid Boy nodded to the other bouncer, who scurried down the driveway into the backyard crowd. "It's his birthday today," Steroid Boy said. "Why you want to ruin his birthday, man?" He sounded almost rationale.

"We don't," Faz said. "We came to wish him Happy Birthday and bring him his birthday present."

The man scoffed. "We're all just kickin' it. Nobody is causing any problems."

"And we're hoping to keep it that way," Faz said. He turned to Del. "I'm sure there are noise ordinance violations though, and I'm guessing no one took the time to get a permit for this gathering."

"I agree," Del said.

Faz spoke to the bouncer. "But we aren't looking to ruin everybody's evening and shut down the party. That would be a shame, wouldn't it, on his birthday?"

The smaller bouncer returned and said something in Spanish. Steroid Boy stepped aside and opened the gate. "Little Jimmy said he looks forward to speaking to you."

The crowd seemed to close in around the two detectives as they walked down the driveway and into the backyard. More men and women leaned into one another, sat on lawn chairs, and came in and out of the back of the house, the screen door whipping open and slapping closed with a thwack. Overhead, multiple strands of party lights crisscrossed between the cornice of the house roof and a freestanding garage. The sweet aroma of marijuana became much more pungent the deeper into the yard they walked.

The focal point of the party was in the southwest corner. When Del and Faz approached, the crowd parted like the Red Sea. Little Jimmy sat in a brown leather chair, the price tag still dangling from the side. Shirtless, his body was riddled with tattoos from his shoulders to his wrists and across his hairless chest, including what looked to Faz to be a portrait of Big Jimmy tattooed over his heart. Multiple gold chains also dangled from his neck, some with crosses. The waistband of his red underwear protruded above his jeans.

Little Jimmy smiled up at them and stretched out his arms, as if to welcome them. When he did, the man seated beside him pulled back the rotary tattoo machine he'd been using to ink Jimmy's left shoulder. Jimmy had a joint between his lips. He took a hit, removed the joint, and handed it to a woman seated on the arm of the chair. He exhaled and slapped the arm of his chair. "Detective Fatso, how do you like my birthday present?"

Little Jimmy had his old man's facial features but that was where the similarities ended. Big Jimmy had been powerfully built, with beefy arms and legs, though Faz doubted the man had ever lifted a weight in his life. Big Jimmy also had an air about him similar to a seasoned politician. Well-spoken, he was beloved in the South Park community because he'd donated frequently to public causes, like the community center. It was a tactic the cartels in Mexico and the Italian Mafia used to ingratiate themselves with the neighborhood. Little Jimmy wasn't his old man. He was thin, though muscled, probably from dedicated weight lifting and possibly steroids. He shaved his head and sported a thin black goatee and he wore the same black sunglasses. He also spoke like the other fools—in clipped English sprinkled with a lot of slang and profanity.

"Good move leaving on the price tag," Faz said. "I think you might have to return it. It's not going to fit through the back door."

Little Jimmy nodded. "Good point. Maybe I'll drop it down the chimney, like Santa Claus." The tattoo artist started again. "You want a tattoo, Detective? I get one every year on my birthday. Julio is the best around, man. I'll set you up for free."

Faz shook his head. "I never caught the bug, Jimmy. I just go to dinner on my birthday."

"I can tell, man. You look like you put on a lot of weight since I last saw you."

"Nah, you were just a lot smaller. I've always been this size."

Little Jimmy laughed and looked to Del. "Who's this, your younger brother? How come you're not skinny like him?"

"Bad genes, I guess," Faz said.

"You got to be careful. You'll give yourself a heart attack or a stroke, man."

Faz pointed. "I like the tattoo of your father. Nice resemblance."

Little Jimmy did not look down at the tattoo on his chest. His smile vanished. His mood darkened. "I got that when I was fifteen so I could always remember what he looked like. Sometimes it's hard for me to remember because I was so young when he died." He paused. Then he said, "But you seem to be doing all right. I heard you were a big-shot homicide detective now. So tell me, Detective Fatso. Why are you here at my birthday party? You looking for a homicide?"

"It's Fazzio," Del said in a tone that Faz had heard before. You didn't want to piss off Del. He'd take down the entire party by himself when angry.

Jimmy turned his gaze to Del. "That's what I said. Maybe you need to clean the wax out of your ears."

"I think you'd be surprised by what we've heard," Del said.

"We already have a body, Jimmy," Faz said. "You know that. You drove past the apartment building in a car making like a pogo stick. Tell me, why would you do that? Seemed discourteous and disrespectful to me."

"Nah. I didn't mean nothing. Just curious, man. A lot of people standing on the sidewalk watching. I wanted to see what all the excitement was about."

"You wouldn't know anything about that shooting, would you, Jimmy?" Faz asked.

Jimmy shook his head. "Me? No, man. I don't know nothing about that."

Faz looked to Del before reengaging Jimmy. "Really? Because we have some people telling us you do know something about it, that maybe it was you who gave the order to have Monique Rodgers killed."

Little Jimmy smiled. "Ah, now you're just messing with me, Detective Fatso. Ask these guys. They'll tell you. I'm a lover, not a fighter." He puckered up, and a woman bent and kissed him on the lips. "You see? Why would I know anything about that?"

"For the same reason your old man gave the order to have the members of that rival gang killed," Faz said. "Because you aren't very bright."

Jimmy stood abruptly, causing the tattoo artist to pull away quickly and the woman to fall into the chair. A trickle of blood inched down his bicep. *"Baja la música,"* he yelled. A moment later the music stopped. Jimmy removed his sunglasses and stepped into the center of the yard, eyeing Faz like a prizefighter.

"Don't insult my father, Detective Fatso. Not on my birthday. Not in my backyard." He glared for another moment, then he smiled and turned, arms spread wide. He shouted, "Listen up, man. Detective Fatso here wants to know if anyone knows anything about a shooting in South Park. Anybody know anything?"

The question was greeted by head shakes, mumbled denials, and silence. Dark eyes bored into Del and Faz. Jimmy looked around the yard for several seconds, then he looked back to Faz. He took a step closer, close enough for Faz to smell the marijuana on his breath. His eyes were glassy, mud-brown pools. "You see, Detective, I'm trying to help the police here. Nobody knows nothing about no shooting or dead body. I'll tell you what I'm going to do though. I'm going to keep my ears open for anybody who says they do know something. Yes, I will. I'm going to be paying very close attention to anyone who says anything."

He smiled.

Faz said, "So am I, Jimmy, and when I hear your name, I'm going to come back here, and the next time we talk, it won't be in a backyard. We'll be talking in a holding cell downtown. I'm going to put you in jail, Jimmy. Just like I put your father in jail, and we both know what happened to him." Faz eyed Jimmy up and down. "And he was a lot bigger and, I'm guessing, a lot tougher than you."

Jimmy smiled, a defiant, broad grin. "Then I'll see you when I see you," he said. He turned to his crowd and yelled, "Man, what kind of party is this? Somebody turn on some fucking music."

The music kicked on again.

Little Jimmy plopped down into his recliner, still watching Faz. The tattoo artist wiped his shoulder with an antiseptic wipe and went back to work coloring his creation. Del and Faz turned to leave.

"Detective Fatso?" Jimmy said. Del and Faz reengaged him. "You didn't ask me about my birthday tattoo. Aren't you curious?"

"Not really," Faz said. "My dad always said only fools get tattoos."

Little Jimmy turned his shoulder. On his bicep was a tombstone. He smiled. "I'm keeping this one reserved. I ain't never going to forget you, Detective. No sir. I'm going to remember you."

Faz smiled. "I'm flattered, Jimmy, and inspired. Maybe I will get a tattoo. Maybe I'll have Julio ink a picture of you right on my ass, so I can always remember what a piece of shit you are."

CHAPTER 18

Tracy watched the hounds bump and jostle one another, barking as they fought their way out the front door to greet her. It was nice to be loved, even if it was just a Pavlovian response to the sound of her truck crunching the gravel drive. Dan stepped out after them, watching Tracy from the doorway. His love was not Pavlovian, and it made Tracy feel special. Dan had apparently worked late, still dressed in his suit, tie pulled down and shirt collar unbuttoned.

Tracy pushed out of the truck and stepped down from the cab, petting the dogs as they circled her. "Did you boys go for a run yet? You don't look like it. You look full of energy." Nearing the front door, she said to Dan, "Thought you would have been home hours ago—nice day like this. I expected to find you lying out on the deck soaking up the sun in your birthday suit."

Dan's lips curled into a bemused smirk. He spoke in an Irish brogue. "Not this fair-skinned Irishman. We tan the way lawyers tell the truth, never on purpose and never very well." He gave her a kiss and stepped aside so she could enter. The dogs remained outside. Dan left the front door partially open, though the dogs showed no interest in coming inside. They could get on the scent of a rabbit or a squirrel and run around the yard entertained for hours.

Tracy dropped her briefcase onto one of the chairs at the dining room table and shrugged out of her coat, draping it over the back. "I take it from their greeting that you didn't get them out yet?"

Dan continued the brogue. "I hate to be the one to break this to you, but when they charge out the door it isn't love. It's more like a jailbreak. I just barely beat you home."

She wrapped her arms around him. "And what about you—do you come out because it's a jailbreak?"

"I'd break out of any jail to be close to you," he said, kissing her.

The sun had nearly set, casting the interior of the farmhouse in streaks of light. A breeze drifted through the house from the open door, bringing the smell of dried grass. "Before we get started here," he said, still smiling as Tracy gave him small kisses, "I was thinking of changing my clothes and going for a run before it gets much darker. You want to go?"

She hadn't exercised in several days and could feel the tension in her shoulders. "I'll go, but only if you promise to lose the accent."

Dan bit his lower lip, scowled, and began to shadowbox around her, speaking in a very good impression of Muhammad Ali. "I can't help it. The words are just so pretty. They're pretty, Howard, just like me. Look at this face. Fifty fights and I've never been cut."

Tracy laughed and shook her head. "Forget the dogs, you definitely need a run."

After changing into running clothes, they stretched for a few minutes before starting out along a dirt trail behind the house that meandered toward the tree-lined hills. The dogs loped in front of them, changing directions as their noses dictated. Since moving to the farm, Dan had mapped out different runs of different lengths, depending on how far they wanted to go, and how much light they had to do it. The early evening temperature had cooled, with a light breeze blowing through the trees, though it remained warm enough that Tracy didn't need a sweatshirt, and her muscles quickly loosened. She carried a water bottle. So did Dan. Her doctor said running was fine the first few months of her pregnancy if she felt up to it, but he admonished her not to get dehydrated. Dan had become the water Nazi.

"So why are you so late?" Dan said in between breaths, both of them still trying to catch their wind, which for Tracy was becoming more and more difficult as her pregnancy progressed. Their running shoes pounded the dirt trail in an uneven pace.

"I don't think I told you. I got a call from Katie Pryor. Do you remember her?"

"Police officer who lives in West Seattle? You want to stop and catch your wind?"

"No, let's just slow the pace a bit."

Tracy felt her breathing syncing with her stride as they started up the first incline, Dan in front to accommodate the width of the trail. "She switched positions a few months ago. She's working the missing persons unit."

"Didn't you help her get the job?"

"I did. She called because she's working a case involving a young woman gone missing. She has a bad feeling about it and asked if I'd take a look."

Dan gave her a sidelong glance, clearly concerned, given what had happened to Tracy's sister. "How long has the woman been missing?"

"Since Monday night, but the circumstances are unusual."

Rex and Sherlock sped past them.

Tracy explained what she knew about Kavita Mukherjee's disappearance and her relationship with her family. When she'd finished, Dan said, "So you don't know if the woman was just upset and needed some time alone or if something has happened to her."

"Unfortunately, when it's a young woman, it's usually the latter."

"But you don't know."

"No."

"Are you working it?"

"Katie asked me for my help. I spoke to the roommate and the family tonight."

"And are you avoiding answering my question because you don't think Nolasco is going to let you work it?"

"I'm not avoiding it . . . but yeah, I doubt Nolasco will allow it. Then again, last year we ignored a missing persons case and they found the woman cut up in garbage bins all around the city. A mandate came down for us to take a more aggressive approach, especially in the first forty-eight hours."

"Okay, but why *you*? You're in trial."

"Closings were today. Besides, I know what this is like, Dan, and I don't mean that in an irrational way. I know what the family is going through because I've been through it. They need an answer. I don't want anybody to have to wait twenty years the way I did . . . the way my family waited. It destroyed my father and my mother."

"I'm just worried about the additional stress, especially with the pregnancy."

"I know and I appreciate your concern, but stress comes with the job," she said. They continued on for several seconds. Then she changed the direction of the conversation. "Interesting family dynamics though. The father definitely projected as the head of the house, but the mother seems to be the one who actually wields the power. If looks could kill, her youngest son would have keeled over dead when he said he'd texted his sister."

"And the daughter's lack of communication with the parents is all because the mother wants her to move home and agree to an arranged marriage?"

"I got a sense there was more to it, but that appears to be the trigger," Tracy said.

Dan used the tail of his tank top to wipe sweat dripping down his forehead. He slowed at one of his designated turnaround spots and they jogged in place. "How are you feeling? You want to turn back or continue?"

"I'm good to go on," she said.

"You sure? Our little tadpole all right? You drinking enough water?"

"I'm fine," she said and squirted a stream of water into her mouth.

With the sun nearly below the horizon, the trail had become immersed in shades of gray. Dan led on.

"I have to say," Tracy continued, speaking to the back of Dan's head when he again ran ahead of her where the trail narrowed, "that an arranged marriage sounds barbaric—like putting livestock on the auction block and having all their parts and pedigrees considered. Only now they apparently do it on the Internet."

"I thought the Internet was for porn," Dan said. They'd watched the musical *Avenue Q* earlier that season at the Seattle Rep, and the song—"The Internet Is for Porn"—had stuck in his head. "Don't be so quick to judge."

"You don't see it as barbaric?"

"When I practiced in Boston I had a secretary who was Indian and in an arranged marriage. She seemed happy. I'm just saying, I don't think it's our place to judge what we don't understand. The percentage of divorces is lower than in America."

"The mother said the same thing," Tracy said.

"There's also a strong sense of duty to the family, including grandparents. Unlike Americans, they don't just stick us old folk in a home."

"The father's parents lived in the house," Tracy said, thinking of the elderly couple on the couch who hadn't spoken a word or revealed any outward sign of emotion.

"From what I understand, the parents and children care for the grandparents. When the son gets married, his wife moves in and the cycle continues."

Tracy shot him a glance. "Are you serious?"

Dan shrugged. "Jayanti, my secretary, moved in with her husband's parents. She'd come to work some days bleary-eyed and dragging. She'd work all day, then go home and cook dinner, do the laundry, and help her kids with homework. She said it was the Indian way, that someday her son and his wife would take care of her and her husband."

Dan led Tracy down an incline and she stutter-stepped so as not to step on the heels of his shoes. She could feel a twinge of discomfort in her knee from an old injury. "Did she say she even loved the guy?"

"I don't remember." Dan spoke while glancing over his shoulder. "I met him at firm functions. He seemed like an okay guy. I don't know. I'm just saying it's not really our place to judge. Look at us. We got married quickly."

"We lived together for two years."

"Still felt quick," Dan said.

Tracy punched him between the shoulder blades and Dan laughed. The trail widened again and she sped up to run side by side. "I'd prefer that our son or daughter love the person they marry and the two can't keep their hands off each other."

"Hey," Dan said. "That might be my daughter you're talking about." He again imitated Muhammad Ali. "I'll knock the fool out."

"I think that's Mr. T, not Muhammad Ali."

Dan laughed. "Speaking of not being able to keep our hands off each other . . ."

"Who said anything about us?"

"Hey, you initiated the launch sequence when you got home. Don't expect me to abort the launch now. I'll race you home? Winner gets to undress the other."

"As long as you promise not to laugh at my belly."

Dan smiled. "I could get a sympathy belly so you don't feel self-conscious."

"Spare me," she said.

He patted his stomach. "No, spare me."

"You're a goober."

He increased his pace as they came out of the hills along the dirt trail and raced for home.

CHAPTER 19

Faz kept the window down on the drive home, hoping the cool temperature would help calm him. He and Del had gone to Little Jimmy's to push buttons, something they usually excelled at, but Little Jimmy had pushed a few buttons of his own. Faz didn't like being called "Detective Fatso" but he could dismiss it as juvenile; what really bothered him was the way Jimmy had flaunted the killing. He was behind it, Faz was sure of it, and he was daring Faz to prove it.

He parked in his drive and shut off the engine. The aroma from Vera's tomato plants assaulted him through the open car window. Another month and they'd have enough tomatoes to stew and fill jars that Vera would give to appreciative neighbors as Christmas gifts.

Maybe. Christmas was still months away and maybe no longer guaranteed. "Shit," he said, and told himself not to go there, not to think about down the road.

He looked up at the basketball hoop and thought of Antonio. Vera did not want their son to know about her cancer until they had more information. She'd told Faz that Antonio had enough stress pursuing his own restaurant and finding the right moment to propose to his girlfriend. Faz didn't know if not telling Antonio was the right thing to do. Antonio was no longer a child and Vera was his mother. On the other hand, Faz better understood, now more than ever, that this was Vera's way—to not worry them about things they could not control.

He got out of the car and spotted the wheelbarrow along the side of the house. It contained a bag of potting soil and Vera's bucket of gardening tools. He looked at the rhododendron Vera had asked him to move the prior week. He'd begged out of her request, saying that the digging and lifting would hurt his back. That had been just an excuse. He saw a vacant spot in the foliage where the plant had been.

"Damn," he said.

Atop the porch steps he reached to insert the key in the lock, then pulled back his hand. What if this were to be his life, coming home late to a dark and empty house? What if Vera wasn't here when Antonio got married or when he opened his new restaurant? The thoughts spun like dust devils, forcing him to step back. He chastised himself. Now was not the time to fall apart or to panic. Vera was going to need him, whether she was willing to admit it or not. He needed to hold his shit together.

Faz took several deep breaths and stepped into the kitchen. The stove light shined down on several pans of banana bread emitting an intoxicating odor. "Vera?"

He pulled his tie from around his neck, clicked off the stove light, and touched the bread. Still warm. She'd been busy.

He walked into the darkened dining room and heard water running through the pipes in the walls—Vera in the shower. At the top of the stairs he came to Antonio's bedroom. It still had Mariners baseball pennants on the walls, and the drapes and bedcovers matched the team's blue-and-turquoise color scheme. Vera had insisted they not change it, saying that when Antonio had children they could spend the night in his room. Faz closed his eyes, wondering if Vera would be here to experience it.

The lamp on Vera's dresser illuminated the room in a soft light. He heard the shower shut off and, not wanting to alarm Vera when she walked into the bedroom, he called out her name.

"Vera?"

"Hey. I'll be out in a minute."

He hung his suit coat on the valet stand and wrapped his tie around the knob. He discarded his shirt in the hamper and sat on the edge of the bed to remove his loafers.

Vera stepped from the bathroom followed by a rolling wave of steam. She wore her light-blue bathrobe, a towel wrapped atop her head. "Hey," she said, bending to kiss him. "How did it go?"

"Huh? Oh, yeah, Latents is going to jump on it first thing in the morning, after we get the search warrant," he said. He didn't tell her that he'd gone out to South Park to talk with Little Jimmy; it only would cause her concern.

"Did you ever find out what motivated the wife to try to wipe down the car?"

"No," Faz said. "Not really our business." He stood and slid his shoes into the rack in his closet. "Del thinks it's drugs. I think she's cheating on her husband. Drugs are something you can at least explain to your spouse, maybe even earn a little sympathy. She wasn't saying anything. We'll probably never know."

"Are you hungry? I could heat up some ravioli and that chicken from the other night? Or I could cut up some banana bread with butter."

"Smelled terrific when I walked in, but I'll wait until morning," he said. "I ate at work." He hadn't. He hadn't been hungry and wasn't at present. "How was your day? Looks like you got a little gardening in."

She smiled and shrugged. "It was okay. I kept busy."

"You got some color. Or is that just from the steam?" Nobody took hotter showers than Vera. Her face looked flushed, even in the dull light.

She went to her dresser, opened a bottle of cream, and spread the lotion across her forehead and beneath her eyes. She was still young, but in that light Faz saw that she'd aged. They both had. He looked in the mirror some mornings and didn't recognize the guy looking back at him. He still felt like he was thirty.

"I got done some much-needed weeding and replanted that rhododendron along the back fence."

"I saw that. I'm sorry. I should have done that for you," Faz said.

She waved him off and rubbed cream on her neck and arms.

"I'm sorry, Vera. I shouldn't have bitched about it."

"Don't start apologizing," she said.

"No, I mean it—"

"So do I!" Her voice snapped.

Faz froze. He watched her reflection in the mirror. She looked down at the dresser. After a moment she said, "Just . . . don't start apologizing for everything like . . . like I'm not going to be here, or like I'm some invalid you have to walk around on eggshells."

"Okay," he said. "I didn't mean anything by it. I just know it was a lot of work moving it."

Vera nodded. "I got the biopsy results back."

"What?" Faz said, suddenly alarmed. "I thought he said Friday."

"Well, his office called and wanted me to schedule an appointment to come in Friday for the results, but I told them I didn't want to waste any more time and to just tell me over the phone."

Faz felt a lump in his throat. He almost couldn't get the words out. "What did he say?"

"I have a grade two tumor in my right breast."

"What does that mean, grade two? Is that good?"

"He said that tumors vary from one to three so it's not as bad as it could be, but not as good either."

Two out of three, Faz thought. *Shit.*

"Forty percent of the breast is involved. He said it started in the milk duct, then broke through the duct wall and spread to the fatty tissue and to my lymphatic system. My lymph nodes."

Faz felt as though his entire body had been set on fire. "So what do we do now?"

"I contacted an oncologist at Seattle Cancer Care that he recommended, and I got an appointment. The nurse said it was likely we'd discuss a lumpectomy or mastectomy with either radiation or chemotherapy. Possibly both."

"We'll just have them take it off, right? No sense screwing with it. Take the breast off and then either chemo or radiation."

"I don't know," she said. "I assume they'll provide me with options. Maybe they can save it."

"Screw that. Then you worry that it might come back. Take it off. Take the left off too."

She shook her head and turned to face him. "How would you feel if you had testicular cancer and they wanted to cut off your balls?"

Faz felt as if she'd punched him in the gut. "Hey, I didn't . . . I'm just saying it isn't important to—"

"It's important to me! Okay? It's important to me. I don't want to be disfigured." She started to cry. "And I don't want this, Vic. Not now. Not now. Not at this time in my life. I don't want this."

He went to her and hugged her tight. "I know," he said. "And I don't want you to have it either, Vera." And in that moment he realized that the cancer wasn't about him, and never would be. It would impact his life, and maybe his future, but this was about Vera and, for one of the few times in her life, she was afraid. "You just hold on to me, now, Vera. Okay?" he said. "You just hold on."

CHAPTER 20

Thursday, July 12, 2018

Thursday morning, Faz stood in his bedroom sliding his belt through the loops of his slacks and thinking about the previous night. It had been one of the few times in his life that he'd seen Vera scared, truly afraid of what was to come, and that frightened him as much as the doctor's pronouncement that Vera had cancer.

His cell phone buzzed on his dresser. Del. He didn't sound good. "I threw my back out last night after I left Park 95."

"How did you do that?"

"It was stupid. I met Celia and we took a hot yoga class—"

"You did hot yoga?" Faz asked, disbelieving.

"I know I'm going to regret telling you this, but I sweat like a bull in a wool coat. After we got home I needed to get Sonny out for his walk. He'd been inside the entire day. Anyway, he got his leash caught up and when I turned to get him untangled, my back seized. I almost didn't make it home."

"You didn't slip a disk, did you?"

"Nah. I've had this happen before. It's muscle spasms. It happens if I work out, then go out into the cold and turn too quickly. I'm hoping it's just spasms. But at present I can't get out of bed, let alone walk. I'm on muscle relaxants, which make me too loopy to drive. I'm hoping I can get in this afternoon but I'm not so certain I'll make it. Can you call me if Latents gets a hit?"

"Yeah, no worries, but it will likely be this afternoon. I'm taking the morning off to go in with Vera to see an oncology specialist." Faz lowered his voice so Vera would not hear him downstairs. He could smell the aroma of fresh coffee and banana bread. "Vera got the results back last night from her follow-up visit. She has cancer, Del. Stage two." Faz explained what that meant. "It's invaded her lymph nodes."

"Shit, Faz, I'm sorry, man. I was hoping for better news."

"So was I. I just feel so bad for her, Del, so bad that she has to go through this."

"What's the plan?" Del asked. "With Vera, I mean. What's the treatment?"

"We'll find out more this morning. I assume she'll have to decide whether to get a mastectomy, and then a course of radiation or chemo, maybe both."

"Hell, just cut it off. Don't screw around with it coming back."

Faz again looked to the door to make sure Vera was not coming up the stairs. He lowered his voice. "That's what I said, but it isn't that simple. Vera asked how I'd feel if I had testicular cancer and they wanted to cut off my balls."

Del laughed. "She said that?"

"Her emotions are all crazy. I'm learning it's best to just sit and not say nothing."

"Well, you can do that."

Faz sighed. "I owe her a lot more, I know. She talked to me last night for an hour. I didn't know what to do or to say. I just nodded and held her hand."

"Maybe that's all she wants, Faz."

"Maybe. She's scared, Del. So am I."

"Listen, take all the time you need. Take the whole day. I'll find a way to get in and if I can't, I'll work from here."

"That's just it—I can't stay home. Vera doesn't want me hanging around feeling sorry for her. I'm lucky she's letting me go with her to the doctor this morning."

"She may be saying one thing but wanting something else. Just don't feel like you have to rush into the office."

"I'll let you know first thing I hear from Latents. You do the same if you hear before me," Faz said.

"Yeah. Will do," Del said. "Have you told Tracy or Kins yet, about Vera, I mean?"

"No, not yet. Vera wants to wait to tell anyone until after we see the oncologist," he said. "Then I'll let everyone know the lay of the land, including Billy; in case I need to take some time."

"Maybe it's good we have Andrea," Del said. "She can take some of the pressure off both of us."

"Can't hurt," Faz said.

CHAPTER 21

Tracy arrived at her cubicle later than she had intended. She'd dropped off Kavita Mukherjee's computer at the computer forensic division inside the Vice ICAC, which stood for Internet Crimes Against Children. She'd asked a friend within the unit to break the password and put the e-mails on a flash drive for Katie Pryor, since technically Tracy was not yet working the case. Pryor would secure search warrants for the computer and to obtain Mukherjee's bank statements and ATM activity. Pryor would also fill out paperwork for Verizon that she had "exigent circumstances," which were the key words needed to get the service provider to trace Mukherjee's phone and send Pryor the phone's last registered latitude and longitude.

The Violent Crimes Section was in full swing when Tracy arrived, phone conversations and the clatter from computer keyboards mixing with ambient noise from the television. Tracy noticed her computer had not been activated since she turned it off.

Kins sat at his desk with his back to her, talking on the telephone. Faz and Del were both out, though Faz's computer was on. Andrea

Gonzalez was not seated at any of the desks, which was good because Tracy hadn't had the opportunity to fill Kins in on Kavita Mukherjee.

"Hey," Kins said, hanging up his phone and rotating his chair. He checked his watch. "I thought you might be in court; I'm assuming we didn't get a verdict yet."

Tracy shook her head. "Hoetig said he'd call when the jury sends word." She walked over to his cubicle and looked over the top to make sure no one was on the other side. "I have something to talk with you about. Let's grab a cup of coffee."

"Does it have anything to do with the reason why Nolasco came in here asking for you?"

Tracy suspected she knew the reason for Nolasco's visit. "Did he say what he wanted?"

"No. He just said he wanted to see you as soon as you got in. I told him you were waiting on a verdict in Stephenson. What did you do to piss him off this time?"

"Me?" Tracy said, smiling. "I've been on my best behavior."

"Yeah," Kins said. "Sure."

She looked at the two empty chairs. "Del and Faz get a hit on that print?"

"Not sure. Last I heard the car is over at VPR," Kins said, meaning the vehicle processing room. "Del's at home though; he called in and said he threw out his back. I'm not sure where Faz is, maybe Park 95. Del said he was going to deliver search warrants to Latents."

"How bad is Del's back?"

Kins shrugged. "He said it's sore and stiff. He's on muscle relaxants so he can't drive."

"How early did Gonzalez get in?"

Kins shook his head. "Don't know. I haven't seen her yet. What's going on between the two of you? What do you have against her?"

"I don't like the way Nolasco hired her."

"That sounds a little petty, don't you think? She doesn't have control over how she got hired."

Tracy looked over the top of the cubicle wall a second time, then moved closer to Kins's desk and lowered her voice. "I ran into Ron yesterday afternoon on my way back from court. I asked him why he left the A Team. He said he didn't have a choice. He said Nolasco assigned him to the C Team."

Kins gave an unconvinced frown. "Well, he's the captain, Tracy. He can do that. C Team is losing Arroyo. I like Ron, but this seems like a better career decision for him too."

Tracy nodded. "It probably is, but Nolasco told Ron to take the job because the A Team was a dead end, that none of us were retiring or leaving anytime soon."

"Again, that's true; isn't it?" Kins said.

"Yeah, but Nolasco doesn't know that."

"Know what?"

"He doesn't know I'm coming back."

Kins shook his head. "I'm not following. He doesn't know you're pregnant, does he?"

"I haven't said anything to him. But assume he does know—Ron suspected as much, so that's not far-fetched—and assume that's why he hired Gonzalez and moved Ron to C Team."

"I don't follow."

"It's a heck of a lot easier to force me out if he's hiring another woman to take my place—a Hispanic woman as opposed to a middle-aged white male. It would make a discrimination charge almost impossible to prove."

Kins wasn't buying it. "You do realize you sound a bit paranoid, don't you? You really think Nolasco has thought that far in advance?"

"We both know Nolasco has wanted me gone ever since I started here."

"Well, now that's true. You're like the wad of gum on the bottom of his shoe."

"And when's the last time somebody just started in Violent Crimes? How'd Gonzalez jump the wait list?"

Kins started to speak, then paused. "I hadn't thought of that."

"I also don't like the fact that Gonzalez has been at my desk—using my computer to log in to the system."

Kins looked at Tracy's computer. "Do you think she did anything?"

"I don't know. She said in LA they used whatever desk was available."

Kins shrugged. "Then don't worry about it."

Tracy changed subjects. "Listen, before I go looking for Nolasco, I need to run something by you." Tracy told him the details of her call from Katie Pryor and what she'd learned about Kavita Mukherjee's disappearance.

"With everything we have going on, you're not going to convince Nolasco to give us that one. He'll tell you a missing person is exactly what missing persons is for."

"I know," Tracy said. "But he also can't sit on his hands and wait until we start finding body parts in Dumpsters again."

She left Kins and walked to Nolasco's office. Between the high-rises of downtown Seattle she could see the clear blue waters of Elliott Bay against a pale, cloud-free sky. Nolasco's office door was open. Tracy knocked. The captain sat at his desk, talking on the phone. He gestured for her to enter and she sat in one of two chairs. One of the women in another unit once said Nolasco looked like an aging porn star—thin, with a thick mustache and hair parted down the middle that extended over the tops of his ears.

His problem with Tracy stemmed from an altercation they'd had when she'd been a student at the police academy and Nolasco one of her instructors. Nolasco had made the mistake of grabbing her breast during a demonstration on how to frisk a suspect. He suffered a broken nose and severe groin pain, and he developed a sincere dislike of Tracy.

When Nolasco hung up the phone, Tracy said, "You were looking for me?"

Nolasco always looked like he was squinting into bright sunlight, or fighting a headache. "Kins said you were in court waiting on a verdict."

"Still waiting."

"I understand you have a problem with Gonzalez."

He was too easy to read, but Tracy tried not to smile or say something sarcastic, knowing she'd need Nolasco's approval to look into Mukherjee. "No, I had a problem with her using my computer."

"Why?"

Tracy shrugged. "Didn't we discuss this already? That's my desk and my computer, regardless if I'm in court or not."

"I told you I want her to get up to speed on your active files. You got a problem with her reviewing your files?"

Tracy shook her head. "That's why they're accessible. I do, however, have a problem with her gaining access to my privatized files. They're private for a reason. I didn't set it up that way. That's a department policy."

Nolasco eyed her.

"Are we done?" she asked.

"Yeah, we're done."

Nolasco put his head down. Tracy started toward the door and turned back, as if she'd forgotten something. "I got a call from the missing persons unit. They received a report of a missing twenty-four-year-old woman and asked that we take a look."

Nolasco looked up. "How long has she been missing?"

"Since Monday night," Tracy said.

"What evidence is there of foul play?"

"She hasn't communicated with her parents, her roommate, or her friends. She isn't answering her phone or responding to text messages and she didn't report to work. It isn't like her. Last anyone knew she'd left on a date."

"I'm not hearing anything to indicate foul play."

"Isn't that what we're trying to avoid?" Tracy said.

"What does the boyfriend say?"

"Don't know. They don't know his name or if he's even a boyfriend."

"Nobody knows?"

"The roommate was away and the woman wasn't speaking to her family."

"It's not illegal for people to go missing," Nolasco said. "Let MPU handle it until something more develops."

"MPU called me. They didn't want to wait until someone finds an arm in a Dumpster."

Nolasco knew the brass would raise hell if that happened again. It would paint the department as insensitive. Tracy went for the race card.

"She's East Indian."

"Del and Faz might have a print on the Monique Rodgers killer," he said. "And Del hurt his back. If they get a print, Faz is going to need help working that case."

"Okay, if Faz needs my help, I'll help, but I also think we should pursue this one. This is a college grad, applying to medical school."

Nolasco paused, a lizard stuck between a rock and a hard place. She let him contemplate the possible repercussions. "Let MPU take the lead. Provide support where and *if* they need it. We don't take it unless there's evidence of a violent crime."

"Will do," Tracy said, trying not to smile as she departed.

CHAPTER 22

When Faz arrived at Police Headquarters, he went into the men's room and splashed cold water on his face, hoping to hide the evidence that he'd been crying. The cancer specialist, after reviewing an MRI of the mass in Vera's breast, as well as a separate biopsy and CT scan, said that several lymph nodes had been impacted. He recommended that Vera undergo a mastectomy followed by chemotherapy. To ease the news, he said Vera had discovered the mass early and that a reconstruction of her breast could take place at the same time as the mastectomy. Vera took the news hard but, after time to absorb it, and further information from the specialist, she opted not to have both surgeries at the same time, feeling that the potential complications would leave her too weak; she wanted to preserve her strength to get through the chemotherapy that was to follow the mastectomy, and then deal with reconstruction.

As they left the doctor's office, Faz told Vera he would take the entire day off, but she again insisted that he go to work.

"Monique Rodgers's family is depending on you, and you may have a lead," she'd said. "Besides, what are you going to do at home?"

Faz tried to remain stoic while in her presence, but on the drive into the office he kept hearing the doctor's recommendation that they take one day at a time. He knew the doctor meant it as helpful advice, but hearing him tell Vera not to think about the future got him thinking again. Then, FM 98.1, the Seattle classical station, broadcast "Sono Andati" from *La Bohème*, the song when Mimi is dying. Faz lost it.

He felt relief to find the bull pen vacant. Del was at home, and he suspected Tracy and Kins were both in court, maybe to get a verdict. Eager for a distraction, Faz picked up the receiver and called Latents.

Jason Rafferty, who Faz knew well, chuckled when he picked up the line. "You're an eager beaver, Fazzio. What, did you think we wouldn't call if we got a hit on that car you and Del had towed in last night?"

"You're a genius," Faz said, trying to mask his emotions.

"No, you guys in VC are just predictable," Rafferty said.

"I just want to know if I should get my hopes up."

"I understand," Rafferty said, laughing. "Hang on. Let me make a call and see where we're at."

Rafferty put Faz on hold, and Faz rested the phone on his shoulder, then hit "Speaker," suffering to elevator music. As he waited, Andrea Gonzalez stepped into the A Team's bull pen, approached, and nodded to the phone. "Tell me that's not your version of Pandora."

"Pan-what?"

"Music . . . Never mind."

"I'm waiting to hear if Latents pulled a print off that car Del and I had towed in last night," he said.

"Monique Rodgers?"

Faz nodded. "Thanks for getting the search warrant signed."

She looked at Del's empty desk. "Is Del in?"

"He threw his back out last night and is likely out all day. He's hoping to be back tomorrow."

Gonzalez gave this information a nod, then glanced over at Tracy's desk. "I heard Crosswhite is waiting on a jury verdict. You know if she's coming in or not?"

"I don't know. Later I would assume."

Gonzalez smiled. "She and I haven't gotten off to a very good start."

"She'll be fine," Faz said. "Just use her desk."

"I'd rather not," Gonzales said. "Better to let that alone for a while. I just hate sitting in the back away from everything."

"Then use Del's desk."

"Thanks." She dropped her bag beside Del's chair, sat, and manipulated the mouse. "Damn."

"What?"

"I haven't got a password set up yet to get into the files."

"Gumba two!"

"What's that?"

"Del's password. Gumba two! I'm Gumba one!"

Rafferty returned to the phone. "Faz?"

Faz took him off speaker. "Still here."

"Sorry for the delay. Okay, I'm told we have a preliminary finding." Rafferty explained that they had pulled fingerprints and a palm print in the location where the video showed the suspect putting his hand on the car's hood. They couldn't get every fingerprint, but they got enough to eliminate the prints of the husband, the wife, and the son. Del and Faz had taken elimination prints from the Blaismith family before leaving their home.

"We ran it through ABIS," Rafferty said, meaning the Automated Biometric Identification System, which was formerly the Automated Fingerprint Identification System.

The switch in the acronym was an acknowledgment of ever-improving technology. The detectives had been ordered to take a class to keep up, and the technical instructor emphasized that fingerprints were now just one form of biometrics—palm prints, irises, and facial recognition software being the others. The FBI had also changed the name of its system—to "NGI" for Next Generation Identification system—and the instructor touted that system as providing the criminal justice community with the world's largest and most efficient electronic repository of biometric and criminal history. It all sounded very *Star Trek* to Faz, who just wanted one hit, for one suspect.

"Did we get a hit?" he asked.

"Eduardo Felix Lopez," Rafferty said. Faz scribbled the name on a sheet of paper on his desk. "You got that?" Rafferty asked, spelling out the name.

"I got it," Faz said, underlining the name twice, his mind already thinking about how they might tie Lopez to the shooting.

"He's in the system. You going to run him or want us to do it?"

"I'll do it. Did they say when I might get the full report?"

"Sometime later this afternoon. I'll e-mail you the draft to get you started. I know this one's getting a lot of attention from the media. Nail this asshole, huh?" Rafferty said.

"That's the plan." Faz hung up and banged a fist on his desk. "Yes."

"Good news?" Gonzalez asked.

"We got a hit on the shooter, or at least the guy who put his hand on the hood of the parked car. I'm going to call Del, then run him, see if he's got priors and a current address."

"You want me to run him while you call Del?"

"Yeah, could you? This might not get him out of bed, but he'll take great pleasure in hearing it."

CHAPTER 23

Tracy watched the jurors carefully as they entered from the back of the packed courtroom, walking single file, like a chain gang. They did not make eye contact with the defendant, Dr. John Stephenson, or his attorney. Instead, they kept their attention on the worn linoleum or stared at the neutral figure of Judge Miriam Gowin standing behind the elevated bench. Adam Hoetig seemed to also catch this nuance and glanced at Tracy out of the corner of his eye.

Once everyone had taken a seat, Judge Gowin ran the jury through the preliminaries before she asked if they'd chosen a foreperson. The choice surprised Tracy and, based on another sidelong glance, Hoetig. With hindsight, however, the choice of a mother of two children made sense, especially if the verdict was guilty. Stephenson's wife had been a mother.

"Has the jury reached a verdict?" Gowin asked.

The foreperson confirmed that the jury had. Reading from a note card she said, "On the count of murder in the first degree, we the jury find the defendant guilty as charged."

The verdict was like a sex act, everything up until that climactic moment just foreplay that tantalized and teased and sometimes frustrated. The reading of the verdict, followed by the release of tension, left everyone involved exhausted.

Hoetig gave Tracy a subtle nod. Behind them, members of the gallery wept or quietly cheered. Some clenched fists. Others dropped their heads and their shoulders.

Litwin asked that the jurors be polled, and one by one they each uttered a single word. "Guilty."

When it was over, the jury would get a break, likely a couple weeks, then return for the penalty phase, which often took as long as the trial. For the moment, however, their civic duty was completed.

As court adjourned, Hoetig thanked Tracy, and they agreed to grab a celebratory drink at a later date.

"You going back to the office?" Kins asked when he and Tracy met at the courtroom door. He'd been seated in the gallery.

"Not right away. I need to run something down," she said. "I'll catch up with you when I get back."

"Would that something be related to that girl in the University District?"

"Vice has her computer. I got a message that they've unlocked it and downloaded her e-mails."

—

The vice unit looked like a high-tech classroom with computer screens amid other gadgetry. Tracy developed a rapport with members of the unit when she'd worked for CSI in the same building. One of the people with whom she'd worked well was Andrei Vilkotski.

Vilkotski, from Belarus, immigrated to the United States in the early 1990s and was largely considered a genius when it came to computers and other electronic equipment. Rumors surrounded his past, including one that he was formerly a KGB agent, who, when the Soviet Union collapsed, quickly fled the country. None of the rumors were true, except the part about him being a genius with computers.

"Andrei," Tracy said, entering his cubicle. "How's it going?"

Vilkotski turned and shrugged. He looked a bit like a friar, bald but for a ring of hair around the back of his head. "Could be worse," he said, his common refrain. "Let me guess. You've come to take me to lunch and to finally propose to me." His accent remained thick.

Tracy leaned against a corner of his desk. "What would your wife think about that, Andrei?"

Vilkotski made a face as if considering what his wife might think. Then he said, "She'd probably tell me to take my laundry with me and call it an even trade."

Tracy laughed and sat down. "I understand you got into that computer I dropped off this morning."

Vilkotski looked at her over the top of half-lens reading glasses as if surprised. "Would that be the computer Katie Pryor dropped off, unaccompanied by a search warrant granting me permission to break it down?"

Now it was Tracy's turn to be surprised. "You should have received a copy of a signed warrant. I understood Katie obtained one."

Vilkotski's lip curled, this time almost becoming a smile. "If I had a nickel for every time I've heard that, I'd be a rich man."

"Check your in-box. If you don't have it, I can have it sent over to you."

Vilkotski typed. "Lucky for you I don't hold my breath anymore. I would have suffocated many times over, and my skin would be a permanent blue." He paused, seeing an e-mail from Katie Pryor. "What do you know? Look at this." He pointed at his screen.

"You see, Andrei, I wouldn't ask you to do anything illegal."

"Now you sound like Vladimir Putin."

"Would that make you Donald Trump?"

"Without the hair, obviously."

Tracy laughed. "You were able to get into the computer?"

"Please. My grandson could get into the computer, and he's three."

"Grandson?" Vilkotski had told Tracy that he and his wife married young and had children early. Tracy estimated him to be just late forties.

He pointed to a picture of his grandchild tacked on the inside of his cubicle wall. "He spent the weekend at our house. My son and his wife are traveling. I'm still worn out." He reached behind him and grabbed Kavita Mukherjee's laptop along with a flash drive, onto which he'd transferred her e-mails.

"I programmed the computer so that a temporary password will open it. I did so before I received the warrant, so the password is, 'I didn't talk to you and know nothing about this.'"

Tracy smiled. "A little long, don't you think? Is that all caps?"

Vilkotski smiled. "Then the password is 'Password One, Two, Three'—each word starts with a cap."

"Clever."

"I don't have time to be clever. Thanks to your chief, I must now be available twenty-four hours a day, seven days a week, to help you people find stolen iPhones." Vilkotski did not sound happy.

"I heard about that." Seattle Police Chief Sandy Clarridge had issued the edict after a news report that thieves had stolen more than two thousand cell phones during the first six months of the year.

"Yes, well, now it doesn't make me sleep too good."

Tracy grabbed the laptop. "I appreciate the help, Andrei."

"Yeah, yeah," he said.

Tracy could have had Vilkotski e-mail her the download or have Katie Pryor pick up the computer, but she had a different question she hoped he could help her with.

"Andrei, can you track a cell phone?"

"I don't understand."

She gestured to the laptop. "This woman who went missing, I want to track her cell phone. Could I do that?"

"Why don't you just call the service provider and get the longitude and latitude?"

"Yeah, I understand Katie Pryor did that this morning." Not wanting to leave a paper trail that she was pursuing the case, Tracy had everything sent through Pryor.

"I'm just wondering if there is some other way to track her phone, if it's still turned on—without using the Stingray."

Vilkotski feigned shock. Wide-eyed, he said, "Stingray? What Stingray?"

The Stingray was a simulated cell phone tower police could set up to surreptitiously gather information from suspects' phones, as well as to monitor any other mobile device in the area. Most police departments denied having the machine, which was developed for the FBI and provided to local law enforcement only after the department signed a nondisclosure agreement to not discuss the technology. Recent news stories reported that the Tacoma Police Department had used the machine, and ACLU lawyers quickly got worked up. In eternally liberal Seattle, it was better for a thief to commit a crime than to have his privacy invaded.

"Is there another way?" Tracy asked.

Vilkotski gave this a moment of thought. Then he said, "There are always other ways. For instance, there are certain apps that can be shared."

"Such as?"

"For one, did the woman have a Find My Friends app on her phone?"

"I don't know," Tracy said.

"If she did, you might be able to track her phone from a friend's phone."

Tracy thought of Aditi. It was worth a try. She made a mental note. "Okay, any other apps?"

"Many phones have Find My iPhone, but you would need her Apple ID and password."

"How might I get that?" Again, she thought of Aditi as a potential source.

"I would check her computer. Some people put that information under contacts so they don't forget. It is sort of a master key. I do that myself."

Tracy made another mental note to check the laptop.

"Was your woman living with family?" Vilkotski asked.

"No. Why?"

He shrugged. "Families often use one Apple ID so they can share music, movies, and books without having to purchase it multiple times. I do this also."

"And you can share this across multiple phones?"

"Multiple phones and platforms—like laptops, iPads, computers."

Tracy gave that some thought. "What about friends? Can they share an Apple ID?"

"You said this woman is a college student?"

"Recent graduate."

Vilkotski rolled his eyes. "College students never pay for anything if they can find a way to get it for free, and they usually can. They would have made great Bolsheviks."

—

Tracy walked Kavita Mukherjee's computer and the flash drive over to Katie Pryor at the missing persons unit.

"You get anything from the service provider yet?" she asked.

"I just sent in the Exigent Circumstances Request form," Pryor said. She nodded to the computer. "You got the flash drive."

Tracy handed it to her. Pryor inserted the drive and pulled up Kavita Mukherjee's e-mails, those received and those sent. She and Tracy immediately focused on e-mails Mukherjee had received after 5:00 p.m. Monday afternoon. Mukherjee had not responded to any of them. They did not find any e-mails pertaining to her date Monday night, nor did they find an e-mail confirming a hotel or airline reservation.

Tracy booted up the computer and used the temporary password Vilkotski had provided to review Mukherjee's Internet history, looking through her searches for airlines, rental car companies, websites related to other states and foreign countries. She found nothing.

"Let's go to her contacts," Tracy said.

"What are we looking for?" Pryor asked.

"Vilkotski said people sometimes keep their passwords in a master file under a contact. Let's see if she did."

In contacts, Pryor searched the name Mukherjee and pulled up Mukherjee's parents and her two brothers. The others Tracy did not recognize but deduced to be relatives.

"She's not there," Pryor said, meaning no contact information for Kavita.

Tracy thought of her conversations with Aditi Banerjee and with Mukherjee's family. "Type in 'Vita.'"

Pryor did and she got a hit for someone named Vita Kumari. "Who is that?" she asked.

"Don't know," Tracy said.

Pryor opened the contact and scrolled to the notes section. The contact included frequent-flyer account numbers, bank account numbers, log-in names, and passwords. The list was in alphabetical order and Pryor noted a bank account for the Bank of America. "Hang on." She flipped through documents on her desk and confirmed the number to be the Bank of America account number Mukherjee's parents had provided. "That's her bank account," she said.

"She's using a fake name," Tracy said, thinking Mukherjee did so in case the computer was ever stolen.

"Then those are her usernames and passwords," Pryor said.

"Pull up the Bank of America account and try the username and password."

Within minutes, Pryor was on the website. Mukherjee's log-in information worked. The account did not show any transactions after Saturday afternoon. The last transaction had been a withdrawal of twenty dollars from an ATM on University Avenue the previous Thursday, leaving Mukherjee a balance of $1,492. She'd have trouble paying next month's rent.

"Why would she tear up Aditi's rent check?" Pryor asked. "I mean, did she have so much pride she would reject help?"

"It's possible," Tracy said. "Aditi said she was stubborn. Or she could have already made up her mind to either move or to get another roommate."

Pryor continued to scroll through the notes for the contact Vita Kumari. Near the bottom of the list, Tracy said, "Stop. What is that? Is that another bank account?"

"Wells Fargo," Pryor said. "Sure looks like another account."

"Try it," Tracy said.

Pryor pulled up the website for Wells Fargo and entered the corresponding username and password. It took a second to load before they gained access to the account. Tracy whistled. She and Pryor were staring at an account with a balance of $29,230. "Maybe this is why she tore up the check," Pryor said.

Tracy sat back, stumped. "Aditi said she was saving for medical school, but I'm having a hard time believing she saved this much working in a clothing store at minimum wage."

"Her parents?" Pryor said.

"Not if they were intent on her moving home," Tracy said. "Look at the name on the account. Vita Kumari. And the address is a PO box," Tracy said. "She clearly did not want anyone to know about this account."

Tracy ran her hand down one of the columns of numbers; each deposited amount was identical. "Those are direct deposits."

"The same amount deposited on the same day every month," Pryor said. "We can use the routing number to find out who's making the payment, but I'm going to need a search warrant for the bank to get it."

Tracy thought of Aditi, specifically, the way the young woman had looked to her husband, as if embarrassed when Tracy asked her questions about Kavita.

"You feel like taking a drive?" she said. "I might know a way to get a faster answer."

CHAPTER 24

Andrea Gonzalez told Faz that the name Eduardo Felix Lopez had produced a hit for a nineteen-year-old male arrested just two months earlier for possession of a controlled substance—meth. He had provided an apartment in a multistory brick complex in South Park as his home address. That was both good news and bad news. With the address being two months old, Lopez could have moved, or maybe even fled to Mexico, if he was their shooter. There was no phone number associated with the address, nor could they locate a building superintendent to ask whether Lopez remained a tenant. Lopez had several other priors, each for possession, and one for intent to distribute, but no arrests for a violent crime. Nothing in the system indicated Lopez was a member of the Sureños, but if he was dealing drugs in South Park, that seemed a given. Perhaps Monique Rodgers's husband had been correct, and his wife's shooting had been a prerequisite to Lopez's gang initiation.

Faz decided to treat the interview as noncustodial, at least until they determined whether the address was still good. If it was, and if

Lopez was home, they'd ask to search his apartment. If he refused, they'd seek a search warrant for the apartment, specifically seeking the .40 caliber revolver that had killed Rodgers, then sit on Lopez until they had it.

As Faz and Andrea Gonzalez drove out of the police parking structure, she looked up through the windshield at roiling dark clouds to the northeast. "What's going on with the weather? It looks like a biblical plague," she said.

"Thunderstorms," Faz said.

"I thought we weren't supposed to get thunderstorms west of the Rocky Mountains. Earthquakes are what I was told to worry about."

Faz cut down Columbia Street to the on-ramp to the Alaskan Way Viaduct. "We get one or two thunderstorms a year in the Northwest. We got one last year about this same time of year. It caused fires all over Eastern Washington." Faz took the Viaduct south. From their perch above the surface streets he could see whitecaps, stirred by the wind, picking up on Puget Sound. "I watched the storm last year from a ringside seat at Police Headquarters working the night shift. The Space Needle lit up like something out of a science fiction novel."

Gonzalez gave a small chuckle. "And here I thought I'd found nirvana. Eighty degrees, no rain, clear skies. Felt like LA without the smog, the crowds, and the traffic, and still about twenty degrees cooler." Gonzalez looked again at the sky before sitting back. "You think Lopez is our guy?"

"The timing and the location are right."

"He could've heard the shooting and run for cover."

"He could have, but then why the hoodie over his face?"

Gonzalez gave that some thought. "You think he's still around?"

"If he *was* working for Little Jimmy, following orders, it's possible he got sent to LA or to Mexico. We're going to find out."

"And if he's home, what do we say? How do we justify knocking on his door?"

"If he's home we'll say we're canvassing the area, asking if anyone saw or knows anything about the shooting. We'll ask to search his apartment. Most of these guys don't know any better and let us in. If he refuses, we'll call in a search warrant and keep an eye on him until we get it signed."

"You think he'll run?"

"If he was acting on Little Jimmy's orders and they find out we're onto him, he won't have a choice. Little Jimmy will kill him."

—

Tracy called Aditi on the pretense that she wanted to provide an update on the search for Kavita. Aditi and her new husband had temporarily moved into her parents' home, which was less than a mile from the Mukherjee family home. Tracy needed to talk with Aditi in private, away from Rashesh and the rest of her family. She sensed Aditi was holding something back, something about Kavita that she would not discuss in their presence, something that might explain the $30,000 sitting in a bank account under the name Vita Kumari.

On the drive to Bellevue, Pryor received an e-mail from the cell phone provider with the last known longitude and latitude of Kavita Mukherjee's telephone—47.652770 latitude and 122.174406 longitude. "It's a state park," she said, pulling up the coordinates, "and it's very close to both homes."

Pryor showed the phone to Tracy, who felt a pit in her stomach when she saw a heavily wooded area. Pryor's further research revealed the park to be nearly five hundred acres—an ideal place to hide a body. However, Pryor's further research also revealed the park to be heavily trafficked, particularly in the summer, with joggers, walkers, berry pickers, and horseback riders. Odd then that no one would find a body.

Tracy checked her watch. They had just a couple hours of daylight. "Call the canine unit," she said. "Ask if they can stand by in case we need them. We'll go after we speak to Aditi."

Aditi answered the door of her parents' home and, for a brief moment, Tracy thought they'd caught a break and the young woman stood alone, but as the door pitched farther in, Rashesh appeared behind it.

Rashesh invited them into the living room, which looked to be more for show than use. Beige walls. Gray furniture. Brown carpet. A decorative piece of spiraling copper hung on the wall. It took Tracy a second to realize the image was a peacock. Two plastic plants adorned each side of a bay window through which Tracy could see an expansive backyard and, behind it, a thick grove of trees.

"Is that the state park?" Tracy asked, pointing out the window.

"Yes," Aditi said. "Bridle Trails."

"Does Kavita's parents' home also butt up against the park?"

"Not exactly but it's very close," Aditi said.

Tracy glanced at Pryor, who nodded and said, "Are your parents home?"

"No," Aditi said. "They're out."

"We spoke with Kavita's family and a couple of her coworkers yesterday afternoon. I wonder if you can answer a few additional questions?" Pryor said.

"I can try." Aditi adjusted in her seat.

"What type of relationship did Kavita have with her two brothers?" Tracy asked.

Aditi shrugged. "There has always been a sibling rivalry between Vita and Nikhil because they are so close in age."

Tracy noted Aditi's use of the name Vita. "He seems to have pretty strong opinions about his sister's refusing to move home or submit to an arranged marriage."

Aditi appeared to cringe at Tracy's use of the word "submit." "Nikhil is very traditional. He believes it is a waste of his parents' money to send

Vita to medical school. He believes that is a decision for her future husband to make." Aditi smiled at Rashesh, though it looked forced.

Tracy said, "Why would he care if the parents weren't going to pay for it?"

"He considers her actions disrespectful and an embarrassment to the family," Aditi said. "It is just Nikhil's way, as the oldest son. He has always been more traditional than Vita."

"And what about Sam?"

Aditi smiled. "Sam is more like Vita."

"How did Kavita plan to pay for medical school without her parents' help?" Tracy asked.

"She was working and saving money," Aditi said.

"At the store?"

"Correct."

"Anywhere else?"

Aditi shook her head. "Not that I know of. She could have gotten another job while I was away but . . ."

"But she didn't say that she did?" Tracy asked.

"No."

"And she was receiving minimum wage at the clothing store?"

"I believe so."

"So how could she save for medical school?" Tracy asked. "Even with you living there?"

Aditi paused before answering. "We had talked about applying for financial aid and student loans. Living on our own, not declaring our parents' income, Vita was confident we would receive assistance."

"How much had she saved?" Tracy asked.

"I don't know," Aditi said.

"Did she inherit any money from anyone, a grandparent perhaps?"

"I don't believe so," Aditi said. She shifted, looking uncomfortable with the topic.

"I wonder if I could get a drink of water?" Pryor asked, as planned. She turned to Rashesh. "Would you mind?"

Rashesh looked puzzled by the request.

"I'll get it." Aditi started to stand.

"No, you stay here with Detective Crosswhite," Pryor said, trying to keep her tone casual but forceful. "Her questions are directed at you. Would you mind, Rashesh?"

Rashesh, looking somewhat flummoxed, stood and led Pryor out of the room.

Tracy kept her gaze on Aditi, who watched until Pryor and Rashesh had left the room. Then she said, "We can't help if you're not honest with us, Aditi."

Aditi tried to look surprised. "I don't know what—"

"We obtained Kavita's bank records. She has a Wells Fargo account under the name Vita Kumari. It has close to thirty thousand dollars in it."

She watched for Aditi's reaction. The amount seemed to surprise her, but not the fact that Vita had another account.

"A payment of two thousand dollars is being deposited into the account on the first day of each month. We can trace the routing number, but I think you know where that money is coming from."

Aditi looked stricken. "Rashesh cannot know," she said, her voice rushed and almost pleading.

"We don't have to tell him anything," Tracy said. "But *we* need to know."

"I can get away later to speak with you."

Aditi turned when Katie Pryor and Rashesh reentered the room. She sat back with a forced smile and pleading eyes. Tracy was tempted to push her, to tell her they couldn't afford to waste any time; that the longer a person was missing the less likely they would be found alive, but she decided to respect Aditi's request, pursue other lines of inquiry, and go to the park to search for the phone while it remained light out.

"Sam said Vita told him she had a date Monday night. Did she mention a date to you?"

"No," Aditi said. "I did not know."

Tracy looked at the window. "You're familiar with the state park?"

"Bridle Trails?" Aditi said. "Yes."

"Does it have any significance to you and Kavita?"

"We spent a lot of time in that park when we were young," Aditi said. "We used to run the trails and occasionally we'd ride horses. Our families picked blackberries and hunted for chanterelle mushrooms. Why do you ask?"

"Was there any place in particular where you and Kavita would go inside the park?"

"I don't understand."

"Did you have a favorite spot, a place you might meet?"

"No. No place in particular."

Tracy recalled what Andrei Vilkotski had told her and asked, "Did you and Kavita share any apps on your phones?"

Aditi continued to look puzzled by the line of questioning. "I don't think so."

"Did you have an app on your phone called Find My Friends?"

She shook her head. "Do you want me to check?"

"Yes, I do."

Aditi stood, left the room, and returned with her phone, scrolling through the apps. "No. I don't have that one."

"What about Find My iPhone? Do you own that app?" Tracy asked.

"That one I have," Aditi said. "Here." She held up the phone for Tracy and Pryor to see.

"And what about Kavita? Did she also have that app?"

"I believe it comes with the phone, doesn't it?" She looked to Rashesh but he shook his head.

"I don't know," Tracy said. "Did you and Kavita share an Apple account, you know, to download music and movies, books?"

Aditi looked up at Tracy, about to speak. Then she paused, and in her suddenly widening eyes, Tracy could see that the young woman had figured out Tracy's line of questioning and maybe, just maybe, a way for them to find Kavita Mukherjee's phone.

—

Kavita had kept up a happy persona, a perky smile on her face, her emotions carefully tucked away, this one last time. When the date, and the relationship, ended, she left the hotel room feeling the gravity of her day. It felt like too much for her to bear alone, too much for her to handle. She did not want to go back to an empty apartment to sit alone, wondering what the hell had happened in the course of three months. She had always told herself that it was not her dream she was pursuing; it had been their dream, hers and Aditi's.

No longer.

Aditi was married. She would not be attending medical school.

As Kavita drove from the hotel, the sun had begun to set, and the weather had cooled to a comfortable temperature. She drove out of the hotel parking lot without ever looking back and thought that to be a good metaphor for how she would now get through life. She would not look back. There was no time to look back. She had made the decision to share her money with Aditi willingly and without any regret because she knew it had been hard for Aditi to stomach how easy things seemed to be for Vita, though Aditi had never expressed any resentment or jealousy—until Monday night. Maybe Kavita should have known. Throughout their lives Aditi had always been there for Vita, and she had looked upon this as an opportunity to be there for Aditi, to not leave Aditi behind. Wherever Kavita went, to whatever school, she had decided she would not leave Aditi behind.

That had been the plan, anyway.

Kavita sighed. She wondered if things would have been different if she had told Aditi about the money, if it would have made Aditi rethink

Rashesh's proposal. Maybe it would have made the dream of medical school that much closer to a reality, something she could have clung to when her parents had pressured her to marry.

Maybe, but Kavita would never know, not now, and . . . And she couldn't stop and look back. She had to look ahead, had to or she'd go crazy.

The car in front of her braked suddenly. Instinctively, her foot slid from the gas pedal and she slammed hard on the brakes, tires squealing, her body thrown forward against the shoulder strap. The driver behind her also hit his brakes, and his horn. Thankfully, Kavita had not plowed into the car in front of her or been rear-ended.

She pulled to the side of the road. She needed a moment to catch her breath and regroup. She'd been driving on autopilot, and now that she'd stopped, she realized she'd driven in the direction she had driven for so many years—to her parents' home in Bellevue, not to Seattle. She wondered if there was something in her subconscious, something pulling her home. A part of her wanted to go, now more than ever. A part of her wanted to see her family.

But she knew she couldn't go home, not like this, not this emotionally vulnerable, depressed, and defeated. Her mother would seize this opportunity to toss Aditi's marriage in her face, as Mrs. Dasgupta no doubt had done, building up her new son-in-law's family and apparent wealth, relishing the thought of Aditi living in a London condominium, not to mention all of her impending grandchildren.

It must have been painful for Kavita's mother, though not as painful as it was for Kavita. Kavita's pain was born of the loss of someone she loved dearly. Her mother's pain was born of anger and resentment. The two were not the same.

No, Kavita's mother would not console her. She'd lament again about how selfishly Kavita was behaving. She would guilt-trip Kavita for not giving her a son-in-law or grandchildren, and for making her and Pranav look bad to the family's friends. Her father would largely remain silent, not wanting to upset his wife, and Nikhil would start again about tradition and heritage and culture.

Only Sam would be happy to see her.

Sam. *Kavita considered her phone. Sam had sent her a text message earlier, knowing that the news of Aditi's marriage would be upsetting. He had invited her to his soccer game near the university, but she couldn't go. She'd missed his game, missed the chance to see him.*

In the distance, she saw the tops of the two-hundred-foot trees marking the state park, and her memories made her smile. She recalled the games she and Aditi and her brothers had played as children in those woods, and of her family's summer outings picking blackberries to make jam, and hunting for chanterelle mushrooms. She had gone into the park nearly every day as a child. It was like having a five-hundred-acre backyard. And as she grew older, the park had also become Kavita's refuge, a place where she could go when everything had gone wrong. She'd walk among the trees or sit in a quiet place to contemplate and seek answers.

She pulled away from the curb. She wouldn't go home. She didn't need to. She'd go to the park.

CHAPTER 25

Faz turned into the parking lot of the Ridge Apartments, a multistory building at the end of South Cloverdale, which became First Avenue South just past State Route 99. "Let's see if anyone is home," he said.

In the passenger seat, Andrea Gonzalez was checking her cell phone. She slid it inside her suit coat and said, "You sure you don't want to just scope it out, let SWAT come in and serve a warrant?"

Faz glanced over at her. According to Nolasco, Gonzalez had a lot of experience in a tough city, but she was clearly rethinking a noncustodial interview. "You getting cold feet?"

She scowled. "Please, I did this a number of times in LA. I just know from experience that you can prepare for anything and still get it wrong. Times like this it's nice to have a guy at your back with armor and an AR-15 ready to put a round up somebody's ass."

"Maybe so, but this isn't LA, and we're already in the middle of a Justice Department investigation into the use of excessive force. We call in SWAT when it isn't needed and we might have someone else at our back ready to put a foot up our ass." He considered the building.

"Look, most of these people are poor, not criminals. They're trying to live their lives just like you and me, and they don't like guys like Little Jimmy any more than we do, but they have to tolerate him if they're going to live here."

Gonzalez tilted her head. "The real question is how will they tolerate us?"

Faz shrugged. "Don't expect them to roll out the red carpet, or offer you a cold drink, but they'll largely stay out of our way. And chances are, if Lopez is even still here, he'll tell us he didn't see or hear anything, and if he refuses to let us look around, we'll thank him and leave. Once we know he still lives here, we'll get a search warrant."

Faz pushed open the car door and stepped out into a gusting wind. The dark clouds that had hovered on the eastern horizon now filled the sky, coloring it a darkening gray.

Gonzalez came around the back of the car, raising her voice to be heard above a rush of wind. "If locusts start falling from the sky, you're on your own."

At the building entrance, Gonzalez pulled the door handle without a pause and the door opened, despite a black box mounted on the wall indicating the door was supposed to lock by a security latch.

"Saw this a lot in LA," she said as they stepped inside. "The residents lose their keys so often the supervisor gets tired of being called at all hours of the day and night to open the door. They just disengage the automatic lock."

The interior lobby was austere, as in empty. Not a chair, sofa, or potted plant to be found on the well-worn tile. Small interior mailboxes lined the far wall—some open, others missing doors altogether. Those with doors had slots for the name of the tenant, but all were blank. "Saw this also," Gonzalez said. "The tenants protect their anonymity. The less you know about anyone else, the less they know about you."

Gonzalez hit the elevator call button as a stairwell door to their right flung open and a Hispanic man stepped into the lobby, moving quickly. He eyed them but kept walking, pushing out the front door and looking back over his shoulder with a practiced, hardened stare.

The elevator pinged and the doors pulled apart. Gonzalez took a step inside and quickly retreated, a horrified look on her face. Faz didn't have to ask why. The pungent odor of urine swept over him like a wave of toxic gas.

When she could speak, Gonzalez said, "Let's take the stairs."

"Five flights? I don't think so." Faz removed a handkerchief from his pocket, covered his mouth and nose, and stepped inside. Chivalry would have to take a backseat to self-preservation. "You coming?"

Gonzalez took a deep breath and pulled her jacket over her nose and mouth, grimacing as if fighting a massive headache or the urge to puke. Not surprisingly, the elevator didn't stop to pick up any passengers as it ascended.

"Now we know why that guy took the stairs," Faz said, voice muffled by the handkerchief.

When the doors pulled apart they hurried off onto the fifth floor, gasping as if they'd been holding their breath. Faz took a moment to assess their situation. They stood at the south end of the building, the cracked linoleum lit by the fading ambient light through windows at each end of the hallway. The deepening gray should have been more than enough to trigger the light sensors, but none were on.

"They steal the lightbulbs." Gonzalez pointed at a light fixture missing both bulbs, just two bare sockets where the lights should have been. "The landlord finally gives up buying new bulbs."

"Saw a lot of that in LA too?" Faz asked.

The hallway smelled of mildew, the walls scarred and nicked. Lopez lived in apartment 511, which they determined to be the last apartment at the other end of the hall. As they approached, a blue-white flash sparked. Seconds later, thunder detonated, rattling the aluminum-framed windows.

"Told you," Faz said. "Thunderstorms in July."

"Without the rain. That's just crazy," Gonzalez said.

"Oh, you'll get plenty of rain. That starts in a couple of months. Still think this place is nirvana?"

As they neared apartment 511, they stopped talking and took up positions on either side of the apartment door. Faz faced the southern window. Gonzalez faced the long hall they'd just walked. He gave her a slight nod and she reached to knock on Lopez's apartment door, but just as quickly, Faz grabbed her arm and raised a finger to his lips. He thought he'd heard a faint voice through the paper-thin walls. They both listened. Faz heard the voice again and this time Gonzalez nodded. She'd also heard it. It was a male, speaking Spanish.

Gonzalez mouthed the word. "Spanish."

Faz looked at the door to apartment 511, then looked over his shoulder at the door to the adjacent apartment, 509. He pointed to door 509 and said softly. "This one?"

Gonzalez shrugged. "Can't tell," she whispered.

Faz unclipped his gun and rested his hand on the grip. Gonzalez did the same. The walls, thin enough to transmit soft whispers, weren't about to stop bullets if someone started shooting, but there was nowhere to take cover in the cramped hall. Gonzalez raised her fist to knock. Faz heard the voice again, this time definitely coming from the adjacent door. At that same moment he heard the door pull open.

Gonzalez's eyes shifted to a spot over Faz's left shoulder, then widened in surprise—or fear. She stepped toward him as she unholstered and raised her weapon, shoving him off balance.

"Gun!"

—

When Aditi typed in the Apple username and password she and Kavita had shared, the Find My iPhone app produced a blinking blue dot in the southwest corner of the state park. It was roughly in the same location as the last known longitude and latitude pinpointed by the service provider. Tracy and Pryor thanked Aditi and quickly left, telling her they would let her know what, if anything, they found.

As Tracy drove the exterior of the park, taking in its immenseness while trying to find access, her sense of foreboding deepened.

"You'd think somebody would have found a body, wouldn't you?" Pryor asked in a quiet voice. "With as much foot traffic as this park gets?"

Tracy did, but she didn't say it. They had not discussed the ramifications of the blue dot while inside the Dasgupta home. Both knew what that blinking blue light meant—either Mukherjee's phone had been discarded in the park, or she had.

—

Kavita drove with a new sense of purpose. Move forward. Do not stagnate. Have a plan. Execute it. She turned into the parking lot, which was empty but for one other car, likely a runner using the trails. She stepped from her car to the familiar smell of trees and plants, and it transported her back to a simpler time, when everything she had needed—family, friends, and school—was located right here, in this neighborhood.

She moved quickly to the trailhead but stopped and considered her flats—which she'd worn to avoid accentuating her height during her date. She had not brought another pair of shoes, as she had not planned to come to the park. Undeterred, she started up the slope. The sun had dipped below the canopy of trees, filtering through the branches in wedges and shafts of soft light. Kavita had walked the park's trails so many times, knew the trail signs so well, she could find her way blindfolded. After several hundred yards, the trail forked and Kavita took the Trillium Trail, a 1.7-mile loop that circled the interior of the park. Within minutes of breathing in the park's familiar odors she felt better. She contemplated her dilemma and, more important, how to resolve it.

First, she had to determine whether or not to stay in the apartment, at least until she left for medical school. She didn't want Aditi's charity any more than Aditi wanted hers. Now that Aditi had made her choice, Kavita could use a portion of the money she'd earned to pay the rent until she found a new roommate, a graduate student, she decided. It might be difficult to find a roommate in the summer, but in the fall, when the students returned, the apartment would be in high demand for its proximity to the campus. Problem solved.

Next, Kavita would pick up additional hours working at the clothing store so as not to dip too far into her nest egg. The owner liked her. He would give her an additional shift. Being at work more would also help her ward off loneliness, especially at night, when she and Aditi had hung out. To this end, Kavita decided she would also enroll in a night course to study for her MCAT, the medical college application test. Presuming she did well on the test, she'd apply to a select number of medical school programs for admittance the following fall—schools where everything was new and no one knew her. She would start fresh, away from her family. Away from everything.

The thought was, at the same time, liberating and terrifying. She would be leaving everything she had ever known, everyone she had loved.

She got choked up at the thought of leaving her little brother, Sam, and her father. It would feel like a death, not seeing them.

Her sobs came in a rush, unexpected and powerful. She stopped beneath the branches, weeping. After several minutes, she chastised herself and went back to her new mantra. Move forward. She needed to move forward.

She dropped her head and ran, feeling every pebble in the path through the soles of her flats. When she came to where the trail split again, she took the Coyote Trail, running deeper into the park. She pushed herself through her sorrow, until fatigue set in and she had to stop and catch her breath. She walked in circles, her head thrown back, her lungs and chest aching, sucking in air. The daylight had nearly extinguished, the forest now an ever-deepening gray. It was time to go home.

Something moved. She turned.

Something in the brush. She turned again, then a third time. Something circling her.

She turned yet again, but saw only the trees, straight and tall, like darkened sentries. She fought to hold her breath, struggling to listen. The crickets clicked and the unseen insects buzzed. A light breeze caught the limbs of the trees, causing them to moan and creak. A bullfrog croaked.

She took another deep breath, exhaled, and turned to leave.

The weather quickly worsened. Dark clouds had rolled over the Cascade mountain range, and pushed west, toward Seattle. It had all the makings of a violent thunderstorm.

"Could just be her phone," Pryor said again, sounding nervous as Tracy turned onto 116th Avenue NE. "She could have lost it, or gotten rid of it."

Maybe, Tracy thought, though it didn't answer a more fundamental question: What was Kavita doing this close to home, in a state park that clearly had some sentimental value? Tracy couldn't help but wonder if the young woman, overwrought with sadness, had come to a place she knew, and had taken her own life. But even as that thought entered her mind, Tracy dismissed it as contrary to the determined young woman Aditi had described.

"You don't think so, do you?" Pryor asked. "You don't think it could just be her phone."

"I'm trying to remain optimistic but . . . no, I don't think so." Tracy no longer could ignore reason and common sense for something so fleeting as hope. "There doesn't seem to be a good reason she'd discard it, not in a park. If it's just a phone, it's more likely someone else discarded it, and that still leaves questions like, Why? And where is she?"

Tracy slowed at brown signs designating the park entrance. One bore the image of a hiker with a walking staff, the other a cowboy on horseback. She drove into a parking lot and parked beside three cars facing towering trees and thick brush. When she shut off the engine and pushed out into a stiffening breeze, she heard the rush and hum of cars on the 405 freeway a hundred yards to the west.

"Let's photograph the license plates of the parked cars," she said. "I doubt it matters, but let's do it anyway. We can run them later."

Pryor took the photographs as Tracy retrieved the go bag she used to process crime scenes and kept in the storage space behind her seat. She pulled out an SPD hat and threaded her hair through the opening. Then she slipped on a black windbreaker with the same white SPD initials across the back. She removed a flashlight, directed the beam of light at the ground, and handed it to Pryor when she came around the bed of the truck.

A gust of wind rattled the tree branches, causing them to shimmer and shake.

"You remember the lightning storm last July?" Pryor asked.

"Hard to forget. Let's go before it's on top of us and we lose what little daylight we have left."

Pryor considered her phone. "The signal is due east."

They took a well-defined dirt trail, climbing a slope for the first hundred yards. Horse droppings and tiny acorns littered the ground. At the top of the slope, the trail flattened and forked. A stake in the ground indicated it was the trailhead for two different paths. Tracy stopped and Pryor checked the phone again. The Trillium Trail, perhaps six feet wide, proceeded more or less straight, which was also the general direction of the flashing blue dot.

"This way," she said.

As Tracy and Pryor followed the trail, the forest canopy grew thicker, and what ambient light existed faded to shadows. Tracy's father had taught her and Sarah about forests when she and her sister were growing up in a town in the North Cascades. She recognized the heftiest trees to be second-growth western red cedar, perhaps a hundred years old and two hundred feet high. The gaps were filled in by smaller hemlock, Douglas fir, and a few maple and cottonwood trees. The ground cover was dense and consisted of rotting tree trunks, ferns, salal, red elderberry, Indian plum, and low Oregon grape bushes. Though it hadn't rained, the park smelled damp from the abundant ferns. The wind howled, sometimes in gusts that caused the tree trunks to sway and the branches to creak and moan.

After several hundred yards, the trail again forked. The Coyote Trail continued to the left, in the direction of the flashing blue light on the phone. They walked on.

The first chorus of thunder struck—a distant thrum to the east. Tracy briefly contemplated going back to the parking lot, waiting out the storm, and calling for a canine unit, but instead she pushed forward. Seconds later the forest sparked, a dazzling flash of light that caused the air to crackle just before thunder detonated. It sounded like the blast of a shotgun. The storm was moving fast.

"That felt close," Tracy said over the echoing retort.

"Too close," Pryor said, glancing up.

The blue signal on the phone continued flashing. "We're almost there. Come on." Tracy left the main trail for less defined foot trails and climbed another incline, came down the slope, and crossed a footbridge. The trail looped to the south. Between the trees, along the southernmost edge of the park, Tracy could see pitched roofs. She stopped to again consider the blue dot.

"That direction," Pryor said, pointing.

"There's a path," Tracy said, using the beam of her flashlight to highlight an unmarked trail snaking through the underbrush.

Lightning struck again, this time a brilliant spark that lit the area in shades of blue and gray and rippled the air. Almost immediately, thunder exploded, this time loud enough to cause Tracy and Pryor to instinctively duck.

"Shit," Pryor said.

Tracy thought again about turning back, but the blue dot beckoned, ever closer, as did the thought that Mukherjee's phone could be low on power and might soon die. Still, she also knew Pryor had kids at home.

"Why don't you go back to the parking lot," she said. "I can finish this and we'll meet there."

"No," Pryor said, shaking her head, determined. "Let's go. We're almost there."

"Try to stay off the path," Tracy said. "Walk in the underbrush." If there were shoeprints in the path, Tracy knew they could be important.

They slowed their pace, picking each step carefully, shining the light on the bushes and looking for colors that didn't belong. They were walking toward the houses along the park perimeter. Tracy stopped. According to the app, they were directly on top of the flashing blue light. "It's here, somewhere," she said.

They swept their flashlights over the underbrush, walking in a circle, increasing the circumference. The deepening darkness worked against them; Tracy stumbled several times on tree and plant roots. Lightning struck yet again, this time followed by a loud crack and the sound of splintering wood. She looked up in time to see a thin tree shear in two, the top half crashing through the canopy, dismembering limbs of nearby trees as it fell, and hitting the ground with enough force to send tremors through the soles of her feet.

"This is idiotic," she said. It was something the old Tracy would have done, the Tracy who had no family and nothing to lose. She was also putting Pryor and her family at risk. It was time to leave. "Let's go back to the parking lot, let the storm pass, and we'll call for a canine unit."

But this time Pryor was unwilling to give up. "Try calling the phone," she said. "Maybe we can hear it."

It was a smart move. Tracy called the number. They stood very still, listening, trying to hear over the sound of the wind. "You hear anything?" Tracy asked.

"Just the wind," Pryor said.

The call went to voice mail. Tracy disconnected and tried again. Again, they could not hear the phone ringing.

"Let's quickly drive a stake into the ground and mark the area with crime scene tape so we can find it if the phone dies, or the app quits working," Tracy said.

She snapped off a dry branch from a tree and used the knife from her go kit to sharpen one end. Pryor handed her a rock and Tracy pounded the sharp end into the ground, then used the rock and the knife blade to split the top of the stick. She removed a roll of yellow crime scene tape from her bag and forced it into the cut, tying two streamers and giving the plastic a tug to ensure it was tight. When they retreated to the main trail, she'd tie crime scene tape around the trunks of several trees to guide their return—if she could find the main trail. In all her twisting and turning, she could not immediately recall the direction they'd walked.

"Do you remember the direction we came?" she asked Pryor.

Pryor looked around the area. "Didn't we come from over there?" She pointed toward the incline.

"I think you're right," Tracy said.

They walked northeast, side by side, sweeping their flashlights left and right along the brush. Tracy was looking back over her shoulder to determine if she could see the two yellow streamers fluttering in the wind, when Pryor suddenly tugged on her arm, crying out. In the split second it took Tracy to turn back to the trail, Pryor was falling through the brush. Tracy grabbed Pryor's arm and dropped to the seat of her pants to keep Pryor from falling farther. Pryor had stepped through the brush into a hole, one much larger than a depression.

Tracy held Pryor's arm as the young officer scrambled out. They fell back onto the brush, catching their breath.

"Are you all right?" Tracy asked.

Pryor nodded. "I think so." She looked back to the hole. "How deep is it?"

Tracy stood and helped Pryor to her feet. They took small, careful steps, testing the ground with their feet, seeking to determine the circumference of the hole, which was concealed by the foliage. It appeared to be approximately four feet in diameter.

The foreboding feeling returned.

Tracy dropped to her hands and knees at the edge of the hole. Pryor knelt beside her.

"Hold back the plants," Tracy said.

Pryor pushed back the plants and Tracy directed a beam of light into the dark. The circumference of light centered on the broken body at the bottom of the pit, head contorted to the right, dark hair, splayed like the ribs of a fan, covering much of the young woman's face.

They'd found Kavita Mukherjee.

—

Faz stumbled off balance and hit the wall on the other side of the hallway. He'd managed to turn his head enough to see a person emerging from the adjacent apartment door just as three loud shots echoed in the hallway along with three flashes of light. He rebounded off the wall, struggling to recover his balance.

Andrea Gonzalez stood in front of him, her mouth opening and closing, speaking with urgency, though Faz couldn't hear her. The ringing in his right ear deadened all other sound, and it was as if he was watching a silent movie. Every movement passed as if through a thick, clear fluid. Gonzalez pushed him again, this time farther down the wall, away from the door and the possible line of fire, if additional shooters were inside the apartment.

Her voice came back online. ". . . all right? Are you all right?" she asked over the sound of a woman screaming and a baby wailing, presumably from inside the apartment.

"I'm all right. I'm all right," he heard himself say. From the way Gonzalez winced, he deduced he was shouting.

The body of a Hispanic man lay sprawled on the tile floor, blood saturating a white tank top and already running in rivulets along the cracks and seams. The man's jeans sagged low on his hips, revealing black underpants. Faz stepped forward to kick the gun away from his hand, but pulled back his foot when he didn't see a gun. What he saw instead was a cell phone near the man's right hand. He recognized the face from the DMV photo. Eduardo Felix Lopez.

Gonzalez moved inside the apartment while Faz quickly handcuffed Lopez, as was procedure, and checked for a pulse, not finding one.

He stood and followed Gonzalez inside the apartment. A woman sat slumped in the corner, clutching a wailing child to her chest. When Faz swept his gun right to left, briefly taking aim at the woman, she screamed again, something incomprehensible, and turned her head to the wall.

Gonzalez entered from a room to the right, speaking to the woman in Spanish. *"¿Hay alguien más aquí? ¿Hay alguien más aquí?"*

The woman lowered her head against the child.

Faz continued forward, clearing the kitchen, then a bathroom.

When he returned, Gonzalez knelt beside the woman and was pointing to the open door. *"Dime tu nombre. Dime tu nombre."*

Faz had a hard time hearing either of them with the child crying and the persistent ringing in his ears, and he couldn't understand what they were saying.

"El hombre en el pasillo, ¿cómo se llama?" Gonzalez said. When the woman did not answer, Gonzalez gripped the woman's shoulder and turned her. *"¿Cómo se llama?"*

"López," the woman shouted. *"Se llama Eduardo López."*

Gonzalez looked to Faz, then again to the woman. *"¿Quién vive en el apartamento del al lado?"*

The woman pointed out the door. *"El lo hizo. El lo hizo."*

Gonzalez stood, exhaled a held breath, and spoke to Faz. "Like I said, you can prepare for just about anything and still get it wrong. She says Lopez lives next door, in 511, but came over just before we got here."

Faz turned to the hallway, to Lopez's twisted body. The voice they'd heard speaking Spanish had been his, maybe on his cell phone. They'd just killed their only potential link to the Monique Rodgers shooting. Worse, Gonzalez appeared to have shot an unarmed man.

CHAPTER 26

Tracy stood beside her truck in the parking lot of the Bridle Trails State Park waiting for what was certain to be a large contingent of police and forensic experts. Though the physical storm might have passed, the police storm was just starting. And jurisdiction would be the first battle.

Though Kavita Mukherjee lived in Seattle and Aditi Banerjee had filled out a missing persons report with the Seattle Police Department, Kavita's body had been found in Bellevue. Bellevue had its own police force and jurisdiction over the state park and crimes committed therein. Tracy's only conceivable basis for not surrendering jurisdiction was a lack of information—that is, it remained possible that Kavita had been murdered in Seattle and her body dumped in a Bellevue state park.

That would be for the experts to decide.

One thing was for certain: Tracy wasn't about to just give up the case—not until they knew, definitively, what had happened. Her captain, however, might think differently, which was why Tracy called in the location of the body to her sergeant, Billy Williams, and brought up the issue of jurisdiction, deciding to tackle that problem head-on.

She told Williams she intended to work the crime scene, if in fact it was a crime scene, and asked that a team from the King County Medical Examiner's Office and from SPD's CSI unit be dispatched to preserve whatever evidence existed. They could debate jurisdiction later. Billy agreed, but said Tracy would have to fight that battle without him. Williams was on his way to South Park, along with an anticipated throng of brass, and Stuart Funk, the King County Medical Examiner. Faz and Andrea Gonzalez had been involved in a shooting.

After confirming that neither Faz nor Gonzalez had been shot, Tracy told Williams she would meet CSI officers and forensic personnel in the parking lot to give them the lay of the land before leading them to the body.

After disconnecting, Tracy called Kelly Rosa's cell number. Rosa was a forensic anthropologist for the King County Medical Examiner's Office. She had exhumed Tracy's sister's remains from a burial site in Cedar Grove, and was largely considered one of the best forensic examiners in the state, if not the country. Technically, they didn't need a forensic anthropologist; Rosa's skill was in the handling of skeletal remains and decomposed bodies, but Tracy trusted Rosa as much as she trusted Stuart Funk. She wanted someone who would tell her what evidence existed and give an opinion on what had happened. The last thing she wanted was somebody indecisive, somebody unwilling to say whether Mukherjee had been killed elsewhere, and her body moved and dumped into the hole. Rosa would have no problem making that call and likely others.

Tracy also called Kaylee Wright. Wright worked out of the Special Operations Section of the King County Sheriff's Office as a "tracker" or "sign-cutter." She'd hunted down the bodies Gary Ridgway had dumped during his decades-long murder spree, and she had helped Tracy solve a cold case in Klickitat County in which the victim was a young woman who had been killed forty years earlier. Wright had pieced together what had happened to the woman using photographs of footprints and tire tracks originally taken by a young officer who had found the body in a clearing in the woods.

While Tracy waited in the parking lot for the forensic teams, Katie Pryor remained in the woods. Tracy had directed Pryor to establish a perimeter by stringing yellow crime scene tape around the trunks of trees, then to designate a path, other than the foot trail, to and from the grave. A designated path would hopefully preserve whatever evidence might exist on the foot trail, and the larger trails connected to it—footprints in the dirt, strands of hair or clothing snagged in branches, and broken twigs and trampled leaves. Then again, multiple days of summer weather had no doubt enticed horseback riders, joggers, dog walkers, and berry pickers, who might have already trampled any evidence on the park's trails, but Tracy couldn't make that assumption. She needed Wright's expertise to tell her what was evidence and what wasn't.

Kins was the first to arrive from his home in Madison Park, just across the 520 bridge. He parked his blue BMW beside Tracy's truck and got out of the car shaking his head.

"You're always right, aren't you?" he said.

She gave that comment some thought. Then she said, "I wish I wasn't, not in this case."

Sensing her mood, Kins said, "You all right?" Kins knew the details of what had happened to Tracy's sister, and how finding the body of another young woman buried in the woods could impact her.

"Yeah," she said. "Just feel helpless, you know."

"Not your fault."

"Doesn't matter."

"Nothing wrong with feeling bad," Kins said. "I'll quit this job when I stop feeling bad. I'll know then that I'm dead inside." He looked around the parking lot. "So, how'd we get here?"

Tracy explained that Pryor had prepared search warrants for Mukherjee's phone carrier and what she'd learned from Andrei Vilkotski about using Aditi's shared account to track Mukherjee's cell phone.

"So if Nolasco asks, you can say Pryor found the body," Kins said.

"Pryor did find the body," Tracy said. "She nearly fell into the hole on top of it."

"Is this a natural hole, or did somebody dig it?" Kins asked.

"I don't know. I'd guess that it's not natural but it also doesn't look like it's been recently dug. It's deep. I'd say between six and eight feet, and maybe four feet in circumference. It may have been an old well partially filled in over the years and grown over."

That caused Kins to ask the obvious next question. "Could she have fallen in, an accident?"

"Could have, but if she did, it raises another question."

"Why was she here?"

Tracy nodded and pointed. "She grew up in a home close by. She and her best friend lived in houses along that side of the park. It was practically their backyard. But she was estranged from her family and didn't have a reason to come back here."

"If someone killed her, Tracy, it's likely they knew about the hole."

"I agree."

"The roommate?"

"Maybe. Maybe a family member—someone who knows the park and the trails. Either that, or she came back to a place she knew and, distraught, killed herself."

"In the hole? How?" Kins said.

"I don't know. I'm just throwing out possibilities. That's why I called Kelly Rosa."

Kins said, "Any gun?"

"Not that I could see. It could be underneath her, or somewhere in the brush. No sense speculating at this point. We'll know soon enough too."

"Jurisdiction is going to be a problem," Kins said.

"Maybe. She could have been killed and her body dumped here."

"How likely is that?"

Tracy looked around the empty parking lot. "How'd she get here? Her car isn't here. It's parked on a side street close to her apartment. That increases the likelihood that someone killed her someplace else and dumped her body here, which would give us jurisdiction."

"Is Pryor here?"

"I left her at the site to create a perimeter."

Kins looked over his shoulder at the formidable forest. "Better her than me." He zipped closed his jacket. "Did Billy tell you about Faz?"

"Yeah, but not a lot. What the hell happened? Did they have the wrong apartment?" Tracy asked.

"I don't know. Billy gave me the *Reader's Digest* version also. They'll have all kinds of people out there though, including FIT."

FIT stood for the Force Investigation Team. SPD had formed the team of six detectives as part of the federally mandated reforms created in response to the Justice Department's determination that Seattle Police too often resorted to unnecessary force. A federal monitor overseeing those court-ordered reforms had recently applauded the department's response. This wasn't going to help.

Nights like this, Tracy wondered if maybe Kins was right. Maybe she should just stay home after her baby was born.

Faz stood in the hallway. Lopez's body lay beneath a medical examiner's white sheet, an army-green bag close by to transport the body back to the ME's offices after Stuart Funk finished his on-scene examination. An EMT kept asking Faz if he was all right, and Faz kept telling him he was fine, though he had a persistent ringing in his ears that sounded like static when a television went off the air—back before cable and twenty-four-hour programming. He also had a headache. Though he maintained to everyone who asked that he was fine, nobody seemed to want to accept that answer, or maybe the EMTs just didn't have much else to do. They weren't going to save Lopez. Andrea Gonzalez had seen to that. She'd put three bullets in Lopez's chest, damn near one on top of the other.

Tenants living on the fifth floor had been told to stay inside their apartments, and none seemed too intent on disobeying that order. FIT investigators would eventually question every one of them about what they had seen and heard. In the interim, police officers flooded the hallway, the lobby, and the parking lot, along with the throng of brass, which was expected in any officer-involved shooting, particularly with a federal monitor all over their collective ass.

And that looked like it would be a significant problem. Faz had not found a gun beneath or anywhere near Eduardo Lopez's body.

After clearing the neighbor's apartment, Faz had stepped into the hall to call Billy Williams. He'd given his sergeant a shortened version of the events. Billy had come to the apartment building to take command as the ranking officer. He'd also had the presence of mind to call Anderson-Cooper and have them quickly secure a warrant to search Lopez's apartment. Williams's command lasted until Andrew Laub, the Violent Crime Section's on-duty lieutenant, arrived. Upon confirming a fatality from an officer-involved shooting, Laub called FIT.

FIT's sole function was to investigate whether the force used had been justified, and to provide a report to SPD's Force Review Board. Before the Justice Department's mandate, Violent Crime detectives investigated officer-involved shootings. The new FIT unit, therefore, was a clear indication that the Justice Department did not trust them to be objective, which put the two units immediately at odds. FIT investigators had never discharged their weapons, and Faz and the other homicide investigators knew that until you had been through that experience, you couldn't possibly comprehend the games the mind could play on an officer. In the midst of such a stressful situation, the officer often saw things that were either not there or that were different from what the officer thought she'd perceived. They didn't understand how a detective's mind could fill in blanks while struggling to make sense of an often senseless situation. Faz didn't dislike the FIT investigators; like most of the detectives in Violent Crimes he considered them good people performing a shitty job while being highly scrutinized. But that didn't mean he trusted them either.

At present, Laub, Williams, and Johnny Nolasco stood inside Lopez's crowded apartment while FIT investigators questioned Andrea Gonzalez. The FIT lieutenant had already confiscated Gonzalez's weapon and performed a round count. He would also determine if both the firearm and the ammunition were department approved. That was the least of Gonzalez's troubles.

Shooting an unarmed man would be the real shit storm.

And that was the reason for the warrant to search Lopez's apartment. Now more than ever, they needed to find a .38 and pray that gun barrel matched the bullet that killed Monique Rodgers. Killing an unarmed guilty man was a problem. Killing an unarmed innocent man was much worse.

Faz and Gonzalez would both be required to give tape recorded statements and to complete written reports before they could go home. They would then be put on administrative leave and required to meet with a mental health professional before being considered for reinstatement to active duty. For some officers, that process could take more than a year. Then, when the officer did return, they would learn that they'd been assigned to a different unit, creating a stigma of wrongdoing, despite the exoneration.

Faz had called Vera, knowing the story would be broadcast on the evening news. He told her he was fine but had another long night ahead of him, and she should not wait up. When he asked how she was doing she said, "Fine." She did not elaborate.

Faz heard the elevator ping and looked down the hallway to see what fool had stepped aboard and the expression on that person's face when they got off. Del walked off gingerly, one hand clasped over his nose and mouth. He had a wide-eyed look of horror that made Faz laugh, despite the circumstances. To shorten the distance, and not be in view of the brass talking to Gonzalez inside the apartment, Faz met him halfway down the hall.

"Good Lord and Savior, Faz, what the hell is that smell? I thought the body was in the elevator."

Faz smiled. "I would have warned you if I'd known you were coming."

"No, you wouldn't have," Del said.

"No, I probably wouldn't have," Faz agreed.

The levity between two men who'd been through a lot during the past twenty years was a welcome release of nervous tension. "Are you okay?" Del asked.

"I think I'm doing better than you." Faz pointed at Del's shoes, which didn't match. One loafer was a darker shade of brown. "You get dressed in the dark?"

"I can hardly bend over. At least they're both brown," Del said. "Seriously, are you okay?"

Faz nodded. "Yeah, I'm fine. I got a ringing in my ears and a massive headache, but I think that's more from anticipating the amount of paperwork, interviews, and bullshit they're going to throw my way."

"What happened? Billy wouldn't tell me anything."

Faz looked down the hall to be sure no one was approaching. "I really don't know." He pointed. "I was standing right there, facing the door to Lopez's apartment. Gonzalez was on the other side. Next thing I know her eyes get as wide as saucers and she's shoving me into that wall. She fired three times. Bam, bam, bam."

"Wait, so where was Lopez?"

"The apartment next door."

"What was he doing there?"

"Don't know."

"Was he armed?"

Faz shook his head.

"Oh shit. Are you sure it's Lopez?" Del asked, looking at the covered body.

"Yeah, I'm sure."

"That isn't going to play well with the Justice Department. We'd better hope ballistics can match a gun with the bullet that killed Monique Rodgers. It will help, but it won't solve the problem, not for Gonzalez. What did Gonzalez say? Why'd she shoot?"

"She said she saw something silver in Lopez's hand and thought he was taking aim at the back of my head. Turns out it was a cell phone."

Del rubbed a hand over the stubble on his chin. "Well, that's something, I guess."

"I guess," Faz said. "But not having Lopez creates a bigger problem, even if they find a gun and match it to the shooting."

"It isn't the same as a confession," Del said.

"And it doesn't tell us why he did it," Faz said, "or if he was acting on orders. Little Jimmy is the guy we want."

Faz looked down the hall as Larry Pinnacle, a FIT investigator, exited the apartment and approached. Pinnacle greeted Del, then spoke to Faz. "We're ready to head back to Park 95. We're going to need to get a statement before you go off duty."

Faz nodded. "Understood."

As Pinnacle departed, Del said, "That's one guy I never cared for."

"He's all right," Faz said.

"How's Vera?"

"Weepy. It's been tough on her. Late nights like this aren't helping."

"You want me to stop by, tell her what's happening?"

"I called. She's okay."

"Hey, Faz, I want you to know that I'm sorry I wasn't here."

"I know you are. Shit happens. Don't worry about it."

Faz looked down the hall toward the sound of voices that were increasing in volume. The group had moved from inside the apartment to the hallway. Gonzalez turned her head and looked to where Faz and Del stood, just a passing glance before she returned her attention to her interrogators.

"Rough way to start out in a new department," Faz said.

"She might be going home before she ever got started," Del said.

CHAPTER 27

Tracy knew logistics would be the CSI investigators' biggest hurdle. It wasn't like they could just plug in a light to an electrical circuit in one of the trees. CSI had a van that provided power, but there was no way to get the van to the grave site, which was how Tracy now thought of the hole in the ground. CSI's only option was to haul generators to the site, a difficult and time-consuming process. Once accomplished, the investigators expanded the perimeter Pryor had marked with yellow crime scene tape. Anyone who breached this designated area would be required to sign a log-in sheet. Next, they'd erected a tent over the grave, and attached lights to the tent's interior framework, enough light to illuminate the site like an archaeological dig for some lost treasure.

Tracy wished it were so.

CSI did all of this while trying not to disturb the trails leading to the hole any more than Tracy and Pryor already had. Kaylee Wright arrived and worked with the CSI investigators to reestablish Katie Pryor's walking path to the grave site, designated with red tape. Anyone who crossed that tape would have to complete a statement, which was a way to keep the brass from venturing too close to the crime scene. Not that the brass was going to be a problem this night, not with the majority of them flocking to the officer-involved shooting in South Park.

Once she'd reestablished the walking path, Wright used a powerful beam of light to examine the area surrounding the grave, the trails leading to it, and the main walking paths into and out of the park. She was trying to detect patterns, footprints leading to and from the hole, veering off course suddenly, or signs of an altercation, like trampled plants and disturbed soil. CSI would also take a healthy number of photographs and, where possible, cast any shoeprints found.

After Katie Pryor had provided elimination prints of the soles of her work boots, Tracy sent her home. Pryor had protested, but with Kins present, and the missing person having now become a possible homicide, Pryor was no longer needed, though that was not why Tracy sent her home. She sent Pryor home to be with her family.

Kelly Rosa arrived and quickly climbed down a ladder with a CSI photographer to document the grave site and the body's relationship to it. Rosa's first order of business, however, was to confirm a death and to obtain positive identification. Next, she sketched the position of the body relative to the hole. After documenting the site in photographs, Rosa turned her analysis to determining whether Kavita Mukherjee was the victim of a homicide, an unfortunate accident, or had taken her own life.

As this work went on, and although a significant number of police and forensic personnel were present, the site remained respectfully quiet, as if a pall of sadness had descended over the forest, disturbed only by the hum of the generators and occasional hushed voices.

Tracy heard footsteps, and she and Kins backed away from the hole and met Kaylee Wright on the designated path. A senior crime analyst, Wright was about the same age and height as Tracy, but with dark hair and a darker complexion. She carried a pencil and stack of blue index cards on which she'd document the size and shape of each shoeprint found. Her face remained a practiced mask, revealing little about her findings. She kept her voice soft. "I can't say anything definitive, yet."

"But you're picking up something," Tracy said, knowing Wright well enough to make the inference.

Wright frowned. "Maybe. I've been all over the two main trails." She checked notes she'd taken. "The Coyote Trail and the Trillium Trail." She used a pencil on a trail map to crudely identify the location of the two trails and the footpath leading from them to the hole in the ground. "Never thought I'd say this in Seattle, but the prolonged week of warm weather and lack of rain make it tough to find any definitive shoeprints. Usually there are periods in the day—early morning and late evening, in which there is enough moisture in the air that the sole of the shoe will leave an impression. I'm just not finding anything much. I can say that a lot of people have been through here, some on horseback."

"What about the victim? Have you found her shoeprints anywhere near the hole?" Tracy asked. Wright shook her head. "No. And it's a fairly specific sole pattern—a flat, casual walking shoe. If it was around here, I'd recognize it."

"Not exactly the kind of shoe a person wears to walk through a heavily wooded park," Kins said.

"No. It's not." Wright shuffled through her deck of blue cards and showed them the image of the shoe she had drawn. "It's made by American Rag. See the distinct sole pattern?"

Tracy did—four more or less square treads from the top of the toe to the ball of the foot. Eight total squares. "And you're not finding that pattern anywhere along the footpath leading to the hole or around it?" she asked, hoping it meant the body had been moved.

Wright shook her head. "Not on the footpath and not around the hole. However, I did find the print on both the Trillium and on the Coyote Trail, indicating she was headed in this direction."

"So, we know that she walked into the park," Kins said.

"At least for part of the way," Wright said.

"What do you mean?" Tracy asked.

"She was running for another part."

"She was being chased?" Tracy asked.

Wright shook her head. "She started out walking, but at some point, based on her elongated stride, she started to run. Then she stopped. I found her footprints on the trail facing in all different directions. I didn't find any other footprints to indicate she was running from someone."

"But she stopped and was, what, turning in a circle?"

"It appears so."

"She could have gotten lost," Kins said. "She could have been trying to reorient herself."

Tracy shook her head. "Aditi said they knew this park well. She could have thought she heard something," Tracy said. "That would cause her to run in the first place. She might have heard something and took off running, then stopped—either to catch her breath or to look around for anyone following her."

"But you're not finding any footprints of someone giving chase?" Kins said.

"No. And there is just the one set of footprints when she stops and turns."

"But no footprints around the perimeter of the hole?" Tracy asked again for clarification.

"Not hers."

"You would expect to find her print, wouldn't you?" Tracy prompted.

"I would if she walked or ran over there. Even if she fell into the hole, I'd expect to find a shoeprint or a partial shoeprint somewhere around the perimeter. For example, I found Katie Pryor's prints where she stepped and lost her footing, and I found your shoeprint. I also found a flat shoeprint, but only a partial. I'm not sure it's going to be of much help."

"So the logical deduction from the lack of her shoeprint near the hole is that while she may have walked into the park, and at some point started running, for whatever reason, she didn't walk or run to the hole," Kins said.

"No evidence to indicate she did," Wright said.

"So we can rule out that she fell into the hole while running," Tracy said.

"No evidence she did," Wright said. "On its own, it's not much, but if Kelly determines the victim didn't die from falling into that hole, the lack of any shoeprints would certainly support the argument that she was killed someplace else in the park and her body dumped in the hole."

Kins glanced at Tracy. She knew he was thinking that if Wright was accurate, the killer had to have known the hole existed and hadn't just blindly stumbled upon it while looking to discard a body. It also meant they might not get the chance to figure out what had happened. Bellevue would rightfully take jurisdiction.

Wright turned again, this time to the illuminated tent. "I looked closely at the branches covering the hole. I didn't see where any of them had snapped or been broken—other than those Pryor broke when she fell through. I'm also not finding any hair or clothing fibers. And Kelly said an initial review of the decedent's clothing did not reveal any rips or snags. I'd like to look more closely, under magnification, and I'd also like to look at the branches under natural light before I reach any conclusions."

"You're saying that if she did fall into the hole you'd expect to find some evidence of it," Kins said.

Wright nodded. "Right now I'm just not finding any."

"So Pryor's falling was fortuitous, in terms of the evidence you'd expect to find," Kins said.

"It's certainly evidence that a healthy individual would grab whatever was around them to try to keep from dropping into the hole—and we'd find snapped branches and disturbed leaves."

"Whereas, if somebody dumped the body they could have been careful to move the branches to ensure it didn't look disturbed," Tracy said.

"That's at least a working hypothesis," Wright said.

"Then they had to have known the hole was there," Kins reiterated, "which would imply they had familiarity with the park. Any indication anyone came back to try and fill in the hole?"

"No tool marks to indicate that was the case," Wright said.

Tracy nodded to the stack of cards in Wright's hand. "Anything else of interest?"

Wright shook her head. "Not at present, though, again, I'd like to have another look in daylight. The trails have been well used and the darkness doesn't help. As I said, I found disturbed prints of people walking and jogging, and horse hooves, but nothing definitive."

"No prints to indicate someone or some persons carried a body here?" Tracy asked.

"Not yet."

"So, what we have is what we don't have," Tracy said. "We don't have broken branches or foliage to indicate the victim fell into the hole. We don't have snagged hair or clothing fibers, and we don't have the victim's shoeprints near the hole."

"All true," Wright said.

"But we do have the victim's prints on the designated trails to indicate she voluntarily walked into the park and at some point started running in this direction."

"Correct," Wright said.

"Maybe she was meeting someone, someone who knew the park as well as she knew it," Kins said.

Tracy thought of Aditi.

"I'll come back out tomorrow morning in daylight and recheck everything," Wright said. "How long will we have the site?"

"For as long as we need." At least Tracy hoped that was the case. She looked at the tent, and in the bright lights she saw a seasoned-looking man in a navy-blue Bellevue Police uniform talking to one of the CSI detectives. The detective looked around and spotted Tracy and Kins. He pointed in their direction.

CHAPTER 28

Faz sat at a conference room table in the Park 95 building, his hands cradling a cup of lukewarm black coffee. He'd have opted for an espresso, or caffeine IV; he was that tired. Maybe, he thought, he was just getting too old for this crap. Or maybe Vera's illness was taking more out of him than he'd admit. He had enough years to retire on a full pension, like Arroyo, but then what would he do? He and Vera had talked of traveling, seeing those places they hadn't been able to afford and never had the time to visit. He wanted to go back to Italy, where they'd honeymooned, and he'd promised Vera they'd get to Paris and to Barcelona, but now those trips were on hold.

He stretched the fatigue from his legs and cracked his neck, which was where he carried most of his stress. Two Advil had not yet dented the headache that had developed, nor had time silenced the persistent ringing in his ears. His arms and legs felt heavy, and he knew from experience that fatigue was to be expected after the body and the mind had undergone a stressful event. He wanted nothing more than for this night to be over, to go home and get much-needed rest, but he had a feeling the night was just getting started.

"You doing okay, Faz?" Larry Pinnacle asked the question as he walked into the conference room and shut the door. A former burglary detective, Pinnacle had become one of the six FIT investigators when that team formed in 2014. Faz had a brief working relationship with Pinnacle. They'd always been cordial, but that was the extent of their involvement. He didn't really care. He wasn't looking to make a new friend or hang out with the guy; he just wanted to give his statement and get home.

Faz sat up. "Just tired, you know? Let's get this done."

"We'll try to make this as quick as possible," Pinnacle said.

Faz doubted it.

"You've been read your Garrity Rights and signed the form?" Pinnacle asked. Garrity Rights protected public employees from being compelled to incriminate themselves during investigatory interviews conducted by their employers, a protection that stemmed from the Fifth and Fourteenth Amendments to the Constitution, which protected a person from being a witness against himself.

Faz slid the sheet of paper he'd signed across the table. Pinnacle considered it briefly and set it aside. He slowly lowered his body into a chair. He reminded Faz of a walrus, with a drooping mustache that covered his upper lip, and a pear-shaped body and large head. "Good, okay. Any questions before we get started?"

Faz shook his head and Pinnacle adjusted a tape recorder on the table. "We're going to record this, okay?" He hit "Record" without waiting for an answer and edged the recorder halfway between the two of them.

Faz took out his phone and said, "I'm going to record it too." He hit the "Record" button and slid his phone next to the recorder.

Pinnacle looked at the phone but didn't otherwise respond. Then he identified himself, his position, badge number, and his intent to interview Detective Vittorio Fazzio in the officer-involved shooting death of Eduardo Felix Lopez. When he'd dispensed with the preliminaries,

Pinnacle read from a second sheet of paper. Though Faz had never been through the process, he understood from others that FIT followed a written script, and that their investigators had been trained to avoid showing emotion. It had earned them the nickname Robocops.

"Detective Fazzio, you are aware that I will be asking you questions regarding that shooting?"

"Yes," Faz said.

Pinnacle sat back, making eye contact. "Okay, can you first explain to me: What was your purpose at the apartment building in South Park?"

"We had a last known address for Eduardo Lopez."

"Who is . . ."

"Oh, sorry." Faz shook his head to clear the cobwebs and sipped his coffee. "A suspect in the shooting of Monique Rodgers."

"Thank you. Continue."

"The apartment unit was 511. Our purpose was to conduct a noncustodial interview of Mr. Lopez."

"And why wasn't SWAT involved?"

"No need. It was a noncustodial interview."

"Who made that decision?"

"I did," Faz said.

"Did you believe Mr. Lopez to be armed?"

"Unknown."

"So, possibly?" Pinnacle asked.

"Everyone is possibly armed, especially in this day and age," Faz said. "Did I think he was armed and a threat? No."

"You suspected he was your shooter in the Rodgers homicide?"

Faz shrugged. He knew the purpose of the question and wasn't about to fall into the trap of saying yes, then have Pinnacle question why, in that case, he hadn't assumed Lopez would still be armed. "We didn't know he was the shooter. We knew his handprint was on a car parked in the vicinity of the shooting. He could have just been a guy fleeing the shooting who stuck his hand on the hood of a parked car who might have relevant information. That's what we were hoping to determine."

"Did you or your partner want SWAT to accompany you in issuing the search warrant?"

"As I said, there was no need for SWAT or a search warrant. As for what Andrea Gonzalez thought or wanted, you'd have to ask her that question. I'm not going to speculate."

"Did she tell you she wanted SWAT present?"

Faz was trying to determine where Pinnacle was going with his questions, which didn't sound scripted, as he'd been told. "She mentioned in the car that sometimes she felt better when SWAT was involved."

"You remember her saying that?"

"Words to that effect, yes."

"What exactly do you remember her saying?"

Faz blew out a breath. It seemed as though an eternity had passed since he and Gonzalez had been in the car driving to the building. "She said something like she felt more secure having someone with an AR-15 ready to put a round up somebody's ass."

"But you didn't think SWAT should be present?"

"In this instance? No. As I said, it was a noncustodial interview. We had no evidence Lopez was armed or that he was Rodgers's shooter, and there was no indication he knew we were coming and would consider us a threat. So, noncustodial interview."

"What evidence did you have, besides the video of Lopez touching the parked car and leaving his print?"

Faz sipped his coffee and set the cup down, picking at the rim with his fingernail. "That was it."

"Would it have been a reasonable assumption that Lopez would be armed, given that you suspected him to be the shooter of Monique Rodgers?"

"How many times do I have to say this? I'm sure there are videos out there of a lot of guys who were in that area. Should we consider each of them to be armed and a threat? We just wanted to talk to the guy, find out what he was doing over there, if he saw anything, determine if he started acting squirrelly, and take it from there."

"But you didn't ask that question of your chain of command, correct?"

"What question? If we should get SWAT involved? No, I didn't ask them that."

Faz could see the hamster wheel spinning in Pinnacle's head, and he suddenly realized he'd made a mistake—damned if you do and damned if you don't. If they were proceeding under the assumption that Lopez was unarmed, then why had Gonzalez been so quick to shoot? She'd have to answer that question on her own.

Pinnacle quickly pressed on. "So, you went to the apartment for a noncustodial interview."

"And to ask if we could search his apartment."

"Were you looking for anything in particular?"

Faz paused. Then he said, "A gun and a hoodie."

"A hoodie being . . . what exactly?"

"A hooded sweatshirt. In the video, Lopez had a hood pulled over his head."

"What did you deduce from that?"

"Possibly that he was trying to conceal his identity."

"And what type of gun were you searching for?"

"If we had the chance, we were looking for a revolver, a .38. We didn't find any shell casings at the site of Monique Rodgers's shooting. So we were proceeding under the assumption that her shooter used a revolver. The slug that killed her was a .38."

"And what happened when you arrived at the apartment?"

Faz took a moment. With fatigue, the ringing in his ears had become more persistent. He tugged at an earlobe, like a swimmer trying to dislodge water. “I was standing on the north side of the door frame. Detective Gonzalez was standing on the south side.”

“Detective Gonzalez is not your regular partner, is she?”

“No. My regular partner, Del Castigliano, hurt his back and took a personal day.”

“You’d never worked with Detective Gonzalez before?”

“No. She’d just started Monday.”

“Did you have any concerns bringing a detective with unknown experience to execute a dynamic search warrant?”

“I didn’t say it was a dynamic search warrant,” Faz said. A “dynamic” warrant was a label given to a search warrant if the person to be confronted was suspected of being armed and dangerous. “I said it was a noncustodial interview. Did I have any concerns bringing Gonzalez along? No. I understood that Gonzalez had been a detective in Los Angeles and had significant experience.”

“And where did you gain that understanding?”

“That’s what she told me.”

“You didn’t attempt to verify the information?”

Faz chuckled. “Verify how, Larry? Somebody tells me they have experience, I don’t call them a liar.”

Pinnacle remained all business. “So, you didn’t attempt to verify the information?”

Faz didn’t immediately answer. He knew Pinnacle was only doing his job, but what was it about bureaucratic posts that made detectives forget their own experiences and become officious assholes? “I assumed, since she’d been hired to the Violent Crimes Section, that she’d been properly vetted during the interview process, but that’s above my pay grade. Maybe that’s a question better asked of Lieutenant Laub or Captain Nolasco.”

“You were describing what happened when you arrived at the apartment.”

Faz paused to recall where he'd left off. He was starting to feel like this was an interrogation designed not to get his recollection but to trip him up—get him talking, change subjects, create confusion, anything so he couldn't pick up on a rehearsed thread. Faz had used similar tactics conducting his own interviews. Only this wasn't a rehearsed thread, and Faz wasn't a suspect. Or was he? Shit, he was tired, and not just from the evening. He was emotionally tired from the past few days, since Vera's diagnosis. And he wasn't getting any younger.

He took a moment, sipped his coffee. The ringing in his ear persisted and he again tugged on his earlobe.

"Are you all right to continue?" Pinnacle said.

"Yeah, I'm fine," Faz said. After another moment he said, "I was on the north side of the door frame and Detective Gonzalez was on the south side. This was apartment 511. She was about to knock on the door to the apartment when I heard a voice that sounded like it was coming from inside the apartment and I put my hand up to stop her."

"Had you or Detective Gonzalez removed your firearms from their holsters at this point?"

"Not at that point." Faz was trying to recall when he had removed his gun.

"You're sure?"

"Yeah."

"Did Detective Gonzalez identify you both as Seattle police officers?"

"She never got the chance. As I said, I heard someone—"

"What did they say?"

"I don't know. It sounded like the person was speaking Spanish."

"Was the person speaking Spanish?"

"Gonzalez thought so. She mouthed the word 'Spanish' to me, and she speaks the language."

"From where did you hear the voice?"

"Inside the apartment, I thought. But I wasn't certain so I was asking Gonzalez and that's—"

"You didn't know?"

"I wasn't sure. I thought it was from inside Lopez's apartment. So did Gonzalez. But it could have been in the apartment next door."

"Could you hear what was being said?"

"I told you, I could hear it. I couldn't understand it."

Pinnacle made a note on his pad of paper. "Go on."

Had there even been a question? Faz didn't think so, but he was anxious to get the interview over with. "Detective Gonzalez went to knock and suddenly I hear something, a door opening behind me, and I see her eyes go wide, like there's a big surprise behind me."

"She was looking at you or the door to the apartment she was knocking on?"

"She was looking at me—not at me, but just over my left shoulder." Faz made a vague gesture with his hands. "And I see her eyes go wide, big as two saucers. Next thing I know she's taking a step toward me and raising her arm holding her gun over my shoulder."

"Did you hear anything before you saw her looking over your left shoulder?"

"Like I said, I heard the voice speaking Spanish and I heard a door opening behind me."

"Did you turn around to find out?"

"I don't specifically recall that. I was looking at Gonzalez and my focus was on the door she was about to knock on."

"What happened next?"

"She shoved me and I stumbled backward against the other side of the hall."

"She shoved you off balance?"

Faz detected a hint of disbelief in the question. He was six foot four and 270 pounds. Gonzalez was five foot six and maybe 130 pounds. "Yeah, she did, and she raised her arm and yelled *Gun!*"

"She yelled *Gun!*?"

"As she was raising her weapon she yelled *Gun!* and gets off three quick shots one after the other."

"She pushed you backward before or after she yelled *Gun!*?"

"It was all about the same time. She yells *Gun!* as she's raising her right arm, and shoves me with her left arm." Faz used his arms to demonstrate.

"And you said that she yelled *Gun!*?"

"That's right."

"You didn't yell *Gun!*?"

Faz paused, staring Pinnacle in the eyes. "What?"

"You didn't yell *Gun!*?"

"I told you I had my back to the door. Why would I yell *Gun!*?"

"I'm just trying to get the story straight."

"No, you're not. You're provoking me, seeing if I say something that doesn't match with what I already said, and you're pissing me off."

Pinnacle didn't respond to the comment. He said, "You were facing the door you were knocking on, correct?"

"No," Faz said, unable to hide the irritation in his voice and using his hands to explain where he was standing in relation to the door. "I was standing at an angle facing the window at the end of the hall and focused on the door to Lopez's apartment. The door Gonzalez was about to knock on."

"You never saw the suspect come out of the door?"

"How could I? The door was behind me," Faz said, becoming angry.

"I'm just asking."

"And I told you. Let's move on."

Pinnacle seemed to give this some thought. Then he said, "Is there any doubt in your mind that it was Detective Gonzalez who yelled *Gun!*?"

"Do I have any doubt?"

"Yes."

Faz had interviewed enough suspects to detect tells. Pinnacle lowered his gaze and sat back, pen in hand. He thought Faz was lying. "No. I have no doubt," Faz said.

"And you have no doubt that she looked over your shoulder, saw the suspect, and advanced, knocking you out of the way?"

"No, I don't."

"You said she was knocking on the door?"

"I said she was preparing to knock on the door."

"So she was facing the door, preparing to knock on it."

"Right."

"You didn't draw her attention to the suspect?"

"Draw her attention how?"

"You didn't yell *Gun!*"

Faz chuckled. "What is this shit, Larry?" Pinnacle didn't answer. "Did she say I yelled *Gun!*?"

"So you didn't yell *Gun!*"

"I told you, Larry."

"Did you yell *Gun!*?"

"I told you I didn't."

"And you didn't otherwise draw Detective Gonzalez's attention from the door to the suspect coming out of the apartment?"

"I'm done with this shit." Faz pushed back his chair and stood.

"I'll tell you when we're done, Detective."

"No, you won't. I'm done. Or else I want a union representative before any further questioning."

Pinnacle had also stood. He held his pen in one hand but raised both palms. "All right. All right. Let's just move on. Okay? We'll move on."

"What is this shit? Did she say I yelled *Gun!*?"

"Let's move on. Tell me what you recall happening after she pushed you into the hall wall."

Faz adjusted his chair and sat, taking a moment to sip his coffee, which was no longer warm. When composed he said, "My ears were ringing from having her Glock go off by my left ear. The next thing I heard was Gonzalez asking me if I was all right."

"Why, what had happened?"

Faz stared at Pinnacle. "I just told you, she fired three shots close to my ear. I couldn't hear anything she was saying."

"Was she saying something?"

"I couldn't hear."

"But you heard her ask you if you were okay?"

"Eventually, yeah."

"How much time passed before you could hear her?"

"I don't know."

"Seconds? Minutes?"

"No, it was seconds."

"And then what?"

"And then she went into the apartment Lopez had come out of. There was a woman inside, sitting on the floor pressed against the wall. She was shielding a small child. Both were screaming."

"What was the woman screaming?"

"I don't know. I mean, you know, she was crying."

"You couldn't hear her because of the ringing in your ears?"

"Gonzalez asked her something in Spanish and she responded in Spanish."

"What do you weigh?"

Faz paused again. "Is that relevant?"

Pinnacle stared at him. "I don't know."

"I'm about two hundred and seventy pounds."

Pinnacle wrote the number on his pad of paper. Then he sat back. "When Gonzalez went into the apartment, what did you do?"

"I looked at the suspect to ensure he was dead. And I looked for a gun."

"Was he dead?"

"Very."

"Did you find a gun?"

"I didn't see one. I saw a phone near his right hand. I thought maybe he'd fallen on the gun."

"Did you look beneath him?"

"Not then."

"What did you do?"

"I cuffed Lopez, then went into the apartment with Gonzalez and helped clear the rooms."

"What was Gonzalez doing?"

"Like I said, there was a woman and a child in the apartment, huddled in the corner. They were crying, hysterical. Gonzalez was speaking to them in Spanish."

"You couldn't understand her?"

"No. But I'm pretty sure she was asking the name of the man in the hallway."

"And what did the woman tell Detective Gonzalez?"

"She said it was Eduardo Lopez."

"Detective Fazzio, did you ever find a gun?"

"I did not."

"What about inside the apartment? Did you find a gun inside that apartment?"

"The apartment that the woman and child were in? No. We didn't have a search warrant for that apartment, so we only conducted a visual search of the vicinity for our safety."

"And you didn't go into the suspect's apartment?"

"No. We waited for CSI."

"The death of Monique Rodgers . . . that's your only open case, isn't it?"

"That's right."

"You and Detective Castigliano have solved every homicide in your careers. Is that also correct?"

"That's correct."

"And Lopez was your only lead in the Rodgers case, am I right about that also?"

"To this point, yes."

"Anything else you'd like to add?"

"No."

"Then I'll shut off the tape."

Pinnacle did so. Then he looked across the table. "Thank you, Detective. We're done here."

Faz gathered his phone. He wanted to believe Pinnacle, but he knew from experience that this wasn't the end of the matter. Not by a long shot.

CHAPTER 29

Tracy and Kins's conversation with Bellevue Police Department Captain Ray Giacomoto was professional and direct. Giacomoto wanted to know what Tracy and Kins were doing "on this side of the lake" and why they hadn't called his department.

"The victim was a Seattle resident and the missing persons report was filed with Seattle PD," Tracy said. "We didn't come here thinking we'd stumble on a body. We were tracking her cell phone. When we found the victim, I thought it best to get the site processed before any further time elapsed and possible evidence disappeared."

Giacomoto grinned. "We're fully equipped to process a crime scene, Detective. I think you know that."

"Absolutely," Tracy said.

"So what was the rush? Did you know the victim?"

"Only what I've learned through interviews of her roommate and her family. We've been investigating the victim's disappearance for a few days now."

"The body wasn't going anywhere fast," Giacomoto said again.

"No, it wasn't."

"Which would put it in Bellevue jurisdiction."

"Maybe, but I had no way of knowing, and we still don't know definitively that the victim was killed here. There're no footprints around the hole. So the initial opinion of the tracker is she was killed elsewhere and the body dumped here." Tracy didn't say that the initial opinion was Kavita Mukherjee was killed elsewhere in the park. "It has also been a long time since we've had any rain," Tracy said. "And the newsmen were forecasting that thunderstorm. So, as I said, I thought it best to get the site processed before any footprints or other possible evidence might have washed away."

Giacomoto didn't look fully convinced, but for the moment he seemed content to let her do her job. "We're going to want copies of all the reports," he said.

"Not a problem," Tracy said.

"As for jurisdiction, I suspect that's a decision higher up both our chains of command; until then, I'm happy to sit back and let you run this show."

They turned to the sound of someone approaching. Kelly Rosa had climbed out of the hole. She looked very much like an archaeologist on a dig, with dirt clinging to the cuffs of her blue jeans just above sturdy boots, and along the brim of a Mariners baseball cap. Rosa flipped off her headlamp so she didn't blind them and pulled down a mask that had been covering her nose and mouth. She then removed latex gloves and wiped dirt from the tail of her shirt. Her gait was awkward from rubber kneepads.

"That's a new look for you," Kins said, pointing to the pads.

"Saw them at Costco," she said. "They're for tile workers. The knees aren't as young as they used to be."

"I thought you were trying out to be a catcher," Kins said.

"Yeah, well the Mariners could use somebody who can actually hit," she said. Then, after a pause, she said, "I can tell you it wasn't a robbery, or if it was, it was perpetrated by the stupidest robbers on the planet." Barely five feet tall, Rosa had a seven-foot personality. "She has twelve dollars in her pocket along with a Washington State driver's license and a credit card, a gold chain around her neck, and a gold bracelet on her wrist."

"So no robbery and the killer wasn't trying to conceal her identity," Kins said.

"Except for the fact that the killer dumped her in a hole in the ground covered by brush," Giacomoto said.

"Nobody likes a showoff," Kins said.

"You said 'dumped.' So this wasn't an accident?" Tracy said.

"No," Rosa said. "I don't believe it was."

"What do you believe it was?" Giacomoto asked.

Rosa raised an arm and imitated blows to the skull as she said, "She died from blunt-force trauma—several blows to the side of her head. I'd say two, maybe three. We won't know the number without some close-up photography of the injury. She was struck on the right side by something irregular shaped, a rock most likely. I'd have some of these uniforms searching the park for a rock with blood on it."

"Could be like finding a needle in a haystack," Kins said. "A five-hundred-acre haystack."

"Or the killer could have just dropped it and it's still around here," Rosa said.

"You're certain the killer used a rock?" Giacomoto said.

"Not until we do some work under the microscope, but I'd say it's a strong probability."

"So she was killed here in the park?" Giacomoto asked.

"Not for me to say," Rosa said, and Tracy sensed the medical examiner was cutting her some slack. "I can say she wasn't killed in or near the hole, but as to where . . ." She shrugged.

"I'll get some of my uniforms to do a search of the park," Giacomoto said to Tracy. "Have you had someone go over the trails yet?"

Tracy nodded. "It's being done, but I always appreciate another set of eyes."

Giacomoto handed Rosa a card. "I'd like a copy of your report when it's ready," he said before departing.

Rosa's statement made Kaylee Wright's hypothesis—that Mukherjee had been carried to the hole and dumped—one step closer to a theory.

"What else?" Tracy asked.

"There's little blood in the hole. If she fell and hit her head, she would have bled out and I'd expect a lot more. Livor mortis is consistent with the position of the body in the hole," Rosa said, "but that's probably because she was killed and quickly moved." Rosa was referencing the purplish discoloration that, in death, settled in areas of the body closest to the ground. "When was she last seen alive?"

"Monday evening," Tracy said. "Early, around six o'clock."

Rosa turned back toward the hole, talking as if to herself. "No rigor mortis, so she's been dead at least twelve hours, but probably longer than that. She has abdominal discoloration and some bloating indicating at least thirty-six to forty-eight hours, as well as the preliminary indications of marbling of the skin."

"So, Monday night is a possibility," Tracy said.

"Definitely a possibility, but we'll get it figured out and narrowed."

"For somebody to hit her multiple times in the head with a rock . . . ," Kins said.

"Yeah, I know where you're going," Rosa said. "These were significant blows too."

"Somebody angry," Kins said.

Rosa shrugged. "That's for you guys to prove, but I can say the force of the blows are consistent with someone who meant to cause damage. We're getting ready to move the body. Then the site is all yours."

"Any indication of sexual assault?" Tracy asked, mentally going through her checklist and ticking off boxes.

"Won't know for certain until we get her to the lab, but there's no evidence of a struggle, no torn or ripped articles of clothing, no cuts or scratches, fingernails look clean, but again we'll get that figured out."

"Wonder if you can take a little while putting together your report," Tracy said.

"I'm pretty busy," Rosa said, smiling. "And I can be called away at a moment's notice." She winked and walked back to the grave.

As Rosa departed, Tracy said to Kins, "Not a robbery and probably not a rape. Significant blows to the head."

"You said she had no boyfriend?"

"Not that we know of, but she was on a date."

Tracy again turned to the sound of people approaching. This time a uniformed officer holding a clipboard led a woman in brown pants with multiple pockets, boots, and a black heavy-duty Carhartt jacket.

"Detectives," the officer said. "This is Margo Paige. She's the park ranger in charge of this park."

Tracy extended a hand and introduced herself and Kins. "How long have you worked this park?" she asked.

Paige's gaze kept shifting past Tracy to the tent over the hole. She had a soft voice, though deeper than Tracy expected. "About three years now."

"So you're fairly familiar with it."

"As much as one can be, yes."

"Come with me." She led Paige down the path CSI had designated and stopped at the crime scene tape tied to the tent poles. "Are you familiar with that hole?"

Paige looked confused. "Familiar as in what?"

"Did you know it existed?" Tracy asked.

"It wasn't dug?" Paige asked.

"Not recently," Tracy said.

Paige shook her head. "No, I didn't know anything about it. If I had, I would have had it filled in."

"How prevalent are holes like this in this park?" Tracy asked.

Paige looked to be giving the question some thought. "You have to remember this park is just about five hundred acres, Detective, with more than twenty-eight miles of trails, and houses bordering the perimeter, but to my knowledge I'd say that it is not prevalent. In fact, I'm not aware of any others."

"None?" Kins said.

"Not that I'm aware of."

"Any idea what it is? How it got here?" Tracy asked.

Paige nodded. "Given its relative proximity to the houses that butt up against the park," she said, pointing to lights on the back of the homes, "I'd guess it's an old well, probably bootlegged years ago by someone long-since gone."

"Could it be anything else?"

Paige shrugged. "It's possible it also could be erosion from the ball root of a downed tree, exacerbated by the heavy rains we had this past winter. Storms can uproot trees, and rain will erode the soil beneath it and make the ground covering grow faster. How deep and wide is the hole?"

"Six to eight feet deep. Four feet wide, roughly," Tracy said.

Paige shook her head. "No. No way. More likely it's an old well."

"Have you had any incidents of people falling into an old well before?"

"I haven't, no. But I'm aware of an incident that happened about a decade ago, before I got here. As I understand it, a young woman was riding a horse through the park when the horse came out from under her. She said it was like the horse stepped on a trap door. The fall killed the horse. It might have killed the woman but she'd managed to jump off. There could be a report in storage. I can take a look for it tomorrow."

"So the odds that somebody might have just stumbled onto this hole by chance aren't likely," Kins said.

"Hard to say. That horse and rider weren't out looking for a hole. I guess, from my perspective, I'd be asking why, if someone did know of this hole, they didn't tell anyone about it so we could have filled it in."

CHAPTER 30

Faz pulled into his driveway exhausted, frustrated, and confused. Larry Pinnacle could tell him until the cows came home that he just wanted to get Faz's story, but Faz knew when a detective was trying to poke holes in answers and hoping one of those holes might rip open wide enough to cast the whole story in doubt.

The question was, Why?

What Pinnacle had conducted, awkwardly perhaps, was an interrogation, and he'd hinted that Faz's and Gonzalez's stories were not aligning. Pinnacle seemed most interested in who had yelled *Gun!* On the drive home, Faz had gone over a potential scenario in which Gonzalez told Pinnacle that Faz had yelled *Gun!* He concluded there were three potential reasons she might have done so. Either, in the stress of the situation, Gonzalez misremembered what had happened. She was deliberately lying. Or Faz *had* yelled *Gun!*

Faz dismissed option three based on the evidence. How could he have yelled when he had his back to the apartment door from which Lopez had emerged? He didn't see Lopez, let alone conclude that Lopez had been holding a gun. That left options one and two. Gonzalez was either misremembering what had happened, or she was lying.

It would have been easy to conclude Gonzalez was lying to protect her career, but Faz knew it was not that simple. SPD detectives had recently taken a simulated course in de-escalating high-stress scenarios as part of the Justice Department's reforms to reduce the perceived use of violent force. Faz and Del had entered the mandatory training like teenagers being forced to learn a foreign language. They saw little point to it, particularly given their already extended time on the police force. They quickly changed their tune. The class revealed that high-stress encounters with an armed suspect significantly impacted an officer's recollection, even an officer with experience. In fact, two officers working as partners could have drastically different recalls about what had happened, and often both were wrong. Seasoned officers recalled seeing guns where none existed, and mistook hands being raised in surrender for an act of aggression.

Faz couldn't help but wonder if Gonzalez's memory had been similarly tainted.

He looked up at his and Vera's bedroom window on the second floor. He'd called Vera after the interview, but he hadn't said anything of substance. She didn't need any more worry on her plate. He'd told her he was completing paperwork. He was about to tell Vera not to wait up, though she always did, but she'd beaten him to that punch.

"I'm tired. It's been a long couple of days. I'm going to go to bed."

Faz quietly entered through the back door and climbed the stairs to their bedroom. From the top step he could see her shape beneath the covers, illuminated in a shaft of blue-gray light from the window. The four windowpanes created a cross on the quilt, a peaceful tableau that reminded him of a Norman Rockwell painting, a seemingly perfect portrait of life, without a hint of its often harsh realities.

As Faz stepped into the room, Vera stirred. "Vic?" She turned toward the door, her voice groggy from sleep.

"Yeah," he said. "Sorry to wake you."

"No, it's okay. I was watching television. What time is it?"

"It's after midnight."

"What happened?"

"I'll tell you in the morning. Everything is fine. It's all worked out." He sat on the edge of the bed to untie his shoes.

"You're okay?"

"Yeah, I'm good," he said and thought of the hundreds of times Vera had asked him that question and how few times he'd asked her. "You doing okay?"

"I'm fine," she said. "Was it the person who put his hand on the Volkswagen?"

Faz stood and put his shoes inside his closet. "Yeah. It was."

"What happened?"

He undid his belt and slid off his slacks as he spoke. "We were knocking on the door of his last known address, and suddenly the door to an apartment behind me opened and the guy walked out. My partner shot him."

"Del?"

He'd not told Vera that Del had thrown out his back. "No. Del was home with a bad back. It was a new detective."

"Did he kill him?"

He hung the pants on a hook inside his closet door. "She. She killed him. More brass down there than in a marching band. You know how it is now—FIT got involved and I had to go into Park 95 and provide an interview."

"Are you on administrative leave?"

He climbed into bed. "Yeah, but I'm sure it will only be a couple of days. They'll make me see a shrink before I get cleared. It will be fine."

"You sure you're all right?"

"Sure. You know how it is. It's all procedure now—hoops I got to jump through. I'm sure it will go to a review board and I'll get cleared. Go to sleep. Everything is going to be fine."

Faz was glad the lights were off and Vera couldn't see his face. He thought he was a good detective, but Vera could read his expressions like a well-read book. He thought again about the evening, and if there could have been any plausible scenario that he had yelled *Gun!*; if maybe he was the person misremembering what had happened. He was tired, and he'd been under a lot of stress, worried about Vera. It was possible, but . . . No, he couldn't think of a plausible scenario.

"Vic? Is anything wrong?" Vera asked.

He wanted to run his doubts by her. Vera never let him overthink things. But he couldn't this time. He just couldn't add to her worries.

"Nah. It's all good."

"Because you didn't brush your teeth," she said. "And you're sleeping with your socks on."

CHAPTER 31

Friday, July 13, 2018

By the time Tracy and Kins got back to the parking lot, it was early morning, and their day was just getting started. The first thing to do was the one thing Tracy disliked most about being a homicide detective.

By law, the King County Medical Examiner had the responsibility of notifying next of kin of a death, but in situations such as Kavita Mukherjee, when Tracy had already spoken to the family, she took the responsibility upon herself. Other detectives had questioned why she felt the need. The job was hard enough. She had no clear answer. Perhaps it was a form of penance for failing to protect her sister the night Sarah had disappeared. Or maybe her reasoning was more practical. Maybe the fact that she'd been on the receiving end of such news and knew its devastating impact, gave her a perspective other officers lacked, one that she could share with the family members.

Tracy and Kins arrived at the Mukherjee residence at just after six in the morning. She had called from the park to be certain they were home. The father, Pranav, had been preparing to leave for work. Tracy asked him to stay home. He didn't ask why. He didn't ask if they had found Kavita, or if his daughter was alive. He didn't want confirmed what he already suspected in that place deep inside, that place into which human beings pushed the kind of horrific news only a homicide detective could deliver.

When Pranav opened the front door, he and his wife looked upon Tracy as if seeing the angel of death. They tried to read her facial expression, suspecting what she had come to tell them, the news they did not want to hear. As the seconds ticked by, resignation became reality, as it always did, and that reality hit them like a blow to the gut, knocking the breath from their bodies, and bringing a deep and painful grief. Tears trickled from the corners of Pranav's eyes even before Tracy spoke.

"We found Kavita," she said. "I'm sorry. She's dead."

Pranav and Himani grieved alone for a while, then quietly woke their family. They all huddled in their foyer—Himani and Pranav and their two sons, Nikhil and Sam, and Kavita's grandparents. They wrapped arms around each other, consoling one another as best they could. Tracy and Kins allowed the family time, but they also watched their reactions, keenly aware that a significant percentage of victims are murdered by a family member or by someone who knows them.

Nikhil appeared the most composed, as if he'd somehow been resigned to his sister's fate. Sam looked stunned, seemingly not fully comprehending what his father had told him, not at such a tender age. Death was not yet supposed to be a part of his life, the concept still foreign to him. When the reality hit, Sam collapsed onto the bottom step of the staircase, wailing.

Pranav sobbed, great gasps of pain. Himani's grief was more subdued. Her shoulders shook, but she did not wail or moan. Subconsciously, Tracy's right hand migrated to the bump beneath her jacket. She could think of nothing worse than the loss of a child, especially one taken so senselessly, by violence. And in that moment, as the family grieved, she realized what Kins had been trying to tell her in that conference room.

Being a parent was not for the faint of spirit. Being a parent meant exposing a part of your heart to incredible joy and happiness, but also to the possibility of unspeakable despair and agony. It frightened Tracy to think that a knock on the door, so early in the morning, could bring news that would forever change a parent's life.

CHAPTER 32

Faz waited until nine o'clock before calling the union representative and requesting to speak to a lawyer, in case he needed one. He then set up an appointment with the shrink who would hopefully clear him to return to work, though he knew nothing was ever that easy. Sandy Clarridge, Seattle's chief of police, had recently gone to bat for his officers, arguing that investigations of officers be expedited, and that an officer cleared of wrongdoing be allowed to return to his position and his squad.

Still, the process would take time.

Faz initially thought administrative leave might be for the best, given Vera's circumstances. He could provide her with emotional support as they navigated the medical system, but that wasn't Vera's way. She told Faz there was enough change in their lives. She didn't want more. She said the best thing for them both was for Faz to be at work, keeping his mind busy and having a sense of purpose. Staying home, she'd said, would just make him stir-crazy.

At the moment, however, he didn't have a choice.

The knock on his front door surprised him. He hadn't been expecting visitors. When he pulled open the door, Del stood on the sun-drenched front porch. He wore a suit and tie and was on his way into the office.

"Hey," Faz said. "What's up?"

Del handed Faz his morning paper, removed his sunglasses, and looked past Faz to the interior of the home. "Vera home?"

"No. Some girlfriends took her out for the day to try to get her mind on something else."

"How's she doing?"

"Good moments and bad," Faz said. "She gets emotional when Antonio calls or if we talk at all about the future. I'm learning to stay in the present and take it one day at a time."

Del nodded. "Did she get the surgery set up?"

"Three weeks from yesterday."

"That long?"

Faz shrugged. "After the mastectomy, her case will go to a tumor board. They'll decide the best course of treatment, probably chemo is what the doctor told us. But you didn't come over here to talk to me in person about Vera, did you?"

Del shook his head and nodded to the newspaper. "Have you seen the morning paper?"

"I've been avoiding it." Faz stepped back from the door. "Come on in." Del stepped in, still moving gingerly because of his back, and shut the door. He followed Faz through the living room and dining room and into the kitchen. The smell of banana bread still permeated the room, along with fresh-brewed coffee.

"The article is on an interior page of the metro section. It mentions the shooting of an unarmed Hispanic man, and there's an op-ed piece calling it contrary to the Justice Department's recent pronouncement that we'd made significant progress."

"That was to be expected," Faz said. He held up the coffeepot. "You want a cup? Vera brewed it this morning."

"Yeah. Sure. Why not."

Faz got a couple mugs from the cabinet and filled them, handing one to Del. "I was hoping that with Gonzalez and Lopez both being Hispanic, it might at least deter the papers from insinuating the shooting was racially motivated."

"It's never that way, is it?"

"No, it's not."

The news tended to label all police bullets Caucasian, no matter who did the shooting. Faz asked, "How's the back?"

"Yeah, it's better. I still got to be careful how I move for a while, but the pain isn't as bad."

"You want a piece of banana bread?" Faz asked.

"I better not. Vera's banana bread, I'm liable to eat the whole loaf." Del followed Faz's lead to a chair at the kitchen table. The refrigerator hummed and clicked. Out the back door, the neighbor's golden retriever barked, and a Frisbee sailed across the neighbor's yard just above the fence line.

Del sipped from his mug but Faz could tell he was buying time. His partner looked nervous, the way Faz's son used to look when he was about to tell Faz he'd done something stupid.

"What's going on?" Faz said. "Does your being here have to do with last night?"

"What makes you ask that?"

Faz shrugged. "Something about last night is bothering me."

"Yeah?"

"Pinnacle kept asking me questions about whether I was certain Gonzalez had yelled *Gun!*, like he didn't believe me. Didn't believe what I was telling him." Faz shrugged. "Why would I lie?"

"You wouldn't."

"It pissed me off. I thought about it most of the night."

Del set his mug on the table. "Billy called me this morning," he said. "Apparently, your story and Gonzalez's story don't match."

"I figured as much. What did Billy say?"

"He said Gonzalez told the FIT investigators she wanted to have a SWAT team serve Lopez—that she was worried he could have a gun and things could go sideways. She said you indicated SWAT wasn't needed."

Faz frowned. "That's pretty much true. I mean, SWAT wasn't needed. It was a noncustodial interview. Not that she really pushed for them."

"The implication is that maybe it shouldn't have been noncustodial."

Faz shook his head. "Don't you find it ironic—they're worried about us using excessive force and now they're going to question whether we should have descended on Lopez's apartment with tanks and assault rifles? Talk about overkill."

"I agree."

"We had a handprint on the hood of a car, Del. We had no credible evidence Lopez was the shooter or that he was armed. Everything was circumstantial. He had a record for buying drugs, not even selling, and he had no convictions for violent crimes."

"You're preaching to the choir, Pastor Faz."

"We low-key it, talk to him, tell him we're just looking for information about the shooting and whether he'd been in that area and if he saw or heard anything. Maybe catch him in a lie. You and I have done it a million times."

"I know, and I agree, but Gonzalez made you sound like a cowboy. She made you sound like you wanted to take Lopez down."

"A cowboy? Me? Shit, I can't even get on a horse."

"She said you told her Rodgers was our only open case and you intended to close it."

"She said that?"

Del nodded.

"Wait a minute. I didn't say that," Faz said.

"Doesn't sound like something you'd say."

"Why would I tell her Rodgers was our only open case?"

"I didn't think you would."

"How'd she even know?"

Del shrugged. "I don't know."

Faz sat up, more interested. It was one thing to question his actions. It was another to put words in his mouth. "What else did Billy say she said?"

"Billy said Gonzalez told the FIT investigator that she was about to knock on the door of the apartment and identify herself as SPD but that you stopped her."

"That's true. I did. I heard someone speaking Spanish and thought it was from inside Lopez's apartment. Now I don't think it was. I think the voice was from next door, from the apartment Lopez came from."

"There was nobody inside Lopez's apartment, according to Billy."

"Yeah, I know. That's why I think the noise was from next door. What else did Billy tell you she said?"

"She said she was focused on the door, and that you were standing to her left and behind her so that you had a view of the hallway."

"That's not right. I was on the other side of the door frame with my back to the other apartment so when Lopez opened the door to his apartment I could see him and see into his apartment, in case anyone was behind him."

"Yeah, well, she said she was facing the door and heard you yell *Gun!* She says that's why she shot Lopez."

"I figured she must have said I yelled *Gun!*" Faz said.

Del didn't respond. He sipped his coffee, but again, he was using it as a cover, to give himself something to do.

"You think I could have yelled *Gun!*, Del?"

"No. I mean . . . You didn't, right?"

"What's bothering you?"

Del set his mug down. "Look. I know you've been under a lot of stress lately with everything going on with Vera."

"You're wondering about that Force Science class they made us take, if maybe the stress of the situation and the stress from Vera's diagnosis are making me misremember what happened."

"I thought about it," Del said before quickly adding, "but I didn't say anything to Billy. You thought about it too?"

"Of course I thought about it. How could I not?" Faz put down his mug. "Here's the thing, Del. I had my back to the apartment next door. I know because I was looking out the window behind Gonzalez at the dark clouds rolling in. There's no way I could have seen Lopez. I also remember Gonzalez's eyes getting as big as saucers, and her stepping toward me and raising her gun. How could I have seen that if I'd been looking the other way?"

"You couldn't."

"And, if I had been looking at the apartment when Lopez came out, doesn't that beg another question?"

"Why didn't you shoot?"

"Exactly."

Del nodded but he also diverted his gaze.

"What?" Faz asked.

"Witness agrees with her."

"What witness? There was no witness. We were the only two people . . . Wait, the woman inside the apartment?"

Del nodded. "I think so. Billy told me a woman said she heard a man yell *Gun!* and then a woman asking, 'Why'd you say *Gun*? Why'd you say *Gun*?'"

Faz sat back from the table and took a deep breath, exhaling a slow stream of air. He thought for a moment. Then he said, "No way, Del. That woman was screaming and crying, and she had a child in her arms. They were both hysterical. No way she could have heard anything or been paying attention to anything but the child."

"Maybe not, but Billy says that's not what she told the FIT investigators. Look, Faz, Billy said that with the Justice Department investigation hanging over the department, this is going to be scrutinized until we're all sick of it. So I got to ask, is there any chance you could have got it wrong?"

"What?" Faz said.

"Like you said, you've been under a lot of stress these past couple of days."

Faz couldn't believe what he was hearing. "I didn't say that. You did."

"Hey, I'm just asking, Faz. Don't shoot the messenger. You know your mind has been elsewhere and understandably so."

Faz didn't want to take out his anger on Del. "I didn't get it wrong, Del. I don't know what the hell is going on, but I didn't get it wrong. I didn't yell *Gun!* I didn't even see a gun."

"You remember Gonzalez talking to you, saying anything?"

"I don't know, Del. Shit, I couldn't hear a damn thing—my ears were ringing so bad from her firing her gun over my shoulder. When I could finally hear again she was asking if I was all right. That's it. *Are you all right?*"

"Did you tell that to Pinnacle?"

"Yeah. No reason not to—" Faz stopped. The implication set in. "Shit. She's going to say I didn't hear the woman and I didn't hear her asking me why I yelled *Gun!*"

Del nodded. "That's what Billy said too."

Faz rubbed a hand over the stubble on his chin. "I don't need this crap right now."

"I'm sorry to have to drop it on you," Del said. "Maybe the witness also got it wrong, like we learned in that class. Maybe she didn't hear what she says she heard, but just thought she did."

"Or someone suggested what she'd heard," Faz said. "Gonzalez was the first person to speak to her."

"What did she say?"

"I don't know. I was in the hall cuffing Lopez and looking for a gun. When I went in Gonzalez was already talking to her, in Spanish, but I'm pretty sure she was asking the woman the name of the body in the hallway."

"Maybe she was, but maybe she asked her what she wanted her to remember too. You know? *Did you hear a man yell* Gun!*?*"

Faz nodded. "If she did, Del, then she isn't just misremembering what happened. She's lying, and she's getting a witness to lie to support her version of what happened."

"The question is, Why?" Del said. "Protect her career?"

"Maybe," Faz said. "I don't know, but I'm damn sure going to try to find out."

CHAPTER 33

Pranav broke from the family's huddle. He removed his eyeglasses and wiped at his red and swollen eyes. He spoke to Tracy in a voice barely above a whisper. "Do you know what happened?"

"No," Tracy said. "I'm sorry. Not yet. We're waiting for experts to complete their reports." It was, perhaps, the cruelest part of Tracy's job, her inability to tell the family everything she knew, what their investigation had revealed. She had to wait until she knew for certain what had happened, and even then couldn't tell them everything, not without first exonerating each of them.

"Where did you find her?" Himani asked.

They would know the location soon enough, either from news reporters calling or from neighbors, though not the details. "She was in the state park, just down the street."

"Bridle Trails?" Pranav asked, his eyes becoming wide. "She was here, in Bridle Trails?" Tracy could tell that the information, his daughter so close to home, cut like a knife.

"I take it you know the park well?" Tracy asked, wanting to confirm what Aditi had told them.

"Of course." Pranav closed his eyes and let out a sigh. "She was here," he said and again he broke down crying. Tracy and Kins waited. When he had recovered enough to speak, Tracy suggested they sit and talk. Pranav gestured to the table in the dining room and told Nikhil to grab additional chairs from the kitchen.

Tracy and Kins sat across from Pranav and Himani. Nikhil, Sam, and the grandfather filled in the remaining seats. The grandmother went into the kitchen to make tea. From behind Tracy, light streamed through two sidelights, the shafts illuminating dancing dust motes and creating prisms in the beaded chandelier centered over the table. Tracy prompted Pranav with a simple question. "Was Kavita familiar with the Bridle Trails State Park?"

He blew out a breath, as if exhaling evil spirits. His hands formed a temple and he stared at it as he spoke. "Kavita *loved* that park," he said, voice soft. "When the children were young we used to take walks, pick blackberries and salmon berries." He looked to his sons. They did not speak. "We hunted for chanterelle mushrooms." He returned his attention to Tracy and Kins. "It was a quiet place where we could be together as a family, a quiet place to enjoy each other's company."

Pranav broke down again and hung his head. His shoulders shook. Himani, though seated beside him, did not rub his back or otherwise reach out to console her husband.

The grandmother entered carrying a tray with a gray ceramic kettle and tea mugs. She placed the tray on the table at Pranav's side, poured her son a cup, and handed it to him. She poured a second and handed it to her husband. Himani and the boys declined. Tracy and Kins accepted. It had been a long night and she knew the grandmother wanted to feel useful.

Pranav set his mug on the table between his hands without tasting the tea.

"We used to make jam from the berries," Himani said, as if to explain. "We would can them and give the jars to the neighbors." She looked to Pranav before looking again to Tracy. "How did you find her?"

"The phone carrier was able to trace her cell phone," Tracy said, "and provide us with the longitude and latitude." She did not mention the app on the phone or give specifics about the hole in the ground.

Sam raised his head, as if puzzled, or intrigued, then lowered it again.

Nikhil sat up, elbows resting on the table. Tracy watched him closely. Though Nikhil had shed tears, his sorrow did not appear to be as intense as that of the rest of the family. Maybe that was to be expected. Maybe he was displaying a strong front as the oldest son. He seemed to be elsewhere, deep in thought, and his gaze fluctuated between the tabletop and the picture window, though he did not appear to be looking at anything in particular.

He turned his head and engaged Tracy. "How did she do it?"

"I don't understand your question," Tracy said, though she did. She couldn't provide the family with specifics of Kavita's death either. Kelly Rosa had not yet completed her analysis, and the details would be something only her killer knew.

"How did she kill herself?" Nikhil asked.

Tracy kept her eyes on the young man, but in her peripheral vision she saw Pranav and Himani raise their heads, looking between their son and Tracy. Nikhil had served. It was Tracy's turn to return the volley. "Why do you assume she killed herself?" Tracy asked.

Nikhil frowned. "It seems obvious, doesn't it?"

Tracy played dumb. "What seems obvious?"

Nikhil squinted, as if trying to figure out what game she was playing, or perhaps he knew what game and didn't appreciate it. "The last time you came you told us Kavita was upset. Aditi told us Kavita left their apartment upset."

That was true. And Tracy had considered it possible that, overwrought, Kavita took her own life. "We don't know the details of

Kavita's death," Tracy said. "The medical examiner hasn't completed her analysis."

"You must know something," Himani said from the other end of the table. "You saw her? You were there?"

"Yes, we were there," Tracy said.

"But you won't tell us?" Nikhil said.

"We don't know if Kavita took her own life," Kins reiterated. He was the detective they did not know and, therefore, the authoritative voice who could tell them about rules and procedure, without apologizing for it. "You have to understand this is a process. It will *be* a process. And that process is just getting started. We have specialists who are performing their work—"

"And do any of these specialists know whether Kavita used a gun, a knife? It isn't a difficult question, Detectives," Nikhil said, his voice rising and his gaze fluctuating between the two of them.

Tracy watched him closely, analyzing his words. *Were they sincere?* "The medical examiner's analysis will take time," Tracy said again. "As Detective Rowe indicated, when that analysis is completed, we'll provide you with a copy. Until then we would just be speculating. As hard as this is to hear, you're going to need to be patient."

"You mentioned a gun," Kins said to Nikhil. "Do you know whether your sister owned a gun?"

"No," Nikhil said. "I don't know."

"Do you think Kavita could have been murdered?" Pranav asked.

"We're proceeding under that assumption," Tracy said, "until we learn otherwise."

"Who?" Pranav asked. "Who would kill her?"

"Our investigation is just getting started," Kins said. "We'll keep you up-to-date as much as we can, when we can, but we have to proceed under the assumption that your daughter did not take her own life until the evidence proves otherwise, as Detective Crosswhite said."

"This is ridiculous." Nikhil sat back. "Kavita obviously took her own life. Look at the circumstances. Look at where you found her. She was upset and confused. And it would be just like Kavita to do something like this."

"Don't say that!" Sam's voice snapped. High-pitched with emotion, it cracked like a whip. "Don't say that about her!" Sam pushed his seat away from the table and quickly stood. He spoke to his parents. "Why couldn't you just support her? What was so terrible about her being a doctor?"

"Sam," Pranav said, starting to stand.

"No!" Sam said. "She wanted to be a doctor but you wouldn't give her any money and you tried to force her to move home and get married. You're responsible for this."

"Sam!" Himani said.

Pranav had moved toward his son, arms extended, but Sam turned from him. Nikhil grabbed his brother's arm but Sam broke the grip and ran to the front door. He pulled it open and quickly departed, flinging the door shut. The house shuddered.

After a moment of silence, Pranav turned to Tracy and Kins. He looked slightly embarrassed. "I'm sorry, Detectives. This has been a tremendous shock for us all." He took another deep breath. Then he asked, "When can we see Vita? When can we recover her body?"

"We've positively identified her through her DMV records and photographs so there's no need to identify the body. I'll provide you with the phone number of the King County Medical Examiner and the name of a woman with our Victim Assistance Unit. She can assist you as you go through this process. She can advise you when the medical examiner is finished and releases Kavita's body," Tracy said.

"Finished?" Himani said. "Finished doing what?"

"Examining the body," Tracy said.

"We do not want an autopsy." Himani looked stricken. She turned her attention to Pranav. "We do not want Kavita's body defiled."

"In these circumstances," Tracy said, "when the cause of death is in doubt, the King County Medical Examiner makes the determination whether to perform an autopsy. It isn't a matter of choice. It's a necess—"

"And we have no say in it?" Himani said, pressing her palms flat against the table, becoming angry.

"Unfortunately not," Kins said. "But the most important thing is to determine what happened to your daughter."

It was a standard line that did little to appease Himani. Pranav raised his hands. "Of course we want to know what happened," he said. "Thank you for coming, Detectives. As I know you can appreciate, the family now needs time to be alone."

Tracy and Kins stood. "You may get calls from the news media," she said. "You're under no obligation to speak to anyone, and we would recommend that you not do so. The victims advocate can assist you."

"What about friends and family?" Himani said. "What can we tell them?"

"Certainly you can speak to them," Kins said. "But do not tell them anything that we've discussed. Do not provide any details—"

"We don't have any details," Nikhil interrupted, his voice mocking. "We haven't discussed *anything*."

"What do we tell them?" Pranav said.

"Blame us," Kins said. "Tell them Kavita has died and the police are investigating the circumstances and we have asked you not to provide any details until the investigation is completed."

Pranav led them from the room, cutting off further discussion. "We will do as you have asked," he said and opened the door.

"I'm sorry to bring you this news," Tracy said. "I'm sorry for your family."

"What remains of it," Pranav said, and he shut the door quietly behind them.

CHAPTER 34

Del walked into the A Team's cubicle and found himself alone, which was disturbing. His coworkers were what he liked best about the A Team. Their banter and ribbing made an often-intolerable job tolerable. He suspected Tracy and Kins were running down the body Billy said they'd found in a park on the Eastside, though it sounded like they'd also likely lose jurisdiction. Faz and Gonzalez were both on administrative leave, one of them maybe for good.

With quiet time to think, Del wasn't certain what to believe. He'd back Faz all he could. If Faz said he didn't yell *Gun!*, then Del would support him. Still . . .

Del knew what it was like to work while grieving. He'd tried to work through the overdose death of his niece Allie, but some days he couldn't concentrate. His mind would wander and he'd lose large blocks of time. Faz would say something and Del wouldn't even know what the conversation was about. It got so bad he'd considered taking time off. He didn't want anyone to get hurt because he was distracted.

And as much as he loved his niece, their relationship was nothing compared to that of a husband and wife. He couldn't imagine the emotional strain Faz was experiencing.

So, was it *possible* Faz had yelled *Gun!* and he couldn't recall doing so?

Del didn't want to go there. He'd been there himself. He knew. It was possible.

He grabbed his chair with both hands and lowered himself with care, his back still tight.

"Del." Johnny Nolasco walked into their cubicle.

"Captain," Del said, slowly turning.

"How's the back?"

"It's okay," Del said. "Still gimpy."

"You heard we're going to be shorthanded for a while."

"Yeah, I heard," he said. "That's why I came in."

"I just got word that the *Times* is running another article tomorrow morning about the shooting and contrasting it with the Justice Department's recent commendation on the department's improvement."

"They'll milk it for as much as they can for as long as they can."

"The reporter already knows the suspect was unarmed."

"I saw the article this morning. Do we know who leaked that information?"

"Sources," Nolasco said.

The department had a leak. It always had a leak. It was like that folktale of the little boy sticking his fingers in holes to stop the flow of water. The department had long since run out of fingers and toes.

"So we can assume the article isn't going to be pretty," Nolasco said.

"When's the last time they wrote something good about us?" Del asked.

"Yeah, well, the brass isn't going to like it."

"You think they're looking to make someone a scapegoat?"

Nolasco made a face that told Del that possibility was likely. Then he said, "Nobody is sharing that information with me. I just wanted you to know."

Del knew Nolasco was telling him so he could tell Faz. "Thanks, Captain."

"In case anyone calls looking for a comment, refer them to Bennett Lee." Lee was the department's public information officer.

"Yeah, no problem," Del said. "How long before we get Faz or Gonzalez back?"

"I don't know," Nolasco said. "It's likely going to be a while. And you heard Tracy and Kins got a murder last night?"

"I heard. Heard the body was found over on the Eastside though. Why are we handling it?"

"Good question," Nolasco said, clearly displeased. "But for the moment they're going to be tied up. I may need you to jump in on some other files."

"We still got Monique Rodgers," Del said.

Nolasco shook his head. "Gonzalez shot the shooter last night."

"We can't prove it, not without a weapon."

"CSI located a .38 special, a revolver, in Lopez's apartment. Ballistics is running tests this morning. Call over and find out what they got and when we can get it. If they can match the bullet to the gun, we're finished."

Del shook his head, feeling out of touch, though he'd only been gone for a day. "We got witnesses saying the shooting was a hit, that Rodgers was outspoken about the gangs and the drugs."

"Are you working any leads that can get us there?"

"We were just getting started, Captain. Little Jimmy's name popped up and we know the people are afraid of him, that he threatened them."

"We don't have the resources to burn it. If you think there's something there, get it buttoned up and send it over to narcotics. If there's a link between Lopez and Little Jimmy, if Little Jimmy ordered the killing, narcotics has confidential sources in play to get it figured out."

"And if there is evidence Little Jimmy called for the hit?"

"Then we'll take it to the prosecutor."

Del wanted to dispute Nolasco's assessment. He wanted to offer a reasoned counterargument. Problem was, Nolasco was likely correct. Without Lopez, they didn't have a suspect they could manipulate to get to Little Jimmy. And if the bullet and the gun matched, they'd solved Monique Rodgers's homicide. If Little Jimmy had ordered the hit, narcotics would better be able to make that determination using their paid informants.

Nolasco gave Del a nod before departing the bull pen. When he did, Del picked up the phone.

—

Fifteen minutes later, Del hung up. He'd called Faz first and given him a heads-up about what the search warrant had uncovered. Then he'd called ballistics. They gave him the news over the phone and e-mailed the report. The gun and the bullet that killed Monique Rodgers matched. And thank God for that. With the press beating down on the department about the death of an unarmed suspect, at least they could say Lopez wasn't an innocent man. He'd killed Rodgers in cold blood. They had the gun and they had the videotape. Lopez also came out of an apartment with a silver cell phone in his hand, which made it much more plausible that Gonzalez thought he held a gun. At least it gave her a viable argument.

But that was all wishful thinking. In eternally liberal Seattle, where the police were damned if they did and damned if they didn't, the department could expect a shit storm, especially if some enterprising attorney found Lopez's family.

For the moment, Del and Faz were done with the case. As instructed, Del would button up the file and send it to narcotics with a request that narcotics try to establish a link between Lopez and Little Jimmy. He stood from his chair, using the desk for support, and walked to the table in the center of their bull pen. On the shelves beneath it, the A Team kept their working binders. He bent and carefully pulled the binder for Monique Rodgers. As the officer in charge, it was his responsibility to keep that file and the electronic file updated. Del still needed to write up their interview with Tanny from the convenience store, which would explain how they'd obtained the print from the Volkswagen that led them to Eduardo Lopez's last known address. And he needed to add the ballistics report before shipping the binder off to narcotics.

Del brought the binder to his desk, slipped on cheaters, logged in to his computer, and opened the Rodgers file. He looked down the tip of his nose and saw an entry he had not been expecting. The file indicated he had logged in to his privatized files the previous day, which was not possible since he'd been at home, nursing a bad back. He picked up his cell, about to call Faz and ask if he had logged in to the files—they knew each other's passwords—when his desk phone rang.

"Del," Nolasco said when he answered. "Tommy Fritz needs help conducting interviews in that gang-related shooting a week ago. His partner is out. I told him you could lend a hand. Give him a call."

"Yeah, not a problem." Del hung up the phone, still staring at the computer. Then he yelled over the top of his cubicle wall to the team on the other side. "Hey, Fritz? Captain says you need some handholding this afternoon."

CHAPTER 35

Tracy handed Aditi Banerjee brown paper napkins. The young woman continued to dab at tears, attempting but failing to compose herself. Tracy and Kins sat with Aditi in Adirondack chairs beneath the shade of a gold umbrella outside a coffeehouse called the Down Pour. It was a clever play on words, given Seattle's propensity for rain.

Tracy did not rush the young woman. She empathized with her pain, but she was also evaluating her reaction. As Kins had voiced, the killer had to have known the park intimately.

Aditi sucked in a deep breath. It shuddered hard in her chest before she exhaled, shaking her head. She appeared stunned, in a state of shock. She sat back from the table, wrapping her arms around her as if she were cold, though the temperature was already warming, even in the umbrella's shade.

Tracy and Kins had managed to get Aditi out of the house alone, though not without protest from Rashesh.

"Why did Kavita use her nickname and her middle name for the Wells Fargo account?" Tracy said. "Who was she hiding it from?"

Aditi closed her eyes and exhaled. "Everyone."

Tracy looked to Kins. He shrugged. She said, "Why? Where did she get the money?"

Aditi shook her head. "I didn't know the amount was so large."

"Do you know where the money came from?" Tracy asked again.

Aditi nodded, but before she could speak, she again began to weep. Kins held out additional napkins. Aditi took them and staunched her tears. After a moment she said, "Vita was very strong willed." She spoke as if out of breath. "When she made up her mind . . ." She looked at Tracy and swallowed. "We were different in that respect. Vita was not about to do what her parents wanted. She was not about to get married. You had to know her."

"What did she do?" Tracy asked.

Aditi watched a young couple holding hands as they strolled past the table, then redirected her attention to Tracy. "No one can know," she said. "Vita's parents cannot know. It would bring their family great shame." She paused. Then she said, "And Rashesh cannot know."

"Rashesh?" Tracy said. "I don't understand."

"It's complicated."

"Explain it to me."

Aditi sipped her coffee, set the cup down on the table, and took another deep breath. "Vita was not just my friend, Detectives. She was my sister. After our parents had issued their ultimatums that they would no longer pay for our education or our apartment, we stayed up talking very late, discussing what we were going to do. Neither of us knew. It had always been our dream that someday we would become pediatricians and work together. But before we could do that, we had to get through medical school. The tuition alone seemed insurmountable without our parents' financial support."

She took another sip of coffee. Tracy gave her time.

"Kavita was much more determined. Perhaps she was just much more brave. I don't know. I had mentally prepared to move home, but

Vita told me not to do anything until we had to leave the apartment. I agreed to give her time. Another few days passed and Vita came home very excited and animated."

"About?" Tracy asked, gently nudging Aditi forward.

"She'd gotten a job working at a clothing store on the Avenue. It wasn't a lot of money, but her boss said he'd increase her hours when she graduated. She said the money she earned plus my salary working in a chemistry lab on campus would allow us to stay in the apartment for the summer and at least give us additional time to get things figured out. Though I liked the idea of living in the apartment and working, I thought it would be short-lived, because after paying our rent we had little left to live on, let alone to save for medical school tuition. Vita said not to worry, that we'd figure something out. I began looking for student loans and scholarships. A few weeks after Vita started work at the clothing store, she came home, this time more subdued. She said that she'd been talking with one of the women she worked with. I don't recall her name, but Vita said she had several piercings—a nose ring, I believe."

"Lindsay," Tracy said, recalling the young woman from the store.

"Yes. Vita said she'd been explaining to Lindsay our circumstances regarding our parents, and that Lindsay said she had a way for us to make more money. She apparently pulled out her laptop and opened it to an online dating service. She called it 'sugar dating.'"

Tracy had read an article some month earlier published in the *Seattle Times* discussing the websites. It had also been discussed in the office. Young women filled out an online profile with the hope that a "sugar daddy"—an older, wealthy man—would want to date them. The sites promised the young women the potential to meet men looking to lavish them with gifts and money, and zip them around the world on jets and yachts in exchange for the young woman's companionship, which, loosely translated, meant sex.

"And Vita filled out a profile for one of these sites," Tracy said.

Aditi cried and dabbed at her tears. "Lindsay said she'd made five hundred dollars a month, sometimes more. I told Vita the idea was ridiculous, but Vita remained angry and resentful of her parents. She said that if her mother was intent on giving her away to someone she didn't know then she might as well get paid for it."

Tracy sat back. It was not the story she had expected, but it did put things into better perspective. Vita had not just been a recent college graduate living in a relatively safe area. She had placed herself among those in society most compromised, most at risk. It made Tracy think of what Sam had told them, about Vita having a "date" the night she had disappeared.

"And what did you think, Aditi?"

Aditi lowered her eyes. "I said I thought it was ludicrous. But Vita kept telling me that I did not have to sleep with the men, that some men were just looking for companionship. I didn't want to do it, but I felt I owed it to Kavita to try to make more money, that we had come so far together. I had to at least try. I didn't want to disappoint her."

"You created a profile too," Tracy said. She glanced at Kins. The reason for Aditi's desire to keep the information from Rashesh became clear. "What site?" she asked.

"Sugardating.com."

"And what happened?"

"What always happened." Aditi raised her eyes and looked at them. Anger, or bitterness, maybe jealousy, leaked into her voice. "Men took one look at Vita and began responding to her profile. She turned down most and dated a few."

"And what about your profile?" Tracy asked.

Aditi gave a sardonic huff. "I had one or two inquiries, but the men were losers. It became apparent that they weren't looking for companionship."

"They were looking for sex," Tracy said.

"Yes."

"Did you go on a date?"

"Once," Aditi said. "The man was Indian. I thought he would be safe. His profile said he was a computer software engineer and he was opening his own start-up company." She scoffed again. "He was an unemployed computer programmer living in the garage of his parents' home. We went to dinner. On the drive home he pulled into a parking lot and offered me fifty dollars for a blow job."

"I'm sorry," Tracy said.

"It was humiliating. I got out of the car and called Vita to pick me up. That was my one and only date, and that was when I decided I would give in to my parents' desires."

"And what about Vita?"

"Vita was not going to give in that easily. Initially, her dates were like mine, but she just dismissed them. Then she got a message from a man in Medina, a doctor."

Medina was a wealthy community on the east side of Lake Washington with expensive homes and wealthy residents. "Vita met him at a restaurant, and when she came home she said he had offered to pay her a two-thousand-dollar-a-month stipend to be available when he called, which they agreed would be no more than once a week. Vita told me she would split whatever she earned to help fund our medical school tuition. I told her that I couldn't do that, that I wouldn't accept it. I told her not to do it, not to compromise herself."

"But Kavita did," Tracy said.

Aditi nodded. "We didn't talk about it, but I knew she was seeing him."

"Who is this guy?" Tracy asked, becoming angry.

"Dr. Charles Shea." Aditi sat back from the table. "I get the creeps and Vita gets the doctor, a pediatrician no less. It was always that way."

"Was she sleeping with Shea?" Tracy asked.

"I don't know for certain."

"Aditi—"

The young woman raised her voice. "She never told me their arrangement and I didn't ask, Detective." She sat back, catching the anger in her voice. She continued, this time more softly. "I didn't want to know and I didn't want her money. Given the circumstances, and the amount of money you said that she had in her account . . ."

Tracy found it unlikely Kavita would not tell Aditi. "She didn't tell you, Aditi?"

"No."

"Why wouldn't she tell you?"

Aditi frowned. "Because I didn't want to know. And, I think, because Vita felt bad for me and didn't want me to feel worse."

"Felt bad for you?" Kins asked.

But even before Aditi began to speak, Tracy knew why. It was the same reason her sister, Sarah, had been so rebellious as a child, and so fiercely competitive, especially with Tracy. It was tough to live in an older sister's shadow, especially a sister everyone thought was perfect. Tracy wasn't perfect, far from it, but that didn't make it any easier for Sarah to hear. Kavita had been tall, light skinned, and gorgeous. She was also extremely bright. "Was it really that bad, Aditi?" Tracy asked. "So bad that Kavita would sell herself?"

"Kavita would have never seen it that way, Detective. In her mind, she saw this as a business opportunity. That's what she would have told herself. It was a business opportunity that would get her, and me, where she wanted us to go."

"But to put up a profile on the Internet . . . Isn't that what she wanted to avoid, what her mother was doing?" Kins asked.

"Perhaps I can put it in perspective. Ever since we were young, we've heard people talk about how much we are *worth* to our family. Indian women are given away for gifts and tradition all the time in India. In marriage, we are transferred from one family to another. We are not valued as our brothers are valued—for our intelligence and creativity. We are not seen as their equals. We are seen as a commodity. We are seen as brides." Aditi shook her head. "That was never going to be Kavita and this was her way of standing up for herself, of fighting back, of not succumbing to a vicious circle. This was her way of sticking it to her parents and everyone else who said she couldn't do it."

CHAPTER 36

After returning Aditi to her parents' home, Tracy and Kins ran Dr. Charles Shea through the system. He had no priors, not even a parking ticket. The DMV provided his address. A further Google search revealed he was a respected pediatrician with a practice in Bothell. Tracy called Shea's office but was told that he had taken the morning off but would be in that afternoon. They drove to his home on the shores of Lake Washington but encountered a gated entrance. No one answered the intercom and they saw no cars parked in the driveway.

"Probably golfing," Kins said. "Don't all doctors golf?"

Tracy tried to push back her frustration. They had a direction and a sense of purpose but probably little time to pursue Kavita Mukherjee's killer. She suspected that at some point soon, if not already, the brass at Bellevue and Seattle would talk, and she and Kins would be out. They needed to push things.

They waited for Shea outside his home, sipping coffee. "Play out this scenario with me," Tracy said. She'd spent the morning thinking about it. "From what we know, Kavita was using sugar dating to get enough money for her and Aditi to attend medical school, right?"

"That's what Aditi said, but she also said she wouldn't take it," Kins said.

"Forget about that for the moment. Let's just say that was Kavita's intent."

"Okay."

"But then Aditi goes to India and returns married, which means what?"

"I don't know. She doesn't need the money?"

"It means Aditi isn't going to medical school."

"Right. So she doesn't need the money."

"Right. So Kavita suddenly has twice as much money as she thought she had to put toward her medical school tuition."

"Makes sense, I guess."

"So if that's true, what if, after getting the news that Aditi was married and moving to London, Kavita told this guy Shea that she didn't need to see him anymore?"

"And what? He gets angry and kills her? How did Shea know about the old well?"

Tracy shrugged. "I don't know. He works and lives over here. Maybe he knows the park. But forget that for the moment. What if Kavita told Shea she was done?"

"I guess it's possible, Tracy, but—"

"Rosa said the killer was angry. Kavita was a beautiful girl. What if this guy Shea got attached to her?"

"Okay," Kins said. "Time-out. Before we get too far ahead of ourselves, Wright said Mukherjee appeared to have walked into the park. Why would she walk into the park?"

"I don't know."

"And why was Shea in the park?"

"Again, I don't know," Tracy said. "Maybe he runs through the park before or after work."

"And she just happens to be there?"

"Maybe they were running together."

"No, Kaylee said Mukherjee was wearing flats and there was only one set of prints."

Kins was right. Tracy's theory didn't fit with the known evidence. "I'm just saying it's a theory. It's a start," she said.

Kins tried her theory aloud. "He gets upset that she's leaving him, kills her, and dumps the body? Even if he had a gun and forced her to walk into the park, you still have the problem of one set of shoeprints." Kins sat up. "Call Vilkotski. See if Pryor dropped off the phone."

She'd asked Katie Pryor to drop off Kavita Mukherjee's phone to Vilkotski after it had been processed for fingerprints and DNA. Tracy called and the call rang through to voice mail. Vilkotski was either not in or not at his desk. Tracy left a message that she wanted every text message sent to or from Kavita Mukherjee's phone during the past six months.

She hung up and called Pryor, who answered on the second ring. Pryor confirmed that she'd dropped off the phone. "We're going to need another search warrant," Tracy said. "It's for a dating site."

She explained to Pryor what they had learned and asked that she prepare a search warrant to obtain Vita Kumari's dating profile from Sugardating.com, including all communications to or from anyone who had contacted her. She also asked Pryor to run the name Dr. Charles Shea, though she suspected Shea, too, had used a different name on the site.

When she hung up, Kins said, "Run a search on sugar dating. Let's see what we're dealing with."

Tracy typed the words "sugar dating" on her laptop and was assaulted by dozens of websites, from the banal—Seekingarrangement.com—to the more explicit Honeydaddy.com. She limited her search by adding "Seattle" and pulled up an article published in the *Stranger*, an alternative weekly newspaper with a liberal bent. One of the *Stranger*'s reporters had created a profile as a wannabe sugar baby, and went on several dates. She'd even attended a sugar baby conference in, where else, Los Angeles.

"No shortage of wannabe actresses down there looking to supplement their nonexistent acting income," Kins said as Tracy shared her research.

"Not to mention older sleazebags looking to take advantage of those younger women and their dreams."

Kins frowned. "Take advantage?"

"Don't challenge me on this," she said, striking the keys on the keyboard. "There wouldn't be any sugar babies if there weren't any sugar daddies."

"Like there wouldn't be any prostitutes if there weren't any johns?"

"Pretty much," she said.

"I think you're being naïve," he said. "It's the oldest profession for a reason."

"Yes, because there are men who take advantage of women, especially women with a dream, no matter how far-fetched those dreams may be. They exploit them."

"Not all those women have dreams, Tracy."

"No, they don't. Some have given up on their dreams and are just poor and desperate. Does that make it okay?"

"And some are just looking to make money. The men are paying for it and the women accepting it."

"And that makes it okay?"

"If they're over eighteen and participating of their own free will, yes. We'll never stop it, no matter how many resources we devote to it, including you and me."

She'd heard this before. Kins had long been an advocate for legalizing prostitution so police could devote their resources to other crimes. Tracy didn't see it that way. She saw prostitution as the tip of an enormous iceberg that denigrated and devalued women and led to violent crimes such as rape, assault and battery, and murder—not to mention the use of illicit drugs, needle sharing, and the spread of sexually transmitted diseases. A similar argument about police resources had been made to support the legalization of marijuana—that it would allow police to concentrate on other, more serious crimes. It looked good on paper, but then the Mexican drug cartels, realizing they were going to lose a cash cow, plowed under their marijuana fields and planted poppies. They flooded the US market with black tar heroin and created an epidemic leading to much more complex crimes.

"Let's agree to disagree," he said. "Call the newspaper. See if we can meet with the reporter. She might have done much of our legwork for us, which could be useful when we talk to Dr. Charles Scumbag."

An editor at the *Stranger* told Tracy the reporter was a freelance writer named Tami Peterson. He wouldn't give out her phone number but said he'd take Tracy's number and let Peterson know Tracy wished to speak to her.

According to the article, Peterson was twenty-two years old and single. The article included two photographs, one of Peterson at work, the other after she'd primped for her dating site profile. Both revealed her to be attractive—tall and slender with fair skin. In her working photograph, Peterson wore sturdy black-framed glasses, which gave her a studious look. For her profile picture, she'd ditched the glasses to better accentuate blue eyes and long lashes, and she gave the camera a subtle pout that exuded sex appeal. Peterson had used her real name, and indicated she lived in Seattle and loved the theater. As for a dating fee, she'd put "negotiable."

"Look at these websites," Tracy said to Kins. "Date a millionaire! Travel the world on private jets and stay in five-star luxury hotels!"

"Give a loser a blow job in his car!" Kins said, imitating the British accent of the host from the television show *Lifestyles of the Rich and Famous*.

"Can't say that," Tracy said. "Her article says that the topic of sex is expressly forbidden in the profiles, though the couples are encouraged to make their own choices after getting to know one another. What a bunch of crap. They make it sound romantic."

"What, you don't consider Aditi Banerjee's experience romantic?"

"Yeah, that's every girl's dream."

"The real question is, what's a doctor doing on that site?" Kins asked.

"I don't think pond scum is limited to any one profession."

CHAPTER 37

Del stepped from the elevator inside Eduardo Lopez's apartment building, this time with a handkerchief clasped over his mouth. He'd contemplated the stairs, but only briefly. Climbing five flights with a gimpy back was just asking for trouble. By the time he exited the elevator onto the fifth floor, his eyes were watering and he felt nauseated from the smell and holding his breath. He'd take the stairs down—his back be damned.

He'd driven to South Park to tell Monique Rodgers's husband and mother about Eduardo Felix Lopez's death and that ballistics matched the bullet that had killed her to the .38 revolver found in Lopez's apartment. They asked him about Little Jimmy, whether there was any evidence to tie him to the shooting. Del said the investigation was ongoing.

He considered the numbers on the apartment doors as he walked the cracked tile floor. Windows at each end of the hallway provided ambient light, as Faz had described. Technically, Del shouldn't have been at the South Park apartment building. Technically, he should have already buttoned up the file and sent it to narcotics, as Nolasco had instructed. He would do so, but not before he had tied up loose ends, and one burning question.

Del reached the apartment door second from the end, next to what he understood to have been Eduardo Lopez's apartment. He considered where Gonzalez and Faz said they'd stood, and he agreed with what Faz had told the FIT investigator. It made much more sense for Faz to stand to the left of the door frame, not behind Gonzalez, so he could evaluate whoever came to the door and determine whether anyone else was in the apartment and a potential threat—not to mention avoiding a bullet if the person opened the door and fired a weapon.

He knocked on the door of the adjacent apartment. No one answered. He knocked again, more forcefully. The door rattled in the jamb. No answer. He knocked a third time, waited a beat, then put his ear to the door, hearing nothing. When he pulled back, he noticed the door did not contain a peephole, which made it unlikely anyone stood on the other side making him for a cop. More important, Lopez also hadn't had that opportunity before he'd opened the door and walked out.

Del heard a door open and bang shut down the hall. A woman and a young boy exited the stairwell, and the woman lowered the boy to the ground. She carried a plastic bag of groceries in one hand and keys in the other. The boy looked no older than two or three and had something in his hand—a toy dinosaur. As the woman approached, she looked at Del and came to an abrupt stop. She said something under her breath to the boy, gripped his hand, turned and walked back in the direction of the stairwell. The boy looked over his shoulder at Del and the mother quickly admonished him.

"Excuse me," Del said.

The woman did not turn around.

"Excuse me." Del increased his volume and his pace, what his gimpy back allowed. "Ms. Reynoso? Ms. Reynoso." The name was in the FIT reports. Del caught up with the woman just before she pushed the door handle leading to the stairwell.

"Ms. Reynoso?"

"No hablo inglés." She smiled apologetically and looked frazzled.

"¿Hablas español?"

She shook her head. *"Tengo prisa. No puedo hablar ahora."*

She was in a hurry and could not talk now. Del had taken Spanish in high school and he'd worked in Eastern Washington when he first graduated from the Academy. He could speak and understand street Spanish, though he was far from fluent. He didn't need to understand any Spanish to know Reynoso was lying.

He pointed to her apartment door and asked why she had turned around when she'd been coming home. *"Estabas volviendo a casa. ¿Por qué te volviste cuando me viste?"*

"No. No. I can't talk now. I'm late."

"So you do speak English?"

She paused. "*Sí.* Yes. A little."

"Why did you turn around when you saw me?"

Reynoso looked frightened. "Please."

Del held up his badge. "I'm a detective with the Seattle Police Department," he said, though Reynoso seemed unimpressed with his credentials. "I'd like to ask you a few more questions. Do you want to talk in your apartment or here in the hallway?"

Reynoso didn't have to talk to Del at all, but most citizens didn't know this. Resigned, Reynoso nodded to her apartment and they walked the hallway together. At the door, Del gave her some space. The boy looked up at him with both suspicion and trepidation. Del smiled, but it didn't change the look on the kid's face.

Reynoso opened the door and stepped into the apartment. Del looked past her into the apartment, not seeing anyone inside. She put the bag of groceries on the counter and spoke to the boy. *"Daniel, ve a jugar a tu cuarto con tu dinosaurio."*

Daniel looked from his mother to Del, as if afraid to leave her.

"Seguid," she said. *"Haré quesadillas en un rato."*

The boy walked to the door on the other side of the room, glancing back at Del a final time before going through it.

The woman crossed her arms around her body and lowered her chin.

"You were here the other night when Eduardo Lopez was shot. I just want to ask you a few questions," Del said.

"I've already talked to the police. You should ask them." She spoke without raising her gaze.

"I did," Del said. "They sent me back out because your story doesn't match the other witnesses'. They asked me to try to determine why that is, why your story is different."

The woman responded with a shoulder shrug but no words.

"A woman down the hall said she heard a woman yell *Gun!* just before she heard the shots. You said you heard a man yell *Gun!*" There was no such report.

Reynoso shook her head. "I don't know."

Del changed tactics. "How did you know Eduardo Lopez?"

"He lived next door."

"Did you have a relationship with him?"

"No." She shook her head, frowning.

"Then what was he doing here in your apartment?"

"I told—"

"No, you didn't answer that question. No one asked you that question. What was he doing here in your apartment?" Del had read the witness statements, including hers.

She shrugged, buying time. "He just came here."

"You were friends?"

"*Sí.* Yes. We were friends."

"How did you meet?"

"I told you. He lived next door."

"Where did he work?"

"I . . . I don't know."

"What did he talk about?"

"Please," she said. "I have to feed my boy."

"Why did you say you heard a man yell *Gun!*, Ms. Reynoso?"

"Because that's what I—"

"No. It's not what you heard. The police wear body cameras now. Do you know what a body camera is? It's a tiny video camera, Ms. Reynoso. It videotapes everything that happens and records everything that is said." The officers didn't wear cameras, at least not all officers and not yet anyway. That issue was still being negotiated between the city and the police union. Del was just pressing her to see if she changed her story.

"So we know that a man did not yell *Gun!* Why did you say that he did?"

"I don't know. Maybe I make a mistake."

"Ms. Reynoso, you can't get in trouble for telling the truth. But if you lie to a police officer—"

"Please."

"Did someone tell you to say that you heard a man yell *Gun!*?"

"Please."

"Did someone tell you to say that?"

"You tell me to." She raised her voice and her gaze. "You. The police. The woman. She say, 'You heard a man yell *Gun!*'"

Now they were getting someplace. "Did you?"

"I don't know. It was loud and Daniel was crying. I told her I don't know what I hear, but she say again, 'You heard a man yell *Gun!*, didn't you?' So I say, 'Okay, I hear a man yell *Gun!*' Then she say, and you heard me ask him, the other police, 'Why you yell *Gun!*?'"

"Did you hear her say that to the other officer?"

Reynoso shook her head. "I no hear nothing. I just say it because she say to."

"Did she say why she wanted you to say that?"

"She say Eduardo Lopez, he shoot someone. She say I am hiding him and could be in trouble, that I could lose Daniel if I no say it. So I say it."

"Were you hiding Lopez?"

She shook her head, emphatic. "No. He knock on my door and say someone coming to his apartment. He say he need to not be there."

"He knew someone was coming?"

"He say he need a place to go until they go. I tell him I no want to be involved, but he say only for a minute. He say they are immigration."

"So you let him in."

"I was afraid. He had men at his apartment all the time."

"Do you know why?"

She shook her head.

"Was he selling drugs?"

A shrug. "I no know."

"Was he in a gang?"

"I no know."

"Did he say who was coming to his apartment? Who was he hiding from?"

Another shrug. "He just say 'immigration.'"

Del thought of what Faz had told him and moved close to Reynoso's apartment door. "Was he standing by your door?"

She nodded. "He listening. Someone in the hallway, knocking on his door and . . ."

"You heard someone knocking?" Del asked. Faz said Gonzalez never got the chance to knock.

"Yes. They knock hard. Bam, bam, bam."

Del pointed to her apartment door. "On this door?"

"No. His door. Next door."

"You heard someone knocking?"

"Yes. Bam, bam, bam, like that."

Del thought of something else and asked, "Were you talking to Lopez?"

She shook her head. "I no say nothing."

"The officers who came said they heard someone speaking Spanish. Was Lopez speaking to you in Spanish?"

She shook her head, but stopped.

"Do you recall something?"

"Someone call his phone. He speaking Spanish on his phone."

"What did Lopez say?"

"I no know."

"You don't remember anything he said?"

She shook her head.

"Was this before or after you heard someone knocking? Did he get the call before or after someone knocked on his door?"

"After." Reynoso appeared to be fighting the effects of a headache. "Someone bang on the door but Lopez, he just listen. He no answer. Then, no more banging and Lopez, he go to the window," she said, pointing.

Del walked to the window. From it, he could see the parking lot. "He walked over here and looked out the window *after* he heard someone knocking?"

"He hears the knocking. Then he walks to the window, watching. Then he looks at me and he says *'Gracias'* and he starts to leave. Then his phone rings."

It explained why the phone was in Lopez's hand when he walked out the apartment door, and possibly why he had surprised Faz and Gonzalez. Whoever Lopez had been hiding from, whoever had knocked on his apartment door, Lopez believed that person had left, maybe even saw him leave from Reynoso's window. He wasn't expecting anyone to be outside when he opened Reynoso's door, and without a peephole he had no way to check before he did so. Faz and Gonzalez had surprised him.

And he had surprised them.

CHAPTER 38

Tami Peterson lived on Capitol Hill but told Tracy she'd meet them at a corner pub called the Stumbling Monk. She sounded young and enthusiastic, brimming with excitement, and not the least bit intimidated to be meeting detectives. Tracy and Kins hoped Peterson could help them get a better handle on sugar dating, information they might be able to use if Shea were reluctant to talk to them, or if he lied. The more they knew, or Shea thought they knew, the more they could push him out of any comfort zone.

Peterson had been literal when she described the Stumbling Monk as a "corner pub." The entrance to the brick, single-story building faced the intersection of East Olive Way and Belmont Avenue East, just beneath a sign of a bald monk and beer kegs. Kins pulled open a solid wood door with iron bolts and hinges intended to depict a medieval abbey. The décor inside the pub was austere. Half a dozen bar stools lined a nicked and scraped wooden bar. Televisions were noticeably absent, along with their persistent chatter. A bookcase supplied well-worn paperbacks and board games. A handful of people sat on bar stools or at tables and booths, sipping Belgian beers—a handwritten list to choose from on a whiteboard.

Tracy spotted Peterson sliding from one of the booths to greet them. She looked a lot more like her working picture in the newspaper article—black eyeglasses, blue jeans, sandals, and a sleeveless white blouse. The three introduced themselves, and Tracy and Kins slid into the booth across from her. Peterson had a cup of black coffee on the table and her laptop computer open.

"Interesting place," Kins said, considering an old-fashioned bicycle perched on the roof of a closet in the back corner.

"I come down here to write," Peterson said. "It gives me a break from my apartment and at least makes me feel like I got out during the day."

"What do you write?" Tracy asked.

"Whatever pays. Mostly freelance articles, local-scene-type stuff. And, yes, I am one of those people writing a novel."

"Anything published?" Tracy asked.

"Haven't finished it yet," Peterson said. "I'm a great procrastinator. It's sort of a literary romance." She shrugged and sipped her coffee. "My editor said you were interested in the article I wrote on sugar dating. That was almost two months ago."

"We'd like to ask you some questions about your research," Kins said.

"My undercover work as a 'sugar baby.'" Peterson smiled. "Can I ask what this is about? You're both wearing wedding rings so I assume neither of you is interested in creating a profile, though that didn't stop some of the men."

Tracy and Kins returned her smile. "We're working on a case—a young woman apparently did some dating," Tracy said, "and we'd like to find out more about it. From reading the article, it sounds like you put in a lot of time and effort."

"Homicide case?" Peterson asked. The young woman had done her research, and Tracy could see the journalism wheels spinning. She'd be on the Internet the minute they left, trying to figure out who had died, and then she'd try to look up her profile.

"Yes, but we have no information the two are related. We're just starting to run it down."

"But she had a profile and she was dating men from her profile?"

"That's what we're told," Tracy said. "From the tone of your article, I got the impression you didn't think much of the concept of sugar dating."

"You mean my line about it promising a Ferrari and more times than not producing a Kia? I thought I was being subtle."

"We saw through it," Kins said, returning Peterson's smile. "We're highly trained detectives."

"Honestly, I found the whole thing kind of sad. Some of the girls I spoke with saw this as their *Pretty Woman* moment—you know the movie with Julia Roberts?"

Tracy did, and thought the concept of a prostitute and a millionaire falling in love and living happily ever after more than a little far-fetched.

"And that's not how every encounter turns out," Kins said with mock surprise. "I'm shocked!"

"I'm sure some of the sugar daddies tell themselves they're being supportive, helping these girls realize dreams, that they're mentors or something." She shrugged again, a habit. "You can pretty much tell yourself whatever you want to hear and I guess you'll eventually start to believe at least some of it. Other guys I spoke to were more practical. They tell themselves that at least they're not hiring a prostitute."

"And how do the girls rationalize it?" Tracy asked. "Those not living the *Pretty Woman* dream?"

"That's what's so sad. Some of the girls told me they figured they were being used, but at least they were getting paid for it. Some said the money was supplementing their income, and a few said they were still in school and needed the money to pay bills." Peterson shrugged again, this time accompanied by a frown. "From my perspective, everyone was on the hustle and everyone thought they were winning. Nobody really was."

"The websites say these women are making upwards of three thousand dollars or more a month," Tracy said. "I take it you didn't find that to be true."

"The websites say a lot of things." Peterson sat back. "I don't know. Maybe a few are making that much, but I couldn't verify it, and the large majority I spoke with were basically making spending money. I look at it this way—how many guys can afford three thousand dollars a month for a girlfriend?" she said. "From my research, a man can get a really good-looking prostitute for four to five hundred dollars. So, if it happened, I'm betting it wasn't often."

"How are these dating sites even legal?" Kins asked. "Did you find anything about why this isn't considered prostitution? The concept of money for sex seems pretty blatant."

"The websites fly under the radar of local law enforcement because they forbid any specific agreement to exchange cash for sex. From what I was told by vice officers, to be considered prostitution there has to be an explicit agreement that is consummated immediately, or very soon after the agreement is reached. These sites that call themselves dating sites say they're providing companions and that sex is not the primary motivation."

"But it is a motivation," Tracy said, "from your experience?" The article indicated that while at the seminar in Los Angeles, Peterson had been approached by two men wanting to walk across the street to a hotel and have group sex.

"From the research I did, sex was a big part of the package. It always came up. There might have been other things discussed, but sex was definitely on the table."

"What do the website owners say about that?" Tracy asked.

"They say sex is always on the table when two people enter a relationship and begin dating, but neither is obligated to have sex unless he or she wants to." She gave them a rueful smile. "At the same time, these websites let women know up front that these are relationships with no complications and no strings attached. No love is expected or welcomed. So . . . no love, just sex, and the women get paid money. What does that sound like to you?"

"Who signs up on these sites?" Tracy asked.

"No way to know for certain," Peterson said. "Everything is kept confidential; the women are encouraged to use fake names and fake profiles, and I'm sure the men do also. There's a lot of smoke and mirrors, and frankly, a lot of stupidity. Think about the scenario of nineteen-year-old women getting into cars with men they don't know anything about, not even their real names. All they know is what they read on the profile. And often they haven't told anyone what they're doing because they're too embarrassed to be doing it."

"And much of what is on the dating site is probably bullshit," Kins said.

Peterson leaned forward, animated. "I interviewed a mental health therapist for the article, and she said these relationships remind men of that carefree time in their lives when they were young and dating. Except this time the men have the money so they have the power. They control the situation and they can steer the relationship in directions they couldn't when they were just dating. She said the result is a huge power imbalance. The average age of guys using these sites is forty-five. The average age of the women is twenty-six. She said you also have gender imbalance and possibly class and race imbalance, which raises the question of whether the girls are really consenting, or are just so desperate for money either because they've lost their job, can't pay the rent, or can't see a way to make their dream come true working at Starbucks part-time for minimum wage." Peterson shrugged. "Everyone wants to blame the women and give the men a free pass when, really, the men are just as guilty, if not more so."

Tracy glanced at Kins but he ignored her.

Peterson said, "I have to tell you, I never expected I'd be talking to homicide detectives when I concluded the article the way that I did, but I guess it doesn't surprise me."

"How'd you conclude the article?" Kins asked.

"The Internet is a dangerous place," Peterson said, without looking at her computer. "You can go online and protect your identity, but then, so can the person you're targeting. It can be a very deadly game."

CHAPTER 39

Del parked his 1965 hunter-green Impala well back from the basketball hoop, not wanting to have the basketball careen off the rim and hit his baby. Faz stood beneath the rim, cradling a ball in his hands. Del had played basketball with Faz when both were younger and his back wasn't about to seize. Faz was surprisingly agile for his size and proudly proclaimed that he'd played power forward in high school.

As Del got out of the car, he heard a radio broadcasting the final innings of the Mariners game.

"You should have been here an hour ago," Faz said. "Vera made a salmon to die for." He tossed the basketball to Del, who caught it but tossed it back. "I better not. The back is still gimpy. I'm liable to shoot and end up in an ambulance."

Faz banked a shot off the backboard. It kissed the front rim and rolled off.

"How was your day off?" Del asked.

"I'm playing basketball outside, aren't I?" Faz said. "On leave less than twenty-four hours and I'm already going stir-crazy and driving Vera nuts. You want a beer or a glass of wine?"

"No, I'm good. Came by to talk."

"I figured as much." Faz nodded to the patio table and chairs on the deck. "Let's talk outside."

He tossed the ball over his shoulder. It bounced twice and settled in the bushes along the driveway. They heard crowd noise, cheering, coming from the radio on the patio table. "They winning again?" Del asked, pulling out a chair. After a slow start, the Mariners had won nine out of ten games.

"Four to nothing last I heard," Faz said. "Sounds like more."

Del settled across the table from Faz. "I went back to South Park tonight, to Lopez's apartment building."

"Yeah?" Faz smiled. "When we talked this afternoon you said Nolasco told you to send the file to narcotics?"

"I haven't quite gotten around to it." Del smiled. "I had to go out there to tell Rodgers's family about the ballistics report."

"How'd they take it?"

"About as I expected. They still think Lopez worked for Little Jimmy. I told them we were still trying to make that connection. Since I happened to be in the area I decided I'd drive over and talk to Lopez's neighbor."

Faz sat forward, forearms on the table. "Did she talk to you?"

"She wasn't about to." Del told Faz about the encounter in the hallway. "She was scared, Faz."

"Little Jimmy?"

Del shook his head. "No. She's afraid of us, the police."

Faz gave that some thought. "She didn't want anyone to see her talking to you?"

"Maybe, but it wasn't a general fear of the police. It was more specific."

Faz gave him an inquisitive look. "Of what?"

"Of who? Gonzalez. I asked Reynoso who told her to say she heard a man yell *Gun!*"

"And she said Gonzalez told her?" Faz asked.

"After some hemming and hawing she said the woman police officer told her to say she heard a man yell *Gun!*"

"No shit?"

Del nodded. "No shit." He told Faz the details of his encounter at the apartment. "Gonzalez told Reynoso she could get in trouble for letting Lopez into her apartment, that things could get bad for her and for her son."

"Did you tape her?" Faz asked.

He shook his head. "Nah, I was worried she'd spook and clam up. But even if she went on the record, FIT, or whoever else looked into this, would argue that I tainted her testimony and tampered with a witness, especially since I told her you were wearing a body camera so we knew she was lying when she said she heard a man."

Faz sat back from the table. "You said that?"

Del nodded.

"Shit, Del. I don't want you to put your job at risk."

"Yeah, well, there's more to it," Del said. "When Nolasco told me to close down our investigation and send the file to narcotics, I went into the file to update the binder. I saw that Tracy had opened the file Monday and Tuesday afternoon of this week."

"Why would Tracy . . . Wait . . . Tracy was in the Stephenson trial Monday and Tuesday afternoon."

"I know."

"Then . . ."

"There was another record of me logging into the file yesterday, when I was home with a bad back."

"Did you remote in?"

Del shook his head. "No. I was going to ask you the same question."

"Oh shit, Del."

"What?"

"Damn," Faz said. "I let Gonzalez use your computer yesterday, after she gave me a song and dance about her and Tracy having problems. I gave her your password."

Del nodded, thinking about it. "And if she'd used Tracy's computer on Monday or Tuesday, she would have known I was the lead detective on Rodgers, not Tracy, and that she couldn't get into the privatized report files."

"Why, though? Why would she want to get into your files?"

"I don't know. But her interest was clearly Monique Rodgers."

"Did you ask Reynoso why Lopez was at her apartment?" Faz asked.

"I did and she said Lopez needed to hide from someone."

"He knew we were coming?"

"I don't think so."

"Then who?"

"Reynoso said Lopez was inside her apartment when someone knocked on his door. You told me you and Gonzalez never knocked."

"That's true, we didn't."

"So someone got to Lopez's apartment just before you and Gonzalez. Reynoso said they knocked several times, then left. She said after the person stopped knocking, Lopez went to the window and watched the parking lot, and while he was doing that, his phone rang and he started talking in Spanish."

"I heard someone speaking Spanish."

Del said, "I know. I also don't think Lopez was expecting anyone to still be in the hall when he came out. I think he thought whoever he was hiding from had left. There are no peepholes in the doors. So Lopez couldn't have checked the hallway before opening the door. I'm thinking that you and Gonzalez surprised him as much as he surprised you."

Faz recalled something else. "Gonzalez asked to run Eduardo Lopez," he said, leaning forward. "She was there when I got the results from Latents on the handprint. She asked if I wanted help running Lopez."

"So, she knew we had a positive hit on Lopez," Del said. "And when she ran Lopez she had his last known address."

"You think she told Lopez we were coming to pick him up?"

"Maybe," Del said. "But that doesn't explain who came to Lopez's door before you, who Lopez was hiding from."

Faz recalled the man who'd come down the stairs just before he and Gonzalez stepped onto the elevator. The timing was right. "I might have seen him."

"Who?"

"I don't know who, but Gonzalez and I saw a Hispanic man come out of the stairwell when we were waiting for the elevator. He gave us a look . . . and when he left the building he walked in the direction of the parking lot."

"And according to Reynoso, Lopez went to the window and watched him leave," Del said.

"That's just about how long it would have taken for us to get up to the apartment, but if Gonzalez told Lopez we were coming, why'd she shoot him?" Faz asked.

"Maybe she didn't tell him. Maybe she told the other guy, and when he knocked on the door and got no answer he figured Lopez wasn't home."

"Still doesn't explain why she'd shoot him."

"I can't answer that. Not yet," Del said. "All I'm certain about at this point is a dead man can't testify against Little Jimmy. And Gonzalez shooting Lopez pretty much put an end to our investigation, especially since the ballistics for the bullet that killed Monique Rodgers matches the .38 in Lopez's apartment."

"We don't have enough to accuse her," Faz said. "I mean we get Reynoso to say Gonzalez told her what to say and Gonzalez will just deny it."

"And if it comes out that I lied and told her you were wearing a body camera . . ."

"Your balls will be frying right next to mine."

Del nodded. "I'm going to give Los Angeles a call tomorrow and see if I can talk to some people down there, try to find out what they know about her."

"Run an address for her," Faz asked.

"I can't do that. You know that, Faz." Officers were not supposed to run addresses unless the address related to a specific case.

"Just get me an address. I'm going stir-crazy sitting here. Let me keep an eye on Gonzalez while she's off duty. Has anyone checked Lopez's phone to find out who he was calling or texting?"

"Not yet. I drove straight here. I'll get on it tomorrow." Del sat back, shaking his head. After a few moments he said, "What a shit storm."

"A shit storm within a shit storm," Faz agreed.

CHAPTER 40

Armed with a smiling picture of Shea in a medical coat, as well as the DMV report indicating he drove a white 2017 Tesla Model X, Tracy and Kins pulled into the parking structure for the medical complex late Friday afternoon. Tracy had called the clinic again, posing as a mother with a sick daughter, and trying to see Shea that afternoon. She was told he was booked.

Parking spaces for doctors' cars were located on the ground floor closest to the building entrance. They did not see a white Tesla.

"That car has a price tag of about $125,000," Kins said as they pulled into the parking lot and found a parking space. "So I'm guessing we should only see two or three."

"My dad was a doctor and he drove a truck," Tracy said. "If Shea is driving a hundred-thousand-dollar car and living in Medina, he either comes from money or he married into it. It's rare these days for a pediatrician to earn that kind of money in medicine."

"Not to mention spending a couple thousand a month on a concubine."

"Not to mention," Tracy said.

A white Tesla entered the parking structure. "That's his car."

"And that's him," Kins said when Shea pulled into a doctor's parking stall and stepped out. The back doors of the car rose like the wings of a bird.

Tracy and Kins quickly approached. "Dr. Shea?" Tracy said.

Shea had removed a sport coat from the backseat and startled at the sound of his name. His eyes narrowed. "Yes."

Tracy flashed her badge. "I'm Detective Crosswhite. This is Detective Rowe. Can we have a minute?"

"What about?"

"Vita Kumari," Tracy said.

Shea's eyes flashed recognition but he said, "I don't know anyone by that name."

"Yeah, you do," Kins said. "So, don't go there, okay? We know all about the sugar dating, sugar babies, and sugar daddies. You'd be the daddy. She'd be the baby. Am I right?"

Shea instantly deflated, which had been Kins's intent. "What is it you want?"

"Maybe it would be better if we spoke in your office rather than here in a parking lot?" Tracy said.

"Did something happen to Vita?" Shea asked. His concern sounded sincere, but officers said Ted Bundy had also sounded sincere.

"Why do you ask?" Kins said.

"Because I have two detectives standing outside my car telling me they want to talk to me about Vita."

Kins looked at Tracy. "Good point."

"Yes," Tracy said to Shea. "Something happened to her."

Shea looked across the garage to the sliding glass doors of the building. "Follow me." He led them up a stairwell and used a key to unlock an interior door. They followed him along a hallway carpeted with railroad tracks and train cars that meandered past a mural of an African safari with monkeys in the trees, elephants and lions, and a cheetah lying on a branch overhanging a river. They continued down a hall cluttered with weight and height scales, and eye charts.

"Dr. Shea—" A woman in a blue uniform stepped from one of the patient rooms. Her eyes drifted to Tracy and Kins. "I thought you'd left for the evening."

Surprisingly, Shea introduced them as Seattle detectives. "I came back to do a little paperwork. Hopefully I won't be long."

Shea stepped to a door with his name on an engraved plate and pushed it open. The furnishings were austere for someone driving such an expensive car. Shades, the see-through variety, covered his window. He had a view of the 405 freeway.

"Have a seat." Shea gestured to two chairs and moved behind his desk, which had a light veneer, in keeping with the office décor. A large computer screen took up much of the surface. On the wall behind him hung several framed degrees. He'd attended Gonzaga University—the Jesuits would surely not condone his sugar-daddy profile—had obtained his medical degree from the University of Washington, and was board certified in pediatrics. He sat. "You said something happened to Vita?"

"When's the last time you saw Kavita?" Tracy asked.

"Monday night."

"What did you do?"

Shea cleared his throat. He looked younger than his forty-four years. He had a habit of pushing blond strands of a boyish haircut from his forehead. "We went to dinner, then to a hotel in Kirkland, as was our routine."

"Where did you go to dinner?" Tracy asked.

"Lila's Café. It's in Kirkland. The reservation was in my name."

"And the hotel?"

"The Marriott. Also in Kirkland."

"Also in your name?" Kins said.

Tracy kept notes. If Shea was trying to hide anything he was doing a poor job of it.

"No," Shea said.

"Was the reservation under Kavita's name?" Kins asked.

"Yes."

"Fairly bold actions for a married man living in Medina, isn't it?" Kins said. "Weren't you worried about being seen?"

Shea sat back. He loosened his tie and unbuttoned the collar of his shirt. "If anyone saw us at dinner, Vita was a student looking to practice pediatric medicine."

"And what was she at the hotel?" Kins asked. God he could be a sarcastic pain in the ass when they needed him to be.

"We never went into the hotel together," Shea said. "Vita always obtained the room."

"And the hotel management never asked her why she needed a room the same day and time every week?" Kins asked.

"She told them she was in pharmaceutical sales and met with clients on the Eastside early Tuesday mornings. She brought luggage with her."

This was all very neat. "So, this was a standing engagement?" Tracy said.

"For the most part, yes."

"What does that mean?" Tracy said.

"It means we met on Monday nights unless something came up for either of us."

"How would you let each other know if something came up?" Tracy asked.

"We would text. Sometimes we'd call."

Tracy glanced at Kins. "How often did that happen where one of you would have to change your plans?" She didn't care. She was more interested in Shea's comment that they texted each other.

"Rarely. I don't remember it happening."

"And did you text for other reasons?"

"Only to confirm our meetings, and locations."

"You didn't ask if she liked piña coladas and getting caught in the rain?" Kins said, deliberately trying to provoke Shea to determine if he had a short fuse and was easily prone to anger.

Shea looked directly at Kins. "No," he said.

Tracy said, "You used your phone to send these texts? Weren't you worried about your wife reading your messages?"

Shea shook his head. "I never used my phone. We each had burner phones."

"Kavita also?" Tracy asked. This was news to them. Only her personal cell phone had been found in the hole. Shea would have known to take the burner phone if he'd killed her. But then, why would he tell them about it? Could he have thought this through, and decided that if questioned he'd bring up the subject of the burner phones for that very reason, because it wouldn't make sense for him to do so if guilty?

"Yes," he said.

"Did you text to confirm your Monday meeting this week?"

"Yes."

"And did Vita respond?"

"Yes."

"Do you have your phone?"

Shea used a key on his ring and opened the bottom drawer of his desk. He pulled out a cheap cell phone, powered it up, and entered a password. After a minute, he handed Tracy the phone. Kavita Mukherjee had confirmed their date Monday night at 4:14 p.m. She then texted him again at just after five thirty to say she was running late due to traffic. Tracy suspected that wasn't the truth, since that was the night Aditi had come home and told her she was married and moving to London with her husband. More important, whoever had killed Vita had taken her burner phone but not her cell phone. Again, Tracy wondered if the act was deliberate, to throw them off. Shea certainly had reason to do so.

Tracy looked to Kins before redirecting her attention to Shea. "Why Monday nights?"

"My wife has book club the first and third Mondays of every month. Girls' night out. So she says."

"Who watches your daughters?" Tracy asked.

The fact that Tracy knew he had daughters caused Shea to pause, which had been her intent. She wanted Shea to think they already knew a lot more than they did. "We have a nanny."

"Does your wife work?" Kins said.

Shea chuckled at this. "God, no. She's one of the Umberto children. You know, the chain tool shops?"

"I thought I read in the newspaper that the family sold those stores a few years back," Kins said. "A couple hundred million, wasn't it?"

"Two hundred and eighty-six million," Shea said. "But the family remained a part of the board for five years. Last year they didn't like how the stores were being run and bought them back. They have what you might call 'disposable income.'"

"Why did you say *so she says* when I asked where your wife goes on Monday nights?" Tracy asked.

Shea sat back, rocking in his chair. "I suspect that my wife has a boyfriend and it isn't her first."

Kins nodded. "And you thought you'd do the same?"

Shea shrugged.

"So why a sugar baby?" Tracy said.

"Because I can't very well go out and pick up somebody at the local gym or the coffee shop, can I? My wife's family is well known all over the Eastside."

"And if your wife found out it would be the excuse to kick you out, and she'd be gone, along with her money," Kins said.

"Maybe, Detective. She isn't necessarily setting the moral high ground, but with that much money you tend to establish the morals."

"Why don't you just divorce?" Kins said.

"Because we have two daughters under ten who adore their father—their mother not so much. So, we make things work. For them."

"How many sugar babies do you have?" Tracy asked, stumbling over the words "sugar babies."

"I had three. Kavita and two others."

"Where did you find the time? And the stamina?" Kins asked.

"I saw the other two less frequently, maybe once every couple of months."

"You saw those two separately or together?" Kins asked.

Shea took a moment. "Together."

"A threesome," Kins said, continuing to pick at the scab to see if it would bleed.

"How did you keep the payments to Vita and these other two girls from your wife?" Kins asked.

"I made direct deposits from my account into Vita's account. It's numbered. No names. If asked I could say it was the health club payment. Not that it would matter. My wife pays no attention to our finances, especially mine. She doesn't have to. We have a money manager for her trust, but she can pretty much do what she wants with it. My income, by comparison, is minuscule and of little interest to her. I paid the other two girls cash."

"When you saw Kavita Monday night what was she like? What was her demeanor?" Tracy asked.

Shea gave this some thought, as if he'd already forgotten. "She seemed fine, but then, that was part of our agreement."

"Agreement?" Kins asked.

"We had a written agreement forbidding questions about our personal lives or discussing our personal problems."

"Nothing that could put a damper on the sex," Kins said.

"Did Kavita ever mention a boyfriend?" Tracy asked.

Shea shook his head.

"What did you talk about when you were together?" Kins asked.

"Many things. Vita is very knowledgeable on many subjects. She wants to be a pediatrician. She asked me about my practice and my patients. She's very interested in world and local news, and surprisingly knowledgeable about sports, particularly the Seahawks. Our evenings were enjoyable. I looked forward to them."

"So, you didn't notice anything out of the ordinary that evening?" Tracy said.

"Actually, there was something; Vita advised me that she was ending our agreement." Shea said this matter-of-factly, without emotion, and Tracy wondered if he'd rehearsed it, perhaps anticipating this moment also.

"Did she say why?" Tracy said.

"She told me she had enough money to at least start medical school, and that had always been her goal."

"And this came out of the blue?" Kins asked.

"No. She had told me up front that she was trying to earn money to attend medical school, and that she'd quit when she did."

"Did she say anything else?" Tracy asked.

Shea shrugged. "Nothing that I recall."

"Part of the don't-burden-me-with-your-personal-crap clause of the agreement?" Kins said.

"I don't know, Detective. She said there'd been some changes in her life, that she intended to apply to schools in the fall, and to use her free time to study for the MCATs."

"And how did you feel about that?" Tracy said.

"I was happy for her," Shea said without hesitation. "She's a smart girl. She'll make a good doctor."

Tracy noticed the present tense.

"How did you feel about her moving on?" Kins asked.

"Disappointed. I enjoyed our time together and the relationship had become stable. I was going to have to decide whether I wanted to start all over again."

"Were you upset?" Tracy said.

"No," Shea said. "As I said, we both knew from the start that this was not about developing a future relationship. That was never going to happen."

"So how did you feel about her?" Kins asked. "It doesn't sound like it was love. What was it?"

Shea gave that question some thought. "I guess I thought of her as a business associate."

"And this was just, what, her exercising a clause in that business agreement?" Kins said.

"That was always on the table . . . for both of us."

"What time did you leave the hotel Monday night?" Tracy asked.

"Around nine—a little before. It was still light out. I always left at the same time. My wife usually got home from her book club at nine thirty."

"And Vita? When did she leave?" Tracy said.

"I have no idea. As I said, I left before her. She was free to use the room for the night if she chose, or to go home."

"You left her alone in the hotel room," Kins said.

"Always."

"How often did she spend the night?" Kins asked.

"I really don't know."

"Also not something you discussed?"

"No."

"Your nanny can confirm the time that you returned home that night?"

"Yes. As I said, it's always the same time."

"What's her name?" Tracy asked. Shea provided the name of the nanny, and Tracy wrote that down, along with the young woman's phone number. Then she asked, "What name did Kavita check in under?"

Shea shrugged. "I assume Vita Kumari."

Kins sat forward, his arms resting on the desk. "Dr. Shea, did you consider this relationship to be just a wee bit exploitive?"

Tracy wanted to roll her eyes, but given the gravity of the situation, she refrained.

Shea sat back. He looked tired. "Look, Detectives, I recognize the relationship was out of the ordinary. But it worked for me, for both of us." He shrugged. "What were my options? Go out to a bar and pick up women? I wasn't much good at that when I was young. I doubt I would be much better now. Plus, then you're dealing with different people, STDs, and who knows what else. And when did I have the time to go out and do that?" He paused as if awaiting an answer. Then he said, "I heard about this dating site and I created a profile, just to see what might happen. For the first six months, it was pretty much the shits. The women were not very interesting. I was just about to call it quits when I saw this profile of a beautiful young woman. She said she wanted tuition money to attend medical school. It was refreshing. Did it feel wrong? Yes, to a certain degree, but I figured that this way, at the very least, I could do some good with my money."

"So, what, you're just like Sallie Mae?" Kins said, referencing the student loan service.

This time Shea did not back down. "In a sense, I guess I am, Detective."

"And those other two girls who you have the threesome with, are you paying their school tuition also?"

Shea ignored him.

"What name did you use on the site?" Tracy asked.

"Charles Francis," he said. "My first and middle names. You haven't said why you're asking me all these questions. I'm assuming something happened to Vita?"

"She's dead," Kins said. He and Tracy watched Shea's reaction closely.

His eyes narrowed and watered and he pressed his lips together. After a moment he said, “How?” The word caught in his throat. Tracy didn’t think he was acting, but she couldn’t be certain.

“That’s what we’re trying to determine.”

“But you believe someone killed her. That’s why you’re here. You think I had something to do with Vita’s death?”

“Did you?” Kins asked.

“No,” Shea said, looking between them. Then he said, “My God” in a quiet voice. “Do I need an attorney?”

“I don’t know, Doctor, that’s up to you,” Kins said. “We’re just here to ask questions, and try to piece together, as best we can, Kavita’s evening.”

“I left her in the hotel room,” Shea said, “alive.”

CHAPTER 41

Saturday, July 14, 2018

Faz adjusted in his car seat, his body already developing aches and pains from sitting for too long. He had the window down; the temperature remained tolerable, though the weatherman had predicted a weekend high of ninety-two in Seattle. Faz had arrived in Seattle's Capitol Hill neighborhood at just after six that morning. Upon his arrival, he'd driven down the driveway of the three-story apartment building to confirm that Gonzalez's red Audi A8 was parked in one of the tenant stalls. It was a nice car, though an older model. Still, it made Faz wonder if Gonzalez was somehow supplementing her income.

He'd retreated and parked his Subaru facing south on Twelfth Avenue, across the street from the apartment building and the lone driveway out, and settled in to wait. That had been close to six hours ago.

Faz checked his phone but did not find any messages from Del, whom he knew was making phone calls to Los Angeles, trying to get whatever information he could on Andrea Gonzalez. He took a sip of water from one of the bottles in the small cooler on the passenger seat.

He'd told Vera that he had a follow-up visit with a psychiatrist and a meeting with one of the union lawyers, and that he anticipated being out for most of the day. He didn't like lying to her, but given the circumstances, he also didn't want to add to her worries.

Faz sat up when the sun glistened off the polished hood of the red Audi cresting the inclined driveway. The Audi stopped to allow a northbound car to pass, then turned away from him. Faz put the bottle back in the cooler, started the Subaru, and pulled away from the curb.

Faz knew the Capitol Hill area well. Half a block west, at Cal Anderson Park, he and Vera had enjoyed picnics while watching Antonio play baseball and soccer. They were also close to the freeway entrances for Interstate 5. Gonzalez turned left onto Denny Way and took the on-ramp south. Faz stayed in the right lane, several cars behind the Audi, just in case Gonzalez exited suddenly, a trick to detect surveillance. She drove past downtown Seattle, where the traffic became congested and ultimately slowed to a crawl. Faz had to be careful to remain behind the Audi, which was not easy with traffic in the lanes proceeding unevenly. Though he wore dark sunglasses and a Mariners baseball cap, Del said disguising Faz was like trying to hide a grizzly behind a hankie.

Gonzalez drove the Audi past the exits for the International District. She wasn't switching lanes or increasing and decreasing her speed, another technique to detect surveillance. Minutes later, she exited onto Corson Avenue, still heading southwest, toward Georgetown, though Faz suspected Georgetown would not be her final stop. He sat up, feeling nerves of anticipation. At Marginal Way, Gonzalez turned left toward Boeing Field. Faz slowed again when the traffic lightened, not wanting to get too close. He watched Gonzalez turn right on Sixteenth Avenue South toward the South Park Bridge over the Duwamish.

"Bingo," he said.

It was possible Gonzalez was just visiting friends, but the odds of that were about as low as the odds that Sandy Blaismith had driven into South Park to meet with a fitness trainer. Faz didn't believe in coincidences; people usually had a purpose for their actions, and he suspected Gonzalez had a purpose that afternoon.

Gonzalez turned onto Cloverdale, but drove past the house where Faz and Del had confronted Little Jimmy. The car and foot traffic increased, families dressed for the summer weather walked the sidewalks, all seemingly headed in the same direction, like fans walking to the start of a sporting event or a concert.

Gonzalez turned on Eighth Avenue South, then again on South Sullivan. Faz followed and saw signs for the South Park Community Center. Farther down the road he noted white tents pitched on the grass field adjacent to the center. With the window down, he heard the horns of a mariachi band, and he smelled food cooking. When he reached the corner, he decided not to turn, in case Gonzalez was now paying closer attention, but he also had to be careful he didn't lose her in the crowd if she got out of her car.

The Audi slowed and turned into the community center parking lot, though the lot looked to be full. Faz pulled to the curb across the street, blocking a driveway, and watched Gonzalez drive her car onto the lawn. A parking attendant quickly approached her, but whatever Gonzalez said, or showed him—likely her police ID—it was enough for the attendant not to hassle her. When Gonzalez got out of the car, Faz paid particular attention to her clothing—sunglasses, white shorts, tennis shoes, and a blue T-shirt. She reached back inside the Audi and retrieved a floppy hat, placing it on her head. The brim drooped low, partially obscuring her face. Whatever her purpose, Gonzalez did not want to be identified. The hat, however, would make her easier to follow.

She walked across the lawn toward the white tents.

Faz saw a parked car pull away from the curb and quickly took the vacated spot. An enterprising young man approached the driver's side window and asked for a five-dollar parking fee. Faz paid the ransom, ditched his blue windbreaker in the backseat, and crossed Eighth Avenue into the park.

People strolled the lawn, some eating corn on the cob, others soft tacos and churros. The booths displayed Latino art—paintings and other trinkets. Faz picked up a brochure from one of the tables, declined a sample of food, and looked over the crowd for the drooping hat and blue top. He didn't see her.

He migrated through the crowd, listening to the guitars and trumpets. Women in bright-colored dresses danced on a stage. In the center of the grass field, a wrestling ring had been erected and wrestlers, dressed in ornate *luchador* masks, colorful tights, and knee-high boots, mingled with the crowd. Faz continued to search, going from one tent to the next. He crossed the lawn and started up the other side, looking in the booths and at the people lined up for the food trucks. Beads of sweat trickled from beneath his hat and down his temples and cheeks. He jerked to a stop when he saw the hat and blue top disappear around the back of a tent. Rather than follow, he moved farther down the lawn to the other side of the tent. Gonzalez emerged into the gap between the two tents. She had her head down and appeared to be texting on her phone, unaware of Faz's presence. Faz angled his body, as if interested in the wrestlers, but kept an eye on Gonzalez, who lowered her phone and paced. A man walked down the alley. He had his back to the field, preventing Faz from getting a good look at his face. Faz retrieved his phone, as if to take a picture of the wrestlers, flipped the view, and angled the camera until he could see behind him—Gonzalez stood speaking to the man.

Faz was about to snap a picture when someone bumped him, knocking the phone off center. "Sorry," a young man said.

Faz smiled. "No worries." He redirected the phone to the gap between the two tents. Gonzalez and the man were gone. Faz turned, searching. Gonzalez was crossing the field in the direction of her parked car. Whatever she had come to say, she'd apparently said it. Though Faz wanted to follow her, he sensed it more important to follow the man, try to get a picture, and learn his identity. He turned back to the tents but didn't initially see the man. Three tents down, he saw him step into the back of a tent where a woman sold beaded trinkets and two young children sat at a nearby table sliding beads onto string. The man and woman spoke briefly, but Faz saw his face only in profile. The man kissed her and bent and kissed the two children. Then he turned and disappeared out the back of the tent before Faz could get a good look at his face. About to follow, Faz stopped when the man quickly returned, apparently in response to a question from the woman, giving Faz a good look at his face.

He wore dark sunglasses and a baseball hat, but Faz was certain he recognized him.

CHAPTER 42

Tracy called Kelly Rosa. "Did you complete your report yet for Kavita Mukherjee?"

"Working on it," Rosa said. "But you're not the only one calling."

"Bellevue?"

"Yep. Last night before I went home."

"How long can you stall?"

"They're asking for my preliminary findings, so I'd say not long."

Kaylee Wright had said much the same thing when Tracy called her. She'd have to provide Bellevue with something soon.

Tracy and Kins drove to Park 95 to pick up the flash drive onto which Andrei Vilkotski had copied six months of Kavita Mukherjee's text messages from her phone, and to find out where Katie Pryor was on securing other court orders. Tracy loaded the flash drive on her laptop, and she and Kins went through the information. Nolasco had tried to call each of them late Friday afternoon, but they hadn't taken his calls, anticipating that he was calling to tell them to transfer the file to Bellevue.

"Some nasty text messages from her brother," Kins said, stretching his back. "He's a piece of work."

Tracy had typed "Nikhil" into her search window and pulled up his text messages to his sister. She read a message in which Nikhil told Kavita that her disobedience of her mother and father's wishes was juvenile and disrespectful.

> You are causing unnecessary stress and aggravation for the whole family. Are you so ashamed to be Indian that you would go so far as to hurt Ma and Baba? It is time you came home and stopped behaving like a child.

"Do we know Nikhil's whereabouts Monday night?" Kins asked.

"Home with his mother and grandparents," Tracy said. "The father was returning from a business trip to Los Angeles, and Sam spent the night at a friend's home after a soccer game. Should be easy enough to confirm."

"She didn't respond to any of Nikhil's text messages. That had to piss him off, don't you think?" Kins asked.

"Or he was used to it." Tracy read the text messages Aditi had sent Monday night and Tuesday morning expressing concern and imploring Kavita to respond. She also found the text message Sam, Kavita's younger brother, had sent Monday night.

> Hi Vita. I was just thinking of you and wondering what you are doing. I have a soccer game tonight at Roosevelt near your apartment. It's at 6:oo. Ma and Baba cannot attend so it will just be me. I was hoping you would come.

Kavita responded to her younger brother almost immediately.

Hi Sam. Thanks for the invite. I miss you. Today has been very hard. I suppose you heard that Aditi is married? I'm betting everyone knows by now. She came back from India and moved out of our apartment. She's moving to London. Her husband is an engineer. I feel so alone, Sam. I feel like I have lost a sister. I can only imagine what Ma had to say when she heard the news! Mrs Dasgupta must be throwing it in her face. ☹ I wish I could come to your game, but I can't tonight. I have a date.

I'll be thinking good thoughts for you. Text me when the game is over and tell me how you did? I love you, little brother.

"The date had to be with Shea," Kins said.

"Definitely."

"And the last line, asking Sam to text her," Kins said, pointing to the screen. "That's not a woman thinking of killing herself."

Tracy agreed. She read Sam's response sent after the game.

Vita, we won! I didn't score but I played well. Call me when you get home. I'm staying at my friend's tonight so I'll have my phone.

"What did he mean by 'I'll have my phone'?" Kins asked.

"The mother takes his phone at night," Tracy said.

"Shannah does the same thing. If she didn't, the boys would never get their homework done."

Tracy read the message Sam sent Kavita later that evening, after ten at night.

Vita did you get my message? I called but you didn't answer. Call me.

Sam sent a third message Tuesday, after Tracy and Katie Pryor had visited the family.

> Vita? Are you there? The police were here looking for you. Everyone is worried about you. Ma and Baba are worried. I'm worried. Please, if you get this, could you call?

There was also a text message from Nikhil.

> Vita, the police have come looking for you. You need to stop this nonsense and come home.

"Nothing from the mother or father," Tracy said. "That's odd, isn't it?"

"Seems odd to me," Kins said. "Maybe they asked Sam and Nikhil to contact her. I know Shannah would be texting every five minutes."

"Seems odd," Tracy said again, thinking of her own mother and father when Tracy's sister had disappeared. She and her parents hadn't had the luxury of cell phones then.

CHAPTER 43

Faz watched the man exit the back of the tent and walk east, toward Eighth Avenue. Though the man wore a baseball-style hat and sunglasses, Faz was sure he was the same person Faz saw in the lobby of Eduardo Lopez's apartment building just before he and Gonzalez went up the elevator. The man had looked at both of them, though his eyes had lingered on Gonzalez. At the time, Faz had thought the prolonged stare had to do with the man deducing that they were detectives.

No longer.

Gonzalez had come to South Park to give the man a message, or to obtain one, since nothing appeared to have exchanged hands between them. Whatever Gonzalez had said, the man was on the move. So, too, was Gonzalez.

At the very least, Faz needed to get a better picture of the man to possibly help identify him. He walked parallel to and slightly behind the man as they crossed the lawn. When the man reached Eighth Avenue, he turned right and walked south. Faz crossed the street to where he'd parked his car and watched the man until he turned right at the intersection of Eighth Avenue and South Cloverdale. Faz quickly got into the car and pulled a U-turn. At the intersection—a red light—he inched forward to look down the street, but he did not see the man walking down the sidewalk.

Faz swore. He turned the corner, proceeding slowly, searching the building windows and the alleys between them. He heard a powerful car engine turn over. A moment later, a red Chevelle with black hood stripes pulled from a space along a cyclone fence and approached the street. The man sat behind the wheel. Faz drove past, watching in his rear and side mirrors. The car pulled into the street behind him and Faz recognized it as the same car that had driven past Monique Rodgers's apartment complex with Little Jimmy in the passenger seat.

"Now this is getting interesting." He turned right at the next intersection, ensured the driver did not follow, and pulled a U-turn. He turned right at the corner and settled in fifty yards and one car behind the Chevelle. The Chevelle crossed beneath an overpass for State Route 99. Cloverdale curved to the left and became First Avenue South. Faz and Gonzalez had driven this same road to Eduardo Lopez's apartment and he wondered if the driver, too, lived in the apartment complex and was simply going home. A moment later, the road forked. The Chevelle took the fork to the right—away from the front entrance to Lopez's apartment building. "Scratch that thought," Faz said.

The Chevelle continued along the side of the building, to the apartment parking lot in the rear, but he slowed and instead turned right, into a driveway for a public storage complex.

Faz continued past, looking to his left but still unable to read the car's license plate. He continued along a chain-link fence with three strands of barbed wire strung along the top. Halfway down the block, he pulled to the curb beneath the shade from a tree and turned to look out the back window. The Chevelle had stopped at a chain-link gate inside the storage facility. The man had his arm out the window and punched numbers on a keypad. The gate rolled open and the Chevelle drove through and disappeared behind one of the storage buildings.

Faz considered the apartment building across the street. From what had been Eduardo Lopez's apartment, Lopez could have watched the storage facility twenty-four hours a day, seven days a week. Faz also knew from the prior visit that the storage facility was less than a half mile from Highway 509, which intersected Highway 518 near the Seattle-Tacoma Airport and eventually merged with I-5, the main artery extending from the Canadian border to Los Angeles.

It was all very convenient.

If Faz could get the license plate of the red Chevelle, he could hopefully obtain the car's registration and the name of the man Gonzalez had come to meet. He stepped from the car, looking through the fence and between the storage buildings, but he did not see the car.

He counted four rows of buildings with four buildings in each row. They were arranged in a grid so cars could drive between the units.

The driveway sloped uphill to a squat retail store at the back of the lot that likely rented the storage units and, based on signs in the windows, packing materials and U-Haul trucks.

Faz walked toward the store entrance, glancing down the asphalt drives between the buildings as he did, but he did not see the Chevelle. The man had either turned into one of the storage units, or he had parked at the far end of the lot, behind the last buildings. Faz decided the safest thing was to wait in his car until the Chevelle left the complex, then call Del and have him run the plate.

As he walked back down the driveway, he heard the mechanical sound of a motor engaging and saw the entry gate rolling open. A truck idled inside, preparing to leave the facility. When the car drove out, Faz stepped inside before the gate had rolled shut. Now all he needed to do was find the car, snap a picture of the plate, and leave. He noticed security cameras atop the buildings but dismissed them as cameras running on a loop that no one looked at unless there was a theft.

He continued down the asphalt to the intersection between the first two rows of buildings and looked around the corner. He did not see the

Chevelle. He walked past the second row of buildings and again looked, but still did not see the car. He moved to the end of the complex.

As he suspected, the Chevelle was parked at the back of the lot, alongside another red muscle car and a large U-Haul truck.

Faz lifted his phone, about to snap a picture of the license plates, when he heard what sounded like one of the orange doors to the units rolling open and men speaking Spanish. He moved in the only direction he could, along the back of the building. As he walked, he aimed the phone at the Chevelle's license plate and snapped a picture. Then he snapped a picture of the license plate of the second car. He had his head turned, his focus on the license plates.

When he reached the corner of the building, he felt the barrel of a gun press against his temple.

"Do something stupid, Detective, so I can put a bullet in your head."

CHAPTER 44

Early Saturday evening, Tracy and Kins returned to Police Headquarters.

Papers lay scattered across the table in the center of their bull pen, and the aroma of pizza permeated their work space from the MOD Pizza box on Faz's empty desk—late lunch or early dinner. Tracy ordinarily would have said no to pizza, but now that she was gaining weight, no matter what she ate, she figured she might as well enjoy it. She was starving; she and Kins had not eaten since early that morning.

Muted light filtered into the bull pen from the building's tinted windows. The C Team had gone out to eat, and Kins had turned off the flat-screen television so they could concentrate. No voices. No one-sided telephone calls. No click or clatter of keys on keyboards, just silence, and time to again review Kavita Mukherjee's e-mails and text messages to see if they were missing something and to theorize about what could have happened.

Tracy grabbed a slice of pizza and a napkin and returned to consider the papers on the center table. This was how she liked to work—everything in front of her, all at the same time. It forced her to think in a nonlinear manner—sequential thinking too often caused her to consider what should logically come next in an investigation, which could lead to missing something that did not logically follow. It was human nature for the mind to fill in blanks so things made sense, even when no evidence supported doing so. Murders didn't make sense. The vast majority were not meticulously planned, far from it. The vast majority occurred spur-of-the-moment.

Tracy took a bite of pizza. The pepperoni, red bell peppers, and garlic assaulted her taste buds. She and Kins would reek the remainder of the night and quite possibly in the morning. They agreed to work all night if they had to, as on Thursday, knowing that come morning they would likely have to surrender the case.

Tracy picked up Kaylee Wright's preliminary report, which reiterated what she'd told them in the park. Wright had found a few scattered prints that matched the sole of Kavita's shoes at the trailhead near the parking lot—indicating Kavita had walked into the park. She found more prints farther along the trail, though the stride had changed, indicating Kavita had been running. And she found prints in all different directions, as if Kavita had stopped, possibly because she'd heard something. The lack of similar prints along the trail leading to or around the abandoned well was also a clear indication that Kavita had not accidentally stumbled into the hole. The logical conclusion was that her killer had carried her.

When she lacked evidence, Tracy opted for common sense. "Let's assume she was carried to the hole," she said. "For one, Kavita was not small. She was five feet ten and one hundred and thirty pounds."

"A grown man could have carried her, but I agree, that's dead weight," Kins said.

"Charles Shea?" Tracy said. She walked to a whiteboard she'd found in one of the conference rooms and wrote "Shea" in blue.

"We still have to tie him to the park, and come up with a motive," Kins said. They'd called the park ranger, Margo Paige, late Friday afternoon. Paige had confirmed there were no cameras in the Bridle Trails parking lot. Too bad. Shea's car would have been hard to miss. Paige had said she would drive to Seattle on Saturday to look through the storage files for the park, and that she would call them if she found anything of interest.

"Shea could have convinced Kavita to take a walk with him. It was a beautiful night. Maybe he started acting strange, possessive, and Kavita ran to get away from him. She could have been turning in a circle, searching for a way out of the park and away from him when he came up behind her," Tracy said.

"But Kaylee didn't find two sets of shoeprints on the trail. She found just the one," Kins said.

"Kaylee didn't find much, given how dry the trails have been and how much use they get. Shea's prints could have been destroyed by a runner or by horses. Since Kaylee didn't have a print to look for, it isn't so obvious. As for a motive, it could also be as simple as: Shea developed personal feelings toward Kavita and was upset that she was ending their contract."

"Which also fits with your hypothesis that Kavita suddenly had twice as much money to start medical school and that was the reason she ended their relationship," Kins said.

"Which Shea confirmed," Tracy said.

"Okay, so what about the hole? How did he know about it?"

"Again, the simple answer would be that he was familiar with the park."

"But we don't know that he was. Medina isn't that close to Bridle Trails for him to take evening runs."

"I agree."

"I think we should start with who might have known about the hole."

"The family, for certain," Tracy said. "Her father said they took walks in the park together and hunted for mushrooms, which would have taken them off the beaten paths."

"We need to check the airline, determine if his alibi checks out. And add Aditi to that list," Kins said. "And her family. What do we know about them?"

Tracy wrote the names on the whiteboard, then turned and faced Kins. "Not a lot."

"Circle the father and Nikhil," Kins said. "Sam and the mother would have had difficulty carrying the body. Sam doesn't look like he breaks a hundred pounds. And what would be his motivation? I'd put someone random ahead of him."

Tracy wasn't yet buying that the crime was committed by someone random. For one, the theory didn't fit with the forensic evidence. Based on the damage to Kavita's skull—Rosa said the blows were purposeful, a possible indication the killer had been angry. She picked up Kelly Rosa's preliminary autopsy report. Rosa attributed the cause of death to blunt-force trauma to the left side of Kavita Mukherjee's head, just above the temple. Given the nature of the fracturing, Rosa further concluded that Mukherjee had been struck three times, which also supported an argument that the attack had been a possible crime of passion born of rage or anger. Rosa's report further detailed that there was no physical trauma to indicate Kavita had been raped, though she'd had sexual intercourse within twenty-four hours of her death—that having been with Shea.

"No rape," she said.

"And no robbery," Kins said. "Shea would not have needed the money, and he would not have taken her personal possessions because they would have linked her to him."

"He also would have known to take her burner phone," Tracy said. "And that her regular phone would not likely have anything incriminating."

"The report implies the person surprised her," Kins said. "She had no bruises, cuts, or scratches anywhere on her body to indicate she'd put up a struggle or had attempted to defend herself against an attack."

"Mukherjee ran to get away. Shea could have surprised her when she stopped. It would have been dark and difficult to see, and there were certainly enough trees for him to hide behind."

"What if we assume the killer either followed her to the park or was already in the park?" Kins said.

"Then we have a different problem—why did Kavita go there?" Tracy said.

Kins gave it more thought. "Let's assume she was upset about Aditi."

"She *was* upset about Aditi."

"So what if she went there because she'd planned to meet someone there, or someone wanted to meet her there?"

"Not Sam," Tracy said. "He was at a game. And not the father, who was traveling. Not likely she'd want to meet Nikhil or her mother."

"That leaves Aditi," Kins said. "Or someone random. A second sugar daddy?"

"There's no evidence of a second sugar daddy, and her bank account doesn't indicate a series of deposits from a different number. And we have the same problem. Why did she go into the park?"

Kins took a drink of soda, studying the board. "So, what we know is she walked into the park, which we have to assume means she went there voluntarily, or at least seemingly voluntarily."

"I think that's the key," Tracy said. She drew a timeline on the board. "She arrived at the hotel at just after 7:30." Hotel video of the lobby documented the time Mukherjee obtained a room. "And she left at 8:52." A camera in the parking lot captured Mukherjee leaving the hotel alone. "Who knew she was going to the hotel?" Tracy asked.

"Shea for certain," Kins said.

Tracy underlined his name on the whiteboard. "Maybe he didn't leave the hotel. Maybe he was waiting in the car to follow her, without her knowledge."

"What about Shea's wife?" Kins said. "Shea indicated she suspected he was cheating on her. What if she followed him, then followed Kavita?"

Tracy wrote "Mrs. Shea" on the whiteboard. "Neither explains why Kavita would have gone to the park, but let's keep them up there for now." Then she said, "What about Aditi? What if Aditi knew Kavita had a date and knew the details of that date? Shea said he and Kavita kept to a routine and used the same hotel. Aditi might have known that routine."

"So then she lied when she said she didn't know Kavita had a date?" Kins said.

"Maybe . . . or—" Tracy thought for a moment. "Even if she didn't know their routine, she had the ability to follow Kavita using the app on her phone."

"Yeah, but you said she seemed genuinely surprised when you asked her about the shared Apple account."

"She did, but maybe she knew that question was coming. And Aditi could have lured Kavita to the park without following her from the hotel. She was living close by with her parents. She could have called Kavita and asked her to meet before she left for London."

"And the park makes sense because Kavita would not have wanted to go to the house and face the mother and the rest of the family," Kins said. "You said she didn't even want to see them at the apartment."

"That's what Aditi told me."

"So maybe the park is a place they both know and Kavita would have gone there willingly. But what's Aditi's motivation to kill her best friend?"

Tracy paced near the table. "Jealousy?" she said.

"About?"

"Maybe we've been looking at this from the wrong perspective. Maybe, instead of Kavita's perspective, we should look at it from Aditi's perspective?"

"Which is what?"

"For one, Kavita was going to live the life she and Aditi had dreamed of living since they were little girls. In fact," Tracy said, thinking of their conversation with Aditi, "with Aditi no longer going to medical school, Kavita was prepared to get started. It was no longer just a dream. It was a reality."

"That's true," Kins said.

"So what if Kavita told Aditi about the money, about the fact that she had enough for the two of them to at least get started."

"It's too late," Kins said. "Aditi has already gone and got married."

"What if Aditi has regrets, second thoughts, doubts. And this was just like Kavita, Aditi would think. Kavita was the prettier of the two, the one who got all the attention and got all the breaks."

"Including the doctor who is paying for Kavita's medical school, while Aditi got the losers who wanted blow jobs in the car."

"And Kavita did better in school, though Aditi worked harder," Tracy said.

"That would piss you off," Kins said. "It would piss me off."

Tracy paused, considering it. Then she said, "That's a lot for a young woman to have to take."

"It is, but enough to kill her best friend?"

"Crimes of passion or anger don't always have a reason. The person acts on impulse. Consider that Aditi knew the park. She and Rashesh were living close by, and she and Kavita grew up together and played there together."

"You're saying she could have known about the well."

"Could have," Tracy said.

"How did she carry the body?"

"She had Rashesh, or maybe someone else in her family," Tracy said.

"And Aditi could have driven Kavita's car back to the apartment building with someone following her," Kins said. "It fits. But the biggest question is still motivation."

"I agree. So what if Aditi went to India for a cousin's wedding, like she said," Tracy said, thinking out loud as she paced. "And while she's there, her mother and family start in on her about getting married?"

"They likely did."

"The pressure would have been significant, and this time Aditi did not have Kavita for moral support. Rashesh and his family could also have been in on it. Aditi said the fathers had grown up together."

"The two families had this planned," Kins said. "I can see that."

"Aditi said she and Kavita were both under pressure from their families, but that Kavita was the stronger of the two. What if her family used this opportunity, when Aditi was thousands of miles away from Kavita, to pressure her, and Aditi couldn't fend off that pressure alone?"

"She allowed the marriage to happen to satisfy her parents, not because she wanted it? You're saying she, what . . . snapped or something?"

"Not snapped, just that she's in a different country and this man, this successful, single man, shows interest in her. She said that she was ready to submit to her mother's wishes and didn't want to do the sugar dating from the start. Both their families are at the wedding, and the mother's arguments start making sense. Aditi isn't going to be young forever; she isn't going to have a lot of other suitors—a lot of other men, especially in the United States. Here's a man who wants her. At the very least it must have made her feel special. And she's away, in India, at a wedding. Getting married doesn't seem like such a bad thing."

"But," Kins said, "she has to come back to the States, back to her apartment."

"Back to the life that she had before she left, back to reality . . . And suddenly the magnitude of her decision begins to take hold."

"She realizes it was a mistake, a dumb mistake."

"Add to that the fact that Kavita then tells Aditi that she had enough money for both of them to get started in medical school and . . ."

Kins stood, nodding his head the way he did when things made sense. "She realizes how much she's thrown away. How close she had been to the dream."

"She could have been a doctor, just like her best friend," Tracy said. "And now she's not just married, she's moving to London, to another country, to live not only with a man she hardly knows, but with his entire family, and she's going to have to take care of all of them."

"It had to be overwhelming," Kins agreed. "Maybe too much."

"So let's say Aditi knew Kavita was with the doctor—it was a standing date—every Monday night. And she knew the park, and she knew the hole in the ground."

Kins grimaced, still struggling to come to grips with the information. "I hear you, I do. But to kill your best friend? To hit her with a rock?"

"Maybe she didn't set out to kill her. Maybe Aditi asks Kavita to meet her in the park to just talk to her. Maybe Aditi, overwhelmed by everything that had happened, just needed to talk to her best friend, to her sister, without her husband or anyone else present."

"It doesn't sound like she was going to get any sympathy from her parents," Kins agreed.

"She's panicked. She's frightened and not thinking clearly. And the park is a place where she and Kavita grew up together. It represents a time when they both still had their dreams." Tracy paced, trying out her theory, how it sounded when spoken out loud. It sounded right. It made sense. "Maybe Aditi wants help, and Kavita says there's nothing she can do."

"She could get a divorce," Kins said.

"I don't think so. It isn't done. At least that's what Kavita's mother indicated."

"Kavita had thirty thousand dollars, though. She could have helped her."

"But Aditi said Kavita was upset. She'd torn up Aditi's check. Maybe Kavita was still upset at Aditi for getting married without even calling her, without giving Kavita the chance to talk her out of it. Maybe they were both upset with each other. Sisters can be that way. They start arguing and one thing leads to another."

"And Kavita turns to walk away . . ."

"And Aditi, with her life crashing down all around her, angry and overwhelmed, picks up a rock and lashes out," Tracy said.

"We've seen married couples do it, two people seemingly in love and one does something stupid and the other reacts."

"Kavita was going to live Aditi's life, and Aditi hated her for it, at least in that moment," Tracy said.

"It sounds plausible, Tracy, it does, but how do we prove it?" Kins said.

Tracy thought for a moment. "Kavita's phone records. We know that Aditi tried to contact Kavita that night. We need to check for calls to Kavita's cell."

Kins searched through his computer screen, Tracy leaning over his shoulder. "Nothing," he said. "But she could have used the burner cell phone's number."

"Which would explain why it wasn't there," Tracy said. "It would have recorded a phone call from Aditi's cell phone number."

"We're going to need more, and my sense is we're not going to have the time to get it before Bellevue steps in."

"Maybe we can get more." Tracy returned to her desk and picked up the phone.

"Who are you calling?" Kins said.

"Andrei Vilkotski," she said.

CHAPTER 45

Faz never had a chance. The building at the front of the property was not just a retail store; it was also the property's surveillance center. He learned this as he was led inside a room and saw multiple computer screens providing around-the-clock surveillance of every inch of the storage facility from every conceivable angle. He'd been on one of those screens from the moment he stepped onto the property, and they'd been watching. The scope of the camera's coverage confirmed what he suspected, that the storage lockers were holding something much more valuable than other people's surplus home supplies.

The man who had put the barrel of a gun to Faz's head was the same steroid-induced bouncer who'd been standing guard in the driveway of Little Jimmy's home the night of his birthday party. Every vein in his arms looked like bloated worms burrowing beneath the skin, and his shoulders and chest muscles strained the fabric of a blue security shirt. He'd disarmed and handcuffed Faz, and he'd taken his cell phone, which was a problem, because Faz had not had the chance to transmit his location or any photographs to Del.

"I remember you from the other night," Faz said as the guard handcuffed his wrists around a three-inch pipe that ran the length of the wall. "That must have been one hell of a big bee that stung you. You really should consider carrying epinephrine to help reduce all that swelling."

The man looked at Faz like he was crazy but didn't verbally respond. Clearly, he didn't get the joke.

He left and returned minutes later, this time with the man Faz had followed from the park to the storage facility and a third man Faz did not recognize. They all spoke Spanish. Faz couldn't understand what they were saying, but he was pretty sure he knew the topic of their conversation.

How did he get here and what had he seen?

The man Faz had followed walked closer. "You're the detective from the apartment, the one who shot Eduardo."

"Not me," Faz said. "I was just an innocent bystander." He decided it best that he not reveal this guy's relationship with Andrea Gonzalez until he had a better sense about what was going on. "I'm going to need your names for my report."

"You are one stupid shit," the bouncer said.

"That must have been a bitch to spell on your grammar school tests. How about a nickname?"

The bouncer threw a hook, hitting Faz just above the right temple. It felt like he'd swung a sledgehammer. The blow knocked Faz from his feet and he dropped to his knees, though his hands remained extended above him, the cuffs unable to slide down past a metal strap bolted to the wall. His head pounded and he struggled to shake clear the stars assaulting his vision.

"Man," he said. "You guys really need to improve your sense of humor."

The bouncer stepped toward Faz, poised to deliver another blow, but the man Faz had followed stopped him, again speaking in Spanish. It developed into a heated discussion, until the bouncer turned and left.

"You realize I called my partner," Faz said from his knees. "He has your license plate and he knows where I am. So, anything happens to me, *Vaquero*, and you're looking at the mother of all shit storms. If I were you, I'd make a run for the border. We're not interested in you. We're interested in Little Jimmy. Give him up now, and vanish. It might just work."

The man turned his back to Faz, speaking softly to the third man in the room. Whatever he said, the man was not in agreement. He punctuated the air with animated hand gestures. In the mix of incomprehensible words, Faz heard "Little Jimmy" uttered in English multiple times, probably because *Pequeño* Jimmy just didn't have the same menacing ring to it.

After several minutes, the man he'd followed approached. "You're going to have to take that up with Little Jimmy. Here's a warning. He doesn't like you very much."

Faz felt a welt expanding on the side of his head where he'd been punched, and he was still struggling through the pain and the cobwebs. He decided the best defense in this instance was an offense, any offense, even a perceived offense. He shrugged. "You had your chance. All of you. Mark my words. Kill a cop and it's going to be fire and brimstone around here. They'll torch this place, burn down this whole operation, and all of you along with it. If you live, you'll be sharing a cell at Walla Walla. Don't say I didn't warn you."

CHAPTER 46

Kins looked at his watch. "It's after hours," he said. "Andrei isn't going to answer at this time of night."

"He's on that new detail," Tracy said, dialing the number. "Because of the cell phone thefts. And I have his mobile number."

"Put him on speaker."

Vilkotski answered on the fourth ring. "Andrei, it's Tracy Crosswhite and Kinsington Rowe. I have you on speaker."

"So, then I can assume you are not calling to whisper sweet nothings to me," Vilkotski said.

"I could do that, Andrei," Kins said.

"That I could do without," Vilkotski said. "Please don't tell me you're calling because someone stole your cell phone."

Tracy laughed. "We're sorry to call you at home, but we have another question for you about cell phones."

"Could be worse," he said. "I'm listening."

"If I used the Find My iPhone app on my mobile to find another person's phone, would there be some record of it?"

"A record? No. I mean, the person you were attempting to find might know, but that would only be if they took the time to look at the app," Vilkotski said.

"What would they be looking for?" Kins asked.

"The app places an arrow on your home screen, but only for a brief time. I think it is ten seconds, but don't quote me on it."

"You're saying the person would have to be looking at their phone at the time the app was activated, and know what to look for?" Kins asked.

"Exactly."

"Okay," Tracy said. "But I want to know if there is some type of record generated on the phone that is doing the search. For instance would there be some way to find out if I had searched for someone else's phone using the Find My iPhone app on my phone?"

"I don't believe so, but this I would have to research. What are you trying to determine?"

"Well, ultimately," Tracy said, "we'd like to determine if one person searched for another's mobile to find out where they were going."

"How old is the phone?" Vilkotski asked. "The phone your person is using to search for the other."

"I don't know," Tracy said. "Why?"

"Because you could forget about the app and just view the location history of the phone. Do that and you know everywhere the person has been."

Tracy looked to Kins.

"How would I do that, Andrei?" Kins said.

"You don't do anything. The phone does it. Get the phone. It stores the time and place of each location so that it can provide location services, like when you engage Google Maps and your phone knows your location. There were articles about this being an invasion of privacy. Hah." He gave a sharp, sardonic laugh. "This I find amusing. If you want your privacy invaded, you should live in Russia."

"Could someone disable this service?" Kins asked. "Could they turn it off?"

"They could, but that I do not see—not unless they're paranoid."

Tracy looked to Kins, who shook his head to indicate he had no further questions. "Thanks, Andrei," she said. "Hope we didn't disturb anything important."

"Could be worse," he said again. "This has been the highlight of my night."

Tracy disconnected and looked at her watch. "We need to get Aditi's phone."

"It's still just speculation, Tracy."

"Not if we get Aditi's phone and the history shows her at Bridle Trails State Park, it isn't."

"And if she tells us we're crazy and won't give us her phone, then what? I'm not sure we have probable cause."

"She and Kavita shared an account."

"That's not enough. We need something more."

"I agree," Tracy said. "We need her phone."

"That's a bit circular, don't you think? You going to make that argument to a judge: *We need her phone to prove we needed her phone*? We need something else. And if we go out there now and start asking her questions and get nowhere, she could toss that phone in England."

"What about the service provider? Maybe they can send us the records," Tracy said.

"Maybe, but this isn't an emergency like the need to find Kavita's phone. We're going to need a signed search warrant." Kins looked at his watch. "I don't know if we have time. What time did you say she was getting on a plane to London?"

"Tonight. Late."

The telephone on Tracy's desk rang. She spoke to Kins as she crossed the bull pen to answer it. "I say we drive to the airport tonight and take our chances."

She lifted the receiver. "Detective Crosswhite." Tracy listened for a moment, then turned to Kins, who had his back to her and had his cell phone to his ear, likely to update Shannah on when he'd be home. She snapped her fingers twice to get his attention, then picked up a pen from her desk and hurled it at him, hitting him in the back of the head.

Kins turned and Tracy put the caller on speakerphone. "I'm sorry, Ranger Paige, but could you repeat what you started to tell me so my partner can hear?"

"Sure. I was just saying that I went over to Seattle today and looked through the storage materials for the Bridle Trails State Park. I found that report of the rider whose horse fell down a well. I thought you might want it."

Kins approached. "How long ago was that report made?"

"Hang on." They heard the shuffling of papers. "It was nine years ago."

"Was anyone hurt?"

"No. The rider managed to get off before the horse fell. The horse broke a leg and had to be put down."

"Was the well anywhere near Kavita Mukherjee's home?"

"Is that the decedent?"

"Yes."

"I didn't know she lived near the park."

"It was the family home."

"If you provide me the address I can try to figure that out."

Tracy looked to Kins, who turned back to his desk to look up the Mukherjees' address.

"Is there a name on the report?" Tracy asked.

"Yeah, there is. The rider was fifteen years old. It's a foreign name. First name is Aditi. A-D-I-T-I."

Kins spun around at the sound of the name.

"The last name is Dasgupta. Do you need me to spell it? Detectives?"

CHAPTER 47

The back room had no windows. The only light came from the narrow gap at the bottom of the door. Faz had a sense that he'd been in the room for several hours. He'd heard others speaking in the adjacent room, but no one had been in to see him since the man he'd followed to the storage unit had left. He'd examined the pipe to which he had been cuffed, and pulled on the strap that had been bolted into the wall; it wasn't going to come loose.

He'd contemplated yelling, but given the layout of the storage facility, with the retail space at the front now closed, and a swath of trees and bushes at the rear, and the drone of cars from the nearby 509 freeway, no one was going to hear him. Little Jimmy's minions must have deduced the same thing, which was why they hadn't shoved a rag in Faz's mouth. On the other hand, none of them struck him as heirs to Einstein's throne either. It could have just been a mistake.

Instead of fighting a losing battle with the strapped pole, Faz had used his time to figure out when he'd start to be missed, and by whom. That was hard to say. Vera would certainly try to contact him after it got dark, but she was accustomed to his schedule changing quickly, and his frequent need to work late and not getting the chance to speak to her. She also had other, more pressing matters to worry about. Del was not likely to call him. Del was like Faz in that regard. He called if he had important information, or if he needed something. He didn't call to just shoot the shit. Del would also be conscientious of Vera's illness and he'd try to respect their privacy. So, unless Del learned something about Gonzalez from his contacts in Los Angeles, Faz didn't expect to hear from him. In other words, Faz could be in this room for a long time. Then again, maybe not long enough. He was more convinced than ever that Little Jimmy was moving drugs up and down the West Coast, and that he had stumbled onto the epicenter of that operation. With millions of dollars at stake, Little Jimmy couldn't very well let Faz go with a promise not to say anything. Hell, Jimmy didn't even need millions at stake to kill Faz. Like the guy had said, Jimmy hated Faz and held him responsible for Big Jimmy's death. Killing a cop, however, wasn't something anyone in the drug business did lightly, not if they wanted to fly under the radar. So maybe Faz could hope that Little Jimmy would at least be conflicted. Then again, Little Jimmy probably didn't even know how to spell "conflicted."

Faz heard men speaking Spanish on their way to the room. The door opened and the light came on. The bouncer and the man he'd followed entered the room. Behind them stood Little Jimmy, smiling. *Speak of the devil,* Faz thought.

"What is it they say about a patient man?" Little Jimmy asked.

The others in the room didn't have an answer. As Faz had speculated, they weren't about to give Einstein a run for his money.

"Come on, Detective Fatso. You know the answer."

"Can't say that I do, Jimmy."

"Good things, man. Good things come to a patient man."

"I think it's actually 'Good things come to those who wait,' but either way, I wouldn't get too excited if I were you. I'm not exactly a good thing."

"No? What are you going to tell me? Are you going to tell me that everyone knows you're here and they're on their way to rescue you?" His smile broadened. "We checked your phone, Detective. That's right. We got past your password—surprise. We aren't the dumb Mexicans you gringos take us for. You had some nice pictures of Francisco," he said, "but you hadn't sent anything to anybody. The way I see it, nobody knows you're here, man. You're on an island. You're that guy? What's his name?" He turned to ask the others in the room.

"Robinson Crusoe," Faz said.

"No, man, the actor. He talks to the volleyball . . . Tom Hanks. You're Tom Hanks, man."

"And how long do you think that's going to be, Jimmy? How long before people start missing a detective attempting to solve a murder?"

"I don't know. How many people out there love you enough to give a shit?"

"A lot, Jimmy. I'm very popular."

Little Jimmy stepped forward, still smiling. "Not in here you're not." He looked to the bouncer. "Hector here? He wants to take you apart with his hands. What did you do to piss him off so much?"

"I think it might have been the bee comment." Faz looked to Hector. "Was it the bee comment, Hector? The one about reducing the swelling? I was just trying to be helpful."

Hector looked at Faz, clearly still not understanding.

"You're a funny man, Detective Fatso," Little Jimmy said. "Were you this funny when you arrested my old man?"

"I've gotten funnier with age. I figure by ninety I'll be a riot."

"You know what's funny? You thinking you're going to make it to ninety." Little Jimmy laughed and the others joined him.

"I'll see ninety, Jimmy. I got good genes. My grandfathers on both sides of the family lived to their midnineties and both my mother and father are still going strong in their eighties. Did you know my father scuba dives? No shit. He went swimming with sharks just last summer in South Africa."

"Maybe you'll go swimming with the sharks too," Little Jimmy said. "I can arrange it. Seriously, your old man sounds like a tough son of a bitch. What happened to you?"

"I got the looks," Faz said.

Little Jimmy laughed again. "But not the luck. You're going to come up short of your two grandfathers. Me? I don't know how long I'm going to live. My old man, he might have lived a long time, but somebody put him in prison and he got killed."

"That would be a hazard of running drugs, wouldn't it?"

Little Jimmy lost his smile. "Go ahead, Detective, keep making jokes. What do they say? He who laughs the last is the best."

"Close enough," Faz said.

"So go ahead, tough guy, laugh. You're a brave man."

"No, Jimmy, I'm not a brave man. I'm a problem. I'm your problem. I figure you would have killed me already instead of doing this bullshit tough-guy dance, but we both know you can't kill me."

"Yeah, why not?"

"Because it's bad for business to kill a cop. I know you're running drugs. I know that you probably have millions in inventory in those storage lockers out there. Inventory that doesn't belong to you. It belongs to the cartel you're working for. You kill me, you don't think my partner, Del, is going to know about it? What do you think we've been working on? You kill me, and Del is going to rain hell on you and everyone else up and down the coast, from Canada right down to Mexico, to the doorstep of the cartel supplying you. You know how the cartel is going to fix that problem? Do you know how they're going to make sure you can't testify against them when the storm hits? The same way they fixed it when Big Jimmy went to prison. You're going to be playing pinochle with the worms, Jimmy."

Jimmy stepped closer, close enough for Faz to feel his breath on his face and smell the acidic tinge. Jimmy tilted his head to the side and made noises with his tongue through the gaps in his teeth. "What they care about in Mexico is who moves their product the fastest and gets the most money. And that is me, my friend. We won't even be here in twenty-four hours. We'll be like ghosts. Poof. We're gone. Nothing here. Lockers cleaned out. Product all gone. It's gonna be spread far and wide, and I'm going to make so much money I'll live like a king somewhere. And you? Shit, I'm not going to kill you for any business reason. What's the fun in that? I'm going to kill you because you made this personal, *culero*. You disrespected my old man. Then you disrespect me in my own home."

"Respect is earned, Jimmy. I respected your father. He was a man. And I didn't kill him. The people you work for killed him. How much respect you think they have for a boy who works for the men who killed his father?"

The blows came fast and furious. Little Jimmy threw a combination of punches and kicks and the others joined him. Faz tried to bury his head in the space between his arms but it was futile. Unable to cover up, he could do little but take the punishment and the pain, the searing pain. He heard bones cracking and felt blood spraying from his nose and mouth. The beating continued, until he could no longer hear or feel a thing.

CHAPTER 48

Del walked in the front door of his house trying to appease Sonny, who danced on his back legs, pawing at the air, whining. "Okay, okay," Del said. "Take it easy. I know, you think I abandoned you."

His Shih Tzu had been inside the house, or the backyard, for most of the past two days, first because Del's back had prevented him from taking Sonny on their usual walk to the park, and then because of Del's increased workload with Faz on administrative leave. Sonny was less than eight pounds, but Del thought it best, given his gimpy back, that he not pick him up, at least not for another day or two. "Give me a minute to get settled here and we'll go for a walk, okay?"

Sonny, a white-and-brown ball of fur, dashed past Del and pulled his leash off the peg near the front door.

"Yeah, yeah. We're going to go, and you can do your business, but let me do my business first."

Del draped his suit coat on the railing of the staircase and started down the hall. His cell phone rang. He fished for it in his pants pockets, then realized it was still in the inside pocket of his coat. He thought it would be Celia, but the number was not listed. Del answered.

"Detective Castigliano?"

"Speaking. Who's this?"

"I understand you were inquiring about a Detective Gonzalez this afternoon."

"Yeah, that's right. I'm looking for information on where she served in Los Angeles. Who is this? Did you work with her?" He pulled the phone away from his ear to consider the number, which was not on his screen.

"May I ask the reason for your inquiry?"

It was a legitimate question. "I'm just trying to get a little information on her. We had an officer-involved shooting up here and she was part of it. I'm following up. Has she ever had anything like this happen before? And who am I speaking with?" Del had walked into the kitchen, searching through the drawers for a pen that worked and something to write on.

"My name is Jeffrey Blackmon. I'm with the DEA."

"The DEA?"

"I'm ordering you to cease any further inquiries into Detective Gonzalez's background, Detective. Is that clear?"

Del stopped looking through the drawers. "Excuse me? Did you just order me to do something?"

"Cease and desist, Detective. What's happening is beyond you. And yes, that's an order."

"I don't know you from a hole in the wall. And I don't take orders from people I don't know."

"Then let me introduce myself, again. My name is Jeffrey Blackmon and I'm an agent with the DEA."

"And I'm Santa Claus. Now let's prove it."

"I'm the agent in charge of the OCDETF. Look it up."

"Sounds like an eye exam."

"It's an acronym. It stands for Organized Crime Drug Enforcement Task Forces."

"Never heard of you."

"That's intended."

"And you're running an investigation here in Seattle?"

"As well as in other cities, yes."

"And you don't want me asking questions regarding Detective Gonzalez."

"We do not."

"How do I know what you're telling me is the truth?"

"Faith."

Del chuckled. "My faith is limited to my God, and I have some doubts there also. Everything else, I'm going to need proof."

"I believe you were told your investigation into the shooting of Monique Rodgers had come to an end?"

Del thought back to his conversation with Nolasco. "How do you know that?"

"I suggest you follow that order, Detective, if you won't follow mine."

"Are you threatening me?"

"You screw up my operation, Detective, and I'm going to do a lot more than threaten you. You were given an order to back off. Heed that order. Or I will start making calls. I'd prefer not to have to do that."

The line disconnected. Del pulled the phone away from his ear. What the hell had he and Faz stumbled into?

Sonny continued to dance and whine. "Sorry, partner. Work calls." He punched in Faz's cell phone number, but the call went straight to voice mail. Del knew that unless on call, Faz turned his cell off at night and left it in a basket by the back door. He checked the time. He really didn't want to intrude by calling Faz's home number. He didn't know what shape Vera was in, and he knew they were both going through a lot. What he had was interesting, but interesting would keep until the morning.

He went to his contacts and pulled up the cell number for Johnny Nolasco, to find out how big a pile of shit he and Faz might have stepped in.

CHAPTER 49

Tracy called SeaTac Airport as she and Kins sped from the garage to the freeway, a bar of lights flashing out the back window of their pool car. British Airways flight 48 to London's Heathrow Airport was scheduled to depart at 7:30 p.m., and Aditi and Rashesh Banerjee were ticketed to board. That meant they had limited time to get to the airport, which was certainly doable at that time of night with the flashing lights helping to disperse traffic, though maybe not before Aditi and Rashesh had boarded the plane.

"Not sure we're going to make it," Kins said as he changed lanes and accelerated. "Call the Port of Seattle and ask that they be detained."

The Port of Seattle provided the primary police enforcement at the airport. Tracy made the call, identified herself, and provided the names Aditi and Rashesh Banerjee, their flight information, and asked that they be detained.

When they arrived at the airport twenty minutes later, Tracy and Kins moved quickly to the Port of Seattle Police Department's offices on the third floor of the main terminal building. The frosted-glass door entrance was in the esplanade behind the Southwest Airlines ticket counter. Kins had been there once, many years earlier. Tracy had never been.

They identified themselves and were told that Aditi and Rashesh had been held in a conference room, and that Rashesh was not happy about it.

Not happy was an understatement. Rashesh paced the small room, stopping when Tracy and Kins entered to vent his anger. "What is the meaning of this? Why have we missed our flight to London?"

Aditi sat in a chair at the conference room table, looking bewildered. Tracy asked to speak to Aditi alone, which spurred further protests from Rashesh about their missed flight.

"Our luggage is on that flight."

Tracy looked to the Port of Seattle officer. "The bags were pulled off the flight," he said. "They're being brought here."

"What about—" Rashesh started, but Aditi cut him off.

"Rashesh, please." She turned to Tracy. "Is this about Kavita?"

Tracy nodded. "Yes."

Aditi looked at her husband. "Then I must speak to them, Rashesh." She stood and went to her husband, trying to appease him. "If it is about Kavita, then it is important. Please."

Rashesh hesitated before finally departing, accompanied by two Port Authority police officers. After he had left the room, Tracy and Kins took chairs at the table. Tracy pulled a document from the inside pocket of her jacket, unfolded it, and slid it across the table. She'd had Margo Paige, the park ranger, e-mail it to her after they'd spoken on the telephone.

"The park ranger for Bridle Trails State Park called me this evening," Tracy said. "She found this report in their storage at Sand Point. It was filed nine years ago—a young girl was riding her horse when it fell into a well."

"That was me," Aditi said without hesitation and without considering the document. "I was fifteen. My horse died. I was fortunate to get off just before it fell into the hole."

"Kavita was with you?" Tracy asked.

"Yes. She was behind me or she would have been the one who fell into the hole."

Tracy looked at Kins before reengaging Aditi. "You knew there were open wells in the park."

"That one, certainly." Her gaze shifted between Tracy and Kins. "I don't understand. What does this have to do with Kavita's death?"

Tracy and Kins had not revealed to Aditi, to the Mukherjees, or to the media, the circumstances of Kavita's death.

"You and Kavita shared an iCloud account?" Tracy said.

"I told you that we did."

"You could trace her phone, determine her location."

"I suppose. You told me that it could be done." Aditi's gaze narrowed, as if she had a sudden headache.

"Did you trace her phone that night, Aditi? Did you trace it and find out Kavita was going to the state park?"

"Or did you call and ask Kavita to meet you there?" Kins said.

For a moment Aditi did not react. She considered each of them with the same anguished and confused look. Then, slowly, her eyes widened and she sat up, pulling away from the table. "Oh my God," she said. "You think I killed Vita?" She covered her mouth with her hand. "Why would you think that? Why? Vita was my friend. She was like a sister to me." She started to cry.

Aditi looked and sounded sincere, but Tracy had cases in which the killer did not even recall the murder, had even passed a lie detector test. "It must have hurt a lot, Aditi, to realize that you were leaving that sister, that she was going to have the life you wanted—become a doctor, remain independent."

"Of course it hurt to be leaving her," Aditi said, finding her voice. "I loved Vita. But I chose this life."

"Did you?" Tracy asked.

"What?"

"Did you choose it, Aditi, or was it chosen for you?"

"I don't understand." She looked between Tracy and Kins. "I told you. I went to India, to my cousin's wedding, and I met Rashesh there."

"Your parents were there also?" Tracy said.

"Of course."

"Did they pressure you into marrying Rashesh?"

Aditi gave a short laugh, more a burst of air. She sat back in her chair. "Of course they pressured me; it's what they wanted for me. It's what they've always wanted for me."

"Is it what you wanted, Aditi?"

"No. No, I didn't. Not up until that moment. I told you that. Rashesh is a good man. He's a good man and I believe he will love me if he does not already."

"What about your plans, Aditi?" Tracy asked. "What about your plans of attending medical school and becoming a doctor?"

"Someday, maybe I still will," she said. "Rashesh and I have discussed it. He does not want me to be unhappy."

"Are you unhappy?"

"No." She shook her head. "No." She paused a moment. Then she said, "I want to be a mother. I want to raise a family." She blew out a burst of air, seemingly very tired. "I'm not expecting you to understand, Detective, but when I asked myself what I wanted more in my life, the answer was obvious and not difficult. I want to be a mother, to have children. I want to be a wife and I want to have a family. Maybe I can be a doctor someday as well, but if you asked me which would I give up, there isn't even an issue. I'd give up being a doctor."

And in that moment, Tracy knew that Aditi was telling the truth, because she also felt that way. Aditi had not told them of the time her horse fell into an abandoned well because they had not told her where they had found Kavita's body. She looked at Kins and shook her head. "She didn't follow her."

"Kavita? No. Of course not," Aditi said. "Why would I follow her? I could just call her. I wanted to. I wanted to see her very badly and now . . ." More tears. "But I thought it best to give her time to process everything I had thrown at her."

Something tickled the back of Tracy's mind and she asked, "Who knew of your accident in the park, when your horse fell into the well?"

"Our parents, certainly," Aditi said. "The park ranger. Maybe Kavita's brothers. Yes, Vita's brothers knew, though Sam would have been very young at the time, a baby."

Now something else clicked, things falling into place, like when you found a key piece to a puzzle and it led to the other pieces connecting. "Sam shared the same iCloud account, didn't he? You said he shared music and movies with Kavita?"

"Sam and Kavita were very close," Aditi said. "He missed her very much. This was a way for them to stay in contact with each other. It was all the same account."

Tracy looked to Kins, but inside she was chastising herself. How could she have missed it? It was all right there, on Kavita's phone.

CHAPTER 50

Johnny Nolasco had confirmed Jeffrey Blackmon's credentials, and also that Andrea Gonzalez had been working for the DEA for the better part of three years. Nolasco said that the DEA had a large bust in play up and down the West Coast, including Seattle, and Gonzalez was the agent in charge and needed a cover. That information was not for public dissemination and had been orchestrated at a level above Nolasco. That answered one question, but not the most pressing question. Where the hell was Faz?

When he'd disconnected with Nolasco, Del had again called Faz but again his call went to voice mail. He was about to call Faz's home number when the phone rang in his hand. Caller ID indicated the call was from Faz's home line.

"Hey," Del said, answering quickly. "Glad you called. There's some bizarre shit going on. Did Nolasco get ahold of you?"

"Del?"

Del was momentarily confused by the female voice. Then he said, "Vera?"

"Yes."

"Sorry about that. I thought it was Faz."

"He's not with you?"

"No. No, he's not with me. You haven't heard from him?"

"Not since he left the house early this morning. I can't reach his cell and he's not at the office."

"I'm sure it's nothing, Vera. Maybe he stopped for a bite to eat on his way home." But Del didn't believe that to have been the case. Something was wrong.

"Then why isn't he picking up his phone?"

Del didn't know.

After assuring Vera that he'd call as soon as he heard anything, Del hung up and punched in Faz's cell phone number. His call again went immediately to voice mail, leaving Del with a haunting feeling. He paced the back room with the view of downtown Seattle. The windows in the high-rises sparkled with a golden light. The approaching darkness brought its own foreboding sense of dread.

Del called Billy Williams's cell phone. Williams answered and Del explained the circumstances for the call. He told Billy, "He was going to sit on Gonzalez, try to determine where she went, if she met with anyone to cause any suspicion."

"When's the last time you heard from him?" Billy asked.

"I talked to him this morning, before Gonzalez went anywhere. He was sitting outside her apartment."

"And you haven't heard from him? Not a call, text, e-mail?"

"Nothing," Del said.

Williams listened intently, then said he knew nothing about any task force, but that he'd go up the chain of command and call Del back if he heard anything.

Del wasn't about to wait for Billy. He grabbed his coat and stepped out the front door. He knew Gonzalez's home address, which was close by. He slid into the Impala and the engine roared to life. On the drive, he punched in Faz's number yet again, but as before, his call went directly to voice mail.

At Gonzalez's apartment complex, he parked on the street and approached the front door, looking for the register of tenants, not finding one. More and more apartment buildings and condominium complexes were leaving tenant names off the register to discourage solicitors and to provide security, especially for the elderly. This building wasn't huge, but Del estimated it contained at least twelve different units. He pushed a button, waited. A male voice answered and Del asked for Andrea Gonzalez.

"You have the wrong apartment."

"I'm sorry. I must have written it down wrong. Do you happen to know her apartment number?"

"No, sorry."

Del tried another apartment but got no answer. He pushed buttons for a third and then a fourth apartment. The tenants who answered either didn't know Gonzalez or hesitated enough for Del to know they weren't about to give out her apartment to a stranger, even if they knew it. He tried several more but either got no answer or no information.

Frustrated, he stepped back to the walk, feeling just the hint of a breeze on his neck, trying to focus, coming up with nothing. He called Faz's cell phone once again, and again it went to voice mail. He swore under his breath as he made his way back to his Impala.

Inside his car, he called into the night shift and asked for Ron Mayweather. "I need you to fill out a form to get the last known longitude and latitude for Faz's cell phone."

"What's going on, Del?"

"I don't know. He isn't home and he isn't at work and he isn't answering his cell. Can you run it down?"

"Yeah, I'm on it. I'll call you as soon as I hear anything."

CHAPTER 51

Sam Mukherjee stood in the cul-de-sac of his family's home, staring somberly at Kins and Tracy. He wore a helmet, T-shirt, and shorts and held one end of a skateboard, the other end beneath his tennis shoe.

Tracy pushed out of the car door and approached. "Hey, Sam."

Sam flipped the board and caught it. "Hey." He sounded and looked uncertain. "My parents aren't home."

"Do you know where they are?" Tracy asked.

"My father is out making arrangements for Kavita's funeral, I think. My mother went for a walk and hasn't come back." His chin tilted up as if to consider the darkening night sky. Crickets clicked, a chorus coming from the park.

"Do you know where she walked?" Tracy asked.

Sam pointed over his shoulder to the trees. "She usually walks in the park, but she's also usually home by now so . . ."

"Every night?" Tracy said.

"Pretty much," Sam said. "Sometimes my dad goes with her, but not always."

"And your brother, Nikhil, where is he?" Kins asked.

"He's inside." Sam gestured vaguely. "I don't know what he's doing."

"Do you have your phone on you, Sam?" Tracy asked.

Sam pointed to his shirt on the concrete steps of the narrow porch. "Yeah," he said, tentatively.

"I'm going to need to take it, Sam."

"Why?"

Tracy did not want to blow up the young boy's world, but that was inevitable now. "Your mother said she takes your phone at night. Is that right?"

"Yeah. Usually, but . . . she isn't here and it's summer so . . . She hasn't been taking it. Sometimes she forgets. I think with everything that has happened . . . Why do you want it?"

"Did you give your mother your phone Monday night?" Tracy asked.

He shook his head. "No. I had a soccer game and stayed at my friend's."

"But you sent Kavita a text Monday night, right?"

"Yeah. I was worried about her. I heard my mom and dad talking about Aditi getting married in India. My mom was upset about it. I knew Vita would be upset too. I just wanted to find out how she was doing, if she was okay."

"And she told you she couldn't go to your game because she had a date, didn't she?"

"Yeah."

"Did she tell you about other times she'd had dates?"

"Yeah."

"More than once?"

"Couple of times, I think."

"And these were text messages?"

"Usually. Sometimes I called her."

Tracy looked to Kins. They'd discussed the likelihood that if Kavita had told Sam about one date, they'd discussed others, and that information would have been readily available on the boy's phone. "Did you ever track your sister's cell phone, Sam?"

"What?" His confusion sounded sincere.

"Did you ever track Kavita's cell phone to determine where she was?"

"I wouldn't even know how you'd do that. I mean, maybe I would, I guess. But . . . I didn't ever do that. Why would I?"

"Do you know, Sam, if your parents read the text messages you shared with Kavita?"

He shook his head, emphatic. "I deleted those."

"What about other messages to friends? Did your parents read those?"

"My mom did. Sometimes, I mean. It was kind of BS, you know, but she said that since they were paying for my phone I didn't really have a choice."

"You're on your parents' cell phone account, right?"

"Uh-huh."

"Did your parents put any parental safeguards on your phone, safeguards that allowed them to read your text messages? Even the ones you might have deleted?"

Sam was about to respond, but then paused, as if a thought had come to him and it had taken the words out of his mouth. His eyes lost focus and his gaze dipped to the ground. When he reengaged with Tracy, he'd figured out that answer—just as Tracy had figured it out, though he did not yet know the full consequences.

Andrei Vilkotski had confirmed what Tracy suspected as she and Kins drove from the airport to Bellevue. She'd called and asked him about apps parents could use to read their children's phone messages even without having the phone. Vilkotski had said that the number of spyware apps that allowed parents to read their children's e-mails and text messages, even those texts and messages the child thought he had deleted, were too numerous to list. Vilkotski had also confirmed that because Sam shared an Apple account with his sister, his parents could also use his telephone number to track Kavita's cell phone.

So if Sam and Kavita had discussed Kavita dating, then his mother had also known, for some time, and she'd had the ability to track Kavita's phone to determine where she'd been. If she had done so, she would have determined a routine—Kavita's and Dr. Charles Shea's routine—every Monday night, ending in a hotel room in Kirkland.

"I'll handle the older brother," Kins said, moving toward the front door. "Can you handle the mother?"

CHAPTER 52

Faz opened his eyes, or thought he did. The room remained dark. It took another moment for his other senses to come online. When they did, he wished they hadn't. His head pounded—deep, agonizing thumps that beat with his pulse. He realized he was only seeing out of his right eye. His left eye had swollen nearly shut, his field of vision just a slit. When he attempted to sit up, to relieve the pressure of the handcuffs cutting into his wrists, he winced and grimaced from the pain in his ribs, bad enough that he almost cried out. He had to move in stages, mentally preparing himself for the pain before each movement. His shoulders and arms ached where boots and fists had pummeled him, and his ribs burned as though on fire. He was having difficulty catching his breath. Each time he inhaled it brought a searing pain in his side and caused him to cough, which only further intensified that pain.

He lowered his head to his hands and explored his face. His fingers touched warm, sticky fluid trickling from his head down his neck and behind his ears. Blood. A lot of it. Little Jimmy and his minions had beaten Faz like a piñata. He tasted the iron flavor in his mouth, his tongue exploring the insides of his cheeks for cuts and broken teeth.

After his quick physical assessment, he went to work on his surroundings and his circumstances. He remained handcuffed to the pipe in the room and, for all intents and purposes, he was seriously screwed.

The beating, however, had worse implications than the physical damage. It indicated Little Jimmy really didn't care whether Faz lived or died. In fact, the beating indicated that Faz's bluff of a police firestorm if they killed him hadn't worked. Little Jimmy was more concerned with losing tens of millions of dollars of the cartel's product. The cartel would kill Little Jimmy if that happened, which meant Jimmy had no other option but to kill Faz.

Faz realized that he'd been stupid. He should have insisted that his presence was only related to his investigation into the death of Monique Rodgers. Instead, he'd given Little Jimmy another reason to kill him, as if Jimmy needed another reason.

Faz thought of Vera, about leaving her alone to face her cancer, and felt a profound sadness sweep over him and tears pool in his eyes. The sound of men's voices outside the room and keys in the lock focused his thoughts. The overhead fluorescent lights flipped on, sharp and painful, like shards of glass in his eyes. He tilted his head so he could look up through his one good eye.

"Detective Fatso. You look like shit, man." Little Jimmy crouched and grabbed Faz's face, producing a searing pain where his fingers dug into the flesh. He turned Faz's jaw so he could look at him. "So, Detective, you feel like talking or do you want to tell some more jokes?"

"No point, Jimmy," he mumbled. "My jokes are obviously over this crowd's head."

"Then you feel like telling me what you're doing here?"

"I told you. I came here looking for you," Faz said, his voice barely a whisper. "And my partner knows that I did." There was no sense changing the story now.

Little Jimmy smiled. "And you found me. I guess that's why you're a detective, huh? But I told you, I checked your phone and I don't think your phone lies. *¿Entiende?* I don't think you told anyone why you're here. You're alone. You're on an island."

"You said that. You need another metaphor."

Jimmy paused. "I need a what?"

"My luck I'm stuck on the island with you," Faz whispered.

"You got me thinking, *cabrón*. You got me wondering why you're here and why would you have come alone. So I had to check the videotape, you know? To see if maybe you were following someone."

Faz felt his stomach grip.

Little Jimmy stood and nodded to the door. Hector—Steroid Boy—and the third man dragged a body into the room, but the head dangled so Faz could not see his face, though he had a pretty good idea who he was. They dumped the body at Little Jimmy's feet. Jimmy used his boot to roll the man onto his back. Faz had to tilt his head to see. He recognized Francisco, though barely. Francisco's face was swollen and caked with dried blood. His nose shot off at a right angle, and he looked like he had a golf ball beneath his left eye. "You see, Detective, I'm like a plumber—I'm always looking for leaks. And I think maybe I found one."

"Never saw him before," Faz said.

"But you see, it's like I said—the tape don't lie."

"Did you say that? I don't recall."

"You're going to tell me why you followed Francisco, why you took pictures at the fairgrounds, and who's the woman he was talking to? Hmm . . ."

Faz had forgotten about the grainy and unfocused photographs he'd snapped at the outdoor fair before he'd been bumped. He took a moment and came to another realization. Little Jimmy needed information, and that just might be the one thing to keep Faz alive, at least for the short-term. Despite all of his bravado, Little Jimmy was scared. He knew the consequences if he screwed up the cartel's shipment. In the end, he was just as Faz had believed—another punk.

"I don't know what you're talking about," Faz said.

Little Jimmy lifted Faz's head by the hair, yanking it back so Faz could see him. A sharp pain radiated across his scalp and down the back of his neck. Jimmy crouched, eye to eye. "Do you think I'm stupid, Detective?"

Oh, how Faz wanted to answer that question. Instead, he said, "I was coming back to Eduardo Lopez's apartment and I saw him on the street. So I followed him."

"Really? What, you follow all us Mexicans now? I think they call that racial profiling, Detective. I think it's illegal. I'm going to have to call my lawyer."

Faz wasn't sure what to say, though he knew not to say he'd seen the man, Francisco, at Eduardo Lopez's apartment. "I recognized him from the party at your house."

That answer seemed to catch Little Jimmy off guard. He smiled, like a cat before eating the mouse. "And you remembered him? What, you gringos think all us Mexicans look alike?" Jimmy lost his smile. "You're a terrible liar. Francisco wasn't at my party. Francisco was at home with his wife and kids."

"I guess I was wrong. You all do look alike."

Jimmy pulled something from his pocket, a cell phone, though it didn't belong to Faz. "I don't know who Francisco has been texting, but I think maybe it is you? So I check your phone, but no, he's not texting you. So who's Francisco texting, *cabrón*? Hmm? Who is he texting?"

"Maybe he's having an affair," Faz said. "And didn't want his wife to know."

Jimmy stepped back, reached behind his waist, and pulled out a handgun, a shiny silver piece that looked like a small cannon. "Hold him up," he said, gesturing for the others to lift Francisco from the ground.

Faz figured this was it. He was going to die in the back room of a storage facility and likely end up dumped in some body of water with weights around his legs. Vera would never know what had happened to him. Shit, he wondered if Vera would even have the cancer surgery if Faz died. Faz wasn't sure he'd want to go on living without her.

Hector and the other man lifted Francisco under his arms to a more or less kneeling position. His head flopped between his shoulders.

Jimmy put the barrel of the gun to the back of Francisco's head. "I'm going to ask you one more time, Detective. You tell me a joke or you say 'I don't know' and I'm going to blow off the back of Francisco's head. And then his death is going to be on your conscience, just like my father's. So I'm going to ask you again, and if you don't tell me, I'm going to kill Francisco. Then I'm going to kill you, grind you up and feed you to the pigs."

Little Jimmy stepped back and racked a bullet into the chamber of the silver pistol. He again pressed the barrel to the back of Francisco's head. "So, last chance, *cabrón*, who is he texting?"

CHAPTER 53

The park held a quiet tranquility, the way the North Cascades had once felt when Tracy had been a young girl and walked through them early on weekend mornings. Tracy's father had told her that people referred to grottos of trees as God's cathedrals. She understood why. Mornings, when the sun streamed between the trunks, the shafts of light looked like descending angels. Not tonight. Tonight, the remnants of light colored the park in muted grays. No angels here, not in this place, which would be forever marked by evil.

Tracy followed the same trail she'd taken the night she and Pryor ventured into the park, though this time without the blinking blue light to guide her or the ominous feeling that she was about to stumble onto something horrific. Tonight, she knew the way, and she had a different sense of horror, one that she continued to chastise herself for not seeing sooner. Pranav and Sam had not been home Monday night, nor had his parents, not until late. Only Himani and Nikhil had been present.

Tracy veered to her right at the first fork in the road and continued along the outer trail. Bullfrogs croaked, as if alerting one another to her presence. She slowed her pace as she approached the path leading to the hole in the ground, though the hole had since been filled in by the park ranger. The trail crested. Tracy stopped atop that knoll, looking down upon the person standing at the edge of where the hole had once been.

Himani Mukherjee looked very much like a penitent at what would forever be a grave site in one of God's cathedrals.

As if sensing Tracy's presence, or perhaps expecting it, Himani lifted her gaze and turned, but her glance was brief. She let her eyes drift back to her daughter's grave.

Tracy had been thinking of a number of things to say, but now that she had arrived, she didn't feel the need to say anything. She stepped forward and stood at the edge of where the hole had been and waited, nearly a full minute, before Himani finally spoke.

"I don't expect you to understand, Detective." Her voice barely carried over the sounds of the forest.

And on that point, Himani was correct. Tracy did not understand. "Why don't you try and explain it to me," she said.

Himani smiled, though it had a forlorn and defeated appearance. "What would be the point?" she said.

"Closure," she said. "That's why you're here, isn't it, looking for closure? Was there a reason?"

"There were many reasons," Himani said, recovering some of her anger and bitterness that Tracy first had detected the night she went to the Mukherjee home. Then it was gone again. Himani exhaled, and the air shuddered in her chest, but she did not allow herself to cry. "Many reasons to be upset with Kavita," she said softly, as if speaking to herself.

Tracy waited.

"She disrespected her family. She disrespected herself. She embarrassed us in front of all our relatives and friends. At first, her father and I agreed that it would be best to just wait for her to come to her senses. We figured that, in time, she would come home, that she would ask me to find her a suitable husband. And if that didn't work, we thought a more practical reason would bring her home."

"She'd run out of money," Tracy said. "But she didn't come home and she didn't run out of money and you began to wonder why not."

"Even when Aditi returned from India, married, Kavita still refused. She became even more defiant."

"You and Kavita seem very much alike in that regard," Tracy said.

Himani glanced at Tracy, the same look she'd given Sam when he'd confessed that he and Kavita had exchanged text messages. "You don't understand. You don't understand what it feels like to know that your daughter is a whore. I know about hotel rooms, Detective, and about the man she met there. I know why she didn't run out of money, and why she didn't need to come home." She turned and stared at Tracy, and Tracy couldn't help but think again of that word, defiant. Himani's voice hardened. "You didn't have to listen to Aditi's parents go on about Aditi and Rashesh and the money his family has, about the beautiful home in London where they would live, and about all the grandchildren they will soon have." She shook her head, the anger in her voice continuing to build. "You do not understand the humiliation." She spoke the last words through gritted teeth. Then she closed her eyes and her nostrils flared and her breathing became heavy. She gave Tracy a dismissive wave, like she was just a nuisance. "You don't understand. Our ways are not your ways."

"When did you realize you could follow Kavita using Sam's phone?" Tracy didn't believe Himani had learned this on her own. She believed she learned from someone younger, someone more familiar with technology. Nikhil.

Himani shrugged, just a small acknowledgment. "I've monitored Sam's text messages since we bought him the phone and I've tracked his phone to see where he goes. Tracking Vita's phone was not difficult."

"So you saw the text Sam sent Kavita Monday night."

"And Vita's reply," she said. "It was just another of many messages, Detective, and always on a Monday night." It confirmed that Himani had detected Kavita's routine with Shea. For a long moment Himani did not speak and Tracy thought that perhaps she would choose not to say anything more. Then she said, “I had just left the Dasguptas’ home. They had a party for their friends who could not go to the wedding in India. Kavita was not there, though I was not surprised. I had to listen to them brag about Aditi and about their new son-in-law. Pranav was gone, traveling. He did not have to listen to it.” She raised her hands and curled her fingers into her hair as if to hold her skull together. “Their voices rang in my ears like splinters of glass. By the time I got home, my head was pounding.” She gave a wistful sigh. “I went on to my computer and I pulled up the app, and I saw the messages between Sam and Kavita.” Himani looked at Tracy. “Even on the day Kavita learned Aditi had married, Kavita refused to change her behavior. She continued to humiliate us. It was like she took joy in twisting the knife in our backs.”

“She wasn’t going to continue seeing him,” Tracy said. “She’d told him she was through. She was moving on. She was going to attend medical school.”

This seemed to give Himani pause, but only briefly. “It doesn’t change what she had become,” Himani said. “It doesn’t change the fact that she had defiled herself and no self-respecting man would have her.”

Tracy looked at the disturbed soil, bits of broken branches and bruised and battered leaves atop the dirt. Then she looked back to Himani, watching her carefully, waiting for her to continue. When she did not, Tracy said, “Did you send Nikhil to the hotel intending that he kill Kavita?”

CHAPTER 54

Kins told Sam to wait outside and not to enter the house. Then Kins went inside. The lights were off, the house quiet. He removed his Glock, holding it at his thigh.

"Nikhil?" he called out. "It's Detective Kinsington Rowe from the Seattle Police Department. I'd like to talk to you."

No answer.

"Nikhil?" Kins said again as he stepped from the foyer into the living room. The grandmother and grandfather were seated there. They looked at him with a quiet terror.

"Where's Nikhil?" he asked.

The grandfather's eyes shifted to the kitchen but he did not speak.

Kins and Tracy had discussed the possible scenarios on the drive from the airport to Bellevue and agreed that Himani could not have carried Kavita to the hole alone. So, either Himani had killed Kavita and then enlisted Nikhil's help hiding her body, or Nikhil had killed his sister.

Kins moved across the foyer and dining room and stepped slowly to the doorway. He peered into the kitchen. Nikhil sat at the table in the far corner with the lights off, but Kins could see the large kitchen knife, the point pressing against the young man's throat.

Kins took a moment to regain his composure. He spoke calmly. "Nikhil, put the knife down."

Nikhil's eyes found Kins but he did not respond.

Kins slowly stepped into the room struggling with what to say. He thought of his three boys, how close they were. "Your brother's outside," he said. "And your grandparents are in the other room. You don't want them to see this."

"Sam hates me," Nikhil said, voice nearly a whisper.

"No," Kins said. "Sam doesn't hate you."

The blade moved up and down each time Nikhil swallowed or spoke. "Sam loved Vita."

"Yes, he did. But you're his only brother, Nikhil. He's already lost his sister. Don't let him lose his brother."

"He won't care what happens to me."

Kins kept his gun at his side and stood a safe distance from the table. "He will care. No matter what has happened, you'll always be his brother. Don't do this to him. Don't do this to your parents and your grandparents. Put the knife down."

Nikhil did not comply.

"Then tell me what it is you want, Nikhil." Kins wanted to keep the young man talking.

"What I want?"

"Yes, tell me what you want."

"Why did she have to do it?" he said. Tears streamed down his cheeks. "Why couldn't she come home, get married? Was it so bad?"

"I don't know, Nikhil."

"Do you know what she did? She disgraced all of us."

"Maybe she did, Nikhil, but killing yourself is not going to change anything now. It's only going to make things worse. Your brother has already lost a sister and your parents have lost a daughter. Don't make them bury a brother and a son too."

"Baba will wish I was dead," he said.

"No. He won't. No matter what you've done, he will always be your father. You know how I know that?"

Nikhil made eye contact. His eyes at least appeared hopeful, like he wanted the answer, wanted to know that his father would always love him.

"Because I have three sons of my own. And they'll always be my sons, no matter what they've done, no matter how bad it might be, I'll always be their father and they will always be my sons."

"You must be a good father, Detective."

"So is your father. He'll want to help you, Nikhil. Don't hurt him this way. Don't make him bury two children. Put the knife down, son. Let's all sit down and discuss this."

"What is there to discuss, Detective?"

"We can discuss what happened and why. Don't you want to tell me why?"

"I don't know why. It just happened."

"There are people you can talk to, people who can help you understand why. I'm sure you must have been very upset about what was happening. I'm sure your sister made you angry. I'm sure you weren't thinking clearly." Kins noticed a thin red line, then a trickle of blood down the side of Nikhil's neck. "Let me get you some help, Nikhil. There are people who can help you. They can help you to better understand what happened."

"I understand what happened, Detective. And I know what I did."

"Nikhil?"

Kins turned his head at the sound of Sam's voice. The young boy stood in the kitchen doorway.

"Stay out, Sam," Kins said.

"What are you doing?"

"Leave, Sam," Nikhil said.

Sam stepped in. "What are you doing? Put that knife down."

"Leave," Nikhil said, more forcefully.

"Sam, stay where you are," Kins said, then again, more slowly, "just stay where you are. Everyone just take a deep breath and let's all stay calm."

"Get him out of here," Nikhil said, his voice harsh and agitated.

Sam took a step forward. "Put the knife down. You're cut. You're bleeding."

"Get him out, Detective!"

"Sam, your brother wants you to leave."

"Put the knife down, Nikhil."

"You don't know what I've done, Sam. You don't know."

"Put the knife down."

"I'm sorry, Sam," Nikhil said. "I'm so sorry."

CHAPTER 55

Faz didn't have a lot of sympathy for a gang member and likely drug dealer, but he also didn't want to be the reason Francisco died. He knew, too, because Little Jimmy had been stupid enough to tell him, that Francisco had texted someone, and that someone had to have been Gonzalez. If he was right, the longer he could stall, the better the chances of their survival. Others in the room were talking to Little Jimmy in animated Spanish, and it didn't take a rocket scientist to deduce that they were telling him they needed to leave, quickly. Little Jimmy, however, was blinded by his hatred of Faz.

Faz pulled himself up, swallowing the pain. "You know what, Jimmy? I actually liked your old man."

Little Jimmy turned his gaze to Faz, perhaps waiting for the punch line. He kept the barrel of the gun pointed at the back of Francisco's head.

"I didn't agree with what he did, but he had his priorities in the right place. He took care of his family and he took care of his community. Under different circumstances he might have been a politician, and a good one." He smiled. Jimmy looked perplexed, confused, hopefully not more pissed off.

The man at the back of the room interrupted, his voice and his actions more animated. "*¡Tenemos que irnos ahora, Jimmy! ¡Todavía tenemos tiempo!*"

"You know why? You want to know why they killed him?" Faz said, drawing Jimmy's attention back to him. "They killed him because they knew he was his own man, that he did things his own way, that he cared about his people. Nobody told Big Jimmy what to do. Not even the cartel. That's why they killed him. You know what else? He never let his emotions color his decisions. That's why he was such a good businessman. But what about you? What would your father think of you? What would Big Jimmy think of you right now?"

Little Jimmy didn't answer. But Faz had his attention. It was one thing to say that the cartel did not respect him. It was another to say his father would not respect him.

"Maybe I won't be the one putting the cuffs on your wrists, but kill me and I'm still going to be the reason they nail your ass. They're going to come after you, Jimmy. You know they will. You're letting your emotions make decisions for you. You think my partner is going to let this rest, ever? He's Sicilian. Kill me and he's going to make it his life's mission to bring you down. You're not going to be able to take a shit without him being there to watch you wipe your ass. You think you're going to go back to Mexico and live like a king? Think again. How do you think your pals in Mexico are going to like you when they find out you have a detective on your ass twenty-four seven because you killed a cop? You're going to become a liability. And you know what they do to liabilities . . ." Faz smiled. "So if Del doesn't kill you"—he looked at the others—"all of you, they will. You're going to feed me to the pigs? Those pigs won't even sniff me after they've eaten all of you."

Jimmy redirected the gun at Faz, but Faz could see that he was having misgivings. The others, too, had misgivings about killing him, about the ramifications if Jimmy did so.

"Jimmy, no!" Hector said.

"Shut up."

"We have to go. Now," Hector said.

Another man stepped into the office speaking clipped Spanish. Though Faz could not understand what he'd said, he could tell it was urgent, that something was happening. The others also urged Little Jimmy to move. Hector grabbed his arm.

Jimmy looked at Faz. Hector continued to pull on him. The man at the door yelled Jimmy's name. Whatever was happening, it was reaching a critical stage.

Jimmy grunted, swore, then turned and hurried out the door.

Faz exhaled a slow breath, but this was not the time to get cocky. He considered Francisco. "Hey, are you conscious? Hey, can you hear me?"

Francisco slowly turned his head.

"Did you understand what the man at the door just said?"

Francisco spoke in a whisper. "The trucks are here. The drugs are being loaded for shipment. They need to leave." His head again slumped.

"Who did you text?" Faz asked. "Hey, who did you text?"

Faz heard sounds outside, men yelling in both English and Spanish just before their voices were drowned out by the thumping of helicopter blades slicing the stagnant air. A powerful beam of light pierced the window of the outer office, and slatted shadows undulated on the adjacent wall.

CHAPTER 56

Himani raised her head, but her eyes remained focused on the grave. "Nikhil had nothing to do with this," she said.

"Then tell me what you did," Tracy said, not believing her, but wanting to lock down whatever story Himani chose to tell.

"I don't remember what I did, Detective. I just recall Vita falling to the ground, not moving." Himani reached up and touched her head. "She had blood on the side of her head where I hit her. I remember blood on the rock, and on my hands. I dropped it, somewhere in the bushes." She held out her arm in a dismissive gesture.

"What did you do next?"

"I wanted to run from the park into the street to get help, but . . ."

She was lying. She didn't act alone. Nikhil had been there. "How did you carry the body?" Tracy asked.

Another shrug. "I don't know how. I just did."

Tracy did not doubt Himani knew of the hole, possibly from one of her nightly walks. But she did doubt that Himani had carried Kavita's body by herself. It was far more likely she sent Nikhil to bring his sister home, that she had told Nikhil what his sister had become, and he had followed Kavita from the hotel and killed her in the park. In his panic he'd run to his mother, and she had worked to protect her son. It didn't explain why Kavita had come to the park; that was a question to which they might never know the answer. Kaylee Wright would determine whether any of the imprints around the hole in the ground matched Nikhil's shoes or maybe his mother's.

"I didn't expect you to find her," Himani continued. "When you came to our home and said you had traced her phone, I knew it was just a matter of time."

"Did you or Nikhil take her burner phone?" Tracy asked.

Himani turned and looked at Tracy. "I've lost a daughter, Detective. I won't lose a son."

Maybe not, Tracy thought, *though that would be determined in time.* "You can't protect him."

She shrugged. "We shall see what I can do."

So be it. "Turn around," Tracy said, removing the handcuffs from her belt. "I'm going to handcuff you. Then I'm going to read you your rights."

"You see, Detective, I was right," Himani said.

"Really? About what?"

"You don't understand. You don't understand because you're not a mother."

"Not yet," she said. "And never like you."

CHAPTER 57

Kins was about to rush for the knife when Sam spoke again. "Put down the knife, Nikhil. Please!"

Tears streamed down Nikhil's face. Kins watched the knife, watched to see whether the blade drew more blood. Nikhil's arm collapsed, as if he had been holding a heavy weight and could no longer bear the burden. The knife clattered onto the table and fell to the floor.

Sam moved to his brother. Kins stepped forward and kicked away the knife. He didn't know if Nikhil was crying for what he had done or because he had been caught. The two were not the same. Regardless, he believed Kelly Rosa was correct, that the killing had been one born of anger. He waited, letting the brothers have a moment together, suspecting that it would be one they would not likely have again, not for a very long time, if ever.

CHAPTER 58

Faz watched heavily armed men in Kevlar vests burst into the building and clear the rooms.

"Here," Faz called out.

They entered the room in precision movements. Once satisfied the room was clear, they moved to where Francisco lay on the floor and Faz sat with his arms cuffed to the pole. "He's in bad shape," Faz said to the first man to enter. "Take care of him first."

"Are you Detective Fazzio?"

Faz nodded. "Yeah."

Del stepped into the outer room, and when he saw Faz he seemed to give a sigh of relief, though he had the same look of horror he'd had the night he stepped off the elevator at Eduardo Lopez's apartment building. He crossed the room quickly.

"We got help coming," Del said.

For once Faz could not think of anything to say. He nodded. After a moment, he said, "Don't tell Vera I'm hurt. She'll worry."

"I don't think she's going to buy it, Faz."

"Pretty bad, huh?"

"Pretty bad."

"I don't want her to see me, not like this, Del."

"You know Vera. Wild horses wouldn't keep her away."

"Then get me cleaned up. At least get me cleaned up."

"We will, Faz. We got an ambulance coming."

"How did you find me?" Faz asked.

"Too much to explain at the moment," Del said. He put an arm around his partner's shoulders and pulled him close. "Hey, you know how you've always said you have a face only a mother could love? Not so sure anymore."

Faz smiled. "Don't make me laugh. It hurts too much."

—

Paramedics took Faz from the building on a stretcher. The area outside looked like a military zone. Little Jimmy and the rest of his minions lay facedown on the pavement, hands cuffed behind their backs. Around them men and women in body armor and fatigues stood guard. Overhead, a helicopter continued to hover, the thumping of its blades deafening, a bright light shining down on the ministorage facility. More men and women stood near the chain-link fence and the storage units. They seemed to be waiting for someone to give them the word to enter and begin their search, which meant they were waiting for a signed search warrant.

As the stretcher passed Little Jimmy, he looked up from the ground and made eye contact with Faz. Faz smiled. Then he raised his hand, made a gun with his thumb and index finger, and squeezed the trigger, miming the recoil.

Little Jimmy looked away.

The medics slid Faz into the back of the ambulance. Del stood outside talking to Vera on his cell phone. He mouthed the word "Vera" to Faz, who nodded. Del held the phone up to Faz's ear while the paramedic slipped a cuff over Faz's bicep and inflated it to check his blood pressure.

"Hey, Vera," Faz said, struggling to speak in a full voice.

"Vic, are you all right?"

"Yeah, yeah, I'm all right. I got a few cuts and bruises, but they're taking good care of me. Don't worry about me."

Vera was crying.

"Seriously, I'm fine, honey."

Vera was having none of it. "I'll meet you at the hospital," she said. "Have Del call me when you're on your way."

"Yeah, okay," he said. "I'll have him do that. And, Vera . . ."

"Yeah."

"I want you to know that I love you. I know you know, but I want you to hear me say it. And I know you told me not to start apologizing, but I'm sorry I haven't told you that more often. You deserve to hear it, Vera. You deserve to hear it every day. And I'm going to start telling you that every morning."

"I love you too," she said through her tears.

Faz nodded and Del took back his phone.

"She's going to meet us at the hospital. I think maybe you better call her back and prepare her," Faz said.

"Yeah, I'm thinking the same thing," Del said.

Del looked to his right, to where Andrea Gonzalez stood talking with a group of the men and women dressed in windbreakers. "I'm going to let her explain what's going on to both of us. I got the *Reader's Digest* version myself."

"How did you end up here?"

"We traced your phone, got the last known longitude and latitude. I thought maybe you'd gone back to Eduardo Lopez's apartment. By the time I got down here, SWAT was assembling in a parking lot just down the road. Apparently, they got a text that you were here."

"Detectives," Gonzalez said. She looked to Faz inside the ambulance. "How're you feeling?"

"Like somebody stuffed me into one of those industrial-size washing machines with a bag of rocks."

"You up to answering a couple of questions?"

"If you are," Faz said. "You got some explaining to do."

Gonzalez smiled. "Fair enough. How did you get here?"

Faz explained how he'd followed her, and then followed Francisco to the storage facility.

"You're lucky they didn't kill you."

"I talked a good game. I let them think I knew more than I did. I figured they were running drugs and suggested that whoever they were running them for wouldn't be happy with the attention killing a cop would generate. I also told them Del would rain hell down on them."

"Smart. I can tell you the cartel is really not going to like losing this much product."

"So who are you?" Faz asked.

"I'm with the Organized Crime Drug Enforcement Task Forces. I've led a team pursuing this pipeline for more than three years. It's the largest distributor of heroin and meth on the West Coast. We have similar operations going down in every major city, including Vancouver, British Columbia."

"And the guy I followed . . . the guy you met at the carnival, he's an informant?"

"Francisco Mercado." She shook her head.

"Mercado is a Sureño turned informant. Eighteen months ago he had his second child, a boy. We busted him for dealing heroin just before his son's birth. Given the quantities he was dealing, and given that this was his third strike, he was looking at a potential life sentence."

"He agreed to cooperate," Del said.

She smiled. "Agreed is a little strong. He didn't have much choice. Mercado was the guy we needed to get inside and get details on the deliveries and shipments."

"Is that why they moved you up here?"

Gonzalez nodded. "We finally had a viable informant."

"You were his handler," Faz said.

"And our investigation into the death of Monique Rodgers created a potential problem for you," Del said.

"We needed a little more time to get everything set up and in place," Gonzalez said. "Once Rodgers got killed we had to move up our operation."

"What about Eduardo Lopez? Why was Mercado at the apartment that night?"

"Mercado let us know that Little Jimmy put out a hit on you for fifty thousand after you two went to his home and screwed up his party."

"Gee, and I thought we were well behaved," Del said to Faz.

"Some people just don't appreciate us."

Gonzalez said, "When I found out you had a positive print on Lopez and were driving out to talk to him, I sent Mercado to the address to determine if Lopez was home, in case Lopez decided he was going to try to recover the fifty thousand dollars himself."

"So why was Lopez next door?" Faz asked.

"I don't know," Gonzalez said. "I suspect Lopez maybe thought Mercado was on his way to kill him. Word got out that you two had a positive print on the Rodgers shooter and were moving to pick him up. Mercado said he'd heard it on the street. Lopez lived in the apartment so he could keep an eye on this storage facility for Little Jimmy's crew. From what I've been able to piece together, Lopez must have seen Mercado pull into the parking lot and figured he was coming to kill him."

"He went to the neighbors' apartment to hide," Faz said.

Gonzalez nodded. "When Lopez didn't answer his door, Mercado figured he wasn't home and it was okay to knock on the door. That was the text he sent me that afternoon, the one I got in the car just as we arrived. Mercado didn't know Lopez was next door. Neither did I."

"So when Lopez came out, you thought he was coming to kill me?" Faz said.

"I saw something silver in his hand and thought it was a gun. I wasn't happy about killing him, for a lot of reasons. I wasn't happy when I learned it was a cell phone. I would have liked to have taken him alive."

"So why did you tell the FIT investigators I was the one to yell *Gun!*?"

"I needed to get you off the street until we could take down Little Jimmy. I didn't realize you were such a stubborn son of a bitch."

Faz scratched at the back of his head and felt dried blood. It was rare that he and Del didn't figure things out, but they'd both been dead wrong about Gonzalez. "I guess I owe you an apology, and a thank-you."

"Thank Mercado. He's the one who sent the text that you were here."

"What'll happen to him?"

"We'll arrest him and make him go through the process, like he's going to do time with the rest of them."

"Little Jimmy saw the photos I took of you talking with Mercado. He might already be burned."

Gonzalez gave this some thought. "Then we'll assign him to witness protection, and he and his family will have an opportunity to disappear. If he keeps his nose clean, he'll be out. He's got kids now. Maybe that will be enough. Can I ask you a question? Are you always this dogged?"

"He's stubborn," Del said. "It's the Italian in him."

Gonzalez shook her head. "I'm sorry about what happened."

"Don't start apologizing," Faz said, thinking of Vera. "Like I'm not going to be okay."

"Who knew you were a part of the task force?" Del asked Gonzalez.

"Your assistant chief of criminal investigations, Stephen Martinez, arranged to have me transferred into your unit. And your captain."

"Why Violent Crimes? Why not narcotics?"

"Narcotics was too obvious. We needed to keep this quiet until we had everything in place, but then you two pulled the Rodgers shooting and I suspected it could be a problem. I was originally slated for C Team. They had a detective who was retiring and it was a built-in excuse for me to just slide in. When Rodgers got shot I asked Martinez to ensure I got put on your team so I could keep an eye on the investigation and make sure it didn't screw up my bust."

"Tracy didn't care for you too much," Del said.

"I think I blew her secret," Gonzalez said.

"What secret?" Faz asked. He looked to Del, who also looked like it was news to him.

Gonzalez smiled. "You don't know?"

"Know what? Is she quitting?"

"She'll have to, for a while," Gonzalez said. "She's pregnant."

"No," Faz said. "Seriously?" He turned to Del. "Did you know?"

"I suspected, but I wasn't about to ask. My luck she could just be putting on a few extra pounds since her marriage. You know how that is."

"Yeah, I do," Faz said. "Damn. Tracy's pregnant."

"I guess she was trying to keep that under wraps," Gonzalez said. "In another month she's not going to have that choice. The secret will be out. I just happen to know a pregnant lady when I see one."

"You have kids?" Faz said.

"Four."

"Wow," Faz said. "No kidding?"

"I'll take that as a compliment, Detective. What about you two? You got kids?"

"Not me," Del said.

"One," Faz said.

"I thought you Italians always had big families."

"My wife and I got a late start," Faz said. "And then there were complications. She couldn't have any more children."

"I'm sorry to hear that."

"It was uterine cancer." Faz shook his head. He could feel his emotions leaking out. "We just found out she has breast cancer. We're going through that process now."

Gonzalez touched Faz's shoulder. "It's going to be okay. They get better treating it every year, and she isn't alone. She has a lot of sisters. I'm one of them."

"Yeah?"

Gonzalez pointed to her breasts. "You didn't think these were real, did you?"

"No comment," Del said.

They laughed. Then Gonzalez said, "I had a double mastectomy ten years ago. I figured I might as well get something positive out of it. My husband is happy."

Del and Faz laughed, though neither said a word.

"I'll give you my private number. If your wife needs someone to talk to as she's going through the process, if she has any questions, you have her call me."

"Thanks. She'll appreciate that. She's not saying much about it to me."

"Give her some time and some space. It's a pretty overwhelming experience."

Faz looked to Del. "Speaking of Vera."

"Yeah, we better get you to the hospital," Del said. "If you think I can rain down hell, you don't want to see Vera at work."

"This might actually be a good thing," Faz said.

Gonzalez looked skeptical. "How hard did they hit you in the head?"

"Vera's a caregiver," Faz said. "It's what makes her happy."

Gonzalez smiled. "Then she's going to be very happy when she gets a look at you."

CHAPTER 59

Patrol cars awaited Tracy when she came out of the park escorting Himani Mukherjee; Kins had been busy. Red and blue emergency lights spotted the side of the home and the trees behind it. Neighbors had come down their driveways to the street, noticeably concerned, though they could never have guessed what had transpired—and was about to—at their neighbors' house. Tracy placed Himani Mukherjee in the backseat of one of those patrol cars, her hands cuffed behind her back. If Himani was embarrassed, she didn't show it. She held her chin high, defiant, her eyes directed at the seat in front of her. Kins had already placed Nikhil in the back of a separate car, his hands also cuffed. Nikhil, however, had his head down, avoiding the stares.

"The father just got home," Kins said, nodding at the house. "He's inside with Sam, the grandparents, and Anderson-Cooper."

"How's he doing?"

"He's shell-shocked. They all are. He's called an attorney—a friend—and he's supposedly on his way."

"What did Nikhil tell you?" Tracy asked.

"Not much. It was pretty much a standoff. He had a knife to his throat. The younger brother talked him down."

"He didn't say he killed Kavita?"

"Not in so many words, no." Kins looked at Himani's profile in the backseat of the patrol car. "Why? What's she saying?"

"She says she killed Kavita," Tracy said, following Kins's gaze. "She says she hit her with a rock."

"There's no way she carried her to that hole in the ground."

"I know," Tracy said. "She's lying to protect him. She said she'd already lost a daughter and she wasn't about to lose a son."

"Almost sounds rational, doesn't it? Do you think she sent Nikhil to kill his sister?"

"I don't know. They knew she was at the hotel, and they knew she'd come to the park, for what reason we may never know."

"She can't protect him now," Kins said. "Not completely anyway. And if she does, they'll both be tried for Kavita's death, unless one or both of them plea. The son might. But I don't see the mother taking a plea."

Tracy looked at the house. "I feel bad for the father and for Sam, for what they've suffered through and what they're going to suffer through."

Kins shook his head. "I know the daughter's death hits close to home, Tracy," he said. "You doing okay?"

She thought of that horrific day in Cedar Grove, when Sarah's remains were finally found in a shallow grave. Tracy had wondered how she could continue living, what would drive her after she had learned the truth about her sister's twenty-year disappearance. She didn't have an answer then, and didn't until that moment in the bathroom of their Redmond farmhouse, when she'd held the pregnancy stick and saw two irrefutable lines.

Tracy touched her stomach. "Yeah," Tracy said. "I'm okay."

EPILOGUE

Saturday, December 15, 2018

The nurse handed Tracy her newborn baby girl, swaddled in a blanket, a pink beanie covering the crown of her head. Her face was ruby red and her eyes wide open, searching with an unfocused and slightly cross-eyed gaze.

"You're sure that's normal?" Dan said to the maternity nurse. "The crossed eyes."

"Perfectly normal," the nurse said.

"Will her eyes stay blue?" he asked.

"Not always, but given that her mom and dad both have light-colored eyes, I'd say it's a strong possibility."

"And she's healthy? Everything is okay?"

"She's eight pounds and three ounces," the nurse said, chuckling. "She's definitely not malnourished."

They'd induced labor when Tracy went a week past her due date.

The nurse, having completed many of her tasks, grabbed towels and trays and said, "I'll give you some time alone. You have guests in the waiting room."

Tracy looked to Dan, then spoke to the nurse. "Give us a minute before sending them in. And thank you—for everything."

The nurse smiled. "You did all the work. I was just here for support."

After the nurse departed and the door swung shut, Dan walked to the side of the bed, bent down, and kissed Tracy. "So, how are you doing, Mom?"

Tracy smiled through the tears trickling down her cheeks. "She's so perfect, isn't she? She's so innocent."

"Ten fingers, ten toes, two ears, and a nose," Dan said. "I wish our parents could be here to experience this. My mom would have adored her. Spoiled her rotten, but . . ."

"How do you feel?"

Dan smiled. "Like I just climbed Mount Rainier and I'm standing at the top of the world watching the sun rise above the horizon, seeing that first light of a new day and a rainbow of colors. And it still wouldn't be nearly as beautiful as what I'm seeing in this room."

"Don't get too mushy on me. My hormones are going crazy." She started to cry again.

"Hey," Dan whispered. "It's all right. Look at what you just did."

"What we did," Tracy said. She looked down at her daughter. "I just want to protect her, you know? I never want her to fall and skin her knee, or have some boy break her heart."

"We have time before the boys start coming around," he said. "And her mom does own a couple of weapons and is still one of the fastest guns in the West."

"I can teach her to shoot," Tracy said, not having considered it before that moment. "She can compete."

"As I said, she has a little time before we put her in training," Dan said.

Tracy smiled and looked up at him. "So, have you given it more thought?"

"You know I'd be perfectly happy if you wanted to name her Sarah."

"I know," Tracy said. They'd had that discussion one morning while lying in bed thinking up names. A part of Tracy wanted to honor her sister, and to remember Sarah in a special way, a way that brought a smile to Tracy's face instead of a profound sadness. But Tracy didn't want to put that burden on her daughter's shoulders, didn't want her to have any expectations as to who she was, or who she was supposed to be. She wanted her daughter to grow into her own person, to be exactly who she was meant to be. Tracy could never forget that something horrible and tragic had happened to Sarah, something Kavita Mukherjee and thousands of young women had suffered. She didn't want that morbid thought associated with something so innocent and beautiful.

"No," Tracy said. "When I hear our daughter's name I want it to be associated only with something beautiful, something that has always brought a smile to my face."

"Okay," Dan said. "So then what do you want to name her?"

And the name came to Tracy, one that neither she nor Dan had previously discussed, but that now seemed just perfect. "I want to name her after the person who brought color back to my world when I could see only black-and-white. I want to name her Danielle."

Tears filled Dan's eyes. He bent down low, so that their noses touched. "Seriously?" he whispered.

"We can call her 'Dani' for short," Tracy said.

"Okay," he said. "Danielle Sarah O'Leary it is." He kissed Tracy, long and full on the lips.

Then she said, "Why don't you bring them in?"

Dan kissed his daughter and left the room. Tracy found the remote control and raised her bed, Danielle cradled at her side. The epidural had begun to wear off and she could feel the discomfort setting in, as well as the fatigue. Still, her focus remained on her daughter. She couldn't stop looking at her, couldn't stop smiling.

The door to the room pushed open and the nurse walked back in.

"Has she tried to eat yet?"

"Not yet," Tracy said. "She's just lying here taking everything in."

"She is alert, isn't she?" The nurse walked over and gave the baby a closer look. "Give her a few minutes, then try to get her to eat. She'll be hungry. Speaking of which, what can I bring Mom?"

Tracy had to get used to the sound of that: "Mom." "I'd love a cheeseburger and fries . . . and a chocolate milk shake," Tracy said, "with a shot of whipped cream. I figure I have a few more months to be bad."

"Then you might as well enjoy it. What about your husband?"

"Make it two."

"You got it," she said, departing.

The door opened again and Dan walked in, followed by Faz and Vera. Vera walked straight to Tracy, straight to the baby. She wore a fashionable knit hat over the remnants of her hair. When the oncology team told her it would be best to shave her head during the chemotherapy treatments, to avoid the shock of clumps of hair falling out in her brush, Faz had called Tracy and asked if she would come over for moral support. Tracy did so, and she'd visited Vera nearly every day during her chemotherapy treatments, even when Tracy had become as big as an SUV. She brought over home-cooked meals Vera could freeze during the week.

"She's beautiful," Vera said, gushing. "Oh my God. Vic, look at her. She's like a little angel."

Faz stepped to the edge of the bed. "She's gorgeous, Tracy. You done good. You done real good."

His face had healed from the beating. He had scars, but they'd been able to stitch the cut over his eye into his eyebrow and to straighten his nose and shave the bump. He had been off work for almost two months while he recovered from his injuries, which included two cracked ribs. They were still easing him back into the A Team. Vera had taken care of him, despite Faz's protests. It had been good therapy for her, and it had helped her to forget about her cancer and to get through the days.

"How are you feeling?" Tracy said to Vera.

"Isn't that a question I should be asking you?"

"I'm fine," Tracy said. "A little tired and a little emotional, but I couldn't be happier. How did your last treatment go?"

Vera'd had her final chemotherapy treatment two days before Tracy went into the hospital. Faz said the oncologist was more than optimistic her cancer was in remission and would stay that way.

"I'm fine," Vera said. "Honestly, I've never felt more energized than when Dan called and told us you were in the hospital."

"When do you see the plastic surgeon?"

"About a month," Vera said.

"I suggested that we have dinner with Andrea Gonzalez in case Vera wanted to get a look at possible sizes," Faz said.

Vera swatted him with her hand.

"Hey, it's like buying a car, right? You got to go out and take a look to see what's out there."

"You go look," Vera said. "You're not the one who has to carry them around all day."

"Hey, what did you name her?" Faz said to Tracy.

"Danielle," Tracy said. "We'll call her Dani."

"No kidding." He looked at Dan and gave him a nod. "I always wanted to name Antonio 'Faz.' Vera wouldn't let me."

Vera rolled her eyes. "That would be perfect, wouldn't it? Faz Fazzio. You got a restaurant named after you. Be happy with that."

"Is it open?" Tracy asked.

"A week from tomorrow," Faz said. "We want you there with Del and Celia and Kins and Shannah."

"Wouldn't miss it," Dan said.

"It's a dual celebration," Vera said. "Antonio proposed to his girlfriend."

"That's wonderful," Dan said.

"Did Vera tell you she's going to be working at the restaurant?" Faz asked.

"Just a few days a week as the hostess," Vera said.

"No, no. Tell them what Antonio said."

Vera looked reluctant.

Faz said, "He wants Vera to eventually move into the kitchen. What's the word he used?"

"Tournant," Vera said.

"That's it. He wants Vera to become the *tournant* chef. That's the chef who oversees everything in the kitchen. She'll fit right in."

"I appreciate all the attention," Vera said, "but I think there's a certain mother and adorable baby who deserve it a little bit more than me."

Tracy smiled. "Do you want to hold her?"

Vera beamed. "Do I want to hold her? Can a rooster crow? Let me see that little angel." Tracy handed the baby to Vera. "My God, look at how awake and alert she is."

"You better be careful, Tracy. This one could end up a detective," Faz said.

"She's just beautiful," Vera kept saying. "Just the most beautiful thing."

Tracy gave Dan a nod. Dan said, "Listen, before everyone else gets here, there's something Tracy and I wanted to ask the two of you."

Vera, who had been swaying and cooing, stopped moving. Faz looked concerned. He turned to Tracy. "You're coming back, aren't you?"

"That's a decision for down the road," Tracy said.

"You know that Tracy considers you all to be like family," Dan said. "So we were wondering if the two of you would do us the honor of being Danielle's godparents."

For a moment, neither Vera nor Faz spoke. They looked at one another in silence. Then Vera began to cry, tears streaming down her cheeks, which set off Faz. "Wow," he said softly. "That would be an honor. That would be a real honor, wouldn't it, Vera?"

Vera nodded. She moved to Tracy, bent, and kissed her cheek.

"How do you like that," Faz said. "First, I get a restaurant named after me. Then I become a godfather. And don't you worry, Tracy," he said, adopting a very good Marlon Brando impersonation. "Any boys come around your daughter, I'm going to make them an offer they can't refuse."

"Don Fazzio," Tracy said. "God help us. The A Team will never be the same."

ACKNOWLEDGMENTS

The plot of this novel came about after I read separate newspaper articles about arranged marriages in the Indian culture, and about sugar dating. The subject of an arranged marriage, especially with respect to the Indian culture, is both complicated and interesting. My intent in writing this novel was not to cast judgment but simply to raise the topic, and compare it to blind dates, not uncommon in the United States. I called upon good friend and talented writer Bharti Kirchner for help. Bharti read an early draft of this manuscript and also recommended several novels that would assist me in understanding the culture, including her novel *Sharmila's Book*, Anne Cherian's novel *A Good Indian Wife,* and Pulitzer Prize–winner Jhumpa Lahiri's *The Namesake.* Sadly, the basic premise of this novel is both tragic and true.

The whole concept of sugar dating, on the other hand, is troubling. After reading dozens of articles and websites I'm not sure what to think. The websites would have you believe that a certain percentage of American college students are using the service to put themselves through school. The colleges contend there is no way to verify these statements. The article that struck me as the most troubling was one written by a reporter who posed as a sugar baby and attended a seminar in Los Angeles. The most striking quote from that article was the reporter's observation that nearly everyone on the websites used a fake name to protect their anonymity, including the sugar daddies. She called it a "dangerous game" in which young women go on "dates" with older men, sometimes without even knowing their real names.

As with all the novels in the Tracy Crosswhite series, I simply could not write them without the help of Jennifer Southworth, Seattle Police Department, Violent Crimes Section, and Scott Tompkins, King County Sheriff's Office, Major Crimes Unit.

My thanks also to Kathy Taylor, forensic anthropologist, King County Medical Examiner's Office. Her tutelage continues to inspire me. Thanks also to Kathy Decker, former search-and-rescue coordinator of the King County Sheriff's Office and well-known sign-cutter and man-tracker. Kathy has assisted me with multiple novels and I'm fortunate to have access to her wealth of knowledge.

Thanks to Meg Ruley, Rebecca Scherer, and the team at the Jane Rotrosen Agency. Much like a marriage, they've stuck by me in good times and in bad, for richer or poorer, and, I hope, all the days of my writing life. They do so much for me. I just can't say thanks enough.

Thanks to Thomas & Mercer. This is book six in the Tracy Crosswhite series and my seventh novel with the Thomas & Mercer team, and they continue to promote novels one through seven just as hard as they did on the days those novels were launched. I've said this before. They've changed my professional life and the lives of my family. I am so very grateful for all they have done and continue to do for me. They've put my books into the hands of millions of readers—which is all any author wants. Beyond that, they recently donated three hundred copies of my novel *My Sister's Grave* to an autism fund-raising dinner in Los Angeles to assist in the struggle to help those in need. Their generosity was humbling.

Thanks to Sarah Shaw, author relations, who always greets me with a smile on her face and something special for me and my family. Thank you for always brightening my day.

Thanks to Sean Baker, head of production; Laura Barrett, production manager; and Oisin O'Malley, art director. I've also said this before. I love the covers and the titles of each of my novels and I have them to thank. Thanks to Dennelle Catlett, Amazon Publishing PR, for all the work promoting me and my novels. Dennelle takes care of me whenever I'm traveling and it always feels like first-class. Thanks to the marketing team, Gabrielle Guarnero, Laura Costantino, and Kyla Pigoni. Thanks to publisher Mikyla Bruder, associate publisher Galen Maynard, and Jeff Belle, vice president of Amazon Publishing.

Special thanks to Thomas & Mercer's editorial director, Gracie Doyle. She is with me from the concept to the final written novel, always with ideas on how to make the novel better. She pushes me to write the best novels I can, and I'm so very lucky to have her on my team.

Thank you to Charlotte Herscher, developmental editor. This is book eight together and may have been the hardest to write and to edit. She stuck with me, pushed me to make necessary changes, and helped me to polish the novel into something I'm very proud of. Thanks to Scott Calamar, copyeditor. When you recognize a weakness it is a wonderful thing—because then you can ask for help.

Thanks to Tami Taylor, who runs my website, creates my newsletters, and generates some of my foreign-language book covers. Thanks to Pam Binder and the Pacific Northwest Writers Association for their support of my work. Thanks to Seattle 7 Writers, a nonprofit collective of Pacific Northwest authors who foster and support the written word.

Thanks to all of you, the readers, for finding my novels and for your incredible support of my work. Thanks for posting your reviews and for e-mailing me to let me know you've enjoyed my novels.

Thank you to my wife, Cristina, and my two children, Joe and Catherine. I'm looking forward to our next great travel adventure.

ABOUT THE AUTHOR

Photo © 2017 Jeremy Rice

Robert Dugoni is the critically acclaimed *New York Times*, #1 *Wall Street Journal*, and #1 Amazon bestselling author of the Tracy Crosswhite Series, including *My Sister's Grave, Her Final Breath, In the Clearing, The Trapped Girl*, and *Close to Home*. The Crosswhite Series has sold more than 2,500,000 books worldwide, and *My Sister's Grave* has been optioned for television series development. Dugoni is also the author of the bestselling David Sloane series, which includes *The Jury Master, Wrongful Death, Bodily Harm, Murder One*, and *The Conviction*; the stand-alone novels *The Extraordinary Life of Sam Hell, The 7th Canon*, and *Damage Control*; and the nonfiction exposé *The Cyanide Canary*, a *Washington Post* Best Book of the Year; as well as several short stories. He is the recipient of the Nancy Pearl Award for Fiction and the Friends of Mystery Spotted

Owl Award for best novel in the Pacific Northwest. He is a two-time finalist for both the International Thriller Award and the Harper Lee Prize for Legal Fiction and has been nominated for the Mystery Writers of America's Edgar Award. His books are sold worldwide in more than twenty-five countries and have been translated into more than two dozen languages, including French, German, Italian, and Spanish. Visit his website at www.robertdugoni.com, and follow him on Twitter @robertdugoni and on Facebook at www.facebook.com/AuthorRobertDugoni.